THE
MECHANICS OF WONDER
The Creation of the Idea
of Science Fiction

GARY WESTFAHL

University of California at Riverside

LIVERPOOL UNIVERSITY PRESS

To William Spengemann,
George Slusser, and, of course,
Hugo Gernsback

First published 1998 by
LIVERPOOL UNIVERSITY PRESS
Liverpool L69 3BX

© 1998 Gary Westfahl

The right of Gary Westfahl to be identified as
the author of this work has been asserted by
him in accordance with the Copyright,
Designs and Patents Act 1988.

British Library Cataloguing-in-Publication Data
A British Library CIP record is available

ISBN 0-85323-563-5 (hardback)
ISBN 0-85323-573-2 (paperback)

Typeset in 10/12.5pt Meridien by
XL Publishing Services, Lurley, Tiverton
Printed by Alden Press, Oxford

Contents

Acknowledgements

I must first acknowledge my literary instruction at Claremont Graduate School, where I learned many important lessons from Albert Friedman, Marshall Waingrow, Frank Whigham, and William Spengemann (as discussed in 'Academic Criticism of Science Fiction'). Since my research for this book began while I was there, I must also thank these and other professors who assisted me, especially the late Beverle Houston and Langdon Elsbree, though Spengemann played the largest role in transforming my data into a vigorous argument. I thank the staff of Special Collections at the California State University, Fullerton Library for granting me access to many old magazines; Gene Rinkel and the staff of the Rare Book Room of the University of Illinois Library at Urbana-Champaign for providing copies of the H. G. Wells-Hugo Gernsback correspondence; and the staff of the Interlibrary Loan Department of the Rivera Library of the University of California at Riverside, for tracking down several obscure sources. However, most materials were found in the Eaton Collection of Science Fiction and Fantasy, also at the Rivera Library, and I express my gratitude to its friendly and capable staff, including Clifford Wurfel, Daryl F. Mallett, Kristy Layton, Gladys Murphy, and Sidney Berger.

Early versions of some chapters here have previously appeared in print, and I must thank those who published them. First and foremost is Edward James, who published versions of Chapters 1, 2, 7 and 10 in *Foundation: The Review of Science Fiction* as four essays: 'On *The True History of Science Fiction*', '"An Idea of Significant Import"' (my error in the title quotation is corrected here), '"A Convenient Analog System"' and '"Dictatorial, Authoritarian, Uncooperative"'. He also published two letters responding to comments on those articles (in issues numbers 49 and 52), and some passages from them were used in the manuscript; and, as the first person to read a complete manuscript of this book, he provided several helpful suggestions and, later, assisted in arranging for its publication. In addition, Damon Knight reviewed three chapters of the manuscript and inspired some revisions.

The publication of the four articles inspired a number of informative and/or complimentary letters in *Foundation* from Ivan Adamovic, Steve Carper, Steve Jeffrey, Michael A. Morrison, Cecil Nurse, John D. Rickett,

Andy Sawyer, Madawc Williams, and Michael Wippell, and I thank those individuals for writing them. The first *Foundation* article also prompted an interesting telephone call from Harlan Ellison, which inspired one small change in the manuscript.

I thank Robert Philmus, the late R. D. Mullen, and their colleagues at *Science-Fiction Studies* for working with me on a version of Chapter 3 and for publishing the first part of the chapter, using the same title. In particular, Mullen provided important documents and information, including the editorials in the August 1923 issue of *Science and Invention* and the first issue of *Scientific Detective Monthly*. And I thank Donald M. Hassler, editor of *Extrapolation*, for publishing a version of Chapter 4 as 'This Unique Document', and for urging me to finish this book as quickly as possible.

I should single out for special thanks George Slusser, who has been unfailingly supportive regarding all my science fiction research. Truly, he and Spengemann qualify as the godfathers of this book. Yet I also sincerely thank the critics with whom I will vehemently disagree, especially Brian W. Aldiss and Darko Suvin. Their work, after all, inspired me to undertake this project, and I found them both unusually clear in stating their premises, which was helpful in formulating the premises I employ here.

Finally, I thank Robin Bloxsidge, Janet Allan and the other capable people at Liverpool University Press for their preparation of the manuscript; David Werner, Director of Educational Programs in Corrections at the University of LaVerne, for granting me the occasional opportunity to teach science fiction classes; and Patrick J. Moran, Sarah Wall and other colleagues at the Learning Center of the University of California at Riverside, who have provided me with a stimulating and supportive work environment. And of course, I must thank those who most suffered as a result of my work: my children Allison and Jeremy and my wife Lynne; truly, every book I write should really be dedicated to them.

Gary Westfahl
Riverside, California
1 October 1997

The True History of Science Fiction: Introduction

This is the story of the idea of science fiction and how it grew.

Though there were anticipatory comments throughout the nineteenth century, and a crucial prelude to the idea of science fiction in the form of the 'scientific romance', the first true critic of science fiction was Hugo Gernsback, who offered a complete theory of the genre's nature, purposes, and origins. By doing so, he made science fiction a recognized literary form and launched a tradition of science fiction commentaries that would be carried on by various writers, editors, and fans who, despite a lack of literary training, were attempting to analyse and describe the works they were familiar with. While many responded to, incorporated, and built upon Gernsback's ideas, his major successor was John W. Campbell, Jr, who improved and expanded Gernsback's concepts and became a second dominant influence on the genre.

Campbell, of course, did not bring this discussion of science fiction to an end. In the 1950s, several new critical voices emerged, such as H. L. Gold, Damon Knight, James Blish, and Judith Merril, who largely continued and developed Campbell's theories while anticipating the New Wave of the 1960s. Harlan Ellison, who along with Michael Moorcock became a leading spokesman for that movement, then mounted a vigorous challenge to traditional views of science fiction, though he and other commentators ultimately failed to refashion the genre and faded in importance. As this tradition of commentary continued, a new tradition of academic criticism came to the forefront, begun by pioneers like J. O. Bailey, Kingsley Amis, and Thomas D. Clareson. In the 1980s, Bruce Sterling and others offered the new theory of cyberpunk fiction, demonstrating the continuing vigour of the non-academic tradition, while other new voices, notably including feminists like Pamela Sargent and Joanna Russ, brought their own perspectives to bear upon the genre.

All these people are important, and their stories should be fully told; but this volume, to avoid becoming unfashionably long, must necessarily focus on the two people who established that tradition and still dominate and influence its discussions. Without understanding Gernsback's and

Campbell's contributions, which have never been described in great detail, one cannot understand science fiction or its critical tradition.

One might defend such a study in this way: in any serious consideration of a literary period or genre, critics always read and take note of the comments on that literature from its writers and other contemporary critics. Scholars of Renaissance literature examine works like Sir Philip Sidney's *A Defence of Poesie* and George Puttenham's *The Art of English Poesy*; critics of Romantic poetry read William Wordsworth and Samuel Taylor Coleridge's 'Preface' to *Lyrical Ballads* and Percy Shelley's *The Defence of Poetry*; and students of modern poetry look at T. S. Eliot's 'Tradition and the Individual Talent'. They will not necessarily agree with the critical ideas they find; almost invariably they will find them faulty or incomplete. Yet they read and consider them for three reasons: critics have a traditional duty to read the analyses of predecessors, especially the first critics of a given work or body of literature; since the commentaries were either written or read by contemporary authors, they reveal the ideas that influenced those authors; and they provide additional information about the period and environment from which major works emerged.

Regarding science fiction, one would argue that simply examining the genre's major texts is not sufficient: one must also read the commentaries that were published alongside those works. The analogy breaks down in one respect: as critics, Gernsback and Campbell are a far cry from Sidney and Eliot. They and their compatriots had no background in literary criticism and approached this activity with only a naive and simplistic understanding of literary concepts; they did not write polished essays setting forth their theories in an organized fashion, but rather let their ideas dribble out in scattered editorials, articles, introductions, and responses to readers' letters; they often failed to appreciate the relative importance of various concepts or did not see omissions or contradictions in their theories; and they were generally horrible prose stylists. Given their weaknesses, it is unsurprising that Gernsback and Campbell have not been recognized as literary critics and that science fiction critics like Brian Aldiss and Darko Suvin have not rushed to embrace them as distinguished predecessors.

However, the quality of their commentaries is not the issue; their ideas should be considered for all the reasons given above: these people were among the first to analyse science fiction; not only were they, usually, important writers themselves, but they were also read by contemporary authors, influencing and helping to explain their works; and their comments offer information about the atmosphere and environment from which key works emerged.

Based on such arguments, studying the critical ideas of Gernsback and Campbell could hardly be opposed; yes, indeed, one might say, it would be interesting to see what these early figures had to say about the nature and purpose of science fiction. And on these grounds, I could present this book as a valuable contribution to science fiction scholarship.

However, it is not my purpose to be unobjectionable, and these are not the grounds on which I choose to defend my work.

In fact, I would go much further and argue that, in the case of a literary genre which emerges as a widely acknowledged historical fact, major works of contemporary criticism constitute far more than an interesting accompaniment to or alternate source of information about that genre; they are in fact *parts of the genre themselves*. From this perspective, *A Defence of Poesie* is an essential component of Renaissance literature; the 'Preface' to *Lyrical Ballads* is part of Romantic poetry; and 'Tradition and the Individual Talent' is a key element in twentieth-century poetry. In these cases, criticism functions as the necessary binding force that creates, sustains, and preserves the integrity and identity of the genre. Thus, a study of science fiction that does not take into account its own accompanying critical tradition is not only weakened by that omission, but is fatally flawed.[1]

If critics are free to ignore contemporary criticism in a genre and look only at texts, then the door is open for them to define the genre in any way they choose, select as exemplars any works they choose, and reach any conclusions that they choose.

The dangers can be illustrated by a hypothetical example: imagine a critic of Romantic poetry who decides that the genre's true spirit is found in the satirical works of later Romantics like Shelley's 'England in 1819' and Lord Byron's *Don Juan*; so she defines Romantic poetry as a special form of satirical verse. She then writes *The True History of Romantic Poetry*, beginning in Chapter One with the true father of Romantic poetry— Alexander Pope. In later chapters she discusses other major Romantic poets like Henry Fielding, Samuel Johnson, and Oliver Goldsmith. Finally, before examining the key works of Shelley, Byron, and their successors, she pauses to castigate Wordsworth and Coleridge, those misguided fools who completely misunderstood Romantic poetry and whose idiotic ideas almost destroyed the entire genre.

Such a study, one hopes, would be laughed at and ignored.

Yet my example is analogous to the critical approach taken in the two most important and influential critical studies of science fiction: Brian Aldiss's *Trillion Year Spree: The History of Science Fiction* (originally titled *Billion Year Spree: The True History of Science Fiction*) and Darko Suvin's *Metamorphoses of Science Fiction: On the History and Poetics of a Literary Genre*.

In the case of Aldiss, he implicitly begins by observing that there are many works commonly accepted as science fiction that might be construed as Gothic fiction; ignoring the fact that there are innumerable science fiction works that cannot plausibly be fitted into this mold, he defines science fiction as 'the search for a definition of mankind... characteristically cast in the Gothic or post-Gothic mode' (p. 25). With this definition, he looks back to find the first work of Gothic fiction that involves science and decides that Mary Shelley's *Frankenstein* represents the origin of science fiction— ignoring the fact that the novel was not regarded as anything new in its time and was not strongly associated with works of scientific fiction until 1907, almost a century after its publication.[2] Proceeding in chronological order, frequently giving added emphasis to authors who best fit the Gothic characterization while proceeding to more modern illustrations of that definition, he pauses to condemn Gernsback as 'one of the worst disasters ever to hit the science fiction field' (p. 202).

Suvin seems to begin by noting in certain contemporary science fiction works features that suggest a definition of science fiction as 'the literature of cognitive estrangement' (p. 4).[3] Dismissing all works which lack these traits as 'subliterature' (p. 36), he looks back to find a broad range of classic texts, including Lucian's *True History*, Thomas More's *Utopia*, François Rabelais's *Gargantua and Pantagruel*, and Jonathan Swift's *Gulliver's Travels*, which fit his definition and proclaims this body of work to be 'the largely suppressed SF tradition' (p. 88) which 'significant writers... were quite aware of... and explicitly testified to' (p. 12)—ignoring the fact that, as he also acknowledges, he is the first critic to perceive and discuss this tradition. While going on to modern works like Karel Capek's *War with the Newts* and Ivan Yefremov's *Andromeda*, he occasionally pauses to relegate Gernsback to 'the compost heap of juvenile or popular subliterature' (p. 22).

What unites these theories and my example is this: all three critics take a term that has a meaning rooted in history and established usage, twist and distort that term beyond recognition, and then employ that term as a club with which to bludgeon those who created and developed the genre that term describes.

I realize that Aldiss and Suvin would not so characterize their theories: Aldiss asserts at one point that science fiction is the historical outgrowth of the Industrial Revolution, and Suvin, as noted, claims that there has been an accepted 'tradition' of science fiction since ancient times. Later, I will discuss and refute these arguments; here, I simply note that there is language in the work of both authors clearly suggesting that they are in fact *inventing* the history of science fiction, not *studying* it.

In the 'Introduction' to his *Trillion Year Spree*, Aldiss offers two rebuttals to anyone who might dispute his version of science fiction history. First, he says:

There is an argument which says that SF has no history, and that the story in this book is another generalization, and a false one... This argument... is ingenious—too ingenious. It is an argument which pays attention to the aims of the writer. A history of science fiction, however, must pay attention to the interests of the reader. And to the reader of science fiction, Thomas More's Utopia is as interesting as Burroughs's Barsoom, or *1984* as *2010*. C. S. Lewis is as rewarding as Robert Heinlein. In this volume, we are entirely on the side of the reader. Definite generic interplays exist. (p. 15)

The logic behind this position is clear: the nature and scope of literary genres must be determined solely by the perceptions of their readers; as a perceptive representative of these readers, I see that this is the nature and history of science fiction; thus, this is the nature and history of science fiction. What Aldiss ignores is that other readers have not perceived his 'definite generic interplays' or have observed quite different connections.

Later in that chapter, he offers a completely different rationale behind his expansive vision of science fiction history:

An argument has been advanced recently which says that it is impossible to write a history of science fiction. That SF consists merely of the worst. That such writers as Gore Vidal in *Messiah*, or Olaf Stapledon in *Last and First Men*, or Doris Lessing in her *Canopus in Argus* series, knew nothing of the continuity of science fiction, of its traditions, or of its rules (which means in fact a few prescriptions laid down by a small clique of, in the main, non-writers); and in consequence cannot be said to be a part of science fiction at all.

This is a fallacy. If we can imagine that a playwright like Eugene O'Neill, or a poet like Thomas Hardy, or a novelist like Gabriel García Márquez, knew nothing of the history of the drama, poetry, or the novel, the fact would in no way lessen the contributions those writers made to their chosen medium, or to the influence they had on those who followed them.

There is no such entity as science fiction. We have only the works of many men and women which, for convenience, we can group together under the label 'science fiction'. (p. 20)

Here, he argues that major writers outside the genre can be included if they have made 'contributions' to the genre or have had 'influence'. Unlike the reader-centred argument, this approach seems to offer a reasonable prospect of resolution; while one cannot anticipate what the next reader of science fiction might believe, one can research whether one writer influenced another writer or not. However, problems appear in this methodology as well; since Hindu mythology influenced Roger Zelazny's

Lord of Light, since James Joyce influenced Aldiss's *Barefoot in the Head*, and since John Dos Passos influenced John Brunner's *Stand on Zanzibar*, are we then obliged to add the *Bhagavad Gita*, *Finnegans Wake*, and *U.S.A.* to future histories of science fiction? Obviously not; then we must distinguish between 'important' influences and 'unimportant' ones, between 'major' contributions and 'minor' ones, and we are back to completely subjective criteria.

As if sensing the weakness of this argument, Aldiss then retreats to his completely subjective criterion, stating that 'There is no such entity as science fiction'—we only group certain writers under that label as a 'convenience'. However, there is certainly more to science fiction than that; it is a matter of record that for decades, a large community of writers, editors, and readers have operated on the assumption that science fiction does exist and have expressed consistent views concerning its nature. Aldiss cannot ignore the evidence of this continuing consensus merely because he does not like it and proclaim that 'there is no such entity as science fiction'; it is like arguing that there is no such thing as America, only individual Americans, or no such thing as baseball, only individual players.

As for Suvin, while introducing his definition of science fiction, he refers to 'The novelty of such a concept' and 'this whole new genre' without any sense of contradiction involving his other assertions about the ancient and evident tradition of that literature (pp. 12–13); and, in a particularly revealing passage, he asserts that 'the critical community concerned with SF will have to evolve a theory of the genre which can serve as a framework for its history and criticism' (p. 17)—yet, if Suvin is describing an existing literary tradition, surely he should speak of the need to *discover* a theory of the genre, not to *evolve*, that is, to create such a theory.[4] Finally, after proposing the use of the term 'science fiction' to describe this body of literature, he notes as a possible objection that his 'use of "science fiction" confuses the whole genre with the twentieth-century SF from which the name was taken' (p. 13)—thus acknowledging that he is using the word in a manner utterly alien to its historically accepted meaning.[5]

Perhaps the clearest description of Suvin's methodology is found in his *Victorian Science Fiction in the UK*, where he says that:

> any significant fictional text or group of texts can be centrally interpreted only in interaction with the interpreter's philosophy of history—that is, her/his view of the formal patterns enacting the ideological systems in the discourse at hand. Whoever pretends to an 'objective' neutrality, from whose point of view he can condemn others as 'biased', is fooling either himself or others—usually both (p. xiv).

While some contemporary bias does enter into historical studies, it is one thing to admit that this occurs and see it as a problem to be minimized as much as possible, and another thing to celebrate such bias as the best scholarly approach. That is, all modern observers *reinterpret* history to some extent, but that does not grant them licence to *rewrite* it.

To both men, then, the fact that a large body of tradition and history contradicts their ideas of 'science fiction' is not important; not wishing to dirty their hands with the genre as it existed in history, they skilfully refashion the genre into something they feel is worthy of their critical attention.

Aldiss and Suvin are intelligent and erudite critics who often provide illuminating commentary on individual works; yet we cannot be swayed by their critical acumen into accepting the frameworks they propose for a study of science fiction, or, more importantly, into accepting the premise behind those frameworks. When stripped of other justifications, their theories amount to nothing more than their own personal opinions about science fiction; and everyone is entitled to his own opinion.

That is, if Aldiss sees science fiction as a type of Gothic fiction originating with *Frankenstein*, and if Suvin sees science fiction as a literature of cognitive estrangement whose first modern exemplar is More's *Utopia*, then someone else might, following the lead of Amis in *New Maps of Hell*, define science fiction as a form of satire and select Swift's *Gulliver's Travels* as its origin; or, agreeing with Sam Moskowitz's *Explorers of the Infinite*, one might argue that the space voyage is a central motif of science fiction and select Cyrano de Bergerac's *Voyage dans la Lune* as the first work of science fiction, since it described the first moon voyage based on scientific principles; one might accept the viewpoint of Alexei and Cory Panshin's *The World beyond the Hill* that science fiction represents an attempt to achieve 'spirit' by means of an atmosphere of scientific plausibility and accept Horace Walpole's *The Castle of Otranto* as the first tentative effort of this kind; another might hit upon Brian Stableford's observation in 'Marriage of Science and Fiction' that the 'future war' story of the late nineteenth century was a significant precursor of science fiction and present George Chesney's *The Battle of Dorking* as the earliest work in the genre; one might argue, as I was once prepared to do, that the figure of the scientist and the scientific community is crucial in science fiction and on those grounds select Francis Bacon's *The New Atlantis* as the first work of science fiction; one could accept Lester del Rey's qualified argument in *The World of Science Fiction 1926–1976* that science fiction is as old as literature itself and offer *Gilgamesh* as the origin of the genre; or one could go even further and adopt L. Sprague's and Catherine Crook de Camp's position in *Science Fiction Handbook—Revised* that science fiction, in the guise of 'imaginative literature', might be traced back to the times before the origin of writing, to 'Stories that were told around primitive campfires' (p. 6). Which view is correct? It is all a matter of opinion. And the question of the true character and history of science fiction will boil down to—who is the biggest bully on the block? Some may relish that role, but it hardly constitutes solid grounds for an examination of a literary genre.

To escape from this morass, reconsider my hypothetical critic of Romantic poetry; what would immediately defeat her claims is not simply that she was defying a contemporary consensus, but that she was contradicting a large body of commentary and criticism dating back to the emergence of the genre and the first use of the term which clearly established a meaning for the term 'Romantic poetry' far different from hers. Similarly, I would argue, a working agreement about the true nature and history of science fiction can be achieved only by including in our analysis of it the history of science fiction criticism, accepting that massive body of commentary as a crucial and defining part of that genre; in doing so, we move away from the vague and subjective conclusions of readers and critics and reach the solid ground of historical evidence concerning authors and their influences.

If we accept these principles, then verifiable conclusions emerge: first, there are absolutely no grounds for arguing that anything resembling a 'history of science fiction' actually existed as a historical fact in contemporary perceptions before the nineteenth century; and second, any wide understanding of science fiction as a genre was at best limited and flawed until Gernsback's breakthrough in the 1920s. So, if we define a genre as consisting of a body of texts related by a shared understanding of that genre as recorded in contemporary commentary, then a true history of science fiction as a genre must begin in 1926, at the time when Gernsback defined science fiction, offered a critical theory concerning its nature, purposes, and origins, and persuaded many others to accept and extend his ideas. From that point on, science fiction fits the definition of a historical genre, and we can reasonably speak of a tradition of science fiction. Further, the ideas and texts in that tradition constitute the only unambiguous and unarguable bases for discussions of science fiction.

At this point I anticipate two responses: a cry of anguished protest, and the calm voice of reasoned dissent.

The anguished protest would be that I am proposing a severe, indeed fatal, truncation of science fiction, sweeping away most major authors and leaving only the impoverished texts of the pulp magazines and their successors as proper objects for study; in Aldiss's words, I am limiting science fiction to 'the worst'. Even if my propositions are logical, would science fiction critics of the early twentieth century, for example, ever abandon H. G. Wells, Jack London, Karel Čapek, Aldous Huxley, Olaf

Stapledon, and C. S. Lewis and focus their energies instead on the likes of Gernsback, Edgar Rice Burroughs, E. E. Smith, David H. Keller, and Ed Earl Repp? At a time when the study of science fiction is still struggling to be accepted by a sceptical literary community, it would seem suicidal to present such a lineage as the best science fiction has to offer.

Yet it is hardly improper to examine authors outside Gernsback's tradition in the context of science fiction. Any genre, to delineate and develop itself, looks to authors and works outside that genre for inspiration and models; indeed, Gernsback himself employed Edgar Allan Poe, Jules Verne, Wells and other older writers as exemplars of science fiction, and one cannot deny that those authors and others like Huxley, Stapledon, and Lewis had a lasting influence on the genre. There are also clear parallels and likenesses between those authors and writers who emerged from the science fiction tradition, suggesting that both should be included in diachronic analyses of the genre. So, if Aldiss wishes to focus his critical energies concerning science fiction in the 1930s on Huxley, Stapledon, and Lewis, there is nothing wrong with that; what I object to is lining up Huxley, Stapledon and Lewis in a row and presenting their works as a tradition, as part of the history of science fiction, when such a characterization yokes together three disparate authors who would no doubt be appalled to be in each other's company. In sum, individual works of all types from all times might be considered influences on or examples of science fiction; but terms like 'history' or 'tradition' should be reserved for the one history and tradition of science fiction that can be established by texts, commentaries, and other evidence, and that is the history and tradition launched by Gernsback.

My other point would be this: if science fiction can be admitted to the groves of academe only on the basis of its high literary quality, then the case for science fiction must be based on the demonstrated excellence of the works that emerged from the tradition and label of 'science fiction', not on the number of distinguished works of the past and present outside that tradition which can, with varying degrees of plausibility, be identified as science fiction. After all, there are other groups and genres with prior claims to writers like Mary Shelley, Poe, Wells, Huxley and George Orwell, and it is doubtful that they will ever be accepted entirely—or even primarily—as 'science fiction writers'. And further recruitment of past literary greats will be to no avail; calling William Shakespeare a science fiction writer does not and cannot make science fiction a respectable genre. However, the case for science fiction based on the finest writers who emerged from the genre is, I submit, a strong one: two of them, Ray Bradbury and Kurt Vonnegut, Jr, have already been accepted as major modern writers, though I believe their finest work came when they were still publishing as science fiction writers; many giants of the field—Arthur C. Clarke, Heinlein, Ursula K. Le Guin, Samuel R. Delany, and Ellison, to name only a few—have produced at least a few works which can be called significant; and contemporary writers like Dan Simmons, William Gibson, and Nancy Kress are not simply great modern science fiction writers but are, one can reasonably maintain, great modern writers, period. And many other science fiction writers might be included in such lists. To argue intelligently on behalf of these writers, we need a complete understanding of their true origins; and the ideas of Gernsback and Campbell offer a great deal of insight into their works, while the ideas of More and Mary Shelley offer no insight at all. So, to appreciate properly modern science fiction, we must acknowledge and appreciate its true history, not its imaginary history.

This is as good a time as any to put to rest, once and for all, the basal fallacy beneath the glorious literary constructs of Aldiss and Suvin: the idea that great literature must come from great literature. Thus, for science fiction to be considered worthwhile, it must claim ancestors like More and Mary Shelley. However, not only is the idea logically untenable in itself—where, pray tell, did the first great work of literature come from?—but it is also repeatedly contradicted by literary history. *Gammer Gurton's Needle* and *Gorbuduc* are about as bad as plays get, but we read them with interest today because they launched an era of Renaissance drama that produced—a few decades later—works like *Twelfth Night* and *King Lear*.[6] With notable exceptions, the poems in *Lyrical Ballads* are not outstanding, but that volume is valued today because it directly led to later and greater works, by Wordsworth and Coleridge and others who accepted their premises. There is no contradiction, no shame, in asserting, for example, that the work which best explains and informs Gibson's *Neuromancer* is Hugo Gernsback's *Ralph 124C 41+*;[7] the history of literature is filled with examples of dross that turned into gold, and that is a reasonable characterization of progress in the literature of science fiction from Gernsback to Gibson. The question is simple: are we seeking prestige, or knowledge? The quest for prestige in science fiction leads to Swift, Milton, Shakespeare, and Dante—and into a fantasy world; the quest for knowledge of science fiction leads directly to people like Gernsback and Campbell.

The calm voice of reasoned dissent argues that I am being too nominalistic, too extreme, in asserting that science fiction truly came into existence only when Gernsback proclaimed its existence in 1926, for there are logical grounds for extending the history of science fiction into earlier epochs. These positions can be listed as following: science fiction came as the inevitable result of the development of prose fiction and new prominence of scientific progress in the Industrial Revolution; science fiction materialized when the words 'science' and 'fiction' assumed their modern meanings; science fiction is a form of writing that has emerged at various times in similar historical circumstances and can be discussed as a genre on that basis; science fiction has existed since ancient times as a coherent, though suppressed, literary tradition, clearly established by relationships of influence and borrowing among its key authors; and a wide awareness of science fiction as a genre emerged before Gernsback in the nineteenth century, as shown by various commentaries and widespread acknowledgement of the 'scientific romance' as an accepted category of literature. As I will demonstrate, only the last of these arguments has real validity, and even it has serious flaws.

The case for historical determinism is simply stated: given that the novel and short story were accepted forms at the start of the nineteenth century, and given that science became a major factor in human life at that time, it was inevitable that the two forces would combine to create a genre of science fiction. Aldiss makes the argument obliquely:

> The origins and inspirations for science fiction lie outside the United States, though within the period of the Industrial Revolution. As we might expect. Only in an epoch when a power source more reliable than ocean currents or the wind, faster than the horse, has been developed, can we expect to find a literature that will concern itself with the problems of power, either literal or metaphorical. (p.14)

In *Alternate Worlds*, James Gunn describes the process more clearly:

> The Industrial Revolution brought man-made changes; the great wheel of invention began to accelerate... the world was ready for science fiction, and when the world is ready someone always steps forward to provide or invent what the times require... 'When it's steam engine time people invent steam engines,' Charles Fort said. (p. 52)

This argument, however, is questionable, because recognized literary genres simply do not emerge in this fashion.

Consider two examples: since the eighteenth century and the publication of Adam Smith's *The Wealth of Nations*, the discipline of economics has had a strong and pervasive impact on human life and civilization; indeed, it may be the single most powerful influence affecting the modern world. Yet there has never emerged a literary genre of 'economic fiction'. Similarly, despite the effects of science and other new fields, Christianity has remained a major and important influence up to the present time; yet except for recent and little-regarded products marketed in Christian bookstores, there has never emerged a literary genre of 'Christian fiction'. Clearly, historical determinism alone cannot serve to create literary genres.

What has emerged as a result of the continuing influence of economics and Christianity—and what will inevitably emerge when powerful disciplines impact on modern society—is a number of scattered works by various authors, in various fields, writing at various times, which separately address the issues and concerns raised by that discipline. Thus, looking for literature involving economics, one might bring together works like Daniel Defoe's *Robinson Crusoe*, Charles Dickens's *Hard Times*, Upton Sinclair's *The Jungle*, Sinclair Lewis's *Babbitt*, and John Updike's *Rabbit Is Rich* and prepare a college course on 'economic fiction'. Or looking for literature involving Christianity, one could gather John Bunyan's *Pilgrim's Progress*, Nathaniel Hawthorne's *The Scarlet Letter*, Lew Wallace's *Ben-Hur: A Tale of the Christ*, Robert Sheldon's *In His Steps*, and Lewis's *The Screwtape Letters* for a course on 'Christian fiction'. But no one could argue that these lists of disparate authors constitute actual literary genres that existed and were accepted at the time those works were written. What enables critics to put together similarly incongruous lists of scattered authors and describe the result as a tradition of science fiction is that, in the twentieth century, a genre of science fiction actually emerged, providing a concept that could then be applied, however inappropriately, to a wide range of earlier texts.

Literary genres appear in history for one reason: someone declares that a genre exists and persuades writers, publishers, readers and critics that she is correct. In the case of science fiction, this did not completely occur until Gernsback began his successful campaign on behalf of the genre. Science fiction today exists as a category of literature to be read and studied because of the efforts of Gernsback, not the blind workings of history.

A parallel argument based on linguistics might be derived from comments offered by Brian Stableford in his article on 'Proto Science Fiction' in *The Science Fiction Encyclopedia*:

> It seems reasonable to argue that we cannot meaningfully characterize something called 'science fiction' until we can meaningfully characterize (a) 'science' and (b) 'fiction' in meanings close to those held by these words today... [A] modern definition [of science] did not appear until 1725... 'fiction' first acquired the literary sense in which we use it today in the late 18th century... Logically, therefore, it would be inappropriate to describe as 'science fiction' anything published in the early 18th century or before. (p. 476)

One could continue this thought and argue that a work can be *appropriately* described as science fiction if it appeared at a time when 'science' and 'fiction' were used in their modern sense. But such an assertion would be linguistically invalid. 'Science fiction' is not a chance combination of noun and adjective; it is a *word*—despite that space in its middle—and has been accepted as a word by all dictionaries. And a word exists when its elements are combined—not when its elements come into existence. The word 'cryogenics' is based on two ancient Greek words meaning 'cold' and 'life'; but 'cryogenics' is not an ancient Greek word and the term cannot be employed to describe Greek science. Similarly, the fact that 'science' and 'fiction' acquired their modern meanings in the eighteenth century is irrelevant; the concept of 'science fiction' existed only when those elements were combined to form a word.

One can also maintain that science fiction works have arisen repeatedly throughout history in response to particular parallel circumstances and are thus related. This argument is at least implicit in Suvin's work when he says that science fiction appears at 'favorable historical moments' (p. 88); in addition, this approach to literary genres is specifically sanctioned by Marxist critic Raymond Williams, who declares: 'there are undoubtedly continuities of literary forms through and beyond the societies and periods to which they have such relations' (*Marxism and Literature*, pp. 182–83).[8] And Alexei and Cory Panshin's *The World beyond the Hill* links together disparate texts on the grounds that they illustrate how 'SF developed almost subliminally' (p. 10) as an effort to reconcile the desire for transcendence with scientific rationalism. However, a decision to ignore contexts and connect works widely separated in time and space, even on 'historical' grounds, leads right back to the same problem I began with—arbitrary subjectivity. Gerald Prince has frequently claimed[9] that strict application of narratological principles leads to the conclusion that each work constitutes its own genre, and each historical event is surely unique in some way. So, for a critic to claim that two works and their contexts are similar, she must choose certain criteria which she argues are significant to establish their similarities, and must dismiss other criteria which she argues are not significant to ignore their differences. Needless to say, different critics will make different choices, and no consensus will emerge regarding which works constitute the corpus of science fiction.

Suvin's major argument in *Metamorphoses of Science Fiction* is actually a stronger assertion that, even though no one before him noticed it, there has been a 'coherent literary tradition of SF' (p. 88) since ancient times which can be documented in the texts and comments of its many authors. According to Suvin:

> the significant writers in this line were quite aware of their coherent tradition and explicitly testified to it (the axis Lucian-More-Rabelais-Cyrano-Swift-M. Shelley-Verne-Wells is a main example). Also,

certain among the most perspicacious surveyors of aspects of the field, like Ernst Bloch, Lewis Mumford, or Northrop Frye, can be construed as assuming this unity... new data will [not] substantially affect the basic cultural hypothesis of a coherent literary tradition of SF as part of a popular literature that (like many forms of humor and 'obscenity') spread through centuries by word of mouth and other unofficial channels, and penetrated into officially accepted, normative, or 'high' Literature and Culture only at favorable historical moments. (pp. 12, 88)

Many things must be said about this extraordinary hypothesis.

First, this is Suvin's position, and only Suvin's position; to say that certain other prominent critics 'can be construed as assuming' his position simply means that they do not actually support it. I cannot speak about Bloch or Mumford, but I am familiar with Frye's work and can confidently say that nothing resembling Suvin's theories can be found in his writings.

Second, the analogies that Suvin employs to make his assertion plausible are simply not applicable. 'Humour' and 'obscenity' are universal concepts that occur in every culture and transcend literature itself to appear in virtually all aspects of human life; so one can always locate traditions of humour or obscenity in any body of literature. Suvin cannot say that 'science fiction' is such a universally accepted and pervasive idea.

Third, in developing this notion of a 'coherent literary tradition of SF', Suvin repeatedly employs examples from utopian literature, which has been an accepted literary tradition since the Renaissance[10]—in Suvin's words, utopia is 'a literary genre induced from a set of man-made books within a man-made history' (p.62). Suvin lays the groundwork for equating the traditions of utopian literature and of science fiction by asserting that 'utopias... are the sociopolitical subgenre of SF' (p. 95). However, even granting Suvin's argument, there is a logical problem here: the fact that a subgenre exists at a given point in time does not necessarily imply that the entire genre exists at that time. That is, early in its development the novel incorporated the tradition of picaresque literature to the point that the 'picaresque novel' became an accepted subgenre; yet one cannot go back to medieval tales of the *picaro* and maintain on that basis that the novel existed at that time. Similarly, even if utopias are seen as a subgenre of science fiction, it does not necessarily follow that science fiction always existed when utopias existed. At many points, then, Suvin's argument breaks down into two parts: an unnecessary, self-evident argument that a tradition of utopian literature has long existed—once, he slips and simply speaks of 'the utopian tradition' (p. 102), giving away the game—and a weak argument that a tradition of science fiction has long existed.

Fourth, Suvin explicitly acknowledges that he lacks evidence to support his claims and is distorting the record of history:

> in view of the largely suppressed SF tradition, the achievement of each such major writer not only *has to* but also legitimately *can* indicate and stand for the possibilities of a largely mute inglorious epoch... No doubt this perverts somewhat what 'really happened' in cultural and literary history, but no more so than any historical investigation, dealing, as it must always, with a choice from whatever data have survived rather than *wie es eigentlich gewesen* (how it really was). An ideal history—especially a history of culture—would have to be a geology, interested perhaps as much in the hollows produced by absence of data as in the fullnesses produced by their presence, or a geography of the ocean depths as much as of the visible islands. I confess that this book is not such an ideal, although I propose to suggest how SF, sustained by subordinate social groups with which it achieves and loses cultural legitimacy, is like an iceberg showing only a fraction above the silent surface of officially recorded culture, and how the islands limn not only themselves but also the oceans from which they grow. (pp. 88–89)

But we cannot accept Suvin's proposed methodology; no matter how flawed the historical record, history must be based on that record, not on fantasies of what a larger record might reveal. We cannot be sure that a surviving work represents a larger mass of works and opinions; one can imagine a future scholar after a nuclear war who unearths a copy of Lawrence Sterne's *Tristram Shandy* and argues on that basis that a tradition of eccentric, meandering literature existed in the eighteenth century. And Suvin's analogies fail him again: some of the most famous blunders in the history of geology have been arguments based on the absence of data, like Roderick Murchison's conclusion that the lack of fossils from before 600 million years ago proved that God first created life at that time; a look at visible islands reveals little about the topography of the surrounding oceans; and seeing the tip of the iceberg does not allow observers to infer the size and shape of the iceberg.

Finally, Suvin implicitly acknowledges his lack of evidence for a science fiction tradition in the statements he makes and the statements he does not make in the detailed 'History' that occupies most of *Metamorphoses of Science Fiction*. Although Suvin names many writers, I limit my analysis to the authors in his 'main axis' of science fiction history: Lucian, More, Rabelais, Cyrano de Bergerac, Swift, Mary Shelley, Verne, and Wells. First, discussing these and other writers, Suvin repeatedly contrives to incorporate the word 'tradition' into the text, as if, logomorphically, he could will a tradition into existence by naming it; he also makes numerous observations that *convey the impression*—without going so far as to *assert*—that a given author in his tradition was influenced by a previous author or authors. A few examples of this technique: saying that 'The most significant [ancient imaginary voyage] and nearest in spirit to More is a fragment by Iambulus' (p. 94) does not actually claim that More was aware of or influenced by Iambulus; saying that Cyrano's 'satirical technique… will be systemized to overwhelming effect by Swift' (p. 105) does not actually claim that Cyrano influenced Swift; saying that in *Frankenstein* 'We are back on the shores of Houyhnhnmland as seen by Godwin' (p. 130) does not actually claim that Swift influenced Mary Shelley; saying that the 'glimpses of grotesque yet kindred Aliens in [Poe's] "Pfaall" gave the cue to much later space-travel SF' (p. 142) does not actually claim that Poe influenced those later writers; saying that 'Swift can be felt in the conflict of the Starbordians and the Larbordians of [Verne's] *Propeller Island*' does not actually claim that Verne was influenced by Swift; and saying that 'The world upside-down—where strange animals hunt Man, and the subterranean lower class devours the upper class—recurs in Wells, as in Thomas More' (p. 213) does not actually claim that More influenced Wells.[11]

Disregarding all such statements, I carefully read Suvin's passages on the eight writers looking for places where he *clearly maintains*—without coyness or ambiguity—*that there is textual evidence that one author influenced another author*. The results (see Table 1) show Suvin's patchwork 'tradition' falling apart—*based on an analysis of Suvin's own language*.

What Suvin is actually observing should be apparent. Writers are usually voracious readers who seek out earlier authors for ideas and models. If we arbitrarily select certain writers, call them 'science fiction writers', and analyse which other authors influenced them, it is likely that at least some previous authors in our 'tradition' will emerge as influences on later writers. And if we conveniently choose a preponderance of authors who are part of a tradition of utopian literature, the odds increase that we shall find many instances of such influence. But inevitably we will find two other things: the pattern is not complete—certain previous writers who *should* have influenced later writers in the 'tradition' did not influence those writers; and later writers were also influenced by several authors who were not part of the 'tradition'. In short, the writers were creating their own traditions, and we can bring them together as a 'coherent literary tradition' only by selectively ignoring a lack of evidence on the one hand and selectively ignoring conflicting evidence on the other.

It will be noted that, in attacking Suvin's analysis of literary history, I rely exclusively on examination of his own language and statements, not on my own research. This is as it should be. Consider: if a critic proclaims

Table 1: Suvin's 'Tradition' of science fiction

Authors in Suvin's 'tradition' of science fiction	Previous authors in 'tradition' clearly identified as influences on the author	Previous authors in 'tradition' not clearly identified as influences on the author	Authors outside the 'tradition' clearly identified as influences on the author
Lucian			
More		Lucian	Plato (93) Homer (94)
Rabelais	Lucian More (97)		Villon Plato *Navigatio Sancti Brendani* (97)
Cyrano	Rabelais (106)	Lucian More	
Swift	Cyrano (108)	Lucian More Rabelais	Bacon (109)
M. Shelley		Lucian More Rabelais Cyrano Swift	Coleridge (124) Goethe (130) Milton (130) Godwin (136)
Verne	Rabelais (153) Cyrano (162)	Lucian More Swift M. Shelley	Defoe (151) Homer Xenophon Michelon G. Sand (153) Thales Poe Cooper (162)
Wells	Lucian (219) Swift (219) M. Shelley(22) Verne (220)	More Rabelais Cyrano	Milton Bunyan (217) Kepler (219) Flammarion Plato Morris Poe Bulwer-Lytton (220)

in the 1970s that a clear, coherent literary tradition has existed since ancient times that has never been noticed before, the obvious conclusion is that this tradition did not really exist; if it had existed, then surely someone, some time, would have noticed and recorded its existence, no matter how much it had been 'suppressed'. Thus, the burden of proof shifts from those who would deny this tradition to those who would support its existence. And supporters face a daunting task: to prove that Lucian, More, Rabelais, Cyrano de Bergerac, Swift, Mary Shelley, Verne, and Wells constituted a literary tradition, they must prove that More was aware of Lucian, regarded him as a primary influence, and saw his work as a continuation of Lucian's; that Rabelais was aware of Lucian and More, that he saw them as primary influences, that he regarded them as representing a tradition, and that he saw his work as a continuation of that tradition; that Cyrano was aware of Lucian, More, and Rabelais, that he saw them as primary influences, that he regarded them as representing a tradition, and that he saw his work as a continuation of that tradition; and so on. And they must prove these assertions based on *clear and explicit references* in their texts, not vague assertions of general influence. That is the sort of case that must be mounted to support the claim that 'significant writers in this line were quite aware of their coherent tradition and explicitly testified to it' (p. 12); and, in the absence of such a case, we can justifiably disregard Suvin's argument.

A final argument for science fiction histories extending into the past is that there were in fact prior to 1926 both many works clearly related to science fiction and accompanying commentaries establishing an awareness of those works as a genre. This is how H. Bruce Franklin's *Future Perfect* justifies a survey of American science fiction authors from Hawthorne and Poe to Bierce and Twain: 'Slowly, [nineteenth-century] writers and readers became aware that a new form had developed, the "scientific romance". The term "science-fiction" itself was first used, in England, in 1851. As early as 1876 an introduction to a collection of William Henry Rhodes's fantasy and science fiction was discussing "scientific fiction" as a distinctive genre' (pp. x–xi). Similarly, without persuasive documentation, the Panshins claim in *The World beyond the Hill* that:

> from 1870 or thereabouts, it is at last possible to say that a literature that we can recognize as science fiction was visible and acknowledged. After the beginning of the Age of Technology, when an SF novel was published, it would not be looked upon as a unique prodigy. Instead, reviewers might compare it to some earlier story. Writers would consciously answer each other and extend each other's notions. A literary tradition existed. (p. 68)

Two other critics see an emerging 'tradition' of science fiction within more limited parameters: Moskowitz's *Science Fiction in Old San Francisco* argues that there existed a 'San Francisco school of science fiction which flourished during the last decades of the nineteenth century and had been interred almost without a trace' (p. 14). Choosing a later time frame, Stableford's *Scientific Romance in Britain* maintains that a tradition of scientific romances 'was syncretised as a genre in the decade of the 1890s' and endured as a separate genre until after the Second World War (p. 336).

These assertions are formidable for two reasons: first, one cannot deny that as the nineteenth century came to a close, an increasing number of works were published that are clearly related to modern science fiction; and second, Franklin, the Panshins, Moskowitz, and Stableford can locate nineteenth-century critics who seem to discuss an existing genre of science fiction. Apparently, then, one finds my criteria for a discussion of a historical literary genre—a body of related works connected by contemporary commentary—fully satisfied decades before Gernsback's efforts.

However, there are a number of problems in such arguments.

First, these critics, while citing or describing comments by contemporary observers, acknowledge that the testimony they have unearthed is inadequate to establish a widespread awareness of science fiction and so feel a need to offer other defences for discussing the works they address as a genre. As it happens, all of these additional arguments are questionable.

In *Future Perfect*, Franklin begins with an indefensibly broad 'good working definition' of science fiction—'the literature which, growing with science and technology, evaluates it and relates it meaningfully to the rest of human existence' (p. vii)—which literally turns most modern literature into science fiction; indeed, since Franklin observes, 'There was no major nineteenth-century American writer of fiction, and indeed few in the second rank, who did not write some science fiction or at least one utopian romance' (p. ix), he seemingly wishes to incorporate all nineteenth-century American fiction into science fiction on the grounds that they all at some point touched upon scientific issues. Describing all these works as a science fiction genre renders the term meaningless. In a revealing comment, Franklin describes 'Hugo Gernsback and his creation of technocratic science fiction as an autonomous, self-conscious genre' (p. 394); implicitly, then, *non-technocratic science fiction*—the type Franklin wants to discuss—is *not* autonomous and is *not* self-conscious—and thus is, by my definition, not a literary genre at all.

The Panshins define science fiction as a body of works united primarily by a 'subliminal' quest for scientific transcendence—a characteristic which is not clearly defined and, thus, one that only the Panshins can detect. While they at times refer to accompanying criticism, their primary focus is on a small number of selected works which best illustrate their thesis, and contemporary ideas of science fiction emerge as little more than a distraction.

Sam Moskowitz offers this dubious justification for discussing various San Francisco writers as a 'school of science fiction':

> the factor that connects them beyond any chance of argument is not that they wrote for the same magazines and newspapers as [Robert Duncan] Milne at the same time or immediately following (which they did), is not that some of them repeated his plots with variations (which they did), but that in all but a very few of the stories, *San Francisco and its environs was the basic locale*. (p. 23)

Yet writing for the same publications or borrowing plots from one author hardly makes a group of writers a 'school', and the argument that a shared setting does so can be dismissed without comment.

In *Scientific Romance in Britain*, Stableford offers this defence for discussing various writers as a genre:

> Each of these writers was an individual, operating on his own. Each one found his own particular 'philosophy of life'. This is one of the things that makes it hard to classify scientific romance as a genre— it has no shared, unifying central dogma after the fashion of popular romantic fiction. Nevertheless, it *is* a genre and the philosophies which its practitioners developed do have many recurrent themes and motifs... not because they borrowed from one another (though they often did) but because they were in similar situations, drawing upon similar ideative resources. The political opinions and meta-physical ideas of the major writers were very various, but the horizons of possibility that they glimpsed through the lenses of contemporary scientific discoveries and theories were not. (p. 337)

As with the other formulas, Stableford's concept of a genre is too expansive; I need not list the numerous British writers of this century who 'were in similar situations, drawing upon similar ideative resources' but did not write anything resembling science fiction. Second, I suggest that critics, looking at the comments of early observers suggesting knowledge of a science fiction genre, misread the comments with the same contemporary bias that leads many to misread works of that period. In fact, before the emergence of the term 'scientific romance' at the end of the century, all the scraps assembled to represent nineteenth-century science fiction criticism arguably fall into these categories: predictions of, or calls for, a genre of science fiction, which do not suggest any awareness of an existing genre; descriptions of the works and techniques of specific authors, which do not suggest that those authors are part of a larger group; comments on contemporary genres only vaguely related to science fiction; and authors' comments about their own writing, which imply an approach to science fiction as a genre only to modern critics.

Predictions of science fiction include Felix Bodin's comments on 'the novel of the future' (described in Paul Alkon's *Origins of Futuristic Fiction*); Edmond and Jules de Goncourt's pronouncements on 'the literature of the Twentieth Century', something they saw existing only in the works of Poe (cited in Moskowitz, *Science Fiction in Old San Francisco*, p. 196); and Edgar Fawcett's 1895 call for a new genre of 'realistic romance' (discussed by Brian Stableford in 'Marriage of Science and Fiction', pp. 26–27). Another example would be the article in the 5 September 1835 issue of *The New York Herald* which said that Richard Adams Locke, author of 'The Moon Hoax', 'may be said to be the inventor of an entire new species of literature, which we may call the "scientific novel"' (cited in David G. Hartwell, *Age of Wonders*, p. 118).

We must also relegate to this category the writings of William Wilson, who declared that 'Fiction has lately been chosen as a means of familiarizing science in one single case only... We hope it will not be long before we have other works of Science-Fiction' (cited in Moskowitz, 'The Early Coinage of Science Fiction', p. 312). Wilson is unduly celebrated because he first used the term 'science fiction'; however, since his 'one single case', *The Poor Artist* by R. H. Horne, markedly differs from any modern examples of science fiction, and since Wilson failed to mention any works by writers like Mary Shelley, Poe, or Swift that might be better described as science fiction, it is clear that his concept of science fiction, despite some phrases that resonate when taken out of context, was unrelated to the ideas of Gernsback and his successors. Also, as Stableford notes, his call for 'Science-Fiction' went 'unnoticed and unheeded' ('Marriage of Science and Fiction', p. 26); Gernsback surely reinvented the term without knowing anything about him.

In the category of suggestive comments about individual authors should be placed the remarks of William H. L. Barnes, who undoubtedly wrote the introduction to Rhodes's *Caxton's Book*. While Franklin claims he 'was discussing "scientific fiction" as a distinctive genre', it is instructive to examine his actual words:

> His fondness [in his college days] for weaving the problems of science with fiction, which became afterwards so marked a characteristic of his literary efforts, attracted the especial attention of his professors; and had Mr. Rhodes devoted himself to this then novel department of letters, he would have become, no doubt, greatly distinguished as a writer; and the great master of scientific fiction, Jules Verne, would

have found the field of his efforts already sown and reaped by the young Southern student... (pp. 6–7)

Barnes actually provides little support for Franklin's thesis: he describes the stories that Rhodes wrote in the 1840s as 'this then novel department of letters', though Franklin would call authors of that time like Poe and Hawthorne science fiction writers; the only later writer of this type that he names is Verne; and it is not clear that Barnes believes there are many, or even any, others—that is, one can call Aldiss 'the great master of Joycean science fiction' without necessarily implying that he has many compatriots.

Interestingly, there is evidence elsewhere in *Caxton's Book* that Franklin ignores. After reading the introduction, Franklin perhaps glanced at the Table of Contents, saw an essay by Rhodes entitled 'Science, Literature, and Art', and turned to that essay for further evidence that people at that time knew something about science fiction. But Franklin never mentions the essay, with good reason, for in it Rhodes declares that modern literature and art are declining because of the growing power of science: 'Deficient in literature and art, our age surpasses all others in science. Knowledge has become the great end and aim of human life' (p. 274). Thus, not only does Rhodes ignore the possible combination of fiction and science, but he sees them as antithetical forces, one in the process of destroying the other. So, while Barnes *may* have seen something resembling a new genre emerging in Rhodes, that author himself did not—reinforcing the impression that there was no widespread appreciation of science fiction at that time.

Further, the fact that individual works now identified as 'science fiction' were sometimes compared to each other, as the Panshins note, hardly proves that 'A literary tradition existed'. Given similarities in contents, reviewers would naturally link stories about future wars, stories about moon voyages, and stories about lost races; this does not prove that the reviewers perceived anything like an overall genre of 'science fiction'.

While Moskowitz does offer evidence to substantiate his claims regarding a tradition of science fiction in nineteenth-century San Francisco, the comments he assembles prove, when closely examined, to be less than definitive. To support his notion of a 'San Francisco school of science fiction', he employs the quotation from Barnes discussed above; an observation from a review of Verne's *Five Weeks in a Balloon* in the February 1874 issue of *Overland Monthly* that Verne 'has created what may almost be called a new kind of fiction writing' (p. 59), a statement whose adverb 'almost' cannot be overlooked; a report in the 9 March 1878 *Argonaut* that 'Scientific prose fiction was [Rhodes's] forte' (p. 88), which could well be, as in Barnes's statement, a chance combination of adjective and verb; and a comment that a writer named Cooke was of the 'Vernesque school' (p. 168), which could be a polite way of saying that he was imitating Verne. Since Moskowitz by his own account spent years in secret research exhaustively reading every available newspaper and magazine from this period, the paucity of relevant references to a true genre of science fiction emerges.

Moskowitz's other pieces of evidence fall into my third category, references to genres other than science fiction. Despite repeated use of the words 'science fiction', when Moskowitz actually links these stories to a literary tradition, either in his own words or those of contemporary commentators, it is most often that of the scientific hoax story, a common feature of nineteenth-century newspapers which described in journalistic fashion some imaginary invention or event, usually without a narrative framework (pp. 56, 57, 88, 131, 132, 172, 215, 238, 246, 249). Thus his strategy resembles Suvin's use of utopian literature; Moskowitz seizes upon stories in a tradition related to, but not identical to, science fiction and employs them to argue that a tradition of science fiction existed at an earlier time. There was one new term used in San Francisco which Moskowitz refers to a few times—'wonder-stories' or 'wonder-tales' (pp. 26, 211, 249); but the term clearly takes in not only Moskowitz's 'science fiction' but various supernatural tales—ghost stories, horror stories, and fantasies— also published in San Francisco. So, occasional use of the term suggests no particular understanding of a genre of science fiction.

Searching for evidence of a contemporary awareness of science fiction in the nineteenth century, Franklin briefly notes the appearance of 'the science-fiction "dime" novel as a separate form' (p. xi), works usually described as 'invention stories'. However, these simple boys' stories including one marvellous device, while they later had an impact on science fiction, are too limited in scope to be regarded as true precursors of science fiction; even Franklin sees in their existence little support for his claims.

Overall, then, we can make these statements about nineteenth-century readers' perceptions: first, they did recognize a number of separate traditions of literature resembling science fiction. Stableford lists the types in 'Marriage of Science and Fiction': the 'novel of imaginary tourism' (p. 20), which could also be described as the works of Verne and his imitators; the 'futuristic utopian novel' (p. 23), which could also be described as Edward Bellamy's *Looking Backward* and its imitators; 'the war-anticipation story' (p. 24), which could also be described as Chesney's *The Battle of Dorking* and its imitators; and the 'literary exploration of Darwinian theory' (p. 22), which I believe represents less clearly delineated works better characterized as specialized versions of the Lost Race story popularized by H. Rider Haggard. I would add two more traditions: 'invention stories' and the scientific hoax story first exemplified by Locke's 'The Moon Hoax'. While a critic may find many comments about these categories of fiction, there is, I submit, little evidence that contemporaries regularly saw all these works as one broad category; when they did connect them, they tended to group them together with many other types of fantastic fiction that are not today regarded as science fiction, as seen in the term 'wonder stories'. In so arguing, I find an ally in Stableford, who acknowledges in 'Marriage of Science and Fiction' that 'The "tradition" of science fiction before 1900 is a wholly artificial construction which has meaning only in retrospect' (p. 26).

Finally, commentators sometimes seize upon the comments of individual authors concerning their methods and characterize them as science fiction criticism. While not a feature of the critics primarily discussed here, Suvin employs such reasoning at one point in *Metamorphoses of Science Fiction*: 'Poe's notes stressing verisimilitude, analogy, and probability for the wondrous story made him also the first theoretician of SF' (p. 143). Other histories of science fiction regularly refer to remarks by Verne and Wells. The problem is that almost all authors will at times discuss their principles and techniques of writing without necessarily asserting that they are describing and launching a literary genre; such judgements emerge only in retrospect if their authors' works are later incorporated into a genre. When Gernsback constructed a theory of science fiction, employing Poe, Verne and Wells as prominent examples, he necessarily made discussion of their methods into science fiction criticism; at the time, however, there is little evidence that they saw themselves as pioneers and advocates of a new type of literature. An analogous example might be this: A. E. van Vogt once described his technique of introducing a new idea into his stories every 800 words ('Complication in the Science Fiction Story'); if van Vogt is at some time in the future rehabilitated and celebrated as a model for a new genre of 'dream fiction', stories consisting of series of illogically related ideas, then his remarks may be construed as the first literary criticism of this genre. But that does not mean that van Vogt himself was describing or advocating a new genre in his essay.

Overall, I observe parallels between these efforts to minimize Gernsback's importance by finding previous commentators discussing science and fiction and what Stephen Jay Gould decries as ongoing efforts to deny Charles Darwin his status as the originator of the theory of natural selection. In *An Urchin in the Storm*, he writes:

> Disputes about priority, in any case, tend to ring hollow, despite the vigor of their persecution. Ideas are cheap. The use of ideas, the systematic reconstruction of a world in their light, is the stuff of

intellectual revolutions. Patrick Matthew developed the notion of natural selection in 1831—in Darwin's later sense of a creative force. But who among you has ever heard of Matthew? He presented his position in scattered comments of an appendix to a book on naval timber and arboriculture—not the most auspicious location for a reconstituted world. The chief joy in reading Darwin lies in sensing the excitement of a man, not yet thirty, who knows that he holds a key to the reinterpretation of all biological and anthropological knowledge—and who pursues the reconstruction systematically. Matthew never saw the forest for his trees. (pp. 60–61)

Similarly, I would argue, the idea of combining science and fiction is cheap, and there may be many before Gernsback who hit upon or briefly mentioned the idea; but they are unimportant because they did not make anything of the idea. Gernsback is the central figure in the history of science fiction because he not only found, but fully developed the idea of science fiction, and nurtured a widespread awareness of the genre's existence and importance.

There is, however, one literary tradition prior to Gernsback which was unquestionably real, undoubtedly widely acknowledged at the time, and unmistakably influential: the 'scientific romance'. As discussed in Stableford's *Scientific Romance in Britain*, the term was first used by Charles Howard Hinton as the title of an anthology published in 1886 and emerged as a standard expression when Wells appeared in the last years of the nineteenth century (pp. 5, 7). And Wells himself achieved a brilliant synthesis of the previously separated traditions identified by Stableford, employing various elements of all four types in his early works. Here, then, there seems to be solid ground for arguing that there existed prior to Gernsback both a large body of related works and a contemporary awareness that those works constituted a literary genre.

While admitting the strength of the argument, though, I would still maintain that the idea of the scientific romance, as it is seen between 1890 and 1920, was one that was far from universally accepted, weakly developed, and fatally incomplete. Thus, the scientific romance is not really equivalent to the full emergence of science fiction as a genre that was effected by Gernsback.

First, Stableford notes that the term 'scientific romance' was mainly used by book reviewers, and that most publishers and writers did not seem interested in or fond of the term (p. 7). This indicates that the concept was not completely accepted at the time. Another problem described by Stableford is that the tradition of the scientific romance eventually died out, 'sent... into its terminal decay, to be superseded even in Britain by the idea of science fiction' (p. 17). The term's inability to withstand the American challenge suggests a fundamentally weakness in its under-pinnings.

In fact, Stableford identifies the basic flaw in the idea of the scientific romance in his final section, where he observes:

> Most writers of scientific romance who felt called upon to write introductions to their books, or look back over their careers, automatically went on the defensive. They worked from the assumption that the unspoken question facing them was why on earth they bothered to do it. They seem to have imagined this question being posed in a rather contemptuous way... all begin by surrendering the initiative and admitting that fantastic fiction does need an excuse for existing. It is surely a sad discovery to find H. G. Wells, in the preface to his collected scientific romances, offering embarrassed and sarcastic excuses for ever having written them, and promising (after the fashion of a flasher begging mercy from a magistrate) not to do it again now that he has seen the error of his ways. (pp. 331–32)

Here we see what was lacking in the idea of the scientific romance. In order for a literary genre to emerge and prosper, its representatives must argue that the genre has some unique value or special purpose *which can be served by no other type of writing*. Without such a rationale, there is no particular reason for the genre to exist, and no particular reason for anyone to care about its existence. Manifestly, authors of scientific romances did not regard their work as having any peculiar virtues and consequently made no strong commitment to it—Wells himself dismissed his imaginative creations when he told Arnold Bennett, 'I am doomed to write "scientific romances" and short stories for you creatures of the mob, and my novels must be my private dissipation' (cited in Sam Lundwall, *Science Fiction: An Illustrated History*, p. 42). Publishers and readers responded in kind to their absence of belief in the scientific romance, and without defenders in any quarters, the scientific romance was doomed to wither away and die.

Stableford responds to this crucial omission by building upon some later remarks of S. Fowler Wright to offer his own defence of the scientific romance, largely appealing to the value of the human imagination (pp. 333–36); but even this posthumous addition to the idea of the scientific romance fails to achieve its purpose, for Stableford's eloquent arguments apply equally well to fantasies, fairy tales, and surrealistic visions. Even in retrospect, then, a sympathetic critic of the scientific romance seems unable to offer an argument for the *unique* value of the genre.

In contrast, Gernsback launched the idea of science fiction with a set of arguments that could apply *only* to science fiction. While I discuss his theories more fully below, two of his positions can be crudely described: science fiction offered education in scientific principles and facts to the young, and stimulating ideas for inventions to working scientists. While there is more depth to these ideas than these summaries provide, the arguments hardly seem profound or conducive to writing superior literature; but that is not important. Gernsback's ideas had an immediate impact: other publishers began defending the scientific value of their stories, writers started to include more scientific explanations in their stories, and readers wrote letters praising and analysing stories of this type. Soon, expanded versions of these ideas became the basis for a community of interested writers, editors, and readers whose discussions and commentaries provided a stimulating and supportive atmosphere for the nascent genre of science fiction. Simply put, Gernsback made it possible to believe in science fiction; and that belief, more than the literary quality of his initial offerings, enabled his idea of a genre to grow and endure.

The study of Gernsback and the tradition he engendered therefore answers a larger problem that haunts all British and European science fiction critics: when they look at their native literatures in the period from 1890 to 1920, they find more than enough examples of works classifiable as science fiction that are far superior to anything produced in America at that time; but as they extend their chronological surveys past 1920, they watch their own traditions fade and fall apart, while American science fiction expands and grows stronger to the point that, by 1950, American writers and ideas dominated the world, and British and European authors were forced to imitate or respond to the American tradition. Since they had such a tremendous head start in the field, how could this have happened? Swedish critic Sam J. Lundwall, in *Science Fiction: An Illustrated History*, raises the issue emotionally, claiming that science fiction had somehow been 'stolen' (p. 201) by the Americans from the Europeans, but even if one accepts this characterization as accurate, the question remains: if the Americans were only trafficking in a stolen European concept, why was it so successful in America while it was dying in Europe?

The usual answers provided are far from adequate. British and European critics may defensively complain about the traumatic impact of the First World War and later economic and political upheavals, which effectively smothered their previously thriving traditions of science fiction. This argument occurs in the Panshins' *The World beyond the Hill*: 'Neither American self-esteem nor American confidence in science were shaken as they were in Europe by the events of World War I… It was only Americans, among all the people of the West, who retained enough confidence in man and in science to continue with the unsettling and dangerous business of imagining the new SF mythos' (pp. 142–43). But one cannot deny that in the first half of the twentieth century America had problems too—the anti-Communist and anti-immigrant hysteria of the early 1920s and Great Depression of the 1930s—which failed to extinguish American science fiction. And if we accept this argument, a necessary consequence would be that American literature of all types would be dominating the globe—yet this clearly did not occur. It is hard to argue that American poetry, fiction and drama have overwhelmed and overshadowed British and European works in the twentieth century. Thus, the domination of American science fiction is a unique phenomenon demanding a unique explanation.

American critics—distastefully, I think—at times maintain that there is something peculiar in the American spirit which makes for excellent science fiction. Speaking of the nineteenth century, for example, Franklin argues that 'America, for reasons we shall explore in the course of this book, was from the start especially congenial to science fiction... science fiction was somewhere near the center of nineteenth-century American literature. For what other literature could come to terms with all this?' (pp. viii–ix). While one might dismiss this claim as mindless chauvinism, there are also logical problems: if one ignores for the moment Franklin's questionable incorporation of Irving, Hawthorne, Melville, Twain, and other greats into the category of science fiction, what I said previously holds true: the quality of what might be called American science fiction before 1920 is markedly inferior to that of British and European writers. Would anyone care to argue for Luis Senarens and Garrett P. Serviss as the equals of Verne, Kurd Lasswitz, and Wells? If there is something 'especially congenial' to science fiction in the American experience, it is strange that this unusual affinity did not manifest itself until the early twentieth century.

In truth, there is one simple explanation for the growth and superiority of American science fiction: literary criticism. What Gernsback provided was not simply a set of marketing slogans or slick promotions; he offered a complete theory of science fiction which readers, editors, and writers understood and responded to. They began to discuss Gernsback's ideas, endorsing, expanding, or criticizing them, in editorials and letter columns and through informal contacts. Later came fanzines, conventions, and amateur presses producing a large body of commentary concerning science fiction. Because of the stimulating and supportive atmosphere of the commentaries engendered by Gernsback, American science fiction steadily expanded and improved; because of the absence of such commentary, British and European traditions floundered.[12] Simply put, literary criticism made American science fiction great, and that was Gernsback's great contribution to the field.

Not only the American experience testifies to the power of critical commentary: the revival of British science fiction in the 1960s was accompanied by a new burst of critical activity centred on Moorcock's *New Worlds* magazine, and the new strength of European science fiction in the 1970s was accompanied by a new generation of active critics. If these rejuvenated traditions remain in the shadow of American science fiction, that is in part because they have failed to acknowledge and appreciate the value and importance of Gernsback's seminal ideas and the tradition they engendered.

Not all critics completely dismiss Gernsback and his significance. In *Science Fiction: History, Science, Vision*, Robert Scholes and Eric S. Rabkin recognize his influence: 'Though some have disputed critic Sam Moskowitz's claim that Hugo was the "father of science fiction," everyone must admit that he was at least its benevolent uncle' (p. 39). And Gunn's *Alternate Worlds* notes: 'Before Hugo Gernsback, there were science fiction stories. After Gernsback, there was a science fiction genre' (p. 126). Still, these studies strive to accommodate all approaches to science fiction; they do not claim that Gernsback's influence was the single most important factor in the development of science fiction; and, in the context of many bows in the direction of other figures, their tributes to Gernsback have little weight.

More forcefully, Anthony Boucher's 'The Publishing of Science Fiction' says, 'Science fiction as a thing apart developed first in magazines... one man is primarily responsible: Hugo Gernsback... During the depression years magazine science fiction continued along the course on which Gernsback had set it—essentially bad writing of high ingenuity (though other editors were not so careful as Gernsback to see that the ingenuity bore some relation to plausibility)' (pp. 29, 31). And Amis's *New Maps of Hell* credits Gernsback for launching 'modern science fiction' (p. 35), dismisses the 'traditional roll call' of earlier science fiction for 'heavy reliance on accidental similarities' (p. 23), and even rejects efforts to apply the label to Verne and Wells:

> Jules Verne is certainly to be regarded as one of the two creators [footnote omitted] of modern science fiction; the other, inevitably enough, is H. G. Wells. To treat Wells as such, rather than as the first important practitioner in an existing mode, is no denigration. Rather, it takes account of the fact that all his best and most influential stories appeared between 1895 and 1907, before science fiction had separated itself from the main stream of literature, and so were

written, published, reviewed, and read as 'romances' or even adventure stories. (pp. 31–32)

While the word 'creators' implies a more crucial role than I would grant—talented writers in themselves, I argue, cannot 'create' a literary genre—Amis contradicts the claims of Suvin and Stableford that science fiction represented an 'existing mode' when Wells was writing. However, while accepting 1926 as its birth date, Amis is puzzled by what caused science fiction to improve: 'The mode [in 1940] had not come of age—it has yet to do that—but at least its crawling days were over. Why this happened when it did, or at all, I am not sure' (p. 40). In fact, these developments stemmed directly from the critical discussions inspired by Gernsback and carried on by others in the 1930s like F. Orlon Tremaine and Campbell.

The Panshins' *The World beyond the Hill* acknowledges the importance of Gernsback's role, but almost incredulously:

> *Amazing Stories* was an odd, limited and marginal publication that offered very little in the way of fiction which was truly new and different. There can be no question, however, that *Amazing Stories* was a major turning point in the development of science fiction... Strange and wonderful indeed that an explicit formulation of SF as limited and externalistic as this one by Gernsback could manage to serve as an effective summarizing principle for all the different kinds of Technological Age SF story. Yet it did. (p. 170)

However, they ultimately depict Gernsback essentially as a roadblock to the growth of the sort of science fiction which they espouse as central—'Only when Gernsback and all that he stood for were swept out of the way did science fiction flourish' (p. 182)—and fail to recognize the lasting significance of his theories.

Two books—Lester del Rey's *The World of Science Fiction: 1926–1976* and David G. Hartwell's *Age of Wonders*—also proclaim that Gernsback's *Amazing Stories* represents the true beginning of the genre; Hartwell says that Gernsback 'invented modern science fiction in April, 1926' and 'The history of the world of science fiction dates from the birth of conscious separateness, April, 1926' (pp. 23, 118). But both authors are interested not only in the literature but the entire 'world' of modern science fiction—as del Rey's subtitle suggests—and they pay little attention to the role that Gernsback's tradition played in shaping the modern literature.

Another study of science fiction, Paul Carter's *The Creation of Tomorrow*, also begins in 1926, recognizes Gernsback's role in launching the genre, including a brief summary of some of his ideas (pp. 4–5), and pays tribute to the importance of the accompanying critical commentary which began at that time by noting that letter columns of the time offered a 'residue [of] shrewd and apposite criticism' (p. 296). However, historian Carter tends to see science fiction stories and criticism as a discussion of major topics and issues, not of the nature of science fiction, and thus does not fully recognize the contributions of Gernsback and his tradition.

From the viewpoint of a different discipline—sociology—William Bainbridge's *Dimensions of Science Fiction* accepts Gernsback's importance in science fiction history, stating that 'the birthdate of science fiction is often given as 1926, when Hugo Gernsback began *Amazing Stories*'; his definition of the genre—'literature produced and consumed by the science fiction subculture'—is not unlike my own (p. 10); and his discussions often include the words of science fiction commentators. However, Bainbridge builds his picture of science fiction solely on results of a survey of the science fiction community, thus measuring only modern perceptions of the genre, not the history of its development and growth in connection with critical commentaries.

Astonishingly, the strongest support for my position comes from Barry N. Malzberg, a science fiction writer who could not be more dissimilar to Gernsback in his attitudes and style. In *The Engines of the Night*, after noting the 'revisionist' view that Gernsback was harmful to science fiction, he acknowledges that Gernsback created the genre and began its critical tradition:

> At the risk of aligning myself with Hugo Gernsback, a venal and small-minded magazine publisher whose reprehensible practices, long since detailed, were contemptible to his contributors, partners and employees, I think that he did us a great service and that were it not for Gernsback, science fiction as we understand it would not exist... 'Science fiction builds on science fiction', [Isaac] Asimov said once, and that truth is at the center of the form. Before Gernsback gave it a name... the literature did not exist; before he gave it a medium of exclusivity, its dim antecedents were scattered through the range of popular and restricted writing without order, overlap or sequence. It was the creation of a label and a medium which gave the genre its exclusivity and a place in which it could begin that dialogue, and it was the evolution of magazine science fiction— slowly over the first decade, more rapidly after the ascension of Campbell—that became synonymous with the evolution of the field... Without the specialized format of the magazines, where science fiction writers and readers could dwell, exchange, observe one another's practices and build upon one another's insight, the genre could not have developed. (pp. 11–12)

Unlike del Rey and Amis, Malzberg realizes that the criticism surrounding modern science fiction made it a genre and contributed to its improvement; yet he credits Gernsback only with starting the discussion, not with contributing to it. This is unfortunate, for many of the torturous conflicts in the genre that Malzberg emotionally documents can be traced back to Gernsback's theories of science fiction and Campbell's modifications of those theories.

Other critics have occasionally seen the value and power of the commentaries of readers and fans without recognizing who started and influenced those commentaries: Don Fabun's 'Science Fiction in Motion Pictures, Radio, and Television' notes the important role of editors and fans in shaping the modern genre:

> This small, but homogenous, group of SF readers has... a general reverence for a scientific (or pseudoscientific) approach to problems and a general dislike for nonscientific literature... While this science fiction that has evolved from the relationship between magazine editors and the more articulate of the fans ranges all the way from 'space opera' to the sophisticated 'socio-psychological' stories, as a type it conforms to the expression of a myth. (p. 46).

However, the comment is a parenthetical note in a discussion of science fiction in other media and inaccurately summarizes the concerns and priorities of science fiction readers. And Amis acknowledges that 'readers' letters in the magazines often show a genuinely critical attitude, however crude its bases and arguments, and acquaintance with the whole body of a given author's work is commonly appealed to, implying some sort of power to make distinctions' (p. 49); still, as suggested by the words 'crude' and 'implying', Amis is not altogether supportive of this criticism.

All these studies, then, are in one respect superior to those of Aldiss and Suvin in acknowledging that Gernsback and the discussions he engendered were important; however, none of them fully offers the new perspective I propose.

To say that the critical history of science fiction has not been thoroughly studied understates matters considerably; rather, it is habitually rejected without examination. In 'The Short History of Science Fiction', the Panshins take a cursory look at Gernsback's theories and ridicule them with superficial sarcasm. Aldiss describes the 'rules' of writing science fiction as 'a few prescriptions' without indicating that he is familiar with them, and a lack of knowledge is also manifest in Patrick Parrinder's *Science Fiction: Its Teaching and Criticism*. After an inadequate description of the critical ideas engendered by the magazines, he concludes that 'the project of basing a comprehensive rhetoric of science fiction on these highly ambiguous categories is hopeless' (p. 14). Yet Parrinder reveals that he has never read any magazine commentaries: his one quotation from Gernsback is taken from *The Creation of Tomorrow* (pp. 13, 145). Other comments suggest that he literally only looked at the magazines' covers: he summarizes Gernsback by saying that his 'enthusiasms are sufficiently indicated by the titles of some of his other magazines: *Modern Electrics, Air Wonder Stories, Science and Invention'* (p. 13), and he finally dismisses popular criticism of science fiction with a lame joke, imagining 'some benighted researcher… distinguishing between the literary categories of the "amazing," the "astounding," and the "weird" on the basis of the publication policies of *Amazing Stories, Astounding Science Fiction*, and *Weird Tales'* (p. 14). Yet had he studied these magazines, Parrinder would have learned that the adjectives in magazine titles rarely appeared in discussions of the genre, that Gernsback called his magazine *Amazing Stories* reluctantly, after concluding that the title *Scientifiction* would not be popular, and that Campbell despised the name *Astounding* and repeatedly tried to get rid of it.

It will be my task, then, to demonstrate that what Gernsback presented to the world went well beyond 'a few prescriptions' and 'highly ambiguous categories' to emerge as a true literary theory and history of science fiction which were, granted Gernsback's limited ability, reasonably logical and complete, and which have had a lasting and profound impact on the genre; and I will show how that theory and that history were reflected in Gernsback's own *Ralph 124C 41+* and how his ideas had an impact on contemporary writers. After epitomizing several transitional figures, I will then discuss the theory and history of science fiction offered by Gernsback's major successor, John W. Campbell, Jr, who expanded or modified Gernsback's ideas about the nature and history of science fiction, essentially establishing the direction for all future critical approaches to science fiction; and I will discuss how his ideas and their effects can be seen in Heinlein's *Beyond This Horizon* and how Campbell affected contemporary science fiction. Regretfully bypassing the major commentators who followed Campbell, I will finally discuss how this study might be employed to develop a description of modern science fiction and demonstrate the value of the approach I offer to science fiction criticism.

And, in these ways, I will lay the groundwork for a true history of science fiction.

Notes

1 Since this definition of a literary genre provoked the greatest response when I published a draft of this chapter, I will further explain how I can defend this position in these ways:

A. To argue that my definition yields a body of work with the homogeneity and interrelatedness traditionally associated with the term 'genre'. Given the immense number of works involved, defending this point is difficult, but I will attempt the task at the end of Chapter 2 and in Chapter 11.

B. To argue that previous approaches to science fiction using different definitions are either hopelessly subjective or based on questionable assumptions about literary history and development, while other critical approaches that appear to accept my definition but create quite different characterizations of science fiction truly lack the evidence they claim. That is the argument of this chapter.

C. To argue that literary critics in other fields of genre study implicitly or explicitly use the same definition in that they regularly include references to accompanying critical awareness in their discussions. While I offer one example—Wordsworth and Coleridge and Romantic poetry—I do not stress this point because I regard it as self-evident. In graduate-level literature classes, critical texts are always incorporated into discussions of periods and fields of literature; and studies of other genres regularly emphasize the important role played by a founding or major critical voice—tragedy, Aristotle; sentimental comedy, Richard Steele; detective fiction, Poe; and naturalism, Émile Zola.

Now, if someone wishes to argue against my approach to defining science fiction, I envision three basic ways:

A. To argue that my definition yields a body of work which is not homogeneous or interrelated, thus not satisfying traditional expectations associated with the term 'genre'. This case can be made, though I believe that the vast majority of these works do reflect shared assumptions and conventions.

B. To argue that previous approaches to science fiction are in fact not subjective, illogical, or lacking in evidence; yet no *Foundation* readers defended the critics I discuss here.

C. To argue that there are other fields of genre studies in literature which have successfully functioned by ignoring accompanying criticism, so those fields can serve as models for science fiction studies. Yet the sole example I can provide of a context-free approach to literature is the field of 'popular culture'; and, despite its accomplishments, a review of advertisements for faculty positions suggests that it has not become a major area of literary studies.

Indeed, there is an interesting paradox here. Works in the grand literary tradition—call them High Literature—are usually examined in the context of accompanying critical commentary; works outside that tradition—call them Junk—are usually examined without regard to their critical context. I insist on studying science fiction in the manner of High Literature, which leads me to focus on Junk—Gernsback, Campbell, and their colleagues; others insist on studying science fiction in the manner of Junk, which enables them to focus on High Literature—More, Rabelais, Swift, etc. Also, consider that many genres offered by *Foundation* readers as comparable to science fiction—boys' adventures, spy novels, mysteries, westerns, nurse fiction, horror—are Junk, while the examples I employ—Renaissance literature, sentimental comedy, Romantic poetry, naturalism—are High Literature. An approach to science fiction centred on pulp magazines might seem an effort to 'put science fiction back in the gutter'; but I actually demand that science fiction be regarded and studied as true literature.

2 The identification occurred in a review by Ernest O. Baker, as noted by Madawc Williams in a letter to *Foundation* (No. 50). One Gernsback reader, James T. Brady, Jr, did mention *Frankenstein* in his 1928 'History of Scientific Fiction', but clearly knew little of it; discussing European science fiction, he mentions that 'Germany has Wollstonecraft, who wrote "Frankenstein," and many others' (p. 571). Gernsback referred to Frankenstein in a 1931 editorial, 'Wonders of the Machine Age', indicating that he knew of the novel, but never offered it as an example of science fiction. Later, J. O. Bailey's *Pilgrims through Time and Space: Trends and Patterns in Scientific and Utopian Fiction* (1947) was the first prominent work to connect *Frankenstein* with science fiction.

3 Except for a few later quotations identified as from Suvin's *Victorian Science Fiction in the UK* and *Positions and Presuppositions in Science Fiction*, all Suvin page references in this chapter are to *Metamorphoses of Science Fiction*.

4 In *Positions and Presuppositions in Science Fiction*, Suvin in part clarifies and in part changes his position: he says that 'I argued… that genre traditions are legitimately established in retrospect' (as I read *Metamorphoses of Science Fiction*, he did not) and that his book, '(as any other study) was normative in the sense of possessing norms of value induced from both the critic's presuppositions and the texts (see Mukarovsky, *Aesthetic Function*) and reapplied to texts. Furthermore (as different from some studies) my book foregrounded such norms in order to leave its readers the true freedom of knowing what they were reading and being able to thoughtfully agree or disagree' (pp. 75, xii). Suvin thus acknowledges that his vision of science fiction history was established 'in retrospect' (writers were not aware of this tradition, contradicting previous statements) and it is built on his 'presuppositions' (his own value judgements).

5 In a sense, I could stop arguing with Suvin at this point; he admits that his theories have nothing to do with science fiction as that term is generally employed. However, because his use of the term 'science fiction' must be interpreted as a deliberate attempt to replace his own ideas with the traditional concept of the genre, and because his statements are frequently quoted as observations concerning 'science fiction', I will later in this chapter demonstrate that his theories are questionable.

6 After writing this passage, I discovered that Amis used the same analogy while explaining the improvement in science fiction between 1920 and 1940: 'few things are much good to begin with, and the inferiority of early Elizabethan drama is not what makes Shakespeare's appearance remarkable' (*New Maps of Hell*, p. 43).

7 I make exactly that argument in 'The Gernsback Continuum'.

8 Fredric Jameson, less sanguine about diachronic arguments, dismisses Christopher Caudwell while discussing 'what passes for Marxist criticism'—'To read [Caudwell] is indeed to acquire the gradual impression of a figure named Poetry, which, not unlike the Orlando of Virginia Woolf, alters its shape in the course of its successive adventures down through the ages of modern history' (*Marxism and Form*, p. 375)—a comment that seems applicable to Suvin's description of 'science fiction' as 'a coherent literary tradition… that (like many forms of humor and "obscenity") spread through centuries by word

of mouth and other unofficial channels' (p. 88).

9 In 'Formalist Narratology and Fantasy Literature' and elsewhere.

10 Though J. C. Davis's *Utopia and the Ideal Society* argues that utopia itself was not a recognized literary tradition until the twentieth century.

11 Some additional examples: saying that 'More was well aware of such subgenres as the Earthly Paradise' (p. 93) does not actually claim that More was influenced by any work in that genre; saying that Lucian's 'humanistic irony embodied in aesthetic delight became the paradigm for the whole "prehistory" of SF, from More and Rabelais to Cyrano and Swift' (p. 98) does not actually claim that Lucian influenced those writers; saying that 'Jonathan Swift drew on the tradition of the imaginary voyage... After Lucian, More, Rabelais, and Cyrano, the satirical-cum-utopian tradition also had an offshoot in numerous contemporary pretended travels' (p. 107) does not actually claim that the writers influenced Swift; quoting a modern critic to the effect that Swift's Gulliver is 'More's Hythloday [dressed up] to look like Defoe's Robinson Crusoe' does not actually claim that More influenced Swift; saying that 'What Orwell would expose as brainwashing, Mary Shelley shows as just expiation' (p. 129) does not actually claim that Mary Shelley influenced Orwell; saying that *The Last Man* is 'a precursor of the SF biophysics of alienation which extends from Poe to Flammarion to *The Time Machine* and beyond' (p. 137) does not actually claim that Mary Shelley influenced those writers.

12 Asimov noted the importance of Gernsback in establishing American, rather than European, science fiction as a dominant force, without recognizing the importance of Gernsback's ideas and the discussion they engendered: 'How was it, then, that in one generation, science fiction came to be considered a peculiarly American phenomenon, not only here in the United States, but throughout Europe? It came about because, in 1926 in the United States, a man named Hugo Gernsback founded a magazine called *Amazing Stories*, the first periodical published anywhere in the world to be exclusively devoted to works of science fiction' (*Asimov on Science Fiction*, pp. 140–41).

'An Idea of Tremendous Import':
Hugo Gernsback's Theory of Science Fiction

In calling Hugo Gernsback a literary critic propounding a theory of science fiction, I anticipate a sceptical response: for if we define literary criticism as something requiring education and sophistication, Gernsback cannot be considered a literary critic—understandably, because despite native intelligence and strong motivation, people who lack formal training and exposure to literary theories and practitioners will be unable to produce analyses suitable for scholarly presses or journals. And Gernsback never reveals any particular insight into deeper issues of literary criticism and, as an early reader of my work noted with irritation, offers his observations in appalling prose.

Still, we cannot build a concept of literary criticism on the shifting sands of aesthetic criteria; standards of 'good' and 'bad' criticism will inevitably vary, and one man's Aristotle may be another man's amateur. Instead, we must define criticism in functional terms: if commentators raise and attempt to answer those questions which are the traditional concerns of critical theory, and if they provide or produce texts which illustrate and exemplify their ideas, then they are literary critics, no matter how naive or unsatisfactory their work is. By these standards, Hugo Gernsback more than qualifies as a science fiction critic.

Specifically, a critic who seeks to define and describe a literary genre must perform these tasks: she must suggest criteria by which a work can be identified as belonging to the genre without reference to any external context; she must articulate who its characteristic readers and authors are and what unique value or purpose works in the genre have for them; and she must delineate the literary ancestry of the genre and offer exemplary models for authors, readers, and critics. In confronting and wrestling with these questions in a manner that was more thorough and focused than previous commentators, Gernsback deserves credit for being the first significant critic of science fiction.

Before celebrating Gernsback's accomplishments, however, I must answer a common charge that would apparently undermine his significance: that Gernsback's discussions of the theory and history of science fiction stem only from his desire to make money by selling his magazines, and that they can be dismissed on that account. Evidently that is the attitude of Parrinder, who describes Gernsback's 'shrewdly commercial reprint policy' and refers to his stories as a demonstrated success 'in commercial terms' (*Science Fiction: Its Teaching and Criticism*, pp. 2, 13).

Such attacks involving Gernsback's motives are, first, pure examples of the *ad hominem* argument; logically, Gernsback's statements about science fiction should be judged primarily by their merits, not their alleged motives. And one can hardly argue that statements made by persons engaged in marketing literature are always tainted by greed, while statements made by literary scholars are always motivated by a pure search for truth.

Also, characterizing Gernsback as someone whose interest in science fiction was purely mercenary does not seem accurate: no one has denied Gernsback's desire to make money, but little about his career (as discussed in Chapter 5) indicates that was the *only* reason for his attention to science fiction. Gernsback had no economic incentive to begin writing science fiction for his magazine *Modern Electrics*: other science magazines were not doing it, and readers did not demand it, so it was clearly something he wanted to do. Further, long after he stopped publishing science fiction magazines, he continued writing science fiction to amuse himself and his friends, would on occasion write or speak about science fiction, and continued to read science fiction magazines: in 1961, a comment by book reviewer P. Schuyler Miller in *Analog Science Fiction/Science Fact* prompted Gernsback to write a letter in response. This is not the track record of a man who briefly addressed the subject of science fiction only to make a buck.

It is also hard to argue that his editorial statements and decisions to reprint older stories were simply a matter of economic expediency. I defy anyone, for example, to explain how Gernsback's discussions of Roger Bacon and Leonardo da Vinci as nascent science fiction writers ('The Lure of Scientifiction') could help to sell magazines; and his ongoing arguments that science fiction writers should qualify for patents only served as an embarrassment and may have doomed his attempted comeback with *Science-Fiction Plus* in the 1950s. In sum, more than enough available evidence suggests that Gernsback had a sincere interest in science fiction that transcended any mercenary objectives; and, although Aldiss dismissed his ideas as 'a few prescriptions' (*Trillion Year Spree*, p. 20), they in fact constitute the first comprehensive theory and history of science fiction.

Gernsback's basic definition of science fiction was clearly announced in the first issue of his science fiction magazine, *Amazing Stories*: 'a charming romance intermingled with scientific fact and prophetic vision' ('A New Sort of Magazine', p. 3).[1] In that phrase he succinctly listed the three elements he saw as essential in all works of science fiction and established the groundwork for a thorough explanation of the genre.

First, science fiction is a form of narrative fiction—specifically, a 'charming romance'. Gernsback's idea of the romance was no doubt uncomplicated and similar to the definition in *The New English Dictionary*: 'a fictitious narrative in prose of which the scene and incidents are very remote from those of ordinary life' (cited in Holman, p. 459); he may have also been influenced by the previous term 'scientific romance'. Four years later, however, he narrowed the generic category of science fiction by calling it 'thrilling adventure' ('Science Fiction Week', p. 1061), what Northrop Frye describes as the 'naïve' form of romance (p. 259). Thus, while Gernsback was open to science fiction based on other generic models, like the travel tale, the Gothic novel, utopia, and satire (as discussed later), he identified romance or adventure as its central and characteristic mode.

The second and third elements of science fiction were 'scientific fact' and 'prophetic vision'. To Gernsback, 'scientific fact' meant lengthy and detailed explanations of current scientific knowledge and discoveries, equivalent to those found in science textbooks and articles; indeed, Gernsback at one point advised writers to do library research because 'it gives you a good chance to pad your story legitimately from a scientific text book' ('How to Write "Science" Stories', p. 28). These passages are 'intermingled' with the fiction, included in while remaining distinct from it: he spoke of information being 'contained' in the narrative, as in these instructions to contestants in a short story contest: 'The story... must contain correct scientific facts' ('The $500 Cover Prize Contest', p. 213); and their separability from the narrative text was indicated in his 'opinion' that 'the ideal proportion of a scientifiction story should be seventy-five per cent literature interwoven with twenty-five per cent science' ('Fiction Versus Facts', p. 291). And, while Gernsback's own scientific interests were heavily focused on mechanics and invention, he gestured toward including other fields of science: thus, the 'Associate Science Editors' listed on the title page of every issue of *Wonder Stories* who 'pass upon the scientific principles of all stories' included college professors in the fields of botany, entomology, medicine, psychology, and zoology.

The 'twenty-five per cent science' included the third element of science fiction, 'prophetic vision', thorough descriptions and explanations of hypothetical inventions and scientific processes like those found in Gernsback's science magazines and still seen today in magazines like *Popular Science* (the spiritual descendant of Gernsback's *Science and Invention*). While, like the 'scientific fact', written in the manner of nonfiction, prophecy also in itself combines fact and fiction in that, on the one hand, a scientifically grounded prediction of a future discovery might be substantive enough to warrant a patent, so that he once spoke of 'true or prophetic science' as if both accounts of current information and informed speculations about the future could be considered types of science ('Guest Editorial', p. 140). On the other hand, a predicted invention, even if logical or inevitable, cannot be a fact until it is realized; in a different sense of the word, such a description is a 'fiction'. Thus, science fiction consists of fiction, fact, and a third element which is itself a mixture of fiction and fact.[2]

These three different types of writing are not combined randomly, as suggested by the term 'interwoven', describing separate threads brought together as a part of an overall pattern; that is, one cannot in the manner of Tzara cut up pirate novels and chemistry textbooks and glue passages together to form 'science fiction'. Without explicit description, Gernsback demonstrated in his own fiction three techniques for integrating explanatory material into a narrative as part of what I will call his *pedagogical* model for writing science fiction. Two were traditional devices that can be called the *character-pedagogue* and the *narrator-pedagogue*. First, a writer can provide in the story a knowledgeable and loquacious character, paired with an ignorant and inquisitive one, and have the first character provide all necessary information in conversation. This is, of course, the pattern of the ancient dialogue form and most utopian novels and is seen in the characters of Ralph and Alice in Gernsback's *Ralph 124C 41+: A Romance of the Year 2660*. Second, a writer can simply have the created narrating voice or persona explain things to the imagined reader as the need arises; in prose fiction, this technique is at least as old as Henry Fielding and is used in *Ralph* when the narrator steps in to explain devices Alice is already familiar with or the inventions Ralph develops when Alice is not present. Gernsback's third device, the *author-pedagogue*, is more innovative; here, the actual author steps out of the narrative persona to provide information directly to the actual reader in the form of footnotes, diagrams, drawings, photographs, or glossaries—all devices found in *Ralph* or in other Gernsback pieces like 'Exploration of Mars', 'World War III—In Retrospect', and *Ultimate World*. In these instances, science fiction emerges even more clearly as a combination of fiction and nonfiction, as features traditionally associated only with nonfiction are incorporated into a fictional narrative.

This model of science fiction raises one practical issue for the writer: what is the best process for writing stories which combine such different types of material? There were three times when Gernsback touched upon this question. His most explicit answer came in an article he wrote for *Writer's Digest*, 'How to Write "Science" Stories', though his advice there specifically centred on the 'scientific detective' story (a form discussed below). The writer's first step is research, to master current knowledge: 'The whole secret of scientific fiction lies in reading about your subject before you start your story'. Next, the writer simultaneously envisions the story and the element of scientific prophecy: 'Get an idea of what the murderer is going to do... Then think about what clues the detective will find, and what scientific apparatus or methods *he* will use to trace the criminal. If you have a mental vision of your story before hand, and the scientific details at your finger tips, the story will almost write itself as you work' (p. 29).

A somewhat different explanation of the process of writing science fiction was embodied in the symbol that he created for 'scientifiction', first presented on the cover of the September 1928 issue of *Amazing Stories*. In the picture—which Gernsback devised by combining two contest entries— two gears representing 'fact' (science) and 'theory' (prophecy) together move a pen writing on a page, which 'presents the fiction part' ('Results of Scientifiction Prize Contest', p. 3). Here, the genesis of science fiction rests in the author's scientific knowledge *and* scientific speculations, which then generate a narrative, so that the fictional aspects of the form are the last, and presumably least important, stage in the process. This was also suggested in Gernsback's advice to contestants in a short story contest: 'it would be well to submit [your story] to a literary friend or teacher before you enter it into the competition' ('$300.00 Prize Story Contest', p. 677). Seeking 'literary' advice is the final step, not the first step; the story begins with its science.

Finally, years after his period of greatest influence, Gernsback presented a slightly different definition of science fiction and further information about the process of writing it:

> there is still a good deal of confusion about Science-Fiction and what it really is.
>
> Let us therefore analyze the term. *Science*, the dictionary tells us, is: 'Ordered and systematized knowledge of natural phenomena gained by observation, experimentation, and induction'. *Fiction* is: "Imaginative prose literature."
>
> Science-Fiction therefore can be defined... as: *Imaginative extrapolation of true natural phenomena, existing now, or likely to exist in the future.*
>
> Good Science-Fiction must be based on true science—science as interpreted and understood by responsible scientists. In other words, the story should be within the realm of the possible. ('Pseudo Science-Fiction', p. 2).

While the elements of fiction, science, and prophecy remain central, Gernsback now explained that the prediction arises from the science by a process of 'extrapolation'—a term used by John W. Campbell, Jr in the 1940s, and one Gernsback perhaps borrowed from him. And fiction remains the final embellishment in the process—interestingly, Gernsback's 'short' definition did not even mention that element, announcing its relative unimportance.

In all descriptions of the process of writing science fiction, scientific knowledge comes first; and on that foundation, the author may either construct imaginative speculations which then in tandem create a story, or she may simultaneously construct a story and accompanying speculations.

Overall, Gernsback's theoretical model for science fiction is both novel and striking. The scraps of previous commentary on science fiction that one might assemble typically discuss science fiction as literature written *about scientific marvels*, or, in the case of William Wilson, literature written *from the perspective of science*; but to Gernsback, science fiction *must include scientific writing* (perhaps even taken from a textbook). Since he specified an original fictional genre—romance or adventure—as a model, and since he also required that some writing in the genre of nonfiction be incorporated into it, Gernsback's definition is the first *formal* definition of science fiction.[3]

One might object at this point that Gernsback was proposing nothing new: and to be sure, some amount of exposition and explanation, often in a manner resembling nonfiction, is present in almost all fiction. Gernsback himself acknowledged the link when he commented, 'What description of clouds and sunsets was to the old novelist, description of scientific apparatus and methods is to the modern Scientific Detective writer' ('How to Write "Science" Stories', p. 28). However, these passages are traditionally regarded as decorative embellishments—beautiful 'clouds and sunsets' and the like—necessary evils, or at worst signs of authorial ineptitude, one example being the adventure story where the villain pauses before killing the hero to obligingly explain in detail the previously unclear plot machinations. For good reason, story writers are urged to avoid lengthy descriptions and explanations; yet Gernsback virtually demanded that science fiction authors include large amounts of scientific and prophetic exposition and celebrated this material as a necessary empowering ingredient in science fiction. In examining the works of Gernsback and his authors, then, one must realize the long scientific explanations occur not because writers lack the skill to convey information in any other way; rather, they deliberately stop their stories to provide the information as conspicuously as possible. Gernsback was perfectly capable of describing an invention without lengthy explanations,[4] but he chose to include those passages because, in his view, that is what science fiction should provide.

Though one can criticize this approach to science fiction, there is potentially extraordinary power in Gernsback's proposal: a form of writing which is both fiction and nonfiction and thus superior to ordinary fiction— as Gernsback once asserted, science fiction 'should not be classed just as literature' ('Imagination and Reality', p. 579). Since both fiction and nonfiction have their own virtues, science fiction, at least in theory, might combine the best attributes of fiction and nonfiction and become a form of literature that transcends both in quality and importance.

When Gernsback himself explained the value and purposes of science fiction, however, he offered no such exalted ideas. Instead, he straightforwardly proposed that the three elements of science fiction corresponded to three natural types of readers and authors and each element had a special purpose which was uniquely relevant to one group. Thus, he achieved for science fiction what had never been done for the scientific romance, the necessary work in establishing a literary genre: he was targeting potential groups of readers and authors and explaining to them the benefits of reading and writing science fiction.

First, Gernsback saw almost everyone as a potential reader of science fiction; an early editorial described his plan to 'influence the masses' ('Editorially Speaking', p. 483) and he later professed his desire to 'induce' 'every man, woman, boy and girl… to read science fiction' ('Science Fiction Week', p. 1061). He once asked rhetorically, 'Who are the readers of SCIENCE WONDER STORIES?' and answered 'Everybody. Bankers, ministers, students, housewives, bricklayers, postal clerks, farmers, mechanics, dentists—every class you can think of—*but only those who have imagination*' ('Science Wonder Stories', p. 5; author's italics). In 1953, he again argued that science fiction should always 'cater to the masses' ('Status of Science-Fiction', p. 2). Also, despite common misconceptions, Gernsback felt that ordinary readers without scientific training could be science fiction writers and he happily published works by writers who he knew lacked any formal qualifications. Responding to a reader complaining of authors who were 'lamentably weak in their facts', an editor admitted that some writers were not scientists and needed to learn more science: 'the demand for stories of the type we aim to give, should inspire [authors] with the desire to study natural science for the purposes of their work' ('Discussions', *Amazing Stories*, June 1928, p. 272).[5] And, discussing 'scientific detective' fiction, Gernsback gave advice that clearly applied only to prospective writers without a scientific background:

> buy a few really good reference books… To write really good fiction, saturate yourself with the required atmosphere. Read scientific books, visit chemical laboratories and electrical engineering shops…

What you are not sure about—look up at the library... *before you mail your manuscript to us, submit it to some local professor or authority on science, or to a physics teacher, to check the scientific principles involved.* ('How to Write "Science" Stories', pp. 28–29; author's italics)

A second particular audience that Gernsback sought was young people, included in the above list as 'students', implicitly sought as readers with the garish cover illustrations for his magazines, and announced as readers in a 1927 editorial: 'One of the outstanding facts about AMAZING STORIES is the percentage of youthful readers who find food for thought and a great stimulus throughout the pages of the magazine' ('Amazing Youth', p. 625). A later editorial specifically urged 'The average parent' to be supportive of science fiction since it could help 'young men' 'In the school and college room' ('The Science Fiction League', p. 1062). And these 'youthful readers' could also aspire to become writers, as indicated by Gernsback's instructions to contestants in a science fiction story contest to 'submit' their work to a 'literary friend or teacher' ('$300.00 Prize Story Contest', p. 677)—even high school students, it seems, might be successful in the field.

Finally, Gernsback repeatedly asserted that scientists were or should be reading science fiction; he described science fiction stories as those 'that are discussed by inventors [and] by scientists' ('Science Wonder Stories', p. 5) and once commented that 'The professional inventor or scientist then comes along, gets the stimulus from the story and promptly responds with the material invention' ('$300.00 Prize Contest', p. 5). He also advised writers to 'remember that his work will be read by competent scientists among our readers' ('How to Write "Science" Stories', p. 28). And whenever Gernsback knew of writers who had scientific degrees or titles, he would always include them—'E. E. Smith, Ph.D.', 'David M. Keller, M.D'.—to demonstrate that people with such credentials were actually writing science fiction.

Science fiction thus had three audiences—general readers, young people, and scientists—who could also be its writers.

The general readers would most appreciate the fictional element of science fiction since that would provide 'entertainment', the first purpose of science fiction Gernsback identified. This is a frequent theme in his defences of the genre: his first *Amazing Stories* editorial announced 'these amazing tales make tremendously interesting reading' ('A New Sort of Magazine', p. 3); he lauded science fiction for 'providing the most delightful and stimulating entertainment' ('Science Fiction Week', p. 1061), and the first editorial of *Air Wonder Stories* promised 'stories... full of adventure, exploration, and achievement' which were designed to 'entertain' ('Air Wonder Stories', p. 5). And addressing writers, Gernsback stressed the attribute of entertainment: 'As a story, it must be interesting... *Don't* fall into the misapprehension that, because your story has plenty of science in it, a plot is therefore unnecessary' ('How to Write "Science" Stories', pp. 27, 28).

Here one might ask: yes, entertainment is desirable, but why is it important to have entertaining fiction involving science? Gernsback offered this general answer:

> The past decade has seen the ascendancy of 'sexy' literature, of the self-confession as well as the avalanche of modern detective stories.
>
> But they are transient things, founded on the whims of the moment. For the world moves swiftly these days and with it moves literature also.
>
> Science—Mechanics—the Technical Arts—they surround us on every hand, nay, enter deeply into our very lives. The telephone, radio, talking motion pictures, television, X-rays, Radium, super-aircraft and dozens of others claim our constant attention. We live and breathe day by day in a Science saturated atmosphere... No wonder, then, that anybody who has any imagination at all clamors for fiction of the Jules Verne and H. G. Wells type, made immortal by them; the story that has a scientific background, and is read by an ever growing multitude of intelligent people. ('Science Wonder Stories', p. 5)

Simply put, since people now live in a world filled with growing numbers of marvellous gadgets, there is something appealing about a form of literature that mixes narrative with explanations and depictions of marvelous gadgets; science fiction is the natural form of entertainment for a technological age.

While Gernsback is often credited—or blamed—for launching a tradition of strictly juvenile 'entertainment', it should be noted that he also had loftier ambitions for the genre and the type of reading experience it might provide. Specifically, Gernsback wanted to elevate science fiction above other forms of popular fiction as a true form of literature, so that its authors might eventually enjoy the status of genuine literary figures.

At least one critic, Mark Rose, has argued that genres primarily seek to characterize themselves by a process of what George Slusser calls 'assertive division' (pp. 66): 'Comedy asserts that it is not tragedy, the romance asserts that it is not the novel, and science fiction asserts that it is not fantasy' (cited in Slusser, Letter, p. 66); and there are elements of this approach in Gernsback's theory—as in his distinction between 'scientifiction' that might actually be possible and 'fairy tales' which are impossible (in 'Amazing Creations', p. 109). Generally, however, despite Rose's claim,

Gernsback displayed no obsession about distinguishing science fiction from fantasy.[6] Instead he argued that science fiction was distinct from other forms of popular literature like the 'self-confession' story and the 'detective' story; and in creating the Science Fiction League, he announced that 'the public at large should begin to know the benefits of Science Fiction and be turned from meaningless detective and love trash to the elevating and imaginary literature of Science Fiction' ('The Science Fiction League', p. 1062). Thus despite its appearance in the milieu of pulp fiction, science fiction was something different, something superior, and—no doubt added to reassure concerned parents—something less prurient.

Gernsback's other efforts to provide himself and other science fiction authors with an air of literary respectability were muted but emerged nevertheless in his repeated descriptions of science fiction as 'literature' and his expressed fear that the title *Amazing Stories* 'really does not do the magazine justice, and that many people get an erroneous impression as to the literary contents from this title' ('Editorially Speaking', p. 483). Later, he optimistically asserted that science fiction stories are 'discussed... in the classroom' ('Science Wonder Stories', p. 5), though he may have been thinking only of the science classroom, and referring to the development of the 'scientific detective' story, he said that 'Literary history is now in the making' and that superior stories of that type were 'works of art from every point of view' ('How to Write "Science" Stories', p. 28). He once admitted to the hope that his term 'scientifiction' would some day appear in dictionaries, indicating that he wanted his genre at least to attract the attention of lexicographers, if not critics ('Idle Thoughts of a Busy Editor', p. 1085). In addition, his policy of regularly reprinting stories by writers like Poe, Verne, and Wells suggested a desire to offer a suitably literary context for stories by modern writers; and he sometimes praised his writers as modern-day counterparts of those great writers: for example, he claimed that M. H. Hasta's undistinguished 'The Talking Brain' 'compares favorably with Edgar A. Poe's tales. It is an interesting successor to the wonderful story, "The Case of M. Valdemar"' (blurb, 'The Talking Brain', p. 441) and he announced that Samuel M. Sargent, Jr's 'The Telepathic Pick-Up' was 'worthy of a Poe' (blurb, 'The Telepathic Pick-Up', p. 829). In these little signs, one detects a desire that science fiction be accepted as true literature, more elevated 'entertainment', and that its authors be seen as literary figures—a bold wish from the editor of a popular magazine; and, in this way, Gernsback presented one of the central tensions that he built into the genre: the desire to appeal to the 'masses', and the simultaneous desire to project the qualities of true 'literature'.

Still, entertainment of either a simple or refined sort was not Gernsback's main concern; rather, science fiction, with its long passages of scientific material, could offer all readers, and particularly youthful ones, a scientific education. To Gernsback, this was more important than entertainment; and he invariably coupled comments about entertainment with assertions of the educational value of science fiction.[7] Thus, his complete statement in that first editorial read: 'Not only do these amazing tales make tremendously interesting reading—they are also always instructive. They supply knowledge that we might not otherwise obtain—and they supply it in a very palatable form. For the best of these modern writers have the knack of imparting knowledge, and even inspiration, without once making us aware that we are being taught ('A New Sort of Magazine', p. 3). In 'Science Fiction Week', his full statement was, 'No one can doubt, then, that science fiction… is a means of educating the public to the meaning of science, as well as providing the most delightful and stimulating entertainment' (p. 1061). His complete promise in *Air Wonder Stories* was to offer 'flying stories of the future, strictly along scientific-mechanical-technical lines, full of adventure, exploration, and achievement… We must instruct while we entertain' ('Air Wonder Stories', p. 5).[8] Gernsback never abandoned this principle: in 1953, he stated: 'in our present scientific and technological age a large percentage of Science-Fiction readers deliberately choose Science-Fiction *because they want to be informed—not misinformed.* Hence the science content of the story or novel should be reasonably accurate. If it is not, Science-Fiction is not fulfilling its mission' ('Pseudo Science-Fiction', p. 2). In his 1963 Address to the MIT Science Fiction Society, he declared: 'The classic science fiction of Jules Verne and H. G. Wells, with little exception, was serious and, yes, instructive and educational. *It was not primarily intended to entertain or amuse.* These stories carried a message, and that is the great difference between technological science fiction and fantasy tales' (cited in Panshin, 'The Short History of Science Fiction', p. 21).

At the most basic level, science fiction could provide 'education' because its explanatory passages contain scientific information that the reader can absorb: 'most of the stories are written in a popular vein, making it possible for any one to grasp important facts' ('What Do You Know?', p. 759); this made a science fiction story superior to a 'dry text-book', as an editor explained ('Discussions', March 1927, 1181). To emphasize this benefit of science fiction, Gernsback began to include in each issue of *Amazing Stories* a quiz called 'What Do You Know?' with scientific questions that could be answered with facts from the accompanying stories. Even a story with a scientific error could be educational: publishing Geoffrey Hewelcke's 'Ten Million Miles Sunward', Gernsback announced that 'Frankly, though, there is something wrong with the story' and challenged readers to 'See if you can find out what that "something" is' (blurb, 'Ten Million Miles

Sunward', p. 1127); and the next issue provided a discussion of the error by a Harvard astronomy professor (Luyten, 'The Fallacy in "Ten Million Miles Sunward"', p. 25).

According to Aldiss, Gernsback's insistence on scientific accuracy in his stories 'did have the effect of introducing a deadening literalism into the fiction' (*Trillion Year Spree*, p. 204); while I can question the accuracy of this judgement,[9] it should be noted at this point that Gernsback never demanded that every piece of information in a science fiction story adhere to known scientific laws: after all, the very first story in the first issue of *Amazing Stories* was Verne's *Off on a Comet*, a novel in which, as Gernsback admitted in his introduction, 'the author abandons his usual scrupulously scientific attitude and gives his fancy freer rein' ('Introduction to This Story', p. 4). Still, Gernsback could defend Verne's obvious errors as a useful device for introducing other passages of accurate science:

> once granted the initial and the closing extravagance, the departure and return of his characters, the alpha and omega of his tale, how closely the author clings to facts between! How closely he follows, and imparts to his readers, the scientific probabilities of the universe beyond our earth, the actual knowledge so hard won by astronomers! Other authors who, since Verne, have told of trips through the planetary and stellar universe have given free rein to fancy, to dreams of what might be found. Verne has endeavored to impart only what is known to exist. (p. 5)

This willingness to excuse some scientific inaccuracy in pursuit of larger goals was acknowledged in the editorial 'Plausibility in Scientifiction', where he answered a reader who criticized scientific errors in Murray Leinster's 'The Runaway Skyscraper'. While conceding the reader's points, Gernsback responded:

> a writer of scientifiction is privileged to use poetic license, the same as is the writer of any other story. There is rarely a story of this type so perfect as to pass muster with all of its facts, the general theme, and many other points.... authors often take poetic license, sometimes disregarding the scientific facts, although still retaining enough scientific accuracy to make the plot or story seem probable and at the same time interesting. (p. 675)

So, Gernsback argued, science fiction only needed to be *generally* correct, with a *limited* degree of 'scientific accuracy'.

In the letter columns of *Amazing Stories*, a pattern soon emerged: Gernsback and his associates defending authors against readers trying to out-Gernsback Gernsback in detecting flawed science. The official response was always that a science fiction story only had to include *mostly* accurate information: answering a reader who questioned the scientific basis of Wells's *The Time Machine*, an editor replied: 'these stories are fictional, and while the science in them must have some touch of verisimilitude, the whole fabric would lose interest, if it hadn't elasticity enough in it to be stretchable' ('Discussions', July 1927, p. 412). And an editor defended the scientifically impossible 'diamond lens' in Fitz-James O'Brien's story by repeating Gernsback's principle of 'poetic licence' ('Discussions', April 1927, p. 102). These references to 'poetic licence', in a way, refute Aldiss's charge that Gernsback was 'without literary understanding' (p. 204).

In writing fiction which offered generally accurate educational materials, the science fiction writer could benefit by gaining acceptance from the general public as a scientific authority of sorts. Gernsback vigorously promoted himself as such an authority: at the bottom of every editorial page he announced his weekly radio lectures on scientific subjects; as the idea of science fiction took hold, he increasingly used his editorials to provide factual material on scientific subjects instead of discussing science fiction, and he invited readers to write to *Amazing Stories*'s letter column for further information on scientific issues. In these ways, Gernsback was promoting himself, his authors, and his magazine as scientific authorities, places for unlearned general readers to get accurate data about scientific principles and recent discoveries.

Another method by which science fiction could improve the world involved its third element—prophecy—and its third natural audience— scientists; the predicted inventions in science fiction might inspire a scientist to actually invent a new device:

> The author who works out a brand new idea in a scientifiction plot may be hailed as an original inventor years later, when his brain-child will have taken wings and when cold-blooded scientists will have realized the author's ambition.
>
> An author may not know how to build or make his invention of a certain apparatus or instrument, but he may know how to predict, and often does predict, the use of such a one. The professional inventor or scientist then comes along, gets the stimulus from the story and promptly responds with the material invention. It may not always work out that way, but it is conceivable that it might in the future. ('$300.00 Prize Contest', p. 5)

The possibility of material benefits stemming from science fiction became another argument for the genre's unique importance: 'Thus it will be seen that a scientifiction story should not be taken too lightly, and should not be classed just as literature... It actually helps in the progress of the world, if ever so little, and the fact remains that it contributes something to progress that probably no other kind of literature does' ('Imagination and Reality', p. 579). In addition, while he did not elaborate on this point, readers other than scientists no doubt appreciated the prophecy in science fiction as a type of entertainment in itself and as further inducement to support scientific progress; thus, Gernsback praised science fiction as 'a literature that appeals to the imagination' ('Thank You!', p. 99).

By describing possible new inventions in stories, the science fiction writer, Gernsback claimed, might also earn a more tangible benefit—the right to patent his scientific ideas:

> the patent offices of most countries follow scientifiction stories pretty closely, because in many of these the germ of an invention is hidden. It is not necessary to actually build a model to be an inventor; often it becomes necessary, for court proceedings and for patent reasons, to find out who really was the original inventor of a certain device; if the inventor is an author who brought out the device, even in a fiction story, this would, in the long run, entitle him to ownership of the patent, always providing that the device is carefully described, as to its functions, its purpose and so forth.
>
> For instance, in the United States, the inventor would have two years from the publication of the story to apply for a patent. ('Imagination and Reality', p. 579)[10]

Gernsback's suggestion has been repeatedly ridiculed by critics—for example, Damon Knight sarcastically offered him 'a flourish of kazoos for his notion that science fiction authors should be able to patent their ideas' (*In Search of Wonder* p. 284)—but when placed in the context of Gernsback's own theories, not later theories, the proposal has the airtight logic of a syllogism.

The major premise—and where Gernsback disagreed with actual patent law—is the claim that an inventor should have the right to patent an invention based only on a detailed written description of it. The minor premise is that, according to Gernsback's precepts, a science fiction work should incorporate long passages of detailed scientific explanation—including descriptions of proposed inventions. The conclusion is that if a work of science fiction incorporates a detailed written description of an invention, then the author should have the right to patent that invention on the basis of the story. And granting that right to science fiction authors would not only increase their stature as scientific experts but might also provide public acclaim and additional income, since professional scientists could not be trusted to properly acknowledge science fiction as the source of their ideas: 'it takes an author with vision to see ahead and so to start others thinking along new lines. The inventor or scientist may not always admit the truth of this, but the fact nevertheless remains, that both are susceptible to all sorts of outside influences, more than they will admit even to themselves' ('$300.00 Prize Contest', p. 5). Thus, in the framework of Gernsback's theory of science fiction, patents for science fiction ideas were entirely appropriate and necessary.

Still, science fiction did not exactly develop in the manner Gernsback proposed, and his continuing calls for patents on science fiction ideas made him seem ridiculous when he attempted to return to science fiction publishing in the 1950s. In a speech before the 1952 World Science Fiction Convention, reprinted in *Science-Fiction Plus*, Gernsback argued that:

> Perhaps what is needed is a patent reform. Today you cannot patent mere ideas... Unfortunately, many Science-Fiction authors are so far ahead of their times that most of their devices are impractical *at the time they describe them*... I believe that our patent laws should be revised so that ideas which appear feasible and technically sound to a qualified board of technical examiners will be given a 'Provisional Patent'. Let us assume that such a patent has a life of, say, 30 years. If, during this period the inventor cannot demonstrate the workability or feasibility of the device, the Provisional Patent will lapse... ('The Impact of Science-Fiction on World Progress', p. 67)

As Poul Anderson related in conversation, L. Sprague de Camp, familiar with patent law, rose to rebut the proposal; and Gernsback's chance to regain some influence over science fiction perhaps evaporated. Yet, however absurd his specific plans were, Gernsback still anticipated a principle that is now gospel in the Information Age: that ideas in themselves have value. And if science fiction stories are full of ideas with possible value, shouldn't their authors receive something for their creations?

Science fiction could have influence not only by offering specific ideas leading to specific inventions, however; works in the genre could also inspire new discoveries in a more indirect fashion, as Gernsback pointed out in one early editorial:

> An author, in one of his fantastic scientifiction stories, may start some one thinking along the suggested lines which the author had in mind, whereas the inventor in the end will finish up with something totally different, and perhaps much more important. But the fact remains that the author *provided the stimulus* in the first place, which is the most important function to perform. ('Imagination and Reality', p. 579)

This is important: science fiction is not always designed to tell inventors and scientists what to think; rather, it is supposed to make them think. A vision emerges of science fiction writers and readers engaged in a kind of brainstorming session—writers throwing out ideas and readers responding with their own, possibly similar but possibly different, ideas. Thus, beyond the straightforward process of offering blueprints for realizable devices, science fiction can help science progress simply by inspiring creative thought.

By taking this broad view, furthermore, Gernsback could justify science fiction prophecies that were well beyond the reach of modern science. He developed this argument in an editorial defence of A. Merritt's *The Moon Pool*:

> The editorial board of AMAZING STORIES makes this fine distinction: a story, to be true scientifiction, should have a scientific basis of plausibility, so that while it may not seem possible to perform the miracle this year or next, it may conceivably come about 500, 5,000 or 500,000 years hence... In the story by Mr. A. Merritt in the current issue, the author has hit upon a most extraordinary invention, which, as you will find, he calls 'The Shining One'. Here is really a new thought, because 'The Shining One' is neither a human being, nor a god, nor is it electricity, or light, yet it is possessed of some intelligence. Very strange and fascinating, and most exciting. At first thought you might feel that a story of this kind, while highly interesting, really should be classed with fairy tales. You will, however, soon discover your error, because, after all, the thing is not really impossible. While 'The Shining One' may never become a reality, it is conceivable that such an entity might come into existence at some future time, when we know more about science in general and when we know more about rays and radioactivity... ('Amazing Creations', p. 109)

Thus, one could defend even a visionary prophecy because it is 'exciting' and 'might come into existence at some future time'.

As another point of interest, Gernsback, despite earlier criticisms of detective fiction, later launched a magazine of scientific detective stories, *Scientific Detective Monthly*; and his defence of that subgenre in his first editorial emphasized these points: 'In reading these stories, our readers will acquire a good deal of scientific knowledge that they would not, perhaps, get otherwise; and this alone will probably be found a welcome change from the previous standards of detective fiction'; and 'SCIENTIFIC DETECTIVE MONTHLY will not only prove to be a creative force in this type of literature, but actually help our police-authorities in their work, by disseminating important knowledge to the public, and be also a constant warning to the criminal' ('Science vs. Crime', p. 85). Gernsback makes no mention of detective fiction as an interesting puzzle to solve, or as an explanation of how to solve puzzles; rather, the form is defensed entirely as a way to disseminate scientific information and improve scientific work against crime—a specific adaptation of earlier arguments for science fiction as scientific education.

There is a fascinating lacuna, however, in Gernsback's defence of scientific detective fiction. For perfect parallelism to his science fiction theories, Gernsback should have argued that the stories in *Scientific Detective Monthly* were eagerly read by working policemen and scientifically-trained detectives, and that they valued the stories because such speculative works could give them useful ideas for new investigative techniques; but instead, Gernsback only claimed that the magazine was read by 'the public' and that its only 'duty' was 'to chronicle' the scientific detective work which was being or would be done ('Science vs. Crime', p. 85). By definition, then, scientific detective fiction was not as significant as science fiction, which Gernsback asserted was influencing or could actually influence scientific research; and while many reasons have been offered for the failure of *Scientific Detective Monthly*,[11] one hitherto unnoted contributing factor may be that Gernsback simply did not make this form of writing seem particularly important.

For better or worse, Gernsback's vision of science fiction as a medium for scientific education and scientific ideas is the one aspect of his vision which has always been noted, though rarely appreciated; but these proposals involving the roles and purposes of science fiction involve larger, and more complicated, considerations. For arguing that science fiction is important because it offers scientific information and suggestions immediately raises the question: why is science important, and how will science affect human life and society? Like any instructional and inspirational programme, Gernsback's prospectus for science fiction must include some justification for its existence.

In early editorials, Gernsback hinted at larger goals in providing scientific education and ideas in science fiction: for one thing, science fiction could encourage some younger readers to become scientists themselves. Indeed, such stories might be necessary to a scientist's development: 'It is not too much to say,' an editor noted, 'that a person who never reads fiction and who may be most morbidly self-conscious in that regard, is not on the road to become a good scientist' ('Discussions', June 1927, p. 308). Gernsback alluded to this goal when he said that science fiction 'widen[s] the young man's horizon, as nothing else can' and 'keeps [children] abreast of the times' ('Science Wonder Stories', p. 5); and after noting how many young readers obtain 'food for thought and a great stimulus' from *Amazing Stories*, he added, 'if we can make the youngsters think, we feel that we are accomplishing our mission, and that the future of the magazine, and, to a degree, the future of progress through the younger generation, is in excellent hands' ('Amazing Youth', p. 625).

More broadly, the scientific materials in science fiction could help people feel more comfortable about science, encourage them to support scientific progress, and in general improve their own lives. One general reference to these purposes came when an editor said, 'It is interesting to see in our correspondence, how many of our readers take an enlightened view of the field we are trying to cover, making fiction illustrate scientific fact and lead to the development of a proper conception of "the world we live in"' ('Discussions', June 1927, p. 308); and in 'The Science Fiction League', Gernsback observed that a person who is 'converted to Science Fiction... understands what is going on all around him, which his fellow man is usually ignorant of' (p. 1062). However, his most complete explication of the value of science fiction appeared in his proclamation of 'Science Fiction Week':

> Not only is science fiction an idea of tremendous import, but it is to be an important factor in making the world a better place to live in, through educating the public to the possibilities of science and the influence of science on life which, even today, are not appreciated by the man on the street... If every man, woman, boy and girl, could be induced to read science fiction right along, there would certainly be a great resulting benefit to the community, in that the educational standards of its people would be raised tremendously. Science fiction would make people happier, give them a broader understanding of the world, make them more tolerant. (p. 1061)

This second aspect of scientific education and speculation made science fiction a uniquely powerful form of literature—'a world-force of unparalleled magnitude' ('The Science Fiction League', p. 1062): the knowledge it offered should be absorbed because that will literally make 'the world a better place to live in'.

However, there is one other possible purpose in providing scientific facts and predictions in science fiction which Gernsback acknowledged with disapproval: some scientific data, effectively framed, might induce people to *oppose* certain types of threatening scientific progress; that is, the purpose of learning more about science would be not to assist in the improvement of the world but to be better armed to prevent its destruction. In the early years of *Amazing Stories* he published a number of undisguised anti-technocratic works of this type, including Wells's *The Time Machine* and David H. Keller's 'The Revolt of the Pedestrians', thereby granting implicitly that this was a possible purpose in science fiction; but by 1931, Gernsback was seeing so many stories along these lines that he felt the need to criticize them at length:

> Of late, a certain school of thought has cried persistently that all our present troubles, particularly unemployment, are directly traceable to our 'Machine Civilization'... I have rejected [such science fiction stories] because they distorted the facts and, in many cases, were pure out-and-out propaganda against the Machine Age.
>
> Some of the authors, who should know better, maintained in their stories that, little by little, the machines and sciences are becoming a Frankenstein monster, and finally humanity will rise in revolt and destroy all the machines, and go back to the Middle Ages. The usual underlying plot is that, because of capitalistic concentration of wealth, the machines will be ultimately controlled by a few powerful men, who will enslave the entire world to the detriment of humanity... WONDER STORIES will not, in the future, publish propaganda of this sort which tends to inflame an unreasoning public against scientific progress, against useful machines, and against inventions in general. ('Wonders of the Machine Age', pp. 151–52, 286)

In articulating, while not endorsing, two reasons to learn about science through science fiction—to help science make a better world or stop science from destroying it—Gernsback provided two perspectives on the ultimate value of science: it will be the salvation of mankind, or it will be its ruination.[12]

In approving of science fiction which encourages readers to join or support the scientific community, and condemning science fiction which functions to attack that community, Gernsback seems open to the charge embodied in Franklin's unflattering description of his autonomous tradition: 'technocratic science fiction' (*Future Perfect*, p. 394). Franklin and others would maintain that all literature worthy of the name should in some way challenge or undermine commonly held beliefs and existing power structures. Hence, Gernsback's vision of a science fiction devoted to celebrating, and supporting the continuation of, modern technocratic society seems repugnant; as author Bernard Wolfe said in explaining his distaste for science fiction, 'Science has from the beginning been what it most spectacularly is now, the handmaiden of capitalism. Sf has all along been the handmaiden of, as well as a parasite on, science. This is a treason to the profession of writing, which in its serious forms can be a handmaiden of nothing but disdain for, and assault on, that-which-is' ('Afterword', p. 395). I cannot speak about all science fiction, but I can demonstrate that this view does not fully apply to Gernsback; for in fact, his call for a literature which would offer scientific education and ideas must be seen not simply as an effort to support the scientific community, but also as a severe criticism of that community and an attempt to significantly reform it.

Consider this: why is it necessary for science fiction to educate the public about scientific principles and offer stimulating ideas for new inventions? Surely, scientists could do these things themselves. In seeing these two needs for science fiction, Gernsback implicitly offered two criticisms of the scientific community. First, remaining separate from society, scientists had failed to sufficiently educate the masses:

> The average person considers science something too difficult for him to try to understand. With this mistaken idea, thousands of people are endlessly sick year in and year out, and die, simply because of this ignorance. DESPITE THE TREMENDOUS ADVANCE OF SCIENCE, THE WORLD IS MENTALLY STILL IN THE MIDDLE AGES... Talk to the average man and woman about the most obvious scientific achievement of the day, and they will know little about it, or their knowledge will be so superficial that it cannot be used to assist them in their lives or in bettering their condition. This is an unfortunate situation... ('Science Fiction Week', p. 1061)

To remedy this situation, science fiction must provide the scientific information in a more interesting and lively way than the 'dry text-book' coldly proffered by scientists themselves.

Second, Gernsback felt that professional scientists were too often conservative in their thinking, too often unwilling to accept new ideas— a point he repeatedly made throughout his career. As early as August 1923, he pointed out that 'some of our greatest scientific authorities, as late as twenty years ago, proved by mathematics that it was impossible to sustain in the air a machine such as an airplane [and] the news of the X-ray was greeted with derision' ('Predicting Future Inventions', p. 319); in July 1927, he noted, 'Curiously enough... it is the man of science rather than the layman, who, as a rule, is more unbelieving, more arrogant and more intolerant of projected scientific progress' ('Surprising Facts', p. 317), and in June 1953, while noting that younger scientists may have 'educated minds [that] welcome the new and unusual ideas', he complained that 'over a score of rather prominent older scientists and engineers... were appalled at the present-day furor over space-flying. Most of them voiced their complete disbelief that man could ever land on another planet and return alive' ('Skepticism in Science-Fiction', p. 2). To shake such conservative minds out of their complacency, then, science fiction writers, more imaginative than many scientists—especially the older ones—could offer useful ideas in stories which professionals could turn into inventions.

Thus, science fiction could alter the activities of the scientific community in two ways, and doing so, science fiction writers could effectively become junior members of the scientific community, despite their lack of formal training; and as writers are accepted as scientific authorities of a sort, both by the masses and by scientists themselves, science fiction became, in Gernsback's words, 'a tremendous new force in America…. They are the stories that are discussed by inventors, by scientists, and in the classroom' ('Science Wonder Stories', p. 5).

Without a doubt, Gernsback desired this sort of position for himself: although his articles and editorials repeatedly reveal a great knowledge of science and a fertile scientific imagination, Gernsback himself lacked the formal scientific training and background which would qualify him to be a member of the scientific community; even in a era that continued to celebrate the self-taught Edison as the ultimate scientific genius, science in America was becoming an enterprise exclusively for people with college degrees working collectively for businesses, universities, or the government. Gernsback was clearly haunted by his forced exclusion from this community and seemed to be seeking through science fiction some way to achieve the status of a scientist that he could not obtain in the usual manner.

To promote science fiction authors in this way, Gernsback ingeniously crafted his magazines to provide his authors with an aura of scientific respectability, despite their outlandish covers. First, he had *Amazing Stories* printed in the size and shape of a scientific journal, not a pulp magazine; he initially used 'bulky paper… made specially for our requirements' to make his magazine seem weightier than the others, as he once confessed ('Idle Thoughts of a Busy Editor', p. 1085); despite its colourful covers, Gernsback made the printing on the binding of *Amazing Stories* restrained and dignified, so it would look respectable when shelved; and he employed one sequence of page numbers per volume, like a scientific journal, instead of starting every issue anew with page one, like a popular magazine.[13] In these ways, Gernsback tried to appeal to an audience of scientists, to make the point that a science fiction author could be both a valuable spokesman and colleague, a source of insight.

Perhaps the most fascinating feature of a Gernsback magazine came in his later *Wonder Stories*, where each issue included at the beginning a list of seventeen or so scientific experts, most of them college professors, and the statement that 'These nationally-known educators pass upon the scientific principles of all stories'. What Gernsback claimed here was nothing less than a system of *peer review* in science fiction: like articles in a scientific journal, which are always read first by one or more specialists in the field to judge their accuracy and value, science fiction stories in Gernsback's magazines, he asserted, had similarly been reviewed and deemed accurate.

In this way, then, Gernsback's science fiction magazine emerged in theory as a new type of scientific journal written by worthwhile amateurs, who thus could enter the forum of scientific discussion without formal credentials—which, of course, is just what Gernsback sought. Thus, Gernsback's theory of science fiction contains a third implicit criticism of the scientific community—that it is too insular, too separate from the general public—and science fiction, in the way that its authors achieved something of the status of scientists, was one solution, a method for bringing new voices and attitudes into that community.

One can see that, for all their evident naïveté, Gernsback's ideas have a structure and coherence that qualify them as a literary theory: science fiction has three elements—fiction, science, and prophecy—which identify its works with clarity, if not sophistication; it has three corresponding natural sets of readers and writers—the general public, young people, and scientists; and it has three corresponding purposes—to provide entertainment, scientific education, and stimulating ideas for inventions— which can provide writers of science fiction with unique status in the fields of literature and science.

In the early issues of *Amazing Stories*, one can readily observe that Gernsback's ideas were having an influence: in the letters he received, and in the 'Guest Editorials' he published in *Amazing Stories Quarterly*, his readers begin to parrot those themes and ideas. From the very start, readers liked the idea of fiction that included accurate scientific information; one reader said, 'be sure to have the science in the stories correct so that I shall not be obliged to put the ban on them' ('Discussions', February 1927, 1077). A bit later, the first 'Guest Editorial', by a young fan named Jack Williamson, contained these comments:

> The chief function of scientifiction is the creation of real pictures of new things, new ideas, and new machines. Scientifiction is the product of the human imagination, guided by the suggestions of science. It takes the basis of science, considers all the clues that science has to offer, and then adds a thing that is alien to science—imagination. It goes ahead and lights the way... The realization of scientifiction is proverbial. Science has made hardly a single step that scientifiction has not foretold. And science, in return, has disclosed a million new and startling facts, to serve as wings for the scientifiction author's brain... ('Scientifiction, Searchlight of Science', p. 435)

Williamson simply restated Gernsback's arguments about science fiction as an impetus to invention and discovery. In the next 'Guest Editorial', Frederick Dundas Stewart made these remarks:

> What textbook, what lecturer, can illustrate a scientific principle as forcefully or as vividly as a good Scientifiction story? What other method can make science as interesting alike to the advanced student and to the ordinary layman? When facts are woven into stories of life, they become associated with familiar objects and are thereby indellibly [sic] impressed upon the mind. This valuable use of Scientifiction is too often neglected in favor of the more picturesque and fantastic flights of imagination which frequently characterize it. ('Why We Believe in Scientifiction', p. 3)

This was simply Gernsback's argument about the educational value of science fiction.

While Gernsback's immediate impact can be readily documented with numerous references to many other letters and reader editorials of the time, his lasting effects on the field of science fiction must also be emphasized. There is of course the traditional view that Gernsback's influence on science fiction was basically ephemeral. These arguments are usually supported by noting that science fiction which exactly adheres to Gernsback's formula has essentially vanished; and certainly, little contemporary science fiction of any stature at all seems like 'thrilling adventure' that also functions as a kind of corrective adjunct to the scientific community. Thus, many may feel that Gernsback's ideas, while quaint and interesting, have no real relevance to the modern, mature genre of science fiction.

Such an attitude stems from the fact that critics have been asking the wrong question about science fiction.

The question that implicitly motivates most critical discussions of science fiction is: 'What makes science fiction good literature?' This concern immediately obliges critics to examine only science fiction of demonstrable literary quality and thus ignore the vast majority of works in the field; it also tempts them to neglect science fiction itself and instead focus their attention on great works of literature that might, with some effort, be considered science fiction. Thus, Aldiss pauses in *Trillion Year Spree* to look long—and longingly—at Thomas Hardy before reluctantly concluding that he cannot be brought into the fold; and Darko Suvin in *Metamorphoses of Science Fiction* walks through the history of Western literature almost like a kid in a candy store, hardly able to resist picking up another literary giant or two along the way. The final problem is that the qualities that make science fiction good literature turn out to be identical to those that make any works good literature; so critics obsessed with literary quality and focused on inappropriate examples emerge with 'definitions' of science fiction that are little more than definitions of literature, contorted a bit to include a reference to science (Aldiss, maddeningly, puts the word in parentheses). It would be difficult indeed to find some great work of modern literature that is not somehow 'search[ing] for a definition of man' with Gothic overtones, or one that does not reflect some degree of 'cognitive estrangement'.

The better question to ask is: 'What makes science fiction a literary genre?', or 'What makes science fiction science fiction?' Why did a number of highly different works come to be grouped together as a form of literature, and why has the category endured in the face of numerous forces that might have caused it to collapse and die, as happened to so many other types of popular literature that appeared in the early part of the twentieth century? What qualities and characteristics do all of those works share which justify the perception that they are indeed related? While there is a more thorough answer to that question in Chapter 11, the quick answer is simply: Hugo Gernsback.

That is, if one looks only at works in the tradition of modern science fiction and asks what features almost all of them have in common, three clear answers will emerge.

First, one repeatedly finds, coupled with a recurring desire to achieve true literary quality, a devotion to the style and conventions of popular adventure fiction. Examples of melodrama in the cruder forms of science fiction need hardly be listed; but it is indeed striking to note that even in science fiction works with obvious ambitions—C. M. Kornbluth and Frederik Pohl's *The Space Merchants*, John Brunner's *Stand on Zanzibar*, and William Gibson's *Neuromancer* come to mind—the narrative ultimately falls into patterns of hero and villain, danger and rescue, pursuit and capture. I see this not as a sign of artistic naïveté but as a necessary structuring device—a way to maintain control over a form of fiction which otherwise repeatedly threatens to fall apart. Still, authors seem to sometimes feel guilty about their use of popular forms and visibly aspire to write real literature—creating a dilemma well articulated by Norman Spinrad when he asked, 'Is science fiction commercial schlock or is it literary art? Is it visionary literature or militaristic alien-bashing masturbation fantasies for the next generation of gunfodder? Should we take ourselves seriously or are we just in it for Joe's beer money?' (*Science Fiction in the Real World*, p. 222) And the first person to espouse 'thrilling adventure' as the predominant mode of science fiction—and to articulate its aspirations to literary greatness—was Hugo Gernsback.

Second, one sees a repeated inclination not only to present but to explain new scientific developments, or at the very least to adhere to known scientific laws in imagining those developments. To be sure, the explicit intention of explaining and glamorizing science is now specifically attributed only to juvenile science fiction; thus, the dust jacket of Hugh Walters's *Terror by Satellite* announces the author's desire to include recent scientific information and stimulate young readers to be interested in science. However, one continues to see occasional claims that science fiction can provide scientific education: Basil Davenport said, 'I should be the last to claim that I read science fiction in order to learn science; yet I have learned a certain amount, quite painlessly' (*Inquiry into Science Fiction*, p. 41), and writing in *The Los Angeles Times*, Bettyann Kevles—a science fiction writer herself[14]—says, 'Science fiction, like historical fiction, is a sugarcoated way of learning a complicated subject' (Kevles, 'Truth Stranger than Science Fiction', p. 11). Others who disagree with this literal claim still see a broader educational purpose in the genre; thus, after saying that 'People do not read science fiction to learn science any more than others read historical novels to study history', Gregory Benford goes on to admit that 'One of the great strengths of science fiction, though, is its ability to incorporate the landscape of modern science, with all its grandeur and philosophical import, in a way that conventional fiction cannot' ('Plane in Fancy', p. 2)—a version of Gernsback's argument that science fiction teaches 'the meaning of science'.

More broadly, one observes the droning voice of meticulous explanation—and an implicit educational aim—even in more elevated works of science fiction: the scientist who explains his cure for cancer in Theodore Sturgeon's 'Slow Sculpture', the reference file that Case stumbles on to in Gibson's *Neuromancer*, and the didactic Arthur Aspect implanted in the brain of the hero of Gregory Benford's *Great Sky River* and *Tides of Light*. And a concern for accurate scientific information is expressed even in the writings of modern critics with no particular interest in science, like Damon Knight and Harlan Ellison, who pointedly criticize science fiction works with elementary scientific errors.[15] In terms of the larger purposes ascribed to science fiction, this commitment to strict scientific accuracy seems like a bizarre fetish; after all, it would be perfectly possible for an author to make a valid statement about scientific progress and its effects while ignoring or violating a scientific principle or two. The only explanation is that authors wish their works to retain, however faintly, the authoritative aura of nonfiction: if science fiction stories do not always provide scientific information, the argument goes, they certainly do not provide scientific misinformation, and thus are accurate to a certain degree. And the first person to be obsessed with thorough explanation and correct scientific data in science fiction was Hugo Gernsback.

Finally, one notes repeated assertions that works of science fiction are uniquely valuable not simply in predicting but in creating and shaping the future. First, even major authors have freely admitted that they occasionally write stories simply to present and advocate new scientific ideas, exactly as Gernsback proposed: David Brin described his story 'Tank Farm Dynamo' as a 'propaganda piece', designed primarily to publicize his plan for a new type of economical, energy-producing space station (*The River of Time*, p. 206); and after Arthur C. Clarke came up with the idea of communications satellites in 1945, he admitted that 'I kept plugging [the idea] in my books' ('I Remember Babylon', p. 2). Robert A. Heinlein has told the story of how one of his early stories inspired an actual invention, and Benford has noted evidence that in other cases, science fiction stories have performed a similar function.[16] Beyond the issue of suggesting ideas to scientists, John W. Campbell, Jr, as will be noted, later expanded Gernsback's vision to see science fiction as a uniquely powerful way to influence decisions regarding future scientific progress and, quite possibly, save the human race from extinction (as in 'The Place of Science Fiction'). And the first person to make exaggerated claims for science fiction as a force 'making the world a better place to live in' was Hugo Gernsback.

These shared characteristics in the genre of science fiction were all noted, by the way, in Amis's perceptive *New Maps of Hell*. He acknowledged its mixture of lofty aspirations and juvenile adventure in saying, 'The co-presence of the adult with the stupidly or nastily adolescent is highly characteristic of the modern science fiction magazines' (p. 43); while he 'cannot see much justice in the commentators' repeated claim that SF sugars the pill of a scientific education' (p. 53), he admitted that 'justice to the laws of nature… is always an aim—in the field of science fiction' (p. 17); and after listing with bemusement some of the grandiose claims of science fiction writers and critics, he concluded that 'to feel that what one is doing is the most important thing in the world is not necessarily undignified, and indeed is perhaps more rather than less likely to lead to good work being done' (p. 52). While perhaps not fully aware of their origins, then, Amis listed as characteristics of modern science fiction the three key features of Gernsback's theories.

A list of the traits Gernsback proposed for science fiction also illuminates, I feel, the continuing difficulties faced by foreign-language science fiction writers in their efforts to emulate and surpass their American counterparts; simply put, they have not noted, or have failed to see the importance of, Gernsback's problematic but stimulating prescriptions. I now speak about a field I am not an expert in; but in the works of foreign-language science fiction I have read, I consistently find these characteristics: first, either a wholehearted surrender to the formulas of juvenile adventure (*Perry Rhodan* and the like) or a determination to achieve High Literature

(Stanislaw Lem)—without the characteristic and challenging American commitment to fulfil both sets of expectations; second, the absence of an obsessive concern for detailed scientific explanation and scrupulous scientific accuracy—those qualities that give American science fiction its peculiar difficulty and excitement; and third, the apparent lack of any strong belief that this type of writing has unique value or importance—the attitude that provides American science fiction with its sense of purpose and direction.[17] A fresh interest in the principles of Gernsback might improve foreign-language science fiction and the entire genre as well.

For Gernsback's theories are important for one reason: despite their simplicity and contradictions, they worked.

That is, when Gernsback proclaimed the existence of a literary genre founded on his principles, people accepted and embraced the idea, and a vast and variegated body of modern literature grew out of that idea and its underlying principles. And, because I can think of no other commentator in the twentieth century who single-handedly launched a literary movement of the scope and quality of science fiction, Gernsback is arguably the most important literary critic of modern times.

An important principle of life, and of history, is that people cannot choose their own parents. They must accept the parents they have. A science fiction critic may well wish to believe that her field grew out of the philosophical musings of More, the evening discussions of Mary Shelley, Percy Shelley and Lord Byron, or the trenchant visions of Wells. She may wish to believe that her field was based on principles more lofty than adherence to scientific accuracy and practical scientific ideas. But these are the idle fantasies of a peasant girl who dreams that she is secretly the daughter of a king.

If not the father of science fiction, Hugo Gernsback is certainly the father of the idea of science fiction.

And to better understand what they are doing, science fiction critics, like everyone else, need to know their father.

Notes

1 A note on terminology: in 1911, Gernsback first used the term 'scientific novel' in a review of Mark Wicks's *To Mars via the Moon* (p. 371); then, up until 1923 or so, Gernsback described stories as 'scientific fiction'. He next devised the portmanteau word 'scientifiction', which he copyrighted and used almost exclusively until 1929—though he admitted later it was 'Not a very elegant term' (Address to the MIT Science Fiction Society, cited in Panshin, 'The Short History of Science Fiction', p. 21). Thus, this definition and several comments below refer to 'scientifiction'. When he lost control of *Amazing Stories* and was obliged to employ a different term in his new magazines, he began using

'science fiction', although there was one earlier use of that term in an editor's response to a reader's letter in the January 1927 issue of *Amazing Stories*: 'Jules Verne was a sort of Shakespeare in science fiction' ('Discussions', p. 973). I believe I was the first to note this early use of the term; note 5 discusses the authorship of letter responses. I relegate these data to a footnote because there is no indication that Gernsback's ideas about science fiction ever changed, though his terminology did; thus, whether a particular quotation mentions 'scientific fiction', 'scientifiction', or 'science fiction', Gernsback always seems to discuss the same literature and the same theories. An account of the modern emergence of the term 'science fiction' can be found in Moskowitz's 'How Science Fiction Got Its Name' in *Explorers of the Infinite*; the writings of William Wilson with the term were mentioned above.

2 Later, Gernsback identified another characteristic feature of science fiction writing: 'Science-fiction, ever since its beginning, has spoken a language all its own. As it grows, its literature keeps step with its growth—new terminology, new words, new meanings being added constantly'; and he calls this 'language' 'science-fictionese' ('Science-Fiction Semantics', 2). I discuss science fiction neologisms, including those developed by Gernsback, in 'Words of Wishdom' and 'The Words That Could Happen'.

3 Thus, I answer Brian Aldiss's vague charge that most previous definitions of science fiction 'fail because they have regard only to content, not to form' (*Trillion Year Spree*, p. 25).

4 For example, in the first chapter of *Ralph 124C 41+*, Ralph turns on a 'Language Rectifier' when the woman on his Telephot (picturephone) screen is speaking French, and after he hears her speak in English, he talks of having 'rectified' her speech (pp. 26, 27). Thus, without detailed description, readers understand that a Language Rectifier is an instantaneous translation machine.

5 In references to *Amazing Stories*, I attribute responses to readers' letters to an unnamed 'editor'—probably Associate Editor T. O'Conor Sloane—and attribute unsigned blurbs, or introductions, to stories and some unsigned editorial materials to Gernsback. There are three reasons for this: Moskowitz's report that for *Amazing Stories* 'Gernsback himself... wrote the editorials and the majority of the blurbs for the stories' (*Explorers of the Infinite*, p. 227); the fact that several letter responses refer to 'Mr. Gernsback', explicitly denying his authorship; and my judgement that letter responses generally sound like Sloane, while blurbs often sound like Gernsback. Because of the hectic process of preparing each issue, described in Daniel Stashower's 'A Dreamer Who Made Us Fall in Love with the Future' (p. 46), Gernsback surely wrote some responses and Sloane surely wrote some blurbs, so a few statements may be incorrectly attributed. Unsigned materials attributed to Gernsback are listed in the bibliography as 'Unsigned'.

6 Indeed, I suggest that the American genre of heroic fantasy—a reasonably clear line including authors like Robert E. Howard, L. Sprague de Camp, and Lin Carter—emerged as a result of science fiction; that is, these authors needed a generic concept to distinguish their work from science fiction. In this way, despite dictionary definitions, science fiction, historically speaking, is not 'a branch of fantasy'; rather, fantasy is a branch of science fiction. (The status of fantasy as an outgrowth of science fiction is explored in Chapter 11.) Only when fantasy emerged in the 1940s did Campbell introduce and emphasize arguments for distinguishing science fiction from fantasy—as discussed in

Chapter 7.

7 As noted in my 'Evolution of Modern Science Fiction', Gernsback's belief in science fiction as education may have been inspired by the introduction to Mark Wicks's *To Mars via the Moon*.

8 Gernsback also described the educational value of science fiction in 'The Lure of Scientifiction' (p. 195), 'Fiction versus Facts' (p. 295), 'Amazing Youth' (p. 625) and 'Important Announcement!' (p. 581). His longest explanation, in 'The Science Fiction League', was as follows:

> The average parent, and the man in the street, has as yet not discovered the great and fundamental truth that Science Fiction is highly educational and gives you a scientific education, in easy doses—sugar-coated as a rule. The average man is not scientifically inclined and misses much in life because of his poor scientific education. When he is converted to Science Fiction, his scientific education quickly becomes such that, sooner or later, he understands what is going on all around him... In the school and college room, young men are helped along with their scientific education, in an unmistakable manner. This has been pointed out by many educators, time and again. Particularly those individuals who are not mechanically or scientifically inclined are quickly made to grasp the fundamentals of science through science fiction. (p. 1062)

9 One might respond by building on Gregory Benford's frequently-offered version of Robert Frost's comments on free verse—namely, that writing fantasy, as opposed to science fiction, is like playing tennis without a net. That is, the need to adhere to accepted scientific fact actually kindles one's imagination, rather than 'deadening' it, by providing writers with the stimulating challenge of reconciling their extravagant visions with the cold realities of science.

10 Gernsback is no doubt dimly recalling the familiar story of the inventor who tried to patent the submarine, only to be thwarted when Jules Verne's *Twenty Thousand Leagues under the Sea* was presented as evidence that the idea was not original. The problem, of course, is that while that court decision established that a previous description of a device in a science fiction story might *prevent* someone else from patenting it, it did not establish that the author of such a story *could* patent it.

11 Michael Ashley's explanation, for example, is that *Scientific Detective Monthly* 'fell into the chasm between two worlds'—science fiction and detective fiction—and as a result 'was neither sought after by science fiction fans nor detective fans' ('Introduction: An Amazing Experiment', pp. 31–32).

12 Of course, as I will discuss, attitudes about science in science fiction are more complex than this bipolar vision, as seen even in Gernsback's own theories and fiction.

13 R. D. Mullen of *Science-Fiction Studies* pointed out to me in a letter that many pulp magazines in the 1920s numbered pages by volume; still, it is worth noting that Gernsback continued the practice until the very last issue of *Wonder Stories* in 1936, at a time when other magazines like *Astounding Stories* had begun numbering pages by issue—suggesting, perhaps, that Gernsback saw particular value in pagination by volume.

14 Though not a distinguished one, if she is judged by her 'Mars-Station' (discussed in *The Other Side of the Sky*).

15 See, for example, Knight's attack on Charles Eric Maine's *High Vacuum* and its 'gross [scientific] errors' in *In Search of Wonder* (p. 100), or Ellison's critique of the faulty science behind the television movie *The Love War* in *The Other Glass Teat* (p. 40).

16 In 'Science Fiction: Its Nature, Faults and Virtues', Heinlein said, 'I had a completely imaginary electronics device in a story published in 1939. A classmate of mine, then directing such research, took it to his civilian chief engineer and asked if it could possibly be done. The researcher replied, "Mmm... no, I don't think so—uh, wait a minute... well, yes, maybe. We'll try." The bread-boarded first model was being tried out aboard ships before the next installment of my story hit the newsstands' (pp. 28–29; author's ellipses). And in response to Jeffrey M. Elliot's question, 'Is there any evidence to suggest that science fiction actually gives rise to scientific investigation?', Benford replied, 'Certainly. A fellow wrote a paper on this subject not too long ago, in which he documented numerous such cases. I'm personally aware of several people who have invented things by having had them in the back of their mind as a result of a science fiction story they read'. But he concedes that 'Fundamental discoveries, though, like the theory of evolution or the theory of relativity, don't come out of science fiction' (*Science Fiction Voices #3*, p. 50).

17 It now occurs to me that this list of traits also applies to many science fiction films and television programmes, explaining why I find that field so flawed and uninteresting; while two notable exceptions—*2001: A Space Odyssey* and the *Star Trek* series—both had input from science fiction writers and, surely as a result, display all of the above characteristics.

'The Jules Verne, H. G. Wells, and Edgar Allan Poe Type of Story': Hugo Gernsback's History of Science Fiction

Along with his other accomplishments, Hugo Gernsback stands as the first person to create and announce a history of science fiction. As indicated, earlier commentators who seem to discuss the genre, like Felix Bodin, William Wilson, William H. L. Barnes, and Edgar Fawcett, spoke mainly in the future tense—calling for a genre of science fiction—and cited few if any existing examples. However, Gernsback identified a number of past and present works exemplifying the genre, established three major periods in science fiction history, and illustrated while presenting and discussing texts several generic models for science fiction.

In describing Gernsback's version of the history of science fiction, I apparently contradict myself, since I have maintained that there are no solid grounds for a 'history of science fiction' prior to Gernsback and that Gernsback is the proper starting point for an examination of the genre. Yet Gernsback called figures like Poe, Verne, and Wells science fiction writers and even on occasion described them in chronological order as the 'history of science fiction'. The question is: if Gernsback himself was unwilling to begin the history of science fiction with Gernsback, then why should we? This is the logic employed by Stableford when he briefly anticipates—and rejects—the framework of this book:

> On what grounds might we seek to declare: 'Here science fiction began, and works which are in various ways similar that appeared before this time must be termed proto science fiction'? One possible answer is to consider only *labelled* sf as sf, and to decide that sf began in 1926. But Hugo Gernsback clearly believed that sf already existed and that all it lacked was a convenient name—he considered H. G. Wells, Jules Verne and Edgar Allan Poe all to be 'scientifiction' writers... ('Proto Science Fiction', p. 476)

And to be sure, certain statements by Gernsback, cited below, seem to reflect a belief that the genre 'already existed', to an extent.

Still, knowing what we know about Gernsback's theories and the works he discussed, we cannot trust his testimony. For one thing, his comments were motivated in part by expediency: since Gernsback was publishing many of these earlier stories in 'the magazine of scientifiction', he was obliged to describe them as 'scientifiction'—not works of other types he had recently reclassified as scientifiction. More broadly, people never create literary genres out of thin air; invariably, they have in mind past and present works that exemplify the envisioned genre. That is, when Gernsback plucked works out of earlier eras and labelled them 'science fiction', that does not imply a belief that there previously existed a recognized tradition of science fiction. Finally, I am willing to posit that Gernsback himself did not fully understand what he was doing: like later critics, Gernsback may have believed that a genre comes into existence not when a generic relationship between various works is first acknowledged, but when the earliest work included in that relationship was written; and like later critics, Gernsback may have supposed that if an earlier work appears to fit a modern critical formula, then that formula must accurately describe the work's contents and purposes.

To support the idea that Gernsback was creating a literary genre, not building upon an existing one, consider the blurbs that he wrote to reprinted stories and novels by Poe, Verne, Wells, and other early authors: with mind-numbing regularity, their works were described primarily as examples of entertaining stories containing accurate scientific information to educate readers and predictions to suggest new inventions or ideas. In the blurb to *A Trip to the Center of the Earth* (the title he used), Gernsback wrote, 'Not only was Jules Verne a master of the imaginative type of fiction, but he was a scientist of high calibre... Instead of boring a hole into the bowels of the Earth, Jules Verne was probably the first to think of taking the reader to unexplored depths through the orifice of an extinct volcano. He argues, correctly, that a dead crater would prove... perhaps the best route for such exploration' (p. 101). And he described H. G. Wells's 'The Crystal Egg' in this manner:

> Mr. Wells' imagination is not running loose—he knows his science— and while the story at first glance may seem entirely too fantastic, no one knows but that it may, 5,000 years from now be quite tame and of every day occurrence.
>
> If a civilization on another world were sometime to communicate with us, there might be thousands of methods, to us undreamt of, by which this could be achieved. The crystal egg method which Mr. Wells uses in this story may be one of them. We who are accustomed to radio and who can bring voices out of the thin air with a pocket radio receptor, will not think that the crystal egg is impossible of

fulfillment at some future date. (blurb, 'The Crystal Egg', p. 129)

In his statements, Gernsback implied that Verne wrote *A Trip to the Center of the Earth* primarily to suggest such an underground exploration, Wells wrote 'The Crystal Egg' primarily to stimulate interest in a possible new means of communication, and both wrote primarily to provide readers with scientific information. Other cases may be cited where Gernsback seemingly distorted stories in order to describe them as science fiction: consider, for example, his rather incredible defence of A. Merritt's *The Moon Pool* as science fiction (in 'Amazing Creations', p. 109, cited in Chapter 2); and Paul Carter notes that his blurb to Wells's 'The Man Who Could Work Miracles' 'managed tenuously to define the tale as science fiction... surely this was straining at a gnat' (p. 7).

It is hard to say whether Gernsback believed that such considerations actually influenced the writing of these stories; but Verne, Wells, and their contemporaries surely would not have described the works in these terms. Thus, Gernsback did not draw upon a perceived prior history of science fiction and picture his work as its continuation; rather, he took his own concept of science fiction, plucked earlier works out of their historical contexts, and cut them down to size to fit into his new theories.

In establishing the broad parameters of his science fiction history, Gernsback first described the time from the Middle Ages to 1800 as an anticipatory era of 'Proto Science Fiction' (the usual modern term). In 'The Science Fiction League: An Announcement', he declared that science fiction 'goes back to Edgar Allan Poe, and even further' (p. 933) and he discussed the situation during these times at length in one early editorial:

> Scientifiction is not a new thing on this planet. While Edgar Allan Poe probably was one of the first to conceive the idea of a scientific story, there are suspicions that there were other scientifiction authors before him. Perhaps they were not such outstanding figures in literature, and perhaps they did not write what we understand today as scientifiction at all. Leonardo da Vinci... while he was not really an author of scientifiction, nevertheless had enough prophetic vision to create a number of machines in his own mind that were only to materialize centuries later... There may have been other scientific prophets, if not scientifiction writers, before his time, but the past centuries are so beclouded, and there are so few manuscripts of such literature in existence today, that we cannot really be sure who was the real inventor of scientifiction.
>
> In the eleventh century [*sic*] there also lived a Franciscan monk, the amazing as well as famous Roger Bacon (1214–1294). He...

foresaw many of our present-day wonders. But as an author of
scientifiction, he had to be extremely careful, because in those days
it was not 'healthy' to predict new and startling inventions. ('The
Lure of Scientifiction', p. 195)

Interestingly, Gernsback did not dismiss this period on the grounds that
there existed insufficient awareness of 'science', either as a concept or in
its particulars; instead, while there were sporadic individuals in these times
who possessed sufficient scientific knowledge and imagination to write
science fiction, they lacked a satisfactory—and safe—literary outlet for their
visions.[1] (By the way, Gernsback's focus on figures like Bacon and da Vinci
might offer the foundation for an entirely different approach to science
fiction history. All who have delved into the subject—including
Gernsback—have assumed that the most important element in science
fiction is its narrative, so they have searched mainly for earlier works of
fiction with scientific content. But one could claim that imaginative
speculations based on and combined with scientific data constitute the
heart of the genre and construct a history of science fiction emphasizing
prognosticators of this type, including Bacon, da Vinci, and writers ranging
from Giordano Bruno and John Wilkins to Camille Flammarion and
Percival Lowell, and focusing more on works like Francis Bacon's *The New
Atlantis* and Johannes Kepler's *Somnium*, where a slim fictional framework
is employed to present scientific ideas. While these people are acknowledged as potential writers of science fiction, or sources of ideas for science
fiction, it might be interesting to argue that they in fact are central to science
fiction.)

The second era of science fiction, which might be termed its
developmental period, began in the nineteenth century with Poe. The first
editorial in *Amazing Stories* offered this capsule history: 'Edgar Allan Poe
may well be called the father of "scientifiction." It was he who really
originated the romance, cleverly weaving into and around the story, a
scientific thread. Jules Verne, with his amazing romances, also cleverly
interwoven with a scientific thread, came next. A little later came H. G.
Wells, whose scientifiction stories, like those of his forerunners, have
become famous and immortal' ('A New Sort of Magazine', p. 3). Gernsback
clearly regarded Poe, Verne, and Wells as the most important progenitors
of science fiction; indeed, the statement which by its position qualifies as
Gernsback's very first definition of science fiction was simply a list of their
names: 'By "scientifiction" I mean the Jules Verne, H. G. Wells, and Edgar
Allan Poe type of story—a charming romance intermingled with scientific
fact and prophetic vision' ('A New Sort of Magazine', p. 3). And these
names were continually the focus of his surveys of older science fiction;

introducing *Air Wonder Stories*, for example, he announced: 'Years ago, Edgar Allan Poe wrote his immortal "Unparalleled Adventure of One Hans Pfaal," as well as "The Balloon Hoax." Later, the illustrious Jules Verne gave the world his "Five Weeks in a Balloon." Still later, H. G. Wells startled us with his incomparable "The War in the Air." All of these famous stories, it should be noted, fall in the class of scientific fiction...' ('Air Wonder Stories' 5). While Gernsback reprinted other older authors, Poe, Verne and Wells were the ones most frequently seen in *Amazing Stories*;[2] and it is easy to see why Gernsback favoured them.

First, by identifying Poe as the first science fiction writer, Gernsback made the genre an American creation, a tradition appropriately acclaimed by and continued in an American magazine. Poe could also lend a substantial literary reputation to this form of writing when he was labelled its 'father'. Unfortunately for Gernsback, few Poe stories came near his announced standards of scientific explanation and prediction, and he reprinted only six of them. He indirectly acknowledged in early blurbs that Poe was far from an ideal exemplar of science fiction: while Gernsback said Verne was 'a scientist of high calibre' (blurb, *A Trip to the Center of the Earth*, p. 101) and that Wells 'knows his science' (blurb, 'The Crystal Egg', p. 129), all he claimed about Poe was that he might have become 'an enlightened philosopher' (blurb, 'Mesmeric Revelation', p. 124). And though Gernsback regularly celebrated the triumvirate of Poe, Verne and Wells in the 1920s and 1930s—even when he was no longer reprinting their stories—later comments, as in his 1961 'Guest Editorial', cite only Verne and Wells, omitting Poe; indeed, a 1952 remark seemed to deny that Poe wrote science fiction: 'I find no fault with fairy tales, weird and fantastic stories. Some of them are excellent for their entertainment value, as amply proved by Edgar Allan Poe and other masters, but when they are advertised as Science-Fiction, then I must firmly protest' ('The Impact of Science-Fiction on World Progress', p. 2).

Verne served as the best representative of Gernsback's science fiction, since the author regularly included lengthy scientific lectures on many subjects, and since Verne, unlike Poe, had already been celebrated for his 'prophetic vision'. For that reason, the title page of every issue of *Amazing Stories* featured an illustration of 'Jules Verne's Tombstone at Amiens Portraying His Immortality', and Gernsback once went so far as to call Verne 'our favorite author' (blurb, 'Dr. Ox's Experiment', p. 421).

Wells, the third author in Gernsback's triumvirate, posed some problems: though he was an author clearly knowledgeable about and interested in scientific and prophetic matters, his visible aims in writing stories rarely coincided with Gernsback's emphasis on scientific explanation and prediction. As noted, Gernsback had to struggle to fit 'The

Crystal Egg' into his theories, and when he reprinted *The Island of Dr. Moreau*, the blurb simply stated, 'It is, frankly, not a very pleasant story to read... it is our opinion that Mr. Wells has tried to sketch a travesty upon human beings' (p. 637). Not even Gernsback could construe the story as Wells's suggestion for a new type of animal research!

Despite Gernsback's emphasis on Poe, Verne, and Wells, they were by no means the only writers of the nineteenth century whom Gernsback or his colleagues were willing to accept as important contributors to science fiction history.

First there was Luis Senarens, the prolific nineteenth-century author of juvenile 'invention stories'. Though Gernsback never included his name in lists of major authors and never reprinted any of his crude dime novels, he twice published pictorial articles about Senarens, an honuor accorded no other writer,[3] and the articles' titles called Senarens the 'American Jules Verne'—suggesting he could be compared to Verne, at least as an imaginer of wonderful machines (the focus of both articles).

Richard Adams Locke's 'The Moon Hoax' (1835) was reprinted in the September 1926 issue of *Amazing Stories*.

'The Diamond Lens' (1858) by Fitz-James O'Brien, 'the famous author', was in the December 1926 issue (blurb, 'The Diamond Lens', p. 835).

H. Rider Haggard was cited by an editor, answering a reader's request, who said 'We have Rider Haggard in mind' for a reprint, though it never appeared ('Discussions', August 1927, p. 515).

Edward Bellamy was listed by Gernsback along with Poe, Verne, and Wells as writers who 'have proved themselves real prophets' ('A New Sort of Magazine', p. 3).

Garrett P. Serviss was identified by an editor along with Verne and Wells as 'three of our favorite authors' ('Discussions', July 1927, p. 413), was named by Gernsback as one of 'the better known scientifiction writers' ('Amazing Youth', p. 625), and had three works reprinted in *Amazing Stories*: 'The Moon Metal' (1900), in the July 1926 issue; *A Columbus of Space* (1909), in the August, September, and October 1926 issues; and *The Second Deluge* (1912) in the November and December 1926 and the January and February 1927 issues.

A revised edition of M. P. Shiel's *The Purple Cloud* (1901) was reviewed in the December 1930 issue of *Wonder Stories* (p. 761).

Arthur Conan Doyle's name was in an editor's letter response naming as earlier science fiction works 'the Wells, Verne, and Conan Doyle classics' ('The Reader Speaks', June 1931, p. 132).

And, in a general reference, he said in 1934 that 'many prominent authors of unquestioned literary ability have lent their names to Science Fiction' and 'such stories have appeared from time to time in various publications in many languages throughout the world' ('The Science Fiction League', p. 1061).

In associating writers whose careers began in the nineteenth century with science fiction, Gernsback, unlike later historians, did not link their work to larger events in that era; rather, they were people ahead of their time, 'prophets' who anticipated the value of both scientific progress and fiction about that progress. All on his own, Poe 'conceive[d] the idea of a scientific story'. So, according to Gernsback, nineteenth-century science fiction was simply the product of isolated individual geniuses.

To modern critics, Gernsback's account of science fiction history before 1900 will seem inadequate because of major omissions; and lacking literary backgrounds, Gernsback and his associates may have been unaware of possible precursors of science fiction like Kepler's *Somnium*, Francis Godwin's *The Man in the Moone*, or Edward Bulwer-Lytton's *The Coming Race*. Years later, Gernsback publicly apologized for a major oversight in his history. In 1961, P. Schuyler Miller commented in his book review column for *Analog Science Fact/Science Fiction* that 'I have always wondered why, in that collection of classics [the reprints in Gernsback's magazines], we were not given at least one of the stories of the acknowledged Russian pioneer in the theory and practice of rocket flight, Konstantin Tsiolkovsky' ('The Reference Library', May 1961, p. 162). Gernsback wrote back to say that neither he nor Literary Editor Charles Brandt had been aware of Tsiolkovsky's fiction:

> At one time [Brandt] brought to my attention the name of Konstantin E. Tsiolkovsky. I had never heard of him before 1926, and the book Brandt was talking about had nothing to do with Tsiolkovsky's science fiction, but rather with his theoretical space flight and rockets.
>
> As far as I can remember, there wasn't then in existence an English translation of Tsiolkovsky's early work, and while I am fluent in French and German, I cannot read Russian. It would seem that neither Brandt nor I knew of the story 'Beyond the Planet Earth'. If I had heard about it, it is certain that we would have run it sooner or later in *Amazing Stories* or *Amazing Stories Annual*. (Letter to P. Schuyler Miller, cited in 'The Reference Library', *Analog*, March 1962, p. 168)

There are cases, however, where comments by Gernsback and his editors in *Amazing Stories* demonstrate that they were aware of or informed about certain major works of possible relevance but did not want to include them in Gernsback's history of science fiction. Jonathan Swift's *Gulliver's Travels*, for example, was mentioned in two responses to letters ('Discussions', April 1927, p. 99, and June 1927, p. 310), but even though the circumstances were ideal to identify Swift's work as science fiction, the editor failed to do so.[4] Another response noted that 'A writer such as Charles Lamb or Nathaniel Hawthorne, could consider the most ordinary scene and make it literature. But neither could have dipped into science for their subjects, because it would be unfamiliar ground for them' ('Discussions', July 1928, p. 370), thus announcing that those men never wrote science fiction.

Other authors and works, including some that would later be connected to science fiction, were mentioned by Gernsback and his editors but never identified as part of science fiction history. Answering a reader who complained of 'gruesome stories', an editor replied that 'The same might be said of Shakespeare's "Hamlet" and other classics' ('Discussions', February 1927, pp. 1077–78). Gernsback said that 'Baron Munchhausen, in the wildest flights of his imagination, takes a second place to this presentation of Mr. Fosdick's invention' (blurb, 'Mr. Fosdick Invents the Seidlitzmobile', p. 239), and the blurb to Gernsback's *Baron Munchhausen's Scientific Adventures* in 1928 noted that the Baron 'actually lived' and that 'many versions of his adventures exist' (p. 1061). The blurb to Austin Hall's 'The Man Who Saved the Earth' in the April 1926 issue of *Amazing Stories* spoke of 'the Frankenstein which he had unloosed' (p. 75), and a later Gernsback editorial blasted stories where 'The machines and science are becoming a Frankenstein monster' ('Wonders of the Machine Age', p. 286). The blurb to G. Peyton Wertenbaker's 'The Man from the Atom' in the April 1926 issue mentioned 'Alice in the Looking Glass' [*sic*] (p 63). Reacting to a newspaper story on 'Wolf Girls', an editor noted, 'In the *Jungle Book*, Rudyard Kipling enlarges on the association of a child with a band of wolves and has produced some of his most picturesque fiction in this work' ('Discussions', January 1927, p. 970). And one letter response referred to *Erewhon*—though not knowledgeably, saying that 'if we recollect right, [South America] was the location of Samuel Butler's mythical country of "Erewhon"' ('Discussions', September 1927, p. 612).

These references demonstrate that Gernsback and his associates generally had a little knowledge of literary history and specifically knew of a number of writers, including Swift, Hawthorne, and Butler, whose works included imaginative features that might justify the label 'science fiction'; yet they never included these writers in discussions of science fiction history. This suggests that Gernsback's motive for creating a history of science fiction was not simply to provide famous names that could add prestige to the genre; rather, there was some logic behind his decisions to add certain names in that history and to omit others.

Gernsback's third era of science fiction, the modern period, was immodestly marked by the emergence of Gernsback. At one time, Gernsback regarded the crucial date as 1908, when he started publishing

Modern Electrics, a magazine which soon would regularly include science fiction: in 1929, he claimed that 'I started the movement of science fiction in America in 1908 through my first magazine, "MODERN ELECTRICS." At that time it was an experiment. Science fiction authors were scarce. There were not a dozen worth mentioning in the entire world' ('Science Wonder Stories', p. 5). Twenty-three years later, he was a bit more precise in setting a date for the beginning of 'modern science fiction':

> Usually authors not quite familiar with the writer's [Gernsback's] early work set the date of the start of modern science fiction in the year 1926, which date coincides with the first science fiction magazine, 'Amazing Stories'... We would like the correct this view for historical purposes. Modern science fiction, like so many other endeavors, had an orderly evolution... The date which the writer would like to fix is the year 1911, *not* 1926. 1911 was the year in which the writer's novel, RALPH 124C 41+, ran serially in 'Modern Electrics', which, at the time, had a circulation of around 100,000 copies. The novel caused so much comment and brought so much mail from readers that, at the end of the serial in 1912, it was found necessary to continue science fiction in some manner... (*Evolution of Modern Science Fiction*, p. 1)[5]

However, in other writings, Gernsback employed the more common starting date for 'the Gernsback era', the appearance of *Amazing Stories* in 1926: as he said in 1934, 'Not until 1926, when I launched my first Science Fiction magazine, was any concerted movement possible... The movement since 1926, has grown by leaps and bounds until today there are literally hundreds of thousands of adherents of Science Fiction scattered throughout the entire civilized world' ('The Science Fiction League', p. 1061). Whether one chooses the dates 1908, 1911, or 1926, the beginning of modern science fiction should, in Gernsback's view, clearly be attributed in part to his own actions, statements, and publications; still, he did not assert that all the changes and developments in science fiction during this era stemmed from his influence.

On what grounds did Gernsback declare that the early twentieth century was the third and most important period in science fiction history? First, according to Gernsback, it was at this time—not the nineteenth century as others maintain—that science and its products truly became part of everyday life. As he argued in 1929:

> Science—Mechanics—the Technical Arts—they surround us on every hand, nay, enter deeply into our very lives. The telephone, radio, talking motion pictures, television, X-rays, Radium, super-

aircraft and dozens of others claim our constant attention. We live
and breathe day by day in a Science saturated atmosphere.

The wonders of modern science no longer amaze us—we accept
each new discovery as a matter of course... No wonder, then, that
anybody who has any imagination at all clamors for fiction of the
Jules Verne and H. G. Wells type... ('Science Wonder Stories', p. 5)

In the 1920s, then, one need not be a prophet to recognize the importance
of scientific progress and write fiction on the subject.

With this expanding awareness of science, the twentieth century next
brought, Gernsback asserted, an increase in the amount of science fiction
being written. Though it was not his intent, he provided tacit evidence for
this claim by reprinting a number of contemporary works in *Amazing
Stories*.[6] A few came from his own scientific magazines, like George Allan
England's 'The Thing from—Outside' (reprinted in the April 1926 issue of
Amazing Stories) and Jacque Morgan's Mr Fosdick stories (June, July,
August 1926). Some were from other popular magazines, like Austin Hall's
'The Man Who Saved the Earth' (April 1926), Ellis Parker Butler's 'An
Experiment in Gyro-Hats' (June 1926), Murray Leinster's 'The Mad Planet'
(November 1926) and 'The Red Dust' (January 1927), Captain H. G.
Bishop's 'On the Martian Way' (February 1927), Edgar Rice Burroughs's
The Land That Time Forgot (February, March, April 1927), Merritt's 'The
People of the Pit' (March 1927) and *The Moon Pool* (May, June, July 1927),
T. S. Stribling's 'The Green Splotches' (March 1927), and Harry Stephen
Keeler's 'John Jones's Dollar' (April 1927); Gernsback also named Victor
Rousseau's *The Messiah of the Cylinder* as a possible reprint ('Thank You!',
p. 99). One story came from a more respectable source—Julian Huxley's
'The Tissue-Culture King' (August 1927), first seen in the *Yale Review*. Also,
Gernsback had earlier acknowledged another modern work—Mark
Wicks's *To Mars via the Moon*—with a review in the August 1911 issue of
Modern Electrics, probably written by Gernsback himself.[7]

Finally, Gernsback was singularly energetic in recognizing and
reprinting the science fiction of past and present European writers: in the
first issue of *Amazing Stories* he announced that 'A number of German,
French and English stories of this kind by the best writers in their respective
countries, have already been contracted for' ('A New Sort of Magazine',
p. 3). He reported that he would reprint Hans Dominik's *The Might of the
Three*, 'one of the greatest—perhaps *the* greatest—recent scientifiction
story' ('Thank You!', p. 99), though it never appeared. Announcing that
C. A. Brandt was going to join his staff, he mentioned that Brandt had
'made a study, not only of works in the English language, but also in the
German, French, and Scandinavian languages' ('Experts Join Staff of

"Amazing Stories"', 390). And in the April 1929 issue of *Amazing Stories* he published V. Orlovsky's 'The Revolt of the Atoms', described on the previous issue's first page in this way: 'this tale, which comes to us from Russia, is an excellent story of absorbing interest, not only as a piece of fiction, but for the science contained in it also' ('In Our Next Issue', p. 1058). In his later magazine, *Wonder Stories Quarterly*, Gernsback reprinted a number of European novels, including Otto Gail's *The Stone from the Moon* (*Science Wonder Quarterly*, Spring 1930), Otfrid von Hanstein's *Between Earth and Moon* (*Wonder Stories Quarterly*, Fall 1930), Bruno H. Burgel's *The Cosmic Cloud* (*Wonder Stories Quarterly*, Fall 1931), and Ludwig Anton's *Interplanetary Bridges* (*Wonder Stories Quarterly*, Winter 1933), described as 'the outstanding interplanetary story of the decade' ('Good News for Our Readers', p. 5). In 1932, Gernsback discussed his past and ongoing efforts to discover and acknowledge European works:

> I recently went to Europe where I visited Germany, France, England and Belgium. On this trip a number of new connections with foreign authors were made, and there have already been received by us a number of fine new book-length interplanetary novels… It is certain that future issues of the quarterly will present a large variety of foreign interplanetary stories, such as have never been published before in this country.
>
> I was probably the first to bring foreign science fiction authors to the attention of American readers, and am continuing this policy in the future. And I predict that the stories that will be printed in future issues will excel any which have been published in any magazine, including our own, up to this time. ('Good News for Our Readers', p. 5)

While defenders of Gernsback are often accused of neglecting European writers, it should be noted that Gernsback recognized the value and contributions of European writers far more than any American or British critic after him; for instance, the only time von Hanstein and Burgel are cited in Aldiss's *Trillion Year Spree* is when he mentions that Gernsback reprinted their works (p.204).

In gathering together these disparate American, British, and European writers, Gernsback acknowledged another new feature of the third era in science fiction history: the emergence of people who might be considered, in an old-fashioned sense, science fiction scholars. Gernsback described himself as an expert in the field: having 'made scientifiction a hobby since I was 8 years old', he 'probably [knew] as much about it as any one' ('Idle Thoughts of a Busy Editor', p. 1085). With great fanfare, he announced in July 1926, the hiring of Wilbur C. Whitehead, 'a scientifiction fan of the

first rank', and C. A. Brandt, 'the greatest living expert on scientifiction...
There is not a work of this kind that has appeared during the last fifty years,
with which Mr. Brandt is not fully conversant' ('Experts Join Staff of
"Amazing Stories"', p. 390).[8] And through letters, Gernsback began to
receive the input of 'Scientifiction Fans' 'who seem to be pretty well
orientated in this sort of literature' ('The Lure of Scientifiction', p. 195),
and he later described 'the so-called Science Fiction fans, who make it a
point not only to read every scrap of Science Fiction that has ever appeared
in print but actively to collect such stories, tabulate them, give them a
proper rating, etc'. ('The Science Fiction League', p. 1061). Thus, not only
were there more science fiction stories being written, but there were more
people who knew about these stories as science fiction. With this
knowledge available, Gernsback claimed the ability to obtain and make
use of a broader knowledge of previous science fiction than any earlier
commentator, and he asserted at one point that he had 'a list of some 600
to 700 scientifiction stories' ('The Lure of Scientifiction', p. 195).[9]

While Gernsback did not attribute these developments—the growing
prominence of modern science, the increase in the amount of science
fiction published, and the wider and deeper awareness of science fiction—
to his efforts, he did argue that he and his magazines were contributing to
the growth of science fiction by effectively teaching a new generation of
writers how to write science fiction. In itself, establishing a magazine
devoted to scientifically accurate fiction could have this effect; a response
to a reader who complained of authors who were 'lamentably weak in
their facts' explained that writers were still learning about the special
requirements of this genre: 'the demand for stories of the type we aim to
give, should inspire [authors] with the desire to study natural science for
the purposes of their work' ('Discussions', June 1928, p. 272). In addition,
Gernsback and his editors claimed to be making particular efforts to train
individual writers. One letter response stated: 'we think AMAZING STORIES
is doing its part in developing new authors' ('Discussions', June 1928, p.
272). In 1929, Gernsback announced, 'For the guidance of new authors,
we have prepared a pamphlet entitled "*Suggestions for Authors*"' ('$300.00
Prize Story Contest', p. 485), and his 1930 article for *Writer's Digest* on 'How
to Write "Science" Stories' is also evidence of his desire to help writers
produce better 'scientific detective' stories. An editor's letter response
described other efforts to educate writers: 'Science Fiction is in its infancy,
and... the publishers of this, and our sister magazines, spend hundreds,
perhaps thousands of dollars in advertising for Science Fiction writers,
advising them, often teaching them the finer points and sometimes the
fundamentals of their craft' ('The Reader Speaks', *Science Wonder Stories*,
May 1930, p. 1143).[10]

With the new prominence of science, more science fiction being written, a better awareness of the genre, and ongoing efforts to educate writers, the third age of science fiction, in Gernsback's view, was destined to be its greatest. In 1926, Gernsback said, 'We believe the era of scientifiction is just commencing' ('Editorially Speaking', p. 483). In 1928, he described science fiction as 'a new and distinct movement in literature that is gaining more impetus as the months roll by. There was a time when a Scientifiction book or novel was a scarcity. Now, with AMAZING STORIES MONTHLY and AMAZING STORIES QUARTERLY eagerly championing the cause, Scientifiction has excited the attention of hundreds of thousands of people who never knew what the term meant before' ('Results of $300.00 Scientifiction Prize Contest', p. 519). And Gernsback noted in the same year that 'until very recently, there were not enough new scientifiction stories to go around... But times are rapidly changing... More and more authors of the better kind are taking to scientifiction as the proverbial duck takes to water... Already, in our editorial opinion, our modern authors have far eclipsed both Jules Verne and H. G. Wells' ('The Rise of Scientifiction', p. 147). Later, an editor's letter response offered a similar glowing picture: 'we are trying to train authors to an enlightened viewpoint... here and there young writers are emerging who show true ability—a generation of truly effective writers are growing who will challenge Wells and Verne for their laurels' ('The Reader Speaks', *Wonder Stories*, June 1931, p. 132).

The broad dimensions of Gernsback's history of science fiction are thus clear: first, a long period of relative inactivity, when potential authors of science fiction were hampered by the lack of a supportive environment and appropriate medium; second, the nineteenth century, when a few prescient writers, beginning with Edgar Allan Poe, emerged who dealt imaginatively with science in their works; and third, the twentieth century, when the increased impact of science and a growing awareness of science fiction—the latter in part inspired by Gernsback—greatly enlarged the field and would eventually lead to even greater achievements.

A final issue raised by Gernsback's history of science fiction is the question of genre: was science fiction a continuation or offshoot of some previous established genre, and was one particular generic pattern most appropriate for science fiction? As noted, Gernsback primarily built his history of the genre out of three major and noteworthy authors—Poe, Verne, and Wells. Along with the implied example of Senarens, these authors are identified and offered as models of science fiction to readers and aspiring writers; and though Gernsback tried to cast them as similar writers each attempting to fulfil his new theories, his blurbs also acknowledged their differences in generic approach. In this way, basic tensions in his history of science fiction begin to emerge.

In the *Amazing Stories* article on Senarens, his works were accurately characterized as 'stories... of adventure... designed for boy readers' ('An American Jules Verne', p. 270), and while Gernsback never published anything by Senarens, he did describe others' stories as pure and uncluttered adventures: Merritt's *The Moon Pool* was praised as 'packed full of astounding adventure that sustains your breathless interest throughout' (blurb, *The Moon Pool*, p. 111), and Burroughs's *The Land That Time Forgot* was lauded for its 'exciting interest' and 'hair-raising episodes' (blurb, *The Land That Time Forgot*, p. 983). Thus, melodramatic adventure was presented as one generic model for science fiction.

The Poe stories Gernsback reprinted suggest two additional models. First were stories like 'The Facts in the Case of M. Valdemar', in the first issue of *Amazing Stories*, which Gernsback described as having 'a denouement, the most horrifying and terrible in all modern story telling' (blurb, 'The Facts in the Case of M. Valdemar', p. 93). And Gernsback published other frightening stories of this nature: Alexander Snyder's 'Blasphemers' Plateau' is 'a dramatic [and] tremendously gripping story... we see a scientist gone drunk with power, until at the climax of his achievement he acclaims himself to be God' (blurb, 'Blasphemers' Plateau', p. 657). Such stories derive from the generic tradition of the Gothic novel.

However, there is also a light, satirical tone in other Poe tales that Gernsback reprinted, such as 'The Thousand-and-Second Tale of Scheherazade', though that story has a grim anti-scientific edge: fantasy keeps Scheherazade alive, but technology kills her. Gernsback himself wrote a similar satire called 'The Most Amazing Thing (in the Style of Edgar Allan Poe)'—incongruously published as an editorial in 1927—ventured into pure satire in his novel *Baron Munchhausen's Scientific Adventures*, and published three series of stories about ridiculous scientists and their absurd inventions: Clement Fezandie's 'Doctor Hackensaw's Secrets', Jacque Morgan's 'The Scientific Adventures of Mr. Fosdick', and Henry Hugh Simmons's 'Hicks' Inventions with a Kick'. Thus, in these stories from Poe and others, readers would see another generic model for science fiction, satire; indeed, Gernsback twice employed the term while introducing Jack G. Huekels's 'Advanced Chemistry': 'It is a satire that cannot fail to amuse you' (blurb, 'Advanced Chemistry', *Science and Invention*, August 1923, p. 332) and 'In this story, like in many other satires, there will be found a whole lot of truth' (blurb, 'Advanced Chemistry', *Amazing Stories*, March 1927, p. 1127).

Introducing stories by Verne, Gernsback presents two more options for science fiction writers. First, he praised Verne for his accurate geography and descriptions; he said of *A Trip to the Center of the Earth* that Verne's 'intimate knowledge of geography, the customs and pecularities [*sic*] of the various races, made it possible for him to write with authority on any of these subjects' (blurb, *A Trip to the Center of the Earth*, p. 101). On a grander scale, he enthused of Verne's *Off on a Comet*, 'How closely he follows, and imparts to his readers, the scientific probabilities of the universe beyond our earth, the actual knowledge so hard won by our astronomers! Other authors who, since Verne, have told of trips through the planetary and stellar universe, have given free rein to fancy, to dreams of what might be found. Verne has endeavored to impart only what is known to exist' ('Introduction to This Story', p. 5). In such comments, Gernsback acknowledged Verne's links to a long tradition of descriptive travel literature and thus made the travel tale another generic model for science fiction.

Yet Verne was concerned with more than transportation; he also discussed scientific possibilities in an optimistic tone rooted in the utopian spirit found in French literature since Louis-Sebastian Mercier's *Memoirs of the Year Two Thousand Five Hundred*. Gernsback unambiguously presented Verne's *The Purchase of the North Pole* as a noble effort to improve the Earth through science:

> Many people are continually amusing themselves by pointing out the advantages we would have on earth if our planet were not inclined on its axis $23^1/2$ degrees... If there were no such inclination, there would be no seasons... We would have exactly twelve hours of daylight and twelve hours of night at every point on the globe.
>
> Is it possible by any human agency to right the axis of the earth to accomplish this? In this story the versatile Jules Verne tells us how such an attempt was made and what happened. (blurb, *The Purchase of the North Pole*, p. 511)

Though Verne rarely ventures far enough into the future to present major advances, one can clearly see in his vision of an expanding and improving present a future world which will continue to expand and improve—a utopian attitude. Gernsback also acknowledged the model of utopia more directly by listing Bellamy, author of *Looking Backward*, as a figure equal to Poe, Verne, and Wells in the first issue of *Amazing Stories* ('A New Sort of Magazine', p. 3). Thus, the utopia emerges as a fifth generic model for science fiction.

Wells, the other major author in Gernsback's pantheon, first seemed to variously employ all five patterns for science fiction. The spirits of melodrama and the travel tale infuse *The First Men in the Moon*, as pointed out by Gernsback when he called it 'one of the greatest moon tales of adventure ever written' (blurb, *The First Men in the Moon*, p. 775); there are

elements of Gothic horror and dark satire in *The Island of Dr. Moreau*, as
Gernsback acknowledged in the blurb cited; a lighter satirical tone could
be found in stories like 'The New Accelerator', published in the first issue
of *Amazing Stories*; and familiar works like *A Modern Utopia* and *Men like
Gods*, which Gernsback's readers were probably aware of though they were
not reprinted in *Amazing Stories*, displayed Wells's commitment to utopia.[11]
What Wells first added to the list of available genres for science fiction,
already suggested by *The Island of Dr. Moreau*, was the negative utopia or
dystopia, also manifest in reprinted novels like *The Time Machine, When the
Sleeper Wakes*, and *A Story of the Days to Come*.

Reading *The Time Machine*, with its future human race divided into a
benign race of surface people and a malevolent race of subterranean
cannibals, one could dimly detect another generic model for science fiction:
a combination of the utopia and dystopia in which a new race emerges in
the future that transcends human problems, while existing humans remain
untransformed and imperfect. Other Wells novels like *The Food of the Gods*
and *In the Days of the Comet* hint at this model, for both works describe how
a present-day humanity apparently doomed to despair might be
transformed through technology or miraculous intervention into a new
and superior race. Such stories that combine satirical or dystopian
pessimism about the prospects of today's people and utopian optimism
regarding their possible successors were relatively common in the tradition
of the 'scientific romance', as Brian Stableford observed in *Scientific Romance
in Britain*:

> There is a strong vein of misanthropy in scientific romance... A
> frequent corollary... is the declaration that hope for the future (if
> there is any) must be tied to the transcendence of this brutishness,
> by education or evolution, or both. Utopian optimism was smashed
> by the realization that a New World would need New Men to live in
> it, and that we were neither mentally equipped nor spiritually
> equipped to be New Men. Writers of scientific romance disagreed
> about what manner of men those new beings might be, and were
> ambivalent in their attitudes to them, but their very ambivalence
> intensified their preoccupation with the probable collapse of our
> civilisation and its possible transcendent renewal. (p. 338)

And this subject has also been common in later science fiction stories, as
noted in 1955 by Basil Davenport: 'A favorite theme of science fiction had
long been the coming of Superman, the idea that Homo sapiens is destined
to be superseded by some sort of Homo superior' (*Inquiry into Science Fiction*,
p. 15). Such tales could be regarded, then, as a final possible generic model
for science fiction; since no common term for the form exists, I will call it

the tale of transcendence—a story about people made ideal by a fundamental transformation of the human race.

To be sure, these are crude characterizations of complex writers, and I hasten to acknowledge that one can see a utopian spirit in Poe's *Eureka*, and *The Narrative of Arthur Gordon Pym* is clearly modelled on travel literature; similarly, one can regularly find satire in Verne, though this aspect of his work is neglected by Gernsback and usually omitted by translators,[12] and the element of Gothic horror appears in his *Carpathian Castle*. What I seek to describe, in a rough-and-ready fashion, is not these authors themselves, but simply how these three authors would have been perceived by an audience of readers and writers without literary training, based primarily on the stories Gernsback reprinted and the way he described them; and in doing so, I suggest how these authors, as filtered through the mind of Gernsback, actually influenced the emerging genre of science fiction.[13]

Overall, then, Gernsback provided science fiction with both a reasonably complete and coherent chronology of development and a number of applicable generic models from other traditions. Still, since his presentation of this information was chaotic and fragmentary, conveyed through editorials, letter responses, reprinted stories and story blurbs, one can reasonably ask if readers were in fact responding to and understanding Gernsback's history. The evidence for a positive answer lies in the letters readers sent to *Amazing Stories* and Gernsback's other magazines.

In those letters, one sees that readers were listening and responding to Gernsback's version of science fiction history, just as they listened and responded to his theories of science fiction. First, the myth that his readers disliked his reprints of older stories must be laid to rest; to be sure, some letter writers complained about those stories, but others appreciated them. 'I was delighted to see ["The Moon Hoax"], having seen many references to it in past time', one reader said ('Discussions', July 1927, p. 414); another praised Verne, Haggard, Wells, Leinster, Serviss, Burroughs, and England ('Discussions', April 1927, p. 103); a third listed Wells, Verne, Poe, Serviss, O'Brien, A. Hyatt Verrill, and Gernsback as favourite writers ('Your Viewpoint', *Amazing Stories Quarterly*, p. 431); and a fourth said, 'The Moon Hoax was undeniably clever, well written and a fine story all around... I hope... you do not exhaust the supply of Wells', Verne's, and Serviss' stories. They're masterpieces' ('Discussions', July 1927, pp. 414, 413). One letter writer addressed the editor as someone with real curiosity about science fiction history:

It may interest you to know that I have met with an allusion to the 'Moon Hoax' which may interest you; it is from the *North American*

> *Review*, No. 89, October, 1835 (the writer is discussing Carlyle's *Sartor Resartus*): 'In short, our private opinion is, as we have remarked, that the whole story (i.e., *Sartor Resartus*)... [author's ellipses] has about as much foundation in truth as the late entertaining account of Sir John Herschel's discoveries in the moon'. ('Discussions', March 1927, p. 1180)

And, after Gernsback de-emphasized older reprints in the 1930s, readers kept requesting them—so much so that Gernsback was obliged to write an editorial, 'On Reprints', where he claimed the older stories were either outdated in their science or unavailable.

One might argue that these signs of the popularity of reprints were rare, and that Gernsback carefully selected and emphasized such letters to justify his editorial policy. However, evidence to the contrary can be found in another science fiction magazine of the time, Harry Bates's *Astounding Stories of Super-Science*, which from the start emphatically refused to feature reprints. In early letter columns, while one reader did advise, 'Please don't reprint any of Poe's, Wells', or Verne's works' ('The Readers' Corner', April 1930, p. 129), another asked, 'Why not print some (not too many) stories from H. G. Wells, E. R. Burroughs and Jules Verne?' ('The Readers' Corner', June 1930 423). And when two other readers wrote in to say that the magazine's no-reprints policy was 'too bad' and 'a mistake', Bates responded with a long statement, 'About Reprints', defending his magazine's policy of publishing only new works (July 1930, pp. 134–35). Since these requests for older stories appeared in a magazine that did not feature them, one can be sure that their sentiments were both sincere and representative.

Not only, then, did readers accept as genuine, and share, Gernsback's interest in older science fiction, but some also accepted and restated his version of the genre's history. Consider these comments from a reader of *Science Wonder Stories*:

> Science fiction is a new endeavour. Until the advent of Mr. Gernsback, it was strongly individualized, resting in such luminaries as Wells, Verne, Poe, etc. But Mr. Gernsback knew that imagination was inherent in everyone; that suitable expression could be molded by just a little coaxing or incentive. So from all America he culled the outposts of science fiction writers... we ought to keep in mind that science fiction is yet a scrubby infant. Tolerate its indiscretions as you would a child's. ('The Reader Speaks', May 1930, pp. 1142–43)

A young Jack Williamson contributed a reader editorial, 'The Amazing Work of Wells and Verne', where he argued that 'while this form of literature was invented by an American, Edgar Allan Poe, and while America is the land of scientifiction today, Wells and Verne were its first two masters' (p. 140). James T. Brady, Jr wrote another editorial, 'History of Scientific Fiction', which paralleled Gernsback's periods in its discussion:

> Until the time of Poe... there was no scientific literature of an influential character written, with the exception of a few stories by Bergerac (Voyages to the Sun and Moon) and Swift (Gulliver's Travels). The evolution of the type really begins with stories such as 'Scheherazade's Thousand and Second Tale', [*sic*] 'Mesmeric Revelation', and 'The Balloon Hoax'.
>
> For fifteen years after Poe there was a little fiction of this kind written. In 1862, however, Jules Verne turned his pen toward the scientific story and published 'Five Weeks in a Balloon'... In 1985 appeared Wells' 'Time Machine'... It was Wells who carried on the tradition of Verne in England and by giving impetus to the scientific-fiction idea and purifying its technic [*sic*] paved the way for the numerous writers of the present day.
>
> Until this time little had been done since Poe's death in America. There had been one little known writer, Lu Senarens, whose stories (written about 1890) have proved marvelously prophetic... After Wells, however, many American writers entered the field. At the head of a long list are such names as A. Merritt, Garrett P. Serviss and A. Hyatt Verrill. (p. 571)[14]

Here, one sees a reader accepting the dimensions of Gernsback's history of science fiction while adding more names to the canon.

And did Gernsback's version of science fiction history—including its basic structure and its generic models—directly influence later academic scholars? There is one intriguing connection: in 1934, Gernsback founded the Science Fiction League, whose activities were reported in each issue of *Wonder Stories*. In 'The Science Fiction League' column of the May, 1935 issue, P. Schuyler Miller (later to be well known as a science fiction writer, book reviewer, and collector) was quoted as suggesting, 'there is one piece of work which should certainly be undertaken. That is the formulation of a complete and accurate science-fiction bibliography' (p. 1519). The editor of the column agreed, asking for members' input and specifying, 'We particularly want items published a long time ago—ten, twenty, thirty, forty, fifty years or longer' (p. 1520). Two months later, the column reported that:

> J. O. Bailey of Chapel Hill, N. C. has been collecting rare science-fiction for many years and asks us to wait until his bibliography,

which he is putting a great deal of work into, is completed, before we go ahead and publish one of our own... We are sure, from the interesting letter he sent us, that his knowledge of all published science-fiction is practically unlimited and the LEAGUE would probably lose a lot without his aid. (p. 241)

And, as Harry Warner, Jr. tells it, Bailey, who of course later published the first academic study of science fiction, *Pilgrims through Time and Space*, did receive some help from the work of the League, and provided some help in return:

J. O. Bailey, a scholar with almost imperceptibly faint connections with general fandom... announced as early as 1935, through the letter column of *Wonder Stories*, that he was compiling a bibliography of science fiction. Then working for his Ph.D. degree, he abandoned this project, after snaring 5,000 titles, as too big a task to handle. He sent his notes to [H. C.] Koenig, who had helped him to gather information, and the data proved useful to [A. Langley] Searles [who later presented his own extensive bibliography in issues of the *Fantasy Commentator*]. (*All Our Yesterdays*, p. 68)

It is hard to say how helpful Koenig was to Bailey, but he clearly read Gernsback's magazines and had some contact with fan scholars.

In any event, there are parallels between Gernsback's history and academic histories. Gernsback's identifications of writers of science fiction have endured; that is, every writer Gernsback embraced still appears in science fiction histories (though one of them, Haggard, is usually cast as a peripheral figure, as in Aldiss's *Trillion Year Spree*, p. 138). In addition, other histories often follow Gernsback's broad outline: a period of relative inactivity before 1800, a period of significant development in the nineteenth century, and a modern period beginning in the twentieth century. For example, Bailey's first era of science fiction is 'Before 1817' and the final era is 1915 and after, corresponding to Gernsback's three periods (though Bailey further divides the middle period into 1817–1870, 1871–1894, and 1894–1914). Aldiss dismisses science fiction before 1800 as 'Lucian and All That' (the subtitle of the chapter on that era in *Billion Year Spree*), argues that 'The origins and inspirations for science fiction lie... within the period of the Industrial Revolution' (*Trillion Year Spree*, pp. 13–14)—the early nineteenth century—and sees a 'synthesis' emerging in modern American pulp magazines (p. 205). And ironic agreement with Gernsback's choice of Poe as the father of science fiction comes in Marjorie Hope Nicolson's *Voyages to the Moon*: she cites Poe's claim in 'The Unparalleled Adventure of One Hans Pfaal' regarding his 'attempt at *verisimilitude* in the application of scientific principles (so far as the whimsical nature of the subject would permit) to the actual passage between the earth and the moon'; then she exclaims, 'And right here the trouble begins! From this time on, writers of moon voyages will seek for *verisimilitude* and spend their efforts on attempts to make their planetary flights plausible. They will pride themselves on the application of scientific principles, weighing down their imaginations and ours with technological impedimenta' (pp. 239–40). She thus agrees that Poe brought something new to imaginative fiction—not a wonderful new tradition, however, but the death of a great old tradition.

Finally, the genres implicitly identified by Gernsback as models for science fiction—melodramatic adventure, the travel tale, the Gothic novel, utopia and dystopia, satire, and tale of transcendence—are all regularly mentioned in critical discussions of the genre's history. Some are not particularly prominent: the model of 'thrilling adventure' is usually noted only to criticize it as an unfortunate tendency, and only a few critics like Stableford have noted the tradition of stories about a transformed or replaced humanity. The others—travel literature, Gothic novels, utopia, and satire—are noted more regularly.

Of course, later histories of science fiction also differ from Gernsback's, first in their thoroughness and criteria for selection, which are more sophisticated than Gernsback's naïve demands for scientific content and predictions. Yet the spirit of Gernsback's reductionist standards can sometimes be detected in more erudite studies: for example, Bailey's *Pilgrims through Time and Space,* defining 'scientific fiction' as 'a narrative of an imaginary invention or discovery in the natural sciences', includes More's *Utopia,* not because of its larger features, but simply because 'it describes a wonderful machine, the incubator' (pp. 10, 11).

In addition, later histories usually choose slightly different points in time to mark transitions between eras and offer different explanations for those changes. Aldiss begins with Mary Shelley, pushing Poe back to Chapter Two of *Trillion Year Spree,* and says it was Campbell, not Gernsback, who produced the 'synthesis' of modern science fiction noted above; and while acknowledging earlier works in the genre, Suvin calls 1800 the key 'turning point' in science fiction history (*Metamorphoses of Science Fiction* 89), with a modern synthesis emerging with Wells (pp. 219–20). Finally, modern critics focus less on individuals to identify larger cultural and literary developments to explain the growth of science fiction. No doubt Gernsback's history of science fiction is inferior to later versions; but first efforts are rarely the best ones.

A final difference between Gernsback's science fiction history and later versions is that other critics typically choose only one of the genres or traditions offered by Gernsback and see it as central to science fiction. Frederick Kreuziger's repeated descriptions of science fiction as 'popular literature' (in *The Religion of Science Fiction*) identify the genre's central mode as juvenile adventure; Percy C. Adams's *Travel Literature and the Evolution of the Novel* asserts there is a 'close relationship' between travel literature and 'science fiction' (p. 275), and many have seen links between modern science fiction and the tradition of the fabulous travel tale called the 'fantastic voyage'; Aldiss's *Trillion Year Spree* argues that science fiction is predominantly an outgrowth of the Gothic novel; Suvin's formula of 'the literature of cognitive estrangement' in *Metamorphoses of Science Fiction* leads naturally to an emphasis on utopia and dystopia; Amis's *New Maps of Hell* stresses connections between satire and science fiction; and the Panshins' *The World beyond the Hill* envisions a 'search for transcendence' as the focus of science fiction—although they have their own idiosyncratic notion of that term. Thus, modern critics tend to select one generic model, while Gernsback himself expressed only a mild preference for 'thrilling adventure' and accepted all other generic models as appropriate—in spite of the evident contradictions in this advice.

Indeed, Gernsback's theory and history of science fiction can be seen as efforts to reconcile opposites: the needs to function as both fiction and nonfiction; the purposes of providing entertainment, education, and scientific ideas; the goals of simultaneously reaching the general public, enthusiastic youngsters, and scientists as readers; the desires to achieve literary status, reform the scientific community, and make money from patenting ideas; and the obligations to draw from conflicting genres with conflicting attitudes in order to write science fiction. And it is the combination of all these priorities and principles, I argue, that makes science fiction both a fascinating and flawed genre.

As it happens, 'fascinating' and 'flawed' are apt adjectives to describe Gernsback's personal contribution to science fiction history—the novel *Ralph 124C 41+: A Romance of the Year 2660*.

Notes

1 This tentative embrace of writers before 1800 as at least potential authors of science fiction, however, does seem to conflict with an earlier editorial when he announced, 'Two hundred years ago, stories of this kind were not possible' because science was not then a part of everyday life ('A New Sort of Magazine', p. 3).

2 For the record, these are the works by Poe, Verne, and Wells republished by Gernsback, listed by the titles which Gernsback used (in *Amazing Stories* unless otherwise noted): by Poe, 'The Facts in the Case of M. Valdemar' (April 1926), 'Mesmeric Revelation' (May 1926), 'The Sphinx' (July 1926), 'The

Balloon Hoax' (April 1927), 'Von Kempelen and His Discovery' (July 1927), and 'Thousand-and-Second Tale of Scheherazade' (May 1928); by Verne, *Off on a Comet—or Hector Servadac* (April, May 1926), *A Trip to the Center of the Earth* (May, June, July 1926), 'Doctor Ox's Experiment' (August 1926), *The Purchase of the North Pole* (September, October 1926), *A Drama in the Air* (November 1926), *Robur the Conqueror, or The Clipper of the Ai*r (December 1927, January 1928), *The Master of the World* (February, March 1928), and *The English at the North Pole* (May, June 1929—at this time Gernsback had just lost control of *Amazing Stories*, but he was probably involved in the story's selection); and by Wells, 'The New Accelerator' (April 1926), 'The Crystal Egg' (May 1926), 'The Star' (June 1926), 'The Man Who Could Work Miracles' (July 1926), 'The Empire of the Ants' (August 1926), 'In the Abyss' (September 1926), *The Island of Dr. Moreau* (October, November 1926), *The First Men in the Moon* (December, 1926, January, February, 1927), 'Under the Knife' (March, 1927), 'The Remarkable Case of Davidson's Eyes' (April, 1927), *The Time Machine* (May, 1927), 'The Story of the Late Mr. Elvesham' (June, 1927), 'The Plattner Story' (July 1927), *The War of the Worlds* (August, September, 1927), 'Æpyornis Island' (October 1927), 'A Story of the Stone Age' (November 1927), 'The Country of the Blind' (December 1927), *When the Sleeper Wakes* (*Amazing Stories Quarterly*, Winter 1928), 'The Stolen Body' (January 1928), 'Pollock and the Porroh Man' (February 1928), 'The Flowering of the Strange Orchid' (March 1928), *A Story of the Days to Come* (April, May 1928), *The Invisible Man* (June, July 1928), 'The Moth' (August 1928), 'The Lord of the Dynamos' (February, 1929), and 'The Diamond Maker' (*Science Wonder Stories*, June 1929). And a letter from Gernsback to Wells (4 April 1928) requested prices for several other Wells novels: *The World Set Free*, *The Research Magnificent*, *A Modern Utopia*, *The Food of the Gods*, *The War in the Air*, and *Men like Gods*. However, the prices Wells demanded in a letter of 4 May 1928—$500 for *A Modern Utopia*, $1250 for *Men like Gods*, and $1000 for others—were too high for Gernsback to meet.

3 The articles were 'The American Jules Verne' and 'An American Jules Verne'. In contrast, Gernsback published no articles about Poe and only one article each about Verne (Horne, 'Jules Verne, the World's Greatest Prophet') and Wells (Robison, 'H. G. Wells "Hell of a Good Fellow"—Declares his Son').

4 The first letter stated, 'I like scientifiction, but I like it administered so that I can at least swallow it. It would gratify me immensely to see "intelligent lobsters" and "man-eating trees," together with similar hokum, missing from AMAZING STORIES'. The editor responded, 'This critic wants scientific fiction administered so that he can swallow it. One of the greatest fiction stories of the world is "Gulliver's Travels." We wonder if our correspondent would consider that the adventures of Dean Swift's hero were administered so that he could swallow them' ('Discussions', April 1927, p. 99). Since *Gulliver's Travels* is being offered as a distinguished example of worthwhile fiction that cannot be 'swallowed', it would have been entirely natural for the editor to call it 'One of the greatest scientifiction stories'—but he did not. When a later letter called the book 'a fairy story', the editor responded, 'If he regards "Gulliver's Travels" as merely a fairy story, he is missing a great deal... Swift wrote "Gulliver's Travels" as a bitter sarcasm on the way things were done by humanity in this strange world of ours and the fairy story part of it is merely a vehicle for carrying stern and unpleasant facts home to the stolid mind of everyday humanity' ('Discussions', June 1927, p. 310). Here, despite his

complaints, the editor essentially accepts the term 'fairy story', distinguishing it from true scientifiction.

5 This document, found in the library of the University of California at Santa Barbara, must be the privately printed pamphlet mentioned in Harry Warner, Jr's *All Our Yesterdays* (p. 68), which was distributed at the 1952 World Science Fiction Convention.

6 To be sure, while Gernsback was usually frank in admitting that older stories and 'classic' novels were reprints, he rarely acknowledged in blurbs that recent stories were not originals; still, some readers recognized them as reprints. Thus, even though the short stories in the first issue of *Amazing Stories* were not explicitly described as reprints, Gernsback felt obliged to add this note in the next issue: 'Some of our readers seem to have obtained the erroneous idea that AMAZING STORIES publishes only reprints, that is, stories that have appeared in print before. This is not the case' ('To Our Readers', p. 135). And an explicit admission came three years later from T. O'Conor Sloane, who acknowledged that 'The first issue... contained nothing but reprints of the best scientific fiction of the past' ('Amazing Stories', p. 103). While Gernsback's coyness regarding reprints did not fool all his readers, it can be a problem for scholars trying to sort out which stories were originals and which were not: the usually reliable Michael Ashley, for example, calls G. Peyton Wertenbaker's 'The Coming of the Ice' (p. 52) the first original story to appear in *Amazing Stories* (June 1926) in *The History of the Science Fiction Magazines, Volume I*; but Wertenbaker's 'The Man from the Atom (Sequel)' (May 1926)—which was not in the issue of *Science and Invention* which printed the first story—was actually the first. (I thank R. D. Mullen for pointing this out to me.)

7 The review, and the influence of that novel upon Gernsback, are discussed in my 'Evolution of Modern Science Fiction'.

8 Gernsback's praise of Brandt's expertise was sincere, not mere editorial puffery; thirty-five years later, long after he had any motive to exaggerate matters, he again stated that 'I considered Brandt the greatest authority on science fiction anywhere at that time' (Letter to P. Schuyler Miller, cited in 'The Reference Library', *Analog Science Fact/Science Fiction*, March, 1962, p. 168).

9 In reporting what Gernsback *claimed* were the characteristics of the modern era of science fiction, I am not necessarily obliged to investigate the *accuracy* of those claims; still, some discussion of how knowledgeable Gernsback and Brandt actually were is appropriate. Editorials and blurbs show that Gernsback was familiar with Verne's works, and reprints in the first four issues of *Amazing Stories* (before Brandt's arrival) display some knowledge of the relevant literature of the previous thirty years. However, there are other signs that their awareness of science fiction history was not extensive. A letter in the May 1927 issue of *Amazing Stories* referred to 'Wells' "The Lost World,"' and the error was not corrected in the response ('Discussions', p. 205). Gaps in their information are admitted in a letter Gernsback written to M. Craig, H. G. Wells's secretary (18 July 1927), where he said, 'We find that we do not have a complete library of Mr. Wells' shorter scientifiction stories, and therefore would appreciate your sending to us a copy of each, and your bill to cover, so that we can reimburse you for their cost. Also we should like to have a complete list of all of Mr. Wells' stories of a scientific nature, for future reference in scheduling our publications.' A second letter to Wells (3 December 1927) asked permission to reprint 'The Invincible Man' (though this may be a secretary's

error). A third letter (4 April 1928) asked the price to reprint several novels, including *The Research Magnificent*; but since it is a realistic novel, Gernsback and his associates almost certainly had not read it and asked for it only because of its scientific-sounding title. Years later, Gernsback effectively apologized for the limitations of his and other publishers' knowledge of science fiction: 'The S-F fan knows far more about S-F authors, artists, editors and everything that goes into the magazines than do the publishers themselves. And why shouldn't they? Few publishers ever have the necessary time to read as much science-fiction over as long a time as has the arduous S-F fan' ('Status of Science-Fiction', p. 2).

10 Again one can ask whether Gernsback and his editors were *actually* striving to educate writers—as discussed in Chapter 5.

11 Though both novels appeared on a list of requested titles in Gernsback's letter to H. G. Wells cited above (4 April 1928).

12 As discussed in Walter Charles Miller's introduction to his *The Annotated Jules Verne: From the Earth to the Moon*.

13 Because Poe, Verne and Wells are great authors whose works reflect several of the genres which later emerged in science fiction, it is tempting to build a history of science fiction solely around them; Wells in particular, inasmuch as he drew upon almost all of the genres I discuss as Gernsback's choices for science fiction, seems a logical choice as the father of modern science fiction. However, there are two difficulties involved in constructing a history of science fiction around such authors. First, as already discussed, it is a matter of historical record that neither Poe, Verne, nor Wells gave birth to a recognizably distinct and lasting literary genre, and that these writers had an impact on the tradition of American science fiction primarily through their presentation by Gernsback; thus, when we see their footprints in modern science fiction, it is not a case of direct influence, but of their influence as mediated by Gernsback. Second, any constructed history of science fiction from Poe, Verne, and Wells to, say, Heinlein, Asimov, and Gibson will confront one puzzle: what is the origin of the strong element of juvenile, action-packed adventure which so infuses the works of those modern authors and which is not prominent in the works of Poe, Verne, and Wells? The answer is that Gernsback alone, in assimilating the example of Senarens and his successors, added that vital element to the creation of science fiction.

14. Brady does not seem particularly well informed, though: speaking of 'traces' of scientific fiction in older eras, he mentions 'Aristophene's [*sic*] play, "The Clouds"' and 'the Arabian "Thousand Nights and a Night"' (p. 571); and his error regarding the author and nationality of *Frankenstein* was mentioned in Chapter 1.

'This Unique Document': Hugo Gernsback's *Ralph 124C 41+*

Any discussion of Hugo Gernsback's *Ralph 124C 41+: A Romance of the Year 2660* must begin by acknowledging that all previous judgements regarding the novel are largely accurate—that it is a 'tawdry illiterate tale', a 'sorry concoction' (Brian Aldiss, *Trillion Year Spree*, pp. 203, 204), 'deficient as fiction' (Malcolm J. Edwards, 'Hugo Gernsback', p. 252), 'poorly written' (Brian Ash, *Faces of the Future*, p. 65), 'dense and almost preliterate' (David G. Hartwell, *Age of Wonders*, p. 131), 'unreadable' (Anthony Boucher, 'The Publishing of Science Fiction', p. 29, and L. Sprague de Camp and Catherine Crook de Camp, *Science Fiction Handbook—Revised*, p. 23), 'simply dreadful' (Lester del Rey, *The World of Science Fiction* 33), 'full of... appallingly bad writing' (Chris Morgan, *The Shape of Futures Past*, p. 109), a 'pitiable... novel' (Sam Lundwall, *Science Fiction: An Illustrated History*, p. 76), and so on. Truly, if aesthetic quality is the only reason for reading, no one should read *Ralph 124C 41+*.

And, evidently appalled by its artlessness, some critics who regularly condemn *Ralph* apparently have never read it very carefully, or at all. All of Aldiss's specific comments about the novel in *Trillion Year Spree* concern the first three chapters of the novel and are at times misleading: for example, he says that during sleep 'children are fed lessons, and adults—of all miserable things—the contents of newspapers', which he condemns as "simple-minded Victorian utilitarianism" (p. 204). However, while Gernsback mentions lessons and newspapers as an option in using the *Hypnobioscope*, Ralph himself is depicted reading Homer's *Odyssey*, and Gernsback says that 'All books were read while one slept' (p. 50)—reading activities Aldiss might approve of. Also, Aldiss says that the novel 'drifts into outer space and back' (p. 203); but Ralph's adventures in space occupy the last five chapters of the book, except for a brief coda on Earth, to constitute about 40 per cent of the text, a proportion that makes the novel roughly comparable to E. E. Smith's *The Skylark of Space*, another novel which takes a while to get away from Earth. Yet no one would say that *The Skylark of Space* 'drifts into outer space and back'. As for Sam Lundwall, his full statement—'Hugo Gernsback's pitiable Utopian novel, *Ralph 124C*

41+ (1911), in which the intrepid editor-cum-author managed to take away all the sociological, political and intelligent parts and substitute them with machines and monsters without end' (p. 76)—suggests that Lundwall has not even read the book, since there is nothing in the book that even remotely resembles a 'monster'.[1]

However, while conceding its aesthetic weaknesses, I maintain that Gernsback's novel is the one essential text for all studies of science fiction, a work which anticipates and contains the entire genre. It qualifies—perhaps—as the first work of fiction ever published in a science magazine;[2] and while many previous stories happen to accord with later prescriptions for science fiction, *Ralph* was the first work consciously written to display the characteristic styles and contents of both fiction and scientific writing. Thus, Gernsback was the first writer to directly wrestle with the problems created by the genre of science fiction.

What makes *Ralph* fascinating, then, is not that it is an *aesthetic* failure—and certainly, by any measure it is—but that it is a *critical* failure. Aside from its clumsy prose, a handicap that Gernsback never overcame, all the problems in *Ralph* stem directly from the critical ideas that Gernsback would promote in the decades to come, the ideas that would influence all other writers and readers of science fiction. One might say that like a mechanic, Gernsback had taken apart the engine of science fiction to see what made it work—but he could not put it together again. The novel therefore serves as an explanatory matrix for the modern genre, and later works can be fruitfully analysed by exploring to what extent and in what ways those authors dealt with the problems in Gernsback's theories, and to what extent and in what ways they remain plagued by those problems. Given a question involving science fiction, a critic can point to the pages in *Ralph* where the problem is crudely and nakedly expressed; so the special value of *Ralph* is that the conflicts and contradictions in the novel are unusually clear and conspicuous. More talented writers are more successful in reconciling or concealing the inherent problems of science fiction, so one can ignore those writers' roots and impose alien models from other genres to explain them. Refreshed and enlightened by a reading of *Ralph*, critics can gain a better understanding of what it really going on in modern works of science fiction. Therefore, there is more truth than Brian Aldiss knew of in his description of *Ralph* as 'this unique document' (p. 203).

After my first study of *Ralph* persuaded me that it represented a *mixture* of various goals and models, I was able to confirm this picture by examining its textual history, as reported in 'Evolution of Modern Science Fiction'. The first seven instalments of the original, and quite different, 1911–12 magazine version combined the utopia and travel tale and emphasized stimulating scientific predictions; the last five instalments combined melodrama and Gothic horror and emphasized scientific education and entertainment. For the 1925 version, not significantly changed in later editions, Gernsback tried to blend these disparate purposes and stories together, while also adding passages of humour and satire. For my purposes here, it seems best to focus only on the second text (though I use the slightly revised 1950 edition), since this is the version that had an influence on the genre and the version that best represents the picture of science fiction that Gernsback evolved. That is, the 1925 version perfectly displays the pitfalls and possibilities in Gernsback's theory of science fiction, though it slightly preceded Gernsback's published comments on his theory of science fiction, which began a year later.

In writing *Ralph*, Gernsback scrupulously followed his own formula of 'interweaving' narrative with scientific and prophetic exposition. Consider this passage from Chapter 5 of the novel:

> Ralph and his companion strolled about the immense grounds watching the players and it was not long before he discovered that she, like himself, was enthusiastic about tennis. He asked her if she would care to play a game with him and she acquiesced eagerly... In the game that followed, Ralph, an expert at tennis, was too engrossed in the girl to watch his game. Consequently, he was beaten from start to finish. He did not see the ball, and scarcely noticed the net. His eyes were constantly on Alice, who, indeed, made a remarkably pretty picture. She flung herself enthusiastically into her game, as she did with everything else that interested her. She was the true sport-lover, caring little whether she won or not, loving the game for the game itself.
>
> Her lovely face was flushed with the exercise, and her hair curled into damp little rings, lying against her neck and cheeks in soft clusters. Her eyes, always bright, shone like stars. Now and again they met Ralph's in gay triumph as she encountered a difficult ball.
>
> He had never imagined that anyone could be so graceful. Her lithe and flexible figure was seen to its best advantage in this game requiring great agility.
>
> Ralph, under this bombardment of charms, was spellbound. He played mechanically, and, it must be admitted, wretchedly. And he was so thoroughly and abjectly in love that he did not care. To him, but one thing mattered. He knew that unless he could have Alice life itself would not matter to him.
>
> He felt that he would gladly have lost a hundred games when she at last flung down her racket, crying happily: 'Oh, I won, I won, didn't I?'

'You certainly did,' he cried. 'You were wonderful'.

'I'm a little bit afraid you let me win,' she pouted. 'It really wasn't fair of you'.

'You were fine,' he declared. 'I was hopelessly outclassed from the beginning. You have no idea how beautiful you were,' he went on, impulsively. 'More beautiful than I ever dreamed anyone could be.'

Before his ardent eyes she drew back a little, half pleased, half frightened, and not a little confused. (pp. 81–82)

This scene of 'charming romance' might have appeared in any popular novel of its day, since there is no indication of science or science fiction in it. But the next paragraphs are different:

Sensing her embarrassment he instantly became matter-of-fact.

'Now,' he said, 'I am going to show you the source of New York's light and power'...

They alighted on an immense plain on which twelve monstrous Meteoro-Towers, each 1,500 feet high, were stationed. These towers formed a hexagon inside of which were the immense *Helio-Dynamophores*, or Sun-power-generators.

The entire expanse, twenty kilometers square, was covered with glass. Underneath the heavy plate glass squares were the photo-electric elements which transformed the solar heat *direct* into electric energy.

The photo-electric elements, of which there were 400 to each square meter, were placed in large movable metal cases, each case containing 1,600 photo-electric units [which] generated about one hundred and twenty kilowatts almost as long as the sun was shining... this plant supplied all the power, light, and heat for entire New York. One-half of the plant was for day use, while the other half during daytime charged the chemical gas-accumulators for night use.

In 1909 Cove of Massachusetts invented a thermo-electric Sun-power-generator, which could deliver ten volts and six amperes, or one-sixtieth kilowatt in a space of twelve square feet. Since that time inventors by the score had busied themselves to perfect solar generators, but it was not until the year 2469 that the Italian 63A 1243 invented the photo-electric cell, which revolutionized the entire electrical industry. This Italian discovered that by derivatives of the Radium-M class, in conjunction with Tellurium and Arcturium, a photo-electric element could be produced which was strongly affected by the sun's ultra-violet rays and in this condition was able to transform heat *direct* into electrical energy... (pp. 82–84)

Here, Gernsback provides the other elements of science fiction: 'scientific fact'—a brief account of the then-current state of solar energy research—and 'prophetic vision'—a detailed description of a solar power plant of the future. And in these later passages, the tone and texture of the writing is notably dissimilar from the tale of the tennis court.

Looking at the juxtaposition of these two different forms of writing reveals an immediate problem in Gernsback's approach to science fiction. As a reading specialist can relate, reading fiction and reading nonfiction demand entirely different reading styles: fiction is usually read casually and sequentially, but nonfiction either must be read with unusual care, with an initial survey of the material followed by close reading and final review or, in other circumstances, may be scanned over rapidly by a reader looking only for certain information. Thus, a novel like *Ralph* alternately demands two very different styles of reading.

Interestingly, two early readers of Gernsback's magazines recognized this problem and recommended special printing conventions to help them adjust their reading methods. 'Print all scientific facts as related in the stories, in italics,' one male reader advised. 'This will serve to more forcefully drive home the idea upon which you have established your magazine. Personally, when I have some such system blazing forth before my eyes, I am inclined to stop and consider what I have learned, for future reference' (cited in 'Thank You!', p. 99). However, a female reader suggested, 'Do not sacrifice story interest to scientific detail. (Why not block the very technical parts off in small type? Descriptions of machinery, etc.)' ('The Reader Speaks', *Science Wonder Stories*, June 1929, p. 92). Clearly, the first reader was chiefly interested in the explanations, not the story, and wanted italics to draw his attention to those passages for careful study; while the other reader was chiefly interested in the story and wanted the explanatory material in small print so she could scan over it rapidly. Needless to say, no such conventions were adopted, although Gernsback continued the policy of putting certain peripheral explanations in footnotes, thereby isolating and marking certain forms of informative writing; still, for the most part, readers were left with the problem of a text which alternately demanded two entirely distinct reading methods.

A broader problem in *Ralph* involves the requirement that the narrative and expository passages not only be juxtaposed, but 'interwoven'; and, feeling obliged to maintain both a narrative and a steady stream of educational and stimulating explanation, Gernsback is only intermittently successful in doing so.

Some scientific material is essential to the story: when Alice is threatened by an avalanche in Switzerland, Gernsback must explain the science behind the energy beams Ralph generates in New York to remove the danger;

when Fernand abducts Alice with an invisibility device, he must explain the device Ralph hastily invents to locate her; and when Alice is kidnapped and flown into space, he must explain the form of radar Ralph develops to locate one spaceship, and the creation of an artificial comet to divert another spaceship. These explanatory passages are not intrusive, and these incidents are the most exciting parts in the novel.

Other scientific material might be categorized as linked to the story but not essential to it. To account for Ralph's growing love for Alice, Gernsback must have them spend some time together; and there is some logic in having an eminent scientist like Ralph give Alice a tour of various scientific facilities—the solar power plant, the Accelerated Plant Growing Farms, and so on. And while the focus is on describing and explaining the machinery, moments in these scenes bring out Alice's character as an intelligent woman with a sense of humour. Yet the information provided is not otherwise related to the narrative, and while these passages could not simply be removed, Gernsback might easily have depicted other activities which would have fulfilled the same purpose.

Finally, some scientific material is hardly connected to the story at all. At one point, Gernsback introduces an extended discussion of the future's financial system with a single sentence: 'A few days later, Alice, while rolling along one of the elevated streets of the city with Ralph, inquired how the present monetary system had been evolved: "You know," she confided, "I know very little of economics"' (p. 110). And Ralph begins an explanatory lecture, with occasional questions from Alice. However, the material contributes nothing to the narrative, and could easily have been edited out without its absence being noted.

While the incorporation of scientific and prophetic passages in *Ralph* is thus occasionally awkward or inorganic to the story, a more important problem involves Gernsback's three purposes for science fiction; for in many ways, the narrative and expository materials are working at cross purposes. That is, by striving to provide some scientific education and scientific ideas, Gernsback compromises his goal of offering entertainment; and by striving to provide entertainment, he compromises his goal of offering some scientific education and scientific ideas.

As the passage about solar power indicates, the scientific and prophetic passages in Gernsback's novel can be long and detailed, so at the very least, the unfolding story of *Ralph* is often delayed for some time. What is worse, however, is that the expository passages in some cases actually undermine the narrative. A noteworthy instance is the time when Ralph greets Alice and her father, James 212B 422, newly arrived from Europe:

'We had the honor of being the first passengers to arrive by means of the new *Subatlantic Tube,*' said James 212B 422. 'As you are doubtless aware, the regular passenger service opens next week, but being one of the consulting engineers of the new electromagnetic tube, my daughter and I were permitted to make the first trip westward... '

'But you shouldn't have risked your lives, in an untested tube,' [Ralph] exclaimed. And then, the scientist in him to the front: 'Tell me all about this new tube. Busy with my own work I have not followed its progress closely enough to know all its details.'

'It has been most interesting work,' said James 212B 422, 'and we regard it as quite an achievement in electrical engineering... ' (pp. 58–59)

And he proceeds to describe and explain the transportation system at length and even shows Ralph a simple drawing of a tunnel running through the Earth straight from Brest, France, to New York.

The entire scene is absurd. In the previous chapter, Ralph had been seen reading the *New York News* on a form of microfilm, which surely would have described the imminent opening of a 'Subatlantic Tube'. In fact, a scientist of Ralph's stature would virtually have to be familiar with such a project. Even if one argues that Ralph is merely asking for an explanation as a premise for conversing with the father of a girl he is attracted to—and nothing else in the novel suggests Ralph has such social skills—it is still illogical for a common engineer to respond by giving an elementary explanation of the project—complete with a visual aid—to someone known as one of the world's greatest scientists. Further, since James's daughter Alice already knew everything about the project and had just travelled through the new tunnel, it is incredible that she is described as 'an interested listener' (p. 61) to his lecture. In terms of everything readers are told about these characters, the exchange simply does not make any sense.

The scene can be explained, though, in terms of the author's priorities. Having introduced the concept of a subterranean transportation system, Gernsback wishes to explain the scientific principles behind it and to describe how such a system might be built—in order to educate his general readers and stimulate the thinking of his scientist readers. Since the system comes up in the middle of a major event in the novel—Ralph's first face-to-face meeting with its heroine—Gernsback cannot interrupt the scene with a long explanation from the narrator; so he must work the data into the conversation. Ordinarily, Ralph is the logical person to provide lectures on science; but here, he cannot credibly explain the principles behind a 'Subatlantic Tube' to the man who helped build it and who had just travelled through it with his daughter. Thus, the brilliant Ralph must be temporarily cast as ill-informed, so that he can play the listener to James's lecture.

Other inconsistencies and illogical events crop up all the time in *Ralph*. The world of 2660 is linked by instantaneous telephone and television communications, yet Alice and her father are pictured as completely ignorant of American farming methods: 'In the old-fashioned European farms such as Alice knew, only two crops could be grown' (p. 99).[3] In Chapter 2, Ralph is seen using a *Menograph*, a machine that turns thoughts into printed symbols, while in Chapter 9, Ralph excitedly introduces his latest invention, a machine that turns speech into printed symbols—with no mention of the Menograph; but in a world where people can already do nothing but think to produce a written record, a new device that allows them to speak to produce a record would be trivial and unimportant. In early chapters of the novel, Ralph and Alice travel about in various adaptations of cars and airplanes—the *electromobile*, the *aerocab*, and the *Tele-motor-coasters*—apparently powered by conventional means; but in Chapter 9, we learn that Ralph has recently created a form of anti-gravity, used in presenting an 'Aerial Carnival' and sustaining flying 'Vacation Cities'. But a civilization that has learned the secret of anti-gravity would certainly incorporate it into its systems of transportation. In all cases, Gernsback seeks to provide some more scientific information, or a new idea, and does so at any cost.

Any fiction that seeks to be entertaining must make readers feel that its characters and situations are somehow true-to-life and worth caring about; but preoccupied with extraliterary goals, Gernsback repeatedly fails to achieve this atmosphere. At times, Ralph and Alice momentarily start to seem like real people whose problems and concerns can be related to; but then, Gernsback pulls his strings, and they are jerked away to provide or listen to an incongruous lecture on some new scientific topic.

While the desire to educate and offer scientific ideas thus compromises *Ralph* as entertainment, the desire to entertain also compromises the novel as a source of information and suggestions. In setting his story six centuries in the future, Gernsback was clearly obliging himself to present spectacular scientific advances; however, had he strictly limited himself to the known scientific facts of his day in making predictions, the results would have been generally rather dull. For that reason, Gernsback was repeatedly obliged to posit the existence of miraculous substances and rays to make his inventions work. The solar power plant described above, for example, depends on the amazing 'photo-electric element' constructed out of Tellurium and the imaginary elements *Arcturium* and *Radium-M*. Another of Ralph's astounding scientific feats—reviving a dead dog—requires '*Radium-K*', which 'exhibited all the usual phenomena of pure Radium and produced great heat, but did not create burns on animal tissue' (p. 54), 'Permagatol', 'A green gas having the property of preserving animal tissue permanently and indefinitely', and 'powerful F-9 rays' to stimulate the dead dog's brain (p. 54). Such devices clearly weaken the novel's capacity to provide scientific data and useful ideas. First, while Gernsback usually italicizes all imaginary substances, to indicate that they do not now exist, readers unaware of this unstated convention might suppose that he is describing actual elements. Further, inventors who try to put Gernsback's plans into action will be unable to do so without the unavailable elements and their unusual properties, making his suggestions useless to a working scientist; how could a scientist follow Ralph's procedure for reviving the dead without Radium-K, Permagatol, and F-9 rays?

Still, one cannot entirely discount the potential of Ralph to provide scientific information or stimulate scientific thinking. While most modern readers will find its scientific information outdated or simplistic, I did learn from Gernsback the chemical composition of milk. And a would-be inventor just might be able to realize one of Gernsback's ideas by devising some prosaic substitute for the marvellous enabling substance or device. This actually happened once, as Gernsback enthusiastically explained:

> In the year 1911, in my story Ralph 124C 41+, I featured a purely fictional instrument which I termed 'The Hypnobioscope'. This instrument was supposed to impart knowledge and education to the sleeping mind... This was pure fiction and evidently I did not take much stock in it myself, because I never actually tried it. Much to my amazement, however, Chief Radio Man Finney of the United States Navy, who read the story, tried it in 1922, with the result that today in the Pensacola, Florida, Naval Station, students are taught code while they sleep. You may see the students stretched on benches, with helmets over their heads, sleeping soundly, while an operator is sending them code all night long. ('Our Amazing Minds', p. 197)[4]

The Hypnobioscope depended on a direct link between a machine and the user's brain, impossible then and now; but Finney surmised that comparable results could be obtained by having people listen to sounds while they sleep. A letter in the March 1927 issue of Amazing Stories also described several experiments a reader performed in response to stories ('Discussions', p. 1180). It is possible, then, that modern-day engineers might some day incorporate some of Gernsback's ideas regarding solar power plants even if they lack the super-efficient power element Gernsback described.

Clearly, combining disparate forms of writing and goals, as Gernsback proposed, created problems in *Ralph*; but its most striking feature is the way it attempts, and fails, to follow the generic models implicit in Gernsback's history of science fiction: melodrama, travel tale, Gothic horror, utopia, satire, dystopia, and tale of transcendence. In each case, one finds evidence for classifying *Ralph* as part of that genre—and one observes ruinous problems in identifying the novel as a work of that genre.

First, the influence of Senarens and juvenile adventure fiction can clearly be seen in *Ralph*.[5] Its central story line is certainly melodramatic—a virtuous young scientist must rescue his fiancée from a villain named Fernand who has kidnapped her—and its dialogue at times shows the unmistakable influence of melodrama:

> 'You coward,' [Alice] blazed, 'how dare you keep me here! Turn around and take me back at once—at once, do you hear?'
>
> Fernand, in the act of opening her door and going back to his laboratory, paused smilingly.
>
> 'My dear girl,' he said mockingly, 'ask of me anything and I will grant it—except that. You have a temper that delights me. Your smiles will be all the sweeter, later.' (p. 172)

However, despite this occasional fidelity to the form and language of melodrama, Gernsback's special purposes disturbed and distorted the melodramatic structure. One problem is immediately clear: while melodrama, according to Peter Brooks's *The Melodramatic Imagination*, is dedicated to 'Emotions... given a full acting-out... a full emotional indulgence' (p. 41), science fiction mandates unemotional accounts of scientific data and ideas far exceeding the traditional amount of exposition needed to explain the plot, thus compromising the characteristic tone of melodrama. However, the structure is altered as well: for to make melodrama serve the ideology of science fiction, Gernsback had to make Ralph, the hero of his novel, resemble both a conventional hero and a conventional villain, thus threatening the integrity of the melodramatic form.

To explore Ralph's strange character, I offer a model of conflict in melodrama based on the position of Robert Heilman in *Tragedy and Melodrama* that melodrama is 'a polemic form' in 'the realm of social action' (p. 97), that it works with 'whole rather than divided' characters (p. 81), and that particularly in its American form, characters are, in Garff Wilson's words, 'either completely good or completely bad' (*Three Hundred Years of American Theatre*, p. 101). In this framework, I note three important and interrelated themes in the conflict between villain and hero.

The first is *intellect versus emotion*: David Grimsted's *Melodrama Unveiled* notes that August von Kotzebue, one influence on American melodrama, preached that 'impetuous feeling rather than reason or custom was the proper basis of conduct' (p. 13) and that melodramas usually had villains with 'intelligence' (p. 177) and heroes who 'seldom showed signs of great learning or rationality' (p. 210). The villain is usually older, more knowing, and better educated than the hero, is described as cold and calculating, and uses sophistry in making his case, perhaps with logic or the letter of the law on his side in foreclosing a mortgage. But the hero is young, naive, and unschooled, seems emotional and impulsive, and opposes the villain based on basic morality, not subtle reasoning—despite the law, people should not be deprived of their homes.

A second theme is *indirect action versus direct action*. The villain, typically employing what Grimsted describes as 'diabolic subterfuge' (p. 178), has henchmen do the dirty work so he is elsewhere, with a perfect alibi, when the crime is committed, or sets events in motion and leaves, tying the heroine to the railroad tracks or the hero to a log in a sawmill, so that machines, not the villain, will do the actual killing. However, the hero acts on his own without relying on other people or devices; the villain may be absent at the climax, but the hero is always there to save the day.

A third theme is *the élite versus the common man*; Michael Booth's *English Melodrama* notes that 'Melodrama clearly reflects class hatreds. Villains tend to be noblemen, factory owners, squires; heroes peasants, able seamen, and workmen' (p. 62). Thus, the villain is typically a wealthy man, with considerable property, and he may enjoy power over others, the open or covert support of law officers, or an official position; the hero is poor, with no friends in high places, no official cooperation in opposing the villain, and no title or social status. The hero may be seen as a rebel, an outcast, or even, as Booth says, a 'criminal-hero' (p. 64).

These villainous and heroic qualities illustrate Gernsback's dilemma in using melodrama as a model for science fiction: for in celebrating the value of science, Gernsback's theory of science fiction was promoting intellect over emotion; in depicting new inventions to replace manual labour, his theory was advocating indirect action over direct action; and in supporting the scientific community, his theory was favouring the interests of an élite over those of the common man. Yet melodrama was a form that was *directly antithetical to all of these concerns*. His solution was to make Ralph a hero who alternately displayed the attributes of both hero and villain, so Ralph functions as a traditional hero while also advancing Gernsback's untraditional agenda.

The contradictory qualities of Ralph's character emerge repeatedly. Ralph is 'one of the greatest living scientists' (p. 25) who once called love 'nothing but a perfumed animal instinct' (p. 140), but his love for Alice leads this intellect to scream at his servant, lose a tennis game because he cannot concentrate, and madly dash off to save Alice when she is in danger.

Second, he first rescues Alice with scientific indirect action: when Ralph learns an avalanche is about to destroy her faraway home, he tells her to set up an antenna, goes to his laboratory to create a storm of energy, and broadcasts heat to melt away the threatening snow. Yet when Fernand later kidnaps Alice and flies into space, Ralph eschews any complicated scientific scheme and simply gets in a spaceship to go after them. Finally, due to his vast intellect Ralph is 'one of the ten men on the whole planet earth' with 'the Plus sign after his name' (p. 25); because of that title, he enjoys generous financial support and personal access to the Planet Governor who controls the entire world. Yet to maintain Ralph's scientific productivity, the government forbids harmful activity and Ralph 'grew restive under the restraint' (p. 41), calling himself 'nothing but a prisoner' (p. 42). And when the Planet Governor expressly tells him not to pursue Fernand, Ralph defies the order and leaves anyway, effectively becoming an outcast and criminal.[6]

While such a divided character serves to further undermine the narrative logic of Gernsback's story, Ralph's contradictory impulses generate another complexity with more ruinous effects: as Ralph alternately is a heroic hero and a villainous hero, his opponent splits into a villainous villain and a heroic villain.

This pattern is evident in the novel, for Ralph actually has two rivals for Alice's love: Fernand and a Martian, Llysanorh'.[7] Fernand is a standard villain: aloof and uncaring, he wants Alice simply for the satisfaction of conquest; devious and indirect, he seizes Alice with an invisibility device and uses confederates to seize her again; wealthy and well connected, his machinations suggest a high social status. Llysanorh' is completely different—'a very decent chap' who is 'hopelessly infatuated' with Alice (p. 68). She 'could not deny the fact of his genuine… fervent love' (p. 193), even after he kidnaps her; his abduction is an impulsive, individual action; and as a Martian, he is by definition a social outcast, legally forbidden to marry an Earth woman despite his love—thus, he is a victim of society and to Alice seems 'very pathetic' (p. 190). Though finally driven to kidnap and murder Alice, he resembles a melodramatic hero, and one wonders why Gernsback would complicate his narrative with this character; the novel's last chapters are particularly clumsy, as Ralph, having flown to Alice's rescue and confronted Fernand, finds that Llysanorh' has now kidnapped Alice, which forces Ralph to effect a second rescue.

However, Llysanorh's presence can be explained: since Ralph has attributes of both hero and villain, a purely evil character like Fernand is not sufficient to serve as his foil; while Fernand can oppose Ralph when the scientist is emotional and daring, he cannot be his adversary when Ralph is intellectual and prudent. Thus, a second, more sympathetic villain is required as a counterpart to the sometimes unsympathetic hero.

We see the two villains functioning exactly this way in *Ralph*. In response to Fernand's deviousness, Ralph acts directly and personally: when Fernand invisibly seizes Alice, Ralph rushes after her with his new invention, finds where she is hidden, and frees her. When Fernand kidnaps Alice in his spaceship, Ralph flies into space, locates and overtakes Fernand, and confronts him with startling passion and violence, exclaiming 'If you and I ever meet again I will pound your miserable cowardly body into jelly!' (p. 169).

Ralph acts differently in response to Llysanorh's direct actions: learning that Llysanorh' has taken Alice from Fernand and is heading to Mars, Ralph calculates he will not have enough time to overtake Llysanorh's ship before he reaches Mars and arranges to forcibly marry Alice. He then resorts to a trick: in his spaceship laboratory he creates an artificial comet and sends it toward Mars. He reasons that Llysanorh', for the sake of his fellow Martians, will change course to intercept and destroy the comet, giving Ralph time to catch his ship. Though the stratagem works, it seems unheroic to play upon an opponent's altruism; the scheme resembles the moment in a melodrama when the trapped villain grabs an innocent bystander and puts a gun to his head, saying, 'Surrender, or I will kill him'. The difference is that Ralph is pointing a gun at the entire planet of Mars. There is also something cold about Ralph's reaction when he finds that Llysanorh' has killed both himself and Alice: while returning to Earth, he methodically drains Alice's blood and tries to invent a substance that will enable him to bring her back to life. While understandable, these actions are an oddly unemotional way to respond to the death of a loved one.

The pattern emerges: cold and devious Fernand opposes Ralph's passions, while emotional and direct Llysanorh' opposes Ralph's intelligence; a hero who is alternately sympathetic and cold has spawned a cold villain and a sympathetic villain. Thus, when Ralph proclaims his 'fight is to be man against man, brain against brain' (p. 153), Gernsback inadvertently suggests the complexity of his narrative, with one difference: the fight is Ralph the man against Fernand the brain, and Ralph the brain against Llysanorh' the man.

Overall, then, the needless complexity and lack of coherence in *Ralph* is partially explained by the fact that the genre of melodrama is simply not compatible with certain aspects of Gernsback's theory of science fiction, so Gernsback's attempts to reconcile the two do not work at all.

If melodrama does not always seem appropriate, there is another generic model that Gernsback can draw upon—the travel tale. Percy C. Adams, in *Travel Literature and the Evolution of the Novel*, claims, as noted, a 'close relationship' between travel literature and 'science fiction... through the ages from Lucian to Godwin, Cyrano, and Defoe to our day... much of its appeal deriving from new real ways of travel' (p. 275); and certainly, whether one calls them science fiction or not, many earlier works, including those of Verne, Gernsback's 'favorite author', employ the form of travel literature to present imaginative visions. Also, as Adams notes, 'The place of digressions in, as well as their importance to, imaginary voyages, the fiction closest to the travel account, has been pointed out by Aubrey Rosenberg' (p. 206), so the form provides a precedent for the 'digressions' of science and prediction mandated by Gernsback's approach; there is also a tradition, Adams notes, of 'unadorned, clumsy, hurried prose' (p. 247), which seems to fit someone with Gernsback's limited skills.

The basic narrative of *Ralph* can readily be construed as two extended travel tales: first, the visit of Alice to America, with Ralph as her guide, and second, Ralph's journey into space to rescue Alice. In addition, a number of new transportation devices, including the *aerocab, tele-motor-coasters,* the *electromobile,* and the *space flyer,* are introduced and described, further emphasizing the motif of travel. Indeed, L. Sprague de Camp and Catherine Crook de Camp flatly describe 'most of *Ralph 124C 41+*' as 'a travelogue' (*Science Fiction Handbook—Revised,* p. 23), and just about the only literary reference in *Ralph* is to that notable travel tale, the *Odyssey.* Still, the overall mood of *Ralph* seems far removed from the conventional atmosphere of travel literature.

To demonstrate why Gernsback has problems adapting this model to science fiction, I propose a rough model of the essential elements in travel literature. First, the underlying philosophy is that travel is a worthwhile end in itself, a way to broaden one's horizons and become more mature by learning more about the world one lives in; as Adams says, 'movement and action for their own sake were attractive' in travel literature (p. 185).

Second, the writing generally focuses on pure description, to provide readers with a detailed, evocative picture of the places explored: Adams says that in travel tales 'One finds not just descriptions of buildings, reflections on history, quotations from the ancients, and information for science, religion, or politics... [but also] descriptions of nature that are metaphorical, exact, full of color, And obviously those descriptions reflect the admiration of the writers for what they have discovered' (p. 267).

Third, while protagonists may have a few diverting adventures and project a sense of character, their basic role is to be bland and passive, surrogates for readers who cannot go to the exotic places in the narrative; Adams claims that 'Travel literature contributes little of course to the kind of characterization done so well by certain novelists from Richardson to James' (p. 278).

If these principles are accepted as valid features of travel literature, then

Gernsback will obviously display some resistance to them. First of all, to see travel and observation as the focus of science is to harken back to the model of science proposed by Francis Bacon, who believed that scientific progress would emerge from compilations of all previous examinations of nature and the addition of data from new examinations. However, Gernsback was enough of a scientist to know that scientists must go beyond observation to interact with and experiment on what they see, and this is especially true of the process of invention—Gernsback's main preoccupation: while inventors may get a useful idea or two by noting animal behaviour and physiology, their primary work will involve laboratory work and experimentation.

Second, an obvious characteristic of modern science is that it seeks to go beyond observing surface details to understand inner workings; thus, although some description of the outward appearance of an object may be useful, the true scientist will concentrate more on analysis and explanation of its inner workings.

Finally, given the scientist's need to probe into and work with the material at hand, and given Gernsback's stated desire to provide melodramatic adventure, protagonists cannot remain passive, but must continually interact with their environment, and must develop some sort of personality in carrying out that interaction, so the focus of the text shifts away from neutral observation.

For all these reasons, Gernsback continually disappoints readers who would only like a guided tour of an interesting future. Though Ralph takes Alice to various places, the primary setting for most of the novel is his laboratory, where he uses and works on numerous inventions. Even when he flies off into space, he spends almost no time looking around at the universe, offering readers with a glimpse of its wonders; in fact, the only time he looks out of the window is to observe the progress of his artificial comet. Instead, he virtually transforms his spaceship into a portable laboratory, where he successively invents a form of radar, the comet, and a makeshift method for reviving the dead Alice.

Indeed, instead of observing the outside world, Gernsback's *Ralph* concentrates on describing interiors. Its lack of interest in sightseeing is most graphically demonstrated by the first form of transportation discussed in the novel—a tunnel underneath the Atlantic Ocean. And the novel at times displays tunnel vision: while he spends some time describing the exterior of the solar power plant, Ralph emphasizes how the power plant works; and while visiting the Accelerated Plant Growing Farm, Ralph focuses on explaining how various foods are made there. Further, in engaging in active adventures in the manner of melodrama—as described above—Ralph further compromises the mood of travel literature, as derring-do and heroics obscure the futuristic background.

It might be noted that some science in the novel seems devoted to the *prevention* of travel, although this may reflect Gernsback's own opinions, not an inevitable result of his theories. In the first chapter, when Alice is threatened by an avalanche, Ralph is praised because he devises a way to save her without having to leave his laboratory. The invention of *Tele-Theatre*—a form of television—is explicitly celebrated because it eliminates the need to leave one's home to see a play: Alice comments:

> Can you imagine how the people in former centuries must have been inconvenienced when they wished to enjoy a play? I was reading only the other day how they had to prepare themselves for the theater hours ahead of time. They had to get dressed especially for the occasion and even went so far as to have different clothes in which to attend theaters or operas. And then they had to ride or perhaps walk to the playhouse itself. Then the poor things, if they did not happen to like the production, had either to sit all through it or else go home. They probably would have rejoiced at the ease of our Tele-Theaters, where we can switch from one play to another in five seconds, until we find the one that suits us best. (pp. 86–87)

And the Subatlantic Tube is hailed, despite its complete lack of scenery, because it dramatically reduces travel time from Europe to America. Obviously Gernsback does not believe that getting there is half the fun; instead, getting there is a chore which modern science must work to eliminate or minimize. And with such an attitude, it is little wonder that *Ralph* emerges as a rather disappointing example of futuristic travel literature.

Given Gernsback's focus on interiors and an atmosphere of confinement, one might argue that *Ralph* resembles a Gothic novel; indeed, some parts of the work—when Fernand spirits Alice away with an invisibility device, and the climactic scene in the spaceship where Ralph shares quarters with Alice's dead body and methodically drains her blood—might well be exploited by a Poe or Lovecraft. At times, Ralph indulges in thoughts that recall Gothic themes: working on a method that might revive a dead dog, he muses, 'Would he succeed? Had he attempted the impossible? Was he challenging Nature to a combat only to be worsted?' (p. 55). And at the end of the novel, when Ralph actually tries to use that method to bring Alice back to life, that mood is momentarily dominant:

> At the end of two days the sickness left Ralph, but it left him worn and exhausted physically and he was subject to terrible fits of depression. At these times the boundless space about him appalled him, weighing him down with its infinite immensity. The awful

stillness crushed him. Everything seemed dead—dead as was that silent motionless figure that had been a living laughing creature who loved him—it seemed so long ago.

He felt that Nature herself was punishing him for his daring assault on her dominions. He had presumed to set the laws of Life and Death at variance, and this was the penalty, this living death, shut in with the living dead.

At such times a madness of fear and despair would grip him. He would fling himself down at Alice's side, his face buried in her cold inert hand, and sob like a child in his loneliness and agony of spirit. (p. 203)

Not only does this passage recall the tone and message of the Gothic novel, but there is even a specific use of horrific imagery in the reference to 'the living dead'.

However, the mood is transitory, since Ralph soon does bring Alice back to life and thus succeeds in 'set[ting] the laws of Life and Death at variance'. Indeed, despite these moments, *Ralph* is clearly not a Gothic novel, and with Gernsback's priorities in writing science fiction, it could not have taken that form.

Four traditional attributes of Gothic horror stories might be listed as follows: first, there is the dominant sense that the known universe of everyday life is surrounded and enveloped by strange, powerful and inexplicable forces. Critics differ only in whether they see this mysterious atmosphere as good, evil, or morally neutral. S. L. Varnado's *Haunted Presence* sees 'value elements' in the Gothic world but also describes that world as a 'numinous' one, something that cannot be experienced or understood rationally: 'The numinous, then, can be summed up as an affective state in which the percipient—through feelings of awe, mystery, and fascination—becomes aware of an objective spiritual presence' (pp. 18, 15). According to Linda Bayer-Berenbaum's *The Gothic Imagination*, 'Gothicism asserts that transcendence is primarily evil', although acknowledging that it is also 'unfathomable' and 'incomprehensible' (pp. 13, 141, 143). And William Patrick Day's *In the Circles of Fear and Desire* emphatically states that 'the Gothic fantasy defines a world but defines a portion of that world as unknowable. Mystery and suspense serve as signals to us that what we can see, illuminated by the conventions of the genre, is only a part of what is there' (pp. 14–15), and he later repeats that the Gothic is 'a statement of the essential unknowableness of the real' and 'it reveals that [inner] life to be a dark and mysterious thing, perhaps essentially unknowable, or knowable only at our peril' (pp. 61, 68). It is true that sometimes, as in Ann Radcliffe's novels, the phenomena of this mysterious or supernatural universe are finally explained away as fraudulent machinations, thus in a way denying that vision; still, such works present and validate the Gothic world view even if they ultimately retreat from it.

Second, the Gothic novel typically employs settings that emphasize the limits of human perception and powers. Day (pp. 78, 79) and Bayer-Berenbaum (p. 23) discuss the common theme of 'imprisonment' in Gothic fiction, and Varnado (p. 17) lists 'moldering castles' and 'underground passages' as characteristic Gothic locales. The other Gothic environment is vast looming ruins and uncontrolled nature, which dwarf the people in it and, while apparently offering freedom of movement, make them seem small and unimportant. As Day notes:

> The Arctic desert in which Frankenstein and his creature die, the ruined castles and haunted houses of Otranto and Udolpho, the Abbey of St. Clare in *The Monk*, the house of Usher, Bartram Haugh in *Uncle Silas*, Bly in *The Turn of the Screw*, Castle Dracula and the barren moors surrounding Baskerville Hall—the Gothic is full of images of ruins and blasted landscapes... The chaotic world of the Gothic fantasy is an anticipation of the empty landscape of the grimmest versions of the modernist vision. (p. 169)

Varnado adds that typical Gothic depictions of 'Mountain gloom, lonely castles, phantom ships, violent storms, and the vastness of sea and polar regions' reflect the genre's 'numinous reality' (p. 17).

Third, confronting an inexplicable universe, and confined or diminished by the environment, the Gothic protagonist seems essentially helpless: as Day says:

> the Gothic world comes to dominate and control the protagonists, whatever their course of action, reducing them to a state of nonbeing... The Gothic subverts the notion that reality consists of meaningful chains of cause and effect, that meaning resides in patterns of action, that action may result in progress or even bring about change... the novelist does not do away with sequences of action, but rather portrays action in such a way that it is revealed as meaningless... Action can never be progressive, only circular; whatever the protagonist tries to do, his actions must result in his own disintegration... Whenever the protagonist in a Gothic fantasy attempts to accomplish anything, we recognize almost immediately that he is doomed to failure (pp. 19, 44–45)

And this stance, of course, is opposed to the attitude of science; the 'Gothic atmosphere subverts the physical, world of science, the laws of time and space' (Day, p. 35).

Finally, it has been long acknowledged that 'the central emotion of the Gothic is fear', as Day says (p. 5); Walter Scott once praised *The Castle of Otranto* for its 'art of exciting surprise and horror' (cited by Varnado, p. 22). And this overarching sense of dread carries with it the implicit or explicit warning that those who attempt to exceed those limits will inevitably be chastised and punished—the philosophy best expressed in the horror movie bromide, 'there are some things man is not meant to know'.

It is clear, then, that the Gothic vision would naturally be anathema to Gernsback. First, while acknowledging that there remain many things that science has not explained (as discussed below), Gernsback accepted what Louise B. Young called 'the assumption that is common to all scientific thought: there is an order in nature which can be understood by the human mind... the faith that there is some kind of common denominator in the apparent diversity of nature has not wavered' ('Mind and Order in the Universe', pp. 445–46). He could not accept, then, the concept that there are inherent limits to humanity's knowledge of the universe. Rather than seeing people as forever enveloped in an 'unknowable' universe, science posits that people can learn more about the underlying principles of the universe and thus, in a manner of speaking, envelop the universe in the mind of man.

Second, Gernsback is naturally drawn to environments that emphasize human power and possibilities. Ralph is often indoors, but it is by choice, and he inhabits modern structures and scientific laboratories, not haunted ruins. It is in such places that he accomplishes his wonders; thus, by entering his laboratory to generate an energy beam, Ralph triumphs over the avalanche that threatens Alice in Switzerland. And when Ralph does finally venture into a vast and lonely natural setting—space—he first develops a form of radar to locate one spaceship, then he creates an artificial comet to divert another spaceship; thus, he has symbolically mapped that natural world, and by duplicating one of its features, he has symbolically mastered that world. Only for a moment is he 'weigh[ed]... down' by its 'infinite immensity'.

Third, as already indicated, someone who believes in science cannot accept that people are powerless or that their actions are meaningless, and with each successful accomplishment Ralph powerfully affirms 'the physical, world of science, the laws of time and space'. Ralph and his colleagues repeatedly triumph over nature by melting an avalanche, developing methods of artificial farming, conquering the force of gravity, and defying death itself.

Finally, since humanity can gain a better understanding of the world and even dominate and control it, a general attitude of fear and terror is not appropriate; instead, as noted, it only overcomes Ralph for brief intervals. Consider the passage when Alice is taken away by Fernand's 'invisible cloak':

> Then from what secret invisible source did [that sound] emanate—and why?
>
> To the scientist, accustomed to explaining the unexplainable, it was ominous—menacing—
>
> Again he turned to look behind him, along the deserted way, and at that moment he heard a stifled cry from the girl beside him. He whirled to face her, and faced—nothing! He was alone in the empty street!
>
> Unbelieving, doubting the evidence of his eyes, he stared about him, too astounded for the moment, by this mystifying and amazing disappearance to think collectively... As the full force of the catastrophe struck him, something akin to panic seized him. Danger to himself he could have faced with the calm courage of a brave man, but this unseen and unexpected blow from an invisible source smote him with a chill terror that for an instant held him powerless in its grip. (p. 119)

As in other passages cited, Gernsback recalls the Gothic, with terms like 'ominous', 'menacing', 'mystifying', and a 'chill terror'. But it only lasts 'for an instant'. In the passage immediately following:

> That he should have been careless when she was in danger—but this was no time for self-reproaches. To act, and to act at once—that was vital.
>
> Thoughts of high frequency radio waves—of X-rays—of Fernand—
>
> 'Fernand!' he exclaimed aloud, and with the name coherent thought returned. Putting on all possible speed he covered the distance to his home in a few seconds and dashed up to his laboratory, the while his swiftly-working brain attacked the greatest personal problem that it had ever been called upon to solve.
>
> Having experimented with ultra-short waves, he knew that it was possible to create total transparency of any object if the object could be made to vibrate approximately at the same rate as light... (pp. 119–20)

And he quickly 'assemble[s] a detecting apparatus', goes out, and finds where Alice was hidden. Thus, while the moods of melodrama and travel tale can be more sustained throughout the novel, the Gothic mood, in a work like *Ralph*, can only be momentarily—the interval between discovering an apparently inexplicable problem and solving that problem.

Thus, even though Aldiss's *Trillion Year Spree* describes science fiction as an outgrowth of the Gothic novel, the modern tradition actually emerged from principles that were directly antithetical to those of the Gothic novel.[8]

As one way to illustrate the problems of science fiction employing the generic models of the travel tale and the Gothic novel, one might argue that they are in effect opposite genres—the travel tale, celebrating openness, freedom, and unlimited possibilities in an environment of expansive movement and travel; and the Gothic novel, projecting confinement, boundaries, and preternatural limits on human activities in a setting of drab and threatening interiors. In a sense, then, Gernsback is seeking to achieve the mood of travel fiction in some of the settings of Gothic horror; but the result is a failure by both sets of criteria. That is, *Ralph* has the spirit of a travel tale without any travel, and the settings of a horror story without any horror.

To further understand the incompatibility of the Gothic novel and Gernsback's theory of science fiction, consider his last novel, the posthumously published *Ultimate World* (1971). Its story seems to adapt Gothic conventions to science fiction: mysterious, unseen aliens come to Earth, capture people and perform experiments on them, surgically or genetically transform children into super-intelligent beings with telepathic powers, and move an asteroid into Earth orbit and construct a city in its interior. The people of Earth are completely unable to resist or influence, or even to communicate with, the aliens, indicating that they represent a realm beyond human understanding or control; and at the end of the novel, when the aliens battle and are destroyed by other aliens, there is a further suggestion of unknowable forces enveloping the human environment. Here is a perfect framework for a science fiction Gothic novel: an 'unfathomable' and 'incomprehensible' transcendent world, where all human action is 'doomed to failure', and where reactions of 'fear' and 'horror' are natural.

However, Gernsback refuses to move his story in these directions and steadfastly works to impose rational explanations and a sense of calm. After some initial concern about alien abductions and an abortive attack on the aliens, Gernsback's scientist hero DuBois quickly reasons: 'What did the alien invaders do when *we* attacked *them* with our best and most powerful weapons? *They ignored us.* To me this seems a good omen, at least at the moment. It begins to look as though this is a scientific research expedition' (p. 36). Then, 'to allay panic and riots, all governments wisely began soothing their populations by publicizing... that the invasion was a strictly scientific one for research purposes' (p. 43). Thus, despite the awesome nature of these events, reactions of fear and terror are quashed almost immediately, in the manner of *Ralph*.

As the novel proceeds from strange event to strange event, DuBois immediately comes up with plausible explanations for every one of them: the aliens fail to communicate with people because they are so incredibly advanced that they see humans the way humans see ants; their observations and experiments stem from a helpful desire to improve the race of beings they have discovered; and they are transforming Eros to serve as a spaceship to take them to other worlds. While powerless to resist these alien actions, the people of Earth listen to and accept these explanations, quickly learn to regard the aliens as essentially benign, and consistently refuse to become fearful; thus, there are no descriptions of widespread panic or distress in response to the invasion. Remarkably, people placidly adjust to the aliens and go about their daily business, only minimally concerned about the fact that some children have become super-intelligent and telepathic and about the new moon now circling the Earth. In a way, Gernsback's strategy might be likened to Ann Radcliffe's, in that he constructs a Gothic universe and then explains it all away; however, Gernsback first of all fails to arouse any feelings of horror in his presentation of his universe, and he explains it all away as he goes along, instead of offering a final, rational explanation. Even in the face of an imagined situation that clearly recalls the Gothic, then, Gernsback firmly resists that genre's moods and implications.

While Gernsback thus alternately embraces and rejects the patterns of melodrama, travel literature, and the Gothic, there remains a fourth possible model for *Ralph* in Gernsback's history of science fiction—the utopia—and many will wonder why it took so long to consider this possibility. After all, the novel is routinely described as a utopia: Sam Lundwall's full description of *Ralph* was a 'pitiable utopian novel' (Lundwall, p. 76), and Brian Stableford has observed that 'Scientifiction, of course, as Gernsback envisaged it, was an implicitly Utopian literature. Its most fundamental proposition was the notion that the advancement of science would remake the world, irrespective of any political and moral questions, for the benefit of all mankind' (*The Sociology of Science Fiction*, p. 124). Stableford's language does not admit any possible argument: 'Of course' Gernsback envisioned science fiction as 'an implicitly Utopian literature'. And yet, carefully examined, *Ralph* does not seem to be a fully satisfying utopia.

To explore why this is true, I note some basic characteristics of the form: first, as a matter of definition, a utopia presents a society where virtually all citizens are happy and virtually all problems are solved; or, at the very least, the utopia must be a society seriously attempting to become perfect— Chad Walsh's *From Utopia to Nightmare* notes that 'Wells and many modern utopians conceive of utopia not as a final perfection but as a goal and movement towards a goal; it is a *process*. In their terms, to be utopian is simply to have a utopian sense of direction, and work at it' (p. 56). Still, any utopia must either be perfect, or noticeably better than existing society, to convincingly argue its positions.

Second, the utopia is to some extent designed as a thorough model or plan for an entire society. Lewis Mumford described 'the utopia of reconstruction' as 'a vision of a reconstituted environment which is better adapted to the nature and aims of the human beings who dwell within it than the actual one; and not merely better adapted to their actual nature, but better fitted to their possible developments'. Mumford even uses the metaphor of a blueprint: 'It is absurd to dispose of utopia by saying that it exists only on paper. The answer to that is: precisely the same thing may be said of the architect's plans for a house, and houses are none the worse for it' (*The Story of Utopias*, pp. 21, 25).

Finally, a utopia must imply that such radical improvements in human society are possible, and the focus of the utopia must be on describing and defending its proposed 'reconstruction' of the world, not on matters such as plot or characterization.

Gernsback's presentation of the world of 2660 cannot qualify as a true utopia because it fails to fit the pattern of perfection, or even the lesser pattern of progress to perfection; instead, as careful reading shows, it is a manifestly *imperfect* society.[9]

Some imperfections, it is true, might be brushed away as the kind of minor flaws that are traditionally acceptable in the genre of utopia. This society first has evident discontent at the top. The great scientist Ralph is unhappy because of the limitations placed on his life: to maintain Ralph's scientific productivity, the government does not allow him any harmful activities, and, as noted, Ralph 'grew restive under the restraint' (p. 41), calling himself 'nothing but a prisoner' (p. 42). And when Ralph is about to marry, the Planet Governor expresses relief that at least one of his problems—keeping Ralph happy—has been taken off 'his already over-burdened shoulders' (p. 141). However, unhappy overseers who labour to benefit the public are occasionally seen in utopias, even in the first example of the form, Plato's *Republic*.

Other signs of imperfection could also be seen as unimportant. Since Ralph first contacts Alice because of a wrong picturephone connection, this world has not eliminated all technical problems. There is a large and effective police force, Ralph tells Alice about a recent embezzlement scandal (p. 131), and the major action of the novel, after all, consists of three attempted kidnappings of Alice by would-be suitors. Still, creators of utopias do not always feel obliged to posit the complete elimination of all criminal activity, as in the book that gave the genre its name, Thomas

More's *Utopia*. The Martian Llysanorh' is driven to despair because the law does not allow him to marry the Earth woman Alice, and though he later emerges as a major villain, the novel displays remarkable sympathy for his predicament;[10] but the problems of Martians could be dismissed as tangential. And while there have been major famines as recently as a generation ago, and although science is described as constantly struggling to increase food production for the world's growing population (pp. 97–100), the situation, at the moment at least, seems to be under control.

However, there are other problems in Ralph's world which pose a greater challenge to efforts to classify the book as a utopia.

First, there is the comment that Ralph is supplied with criminals 'under sentence of death' to use in his experiments (p. 42). Even in Gernsback's days, criminals were not executed for minor crimes. If there is a regular supply of such convicts available, one must assume that crime in 2660 is not only widespread but serious in nature as well. In addition, when Ralph approaches the spaceship of the villainous Fernand, he quickly produces a device called the *radioperforer* designed to disable the ship and render its occupants unconscious. This is not a machine that Ralph has just invented; instead, it seems to be a standard item in any spaceship's equipment. Thus, Ralph lives in a society which has found it necessary, as a matter of course, to create and regularly use a device to attack and disable other spaceships, indicating that serious crime is common in outer space as well.

Second, Alice is threatened by an avalanche in the first chapter because, she says, the weather-engineers in her district, on strike for more 'luxuries', have sabotaged the equipment. Sporadic individual crime is one thing; but here is a large and organized expression of widespread discontent, and an expression of discontent that endangers people's lives. And, since neither Ralph nor Alice are surprised about this event, one must assume that strikes of this nature are rather common in their world.

Finally, there is even one indication, when Ralph explains the need for flying 'vacation cities', that scientific progress is not only failing to improve human life, but is making it worse: 'with all the labor-saving devices [people] have, their lives are speeded up to the breaking point. The businessman or executive must leave his work every month for a few days, if he is not to become a wreck' (p. 132). Strangely, the 'labor-saving devices' provided by science are not making work easier; they are driving people crazy.

While the vacation cities have arguably solved the problem, Ralph's explanation remains troubling. This society can keep citizens sane only by periodically letting them get away from society. Logically, this problem should be better addressed by effecting large changes in people's daily lives so they will not be constantly pushed to the brink of insanity. The fact that no such changes appear to be on the horizon portends further disarray, not further improvement, in Ralph's society.

Overall, then, not only does *Ralph* fail to emerge as a satisfactory utopia, but one could argue that it is at least potentially a dystopia. That is, a writer like Robert Sheckley or Frederik Pohl could easily take all of the basic background materials in the novel and employ them to present its future world as a dysfunctional madhouse, careening from one crisis to another while scientists and leaders are preoccupied with trivial concerns. Indeed, Chris Morgan claims that the novel 'is not far from being farce' (*The Shape of Futures Past*, p. 109). Certainly, for reasons noted below, Gernsback does not go this far; but the fact that such a characterization can even be momentarily maintained further suggests that the novel is not a true utopia.

With these unmistakable signs of imperfections in the world of 2660, one must wonder why this novel is routinely described as a pure example of utopia. This misreading of *Ralph* stems from the fact that the novel frequently incorporates what might be called utopian tableaux: a new invention is introduced, its marvellous effects are described, and people express extreme happiness about it. For example, referring to the new Subatlantic Tube, Ralph exclaims, 'This new tube is going to revolutionize intercontinental travel. I suppose it won't be long now before we will regard our tedious twenty-four hour journeys as things of the past' (p. 61). Contemplating a statue of the last work-horse in New York, Alice says, 'It is so much better now with electricity doing all the work' (p. 76). 'Alice was much impressed with the automatic-electric packing machines' (p. 88), the narrator notes, and while enjoying the 'aerial carnival', she says, 'Oh, it is like Fairyland. I could watch it forever' (p. 93). Because of such scenes, readers might well see the entire novel as a utopia without noticing the many signs of pain and unhappiness permeating the world of 2660.

If *Ralph* is to be described as a utopia, then, it might be called a pointillistic utopia: there are tiny points of brightness in the foreground, suggesting perfect bliss, but a few steps backwards reveals a broader and different picture of continuing unrest and imperfection. Specifically, one can define the pointillistic utopia as a story involving a society which is manifestly far from perfect and not designed to serve as an ideal counterpart to modern society; and a story in which ongoing scientific developments and new inventions provide small moments of joy and incremental improvements in the human condition, while promising no final perfection, or even significant progress towards perfection.

If this is the kind of work that *Ralph* is, one must ask why Gernsback wrote such a work. Perhaps he was simply an inept writer who failed to notice that he was undermining his carefully projected utopia with thoughtless references to major social problems. However, evidence suggests that *Ralph* was exactly the kind of novel that Gernsback planned to write—or rather, did not plan to write. 'I must confess I do not recall just *what* prompted me to write *Ralph*,' he wrote in his 1950 Preface to the novel. 'I do recall that I had no plan whatsoever for the whole of the story. I had no idea how it would end nor what the contents would be' (p. 8).

If we accept the report as genuine—and we cannot be sure of that, since authors are not always accurate in remembering or reporting how they write—then from the very beginning Gernsback deliberately neglected the careful thought and preparation that must go into crafting a blueprint for an ideal society—which is the second major reason why the novel fails as utopia. That Gernsback did not wish to write a utopia is also suggested by the novel's subtitle—*A Romance of the Year 2660*—linking the work to the unrelated genre of 'romance', a term which, as indicated, suggests little more than adventures in an exotic locale.

In addition to a writing process that could not produce a utopia, there are other problems in considering *Ralph* a utopia: Gernsback focused on subject matter that would not logically yield a utopia, he chose as another model a genre which did not harmonize with utopia, and these choices of writing process, subject and genre were informed by purposes different from those of utopia.

First, although he made gestures toward recognizing fields like biology and psychology as true sciences, Gernsback saw the main focus of science fiction as the hard sciences of physics and engineering; and not being an idiot, he fully realized that marvellous new inventions of this type—*voice-writers, tele-motor-coasters, Language Rectifiers*, and the like—would not, despite their beneficial effects, in themselves produce a perfect or even a near-perfect world. Since he is disinclined to speculate about sciences like psychology and sociology that might have a more direct salutary effect on human society, he must provide his future society both with helpful scientific advances and a host of unresolved social problems. Indeed, there are no indications in the novel that Gernsback believed that science could solve all human problems, or even that all human problems could be solved.

 Second, in also employing the pattern of melodrama, Gernsback was committed to describing an essentially Manichean universe, with forces of light and darkness engaged in a continual struggle which is finally, for the moment, resolved in favour of light. And this contrasts with the world of utopia, where the static or coming perfection of a society in a faraway time or place is implicitly compared to the static imperfection of the writer's and reader's society, with no sense of active conflict or confrontation between the two. In opting for melodrama, then, Gernsback borrowed a narrative model which combined uneasily with that of utopia.

Finally, Gernsback's purposes in choosing such content, and such a form, differed from the common purposes of writing a utopia. As noted, Gernsback saw science fiction not only as a repository for polished scientific ideas but as a kind of brainstorming session—writers throwing out ideas and their scientist readers responding with their own, possibly similar but possibly different, ideas. So a logical reason for writing *Ralph* with 'no plan whatsoever' is that the kind of overall systematic design commonly seen and emphasized in a utopia might inhibit the spontaneous creative thought of both authors and readers.

Also, Gernsback's desire to emphasize the mood of melodrama more than that of utopia may reflect his own perception of the state of scientific knowledge in his day. Commonly regarded as a confident believer in continuing scientific progress, Gernsback was acutely aware of its limitations, as indicated by various statements in his editorials: 'we have as yet not scratched the surface of the possibilities of nature, or come anywhere near the limit of our progress' ('Hidden Wonders', p. 293); 'Why there should be stars and what their purpose is, we have not, as yet, the slightest conception; perhaps in a thousand years we shall know a great deal about all of it' ('Our Amazing Stars', p. 1063); 'when we delve into the mystery of time, we should be most careful, because we are venturing on an uncharted sea, of which but little is known' ('The Mystery of Time', p. 2); and 'we do not know what electricity is; we do not know what light is, in their ultimate states, and there is practically nothing in the entire world that surrounds us, that we know anything about at all' ('The Amazing Unknown', p. 389). Thus, while he believed that many unanswered problems confronting the scientists of Gernsback's era could eventually be resolved—thus distancing himself from the stance of Gothic, which is that the unknown will remain fundamentally unknowable—he could not with assurance predict they would all be resolved—thus distancing himself from the stance of utopia. In this way, staying between these two extremes, Gernsback's world of scientific progress inexorably moves away from utopia towards melodrama, with heroic scientists struggling against a host of mysteries. Thus, *Ralph's* use of melodrama— in spite of the problems noted earlier—may be the best choice for a depiction of a scientist at work.

In sum, Gernsback's theories propose that science fiction should have a characteristic content, form, and purposes which were antagonistic to those of utopia, which led to only a limited form of the genre, the pointillistic utopia.

Next, one might argue for *Ralph* as satire; certainly, there are moments when Gernsback makes fun of Ralph—when he loses a tennis game because he is so smitten with Alice, or when he gets mad at his manservant

Peter for following his orders:

> 'Well, what is it?' came from the laboratory, in an irritated harsh voice.
>
> Peter, in the act of retreating on tiptoe, turned, and once more cocked a solitary eye around the door-jamb. This one feature had the beseeching look of a dog trying to convey by his expression that not for worlds would he have got in the way of your boot.
>
> 'Beg pardon, sir, but there's a young—'
>
> 'Won't see him!'
>
> 'But, sir, it's a young lady—'
>
> 'I'm busy, get out!'
>
> Peter gulped desperately. 'The young lady from—'
>
> At this moment Ralph pressed a button nearby, an electromagnet acted, and a heavy plate glass door slid down from above, almost brushing Peter's melancholy countenance, terminating the conversation summarily... [Later,] he pressed the button that raised the glass barrier, and summoned Peter by means of another button.
>
> That individual, looking a trifle more melancholy than usual, responded at once.
>
> 'Well, my boy,' said Ralph good-naturedly, 'the stage is all set for the experiment that will set the whole world by its ears.— But you don't look happy. What's troubling your dear soul?'
>
> Peter, whose feelings had evidently been lacerated when the door had been lowered in his face, replied with heavy dignity.
>
> 'Beg pardon, sir, but the young lady is still waiting.'
>
> 'What young lady?' asked Ralph.
>
> 'The young lady from Switzerland, sir.'
>
> 'The—which?'
>
> 'The young lady from Switzerland, sir, and her father, sir. They've been waiting half an hour.'
>
> If a bomb had exploded that instant Ralph could not have been more astounded.
>
> 'She's here—and you didn't call me? Peter, there are times when I am tempted to throw you out—' (pp. 52–53, 55–56)

Here one sees Ralph as the classic 'absent-minded professor', so wrapped up in his work that he fails to notice simple events occurring in the world around him. And Gernsback later indulged in pure satire in the opening chapters of *Baron Munchhausen's Scientific Adventures* and in short stories. However, elements of this genre surface only rarely in *Ralph*; and in fact, satire may be the most inappropriate of all vehicles for Gernsback's purposes.

As a model to characterize the nature of satire, one could say first that, as Northrop Frye observed, the satirist has 'moral norms' that are 'relatively clear' (*The Anatomy of Criticism*, p. 223); Leonard Feinberg's *Introduction to Satire* agrees that 'Of course satire relies on norms', though he says these can take a variety of forms (p. 11); Gilbert Highet says satire evokes 'Hatred... based on a moral judgment' (*The Anatomy of Satire*, p. 150); and George A. Test says 'although values vary in importance from one kind of fiction to another, they are central to satire' (*Satire*, p. 14).

A second 'essential' element, says Frye, is 'wit or humor' (p. 223); Highet speaks of satire having 'a degree of amusement' (p. 150) and Feinberg notes the presence of 'both humor and criticism' (p. 4). Test speaks in terms of the qualities of play and laughter: 'looking only at the play elements, we find it permeating satire, from its presence as imagery and wordplay to its animating the very essence of the satiric act or expression', and 'Even a limited and cursory collection of quotations about satire or works of satire reveals that laughter is commonly associated with satire' (pp. 15, 23).

Third, Frye notes that there must be a foundation of 'fantasy or a sense of the grotesque or absurd' (p. 223), an aspect of the genre Test touches on at various points: he argues that 'The personae, caricatures, stereotypes, and fable figures that dominate works of satire put make-believe at the center of the spirit', that 'one of the most common practices of satire [is] creating the illusion that [satirists] are something they are not... there is the illusion that things and persons are other than they normally appear to be', and he says that some 'satire operates allegorically by projecting and playing off against each other two levels of reality: one in which the audience exists, the other the fictive world of satire', an approach he says can include 'utopias, dystopias or negative utopias, beast fables, [and] science fiction' (pp. 21, 130, 188). Feinberg defines satire as 'a playfully critical distortion of the familiar' which can resemble 'a madhouse, a puppet show, a menagerie, a horde of fools, a gallery of rogues, a utopia *manqué* and a beguiling mixture of all these images', and notes that 'All of the great satirists use the grotesque' (pp. 19, 60, 70). And Highet says that 'satire wishes to expose and criticize and shame human life... either by showing an apparently factual but really ludicrous and debased picture of this world; or by showing a picture of another world, with which our world is contrasted. There are therefore a large number of satiric tales in the form of visits to strange lands and other worlds' (pp. 158–59).

Finally, satire must involve 'an object of attack' (Frye, p. 223); or, as Test puts it, 'Satire ultimately judges, it asserts that some person, group or attitude is not what it should be. However restrained, muted, or disguised a playful judgment may be, whatever form it takes, such an act undermines, threatens, and perhaps violates the target, making the act an attack... That satire is an attack is probably the least debatable claim that one can make about it' (*Satire*, pp. 5, 15). Feinberg speaks of the satirist's 'struggle... against the affectations of authority' (p. 14), and Highet agrees that satirists 'wish to stigmatize crime or ridicule folly, and thus to aid in diminishing it or removing it' (p. 241).

However, a form with such priorities hardly coincides with the priorities in Gernsback's theory and writing of science fiction.

First, as noted in discussing utopia, Gernsback's concerns and methods in writing science fiction did not encourage the use or development of a consistent moral attitude. Indeed, concerns for providing entertainment, educating people about science and suggesting inventions do not seem related to moral issues at all.

Second, committed to conveying scientific information, Gernsback must focus on scientific matters and take them seriously; he once praised himself and other founders of the Science Fiction League because 'They believe in the seriousness of Science Fiction' ('The Science Fiction League', p. 1062). Thus, even though Gernsback periodically wrote and championed others' examples of humorous science fiction, a consistently maintained atmosphere of humour or play, then, might serve to undermine the important functions of education and inspiration that science fiction can perform.

Third, while a futuristic environment invariably is in some sense of the term a 'fantasy' or an act of 'make-believe', a science fiction story in Gernsback's sense can in no way reflect a sense of the 'grotesque' or 'absurd'. That is, the satirist constructs an imaginary world purely as an exaggerated version of contemporary reality, as a way to offer commentary on that world; yet Gernsback wishes his readers to see Ralph's world as an actual future possibility, with wonders that might be realized well before 2660, and seeks in effect to make that world real by inspiring scientists to actually build its posited inventions. If Ralph's world is instead seen as simply a 'grotesque', 'absurd' or 'make-believe' version of today's society, then it cannot work in this way. For example, when reading about the *hypnobioscope*—a device that transmits information, including newspapers, directly into a person's brain—Gernsback's ideal reader would think, 'I wonder if I could actually design or construct such a device'; if that reader thinks, 'The author is clearly satirizing how newspapers fill our brains with useless information by making the metaphor literal', then Gernsback's purposes of science fiction cannot be fulfilled.

Oddly enough, I can call upon Darko Suvin as support for this point, although his remarks are directed more at explaining why science fiction is distinct from utopia, not satire:

In [the dogmatic pessimum], the narremes are too explicit or too repetitive, so that the reader's return to the workaday world does not pass through an imaginary aesthetic paradigm. On the contrary, the reader is referred directly to the relationships in the empirical environment (which, conversely, severely limits the possible Other in the tale, the kind and radicality of the novum employed). In other words, these empirical relationships are redeployed so as to present merely a different conceptual grid or general idea. While a conceptual ideological field is always to be found in a work of fiction, it is (at the latest from the French Revolution on) in the significant cases not a static, preordained substitute for a specifically fictional insight or cognizing, but a questioning or problematic 'attitudinal field' *within* the overall fictional cognition. In significant sf this means that the novum will, as explained above, allow for the reader's freedom—in literary terms, that the story will not be a project but a parable. Any sf tale that is not a parable but a linear or panoramic inventory correlative to a general conceptual grid—most clearly the static utopias of the nineteenth century—thus to a degree partakes of non-fiction (of political, technological or other kind of blueprint) and loses to that degree the flexibility and advantages of fiction. (*Positions and Presuppositions in Science Fiction*, p. 71)

Finally, with a focus on scientific information and possible inventions, science fiction has little concern for commenting on human nature in itself. Further, its protagonists are typically scientists or scientifically knowledgeable people; thus, if attacking human shortcomings becomes a priority in writing, science fiction writers would be driven to make fun of scientists and their work. However, Gernsback is committed to celebrating scientists as important benefactors of humanity. For those reasons, while Gernsback can get away with peripheral humour regarding minor characters—like the befuddled storekeeper who cannot keep track of what is going on when Alice is spirited away by Fernand's invisibility device—he cannot afford to make his main characters Ralph and Alice objects of ridicule. That is, a sustained satire on science or scientists would be counterproductive, as apparently observed, for example, in Jacque Morgan's Mr Fosdick adventures reprinted in *Amazing Stories*; and a sustained satire directed at another target would distract the author from scientific subjects.

For these reasons, then, there are only occasional moments of satire in *Ralph*, all quickly followed by a return to a more sombre and straightforward mood. Gernsback cannot allow Ralph to become a consistently comic character, so scenes that might lead in that direction must be immediately contrasted to pictures of a sober, respectable Ralph: thus, Ralph's anger with his servant is followed by a sombre discussion of the Subatlantic Tube; and the laughable spectacle of Ralph's dismal tennis game, as shown, is followed by a businesslike tour of the solar power plant. Other lighter moments in the novel have similar endings: a joke involving children playing with the Tele-Theater is followed by detailed descriptions of new street lighting and the 'automatic-electric packing machines' (p. 88); and a moment of fun with a befuddled shopkeeper is followed by an account of Ralph's perfection of anti-gravity. More broadly, Gernsback notes, but does not dwell upon, the various imperfections of his future society, so as to avoid making the entire story seem like a satire or dystopia.

Still, it must be noted that satire was the typical approach of Gernsback's short stories, with examples including 'Wireless on Mars' (1909), a deadpan news report about a form of matter transmission developed on Mars; 'The Electric Duel' (1923), a description of a duel fought with electrified swords ultimately revealed as a bad dream; 'The Most Amazing Thing (In the Manner of Edgar Allan Poe)' (1927), an updated version of Poe's 'Thousand-and-Second Tale of Scheherazade'; and 'The Killing Flash' (1929), a vignette about an attempt to kill someone by long-distance electrocution that is ultimately depicted as a short story rejected by Gernsback's magazine.[11] Noting that these were all very short stories, and that the satirical passages in *Ralph* are similarly brief, one might posit that a *short* satire presenting scientific information and ideas might indeed fulfil Gernsback's purposes of science fiction, without encountering the ruinous complications created by a sustained effort at science fiction satire.

There is one example of a satirical science fiction story that was successful by Gernsback's measure. In the August 1926 issue of *Amazing Stories*, Gernsback republished one of Morgan's Mr Fosdick stories, 'The International Electro-Galvanic Undertaking Corp.', about a ridiculous scheme to electrically put a metallic coating on dead bodies and use them as statues on tombstones; the scheme goes awry when Fosdick unaccountably experiments on his living assistant. Then, in the March 1927 issue, there was a letter from a reader who was actually inspired to perform an experiment because of the story: 'Fosdick's electroplating story hit me so hard that I immediately coated rats with graphite and plated them with copper, and also insects were coated in the same manner' ('Discussions', p. 1180). Perhaps, then, even a farcical story could inform readers and inspire them to attempt actual inventions in the manner Gernsback described.

Finally, one can discern in *Ralph* the possible combination of utopia and dystopia seen in Wells and noted by Stableford—a vision of the failure of present-day humanity combined with the triumph of some transformed humanity which could be called the tale of transcendence. Here, the transformation of the human race involves the prospect of eliminating death. When Ralph finally catches up with Alice, only to find her dead, he frantically works to preserve her body with a special gas so that he can bring her back to life once they return to Earth; and the novel ends with her successful revival. In this case, a scientific process has been perfected which might bring immortality—and radical change—to human life and civilization. The magnitude of this achievement is foreshadowed and described in Chapter 3 of the novel, where other distinguished scientists witness Ralph's successful experiment involving the revival of a dead dog. One scientist then exclaims:

> Ralph, this is one of the greatest gifts that science has brought to humanity. For what you have done with a dog, you can do with a human being. I only regret for myself that you had not lived and conducted this experiment when I was a young man, that I might have, from time to time, lived in suspended animation from century to century, and from generation to generation as it will now be possible for human beings to do. (p. 65)

With Alice brought back to life, then, she in effect becomes the first of a new type of human being, capable of living and continuing to improve indefinitely. And there is already one small sign—a very small sign, admittedly—that she has matured and grown as a result of her experience; upon awakening, she finally realizes what readers have known since page one—that Ralph's name means 'ONE TO FORESEE FOR ONE' (p. 207). Still, there remains a note of gloom in that not all humans will be able to undergo this transformation; those not especially prepared and older people are excluded, and the latter group may include Ralph himself, who, if his remarkable record of scientific achievements is any guide, must be at least middle-aged. Thus, some humans will advance through life extension, while others will be left behind.[12]

Still, this element is, to say the least, muted in Gernsback's novel. Trumpeting this possibility too strongly, perhaps, would not suit Gernsback's desire to inspire support for scientific progress: for one thing, such a transformation of humanity might make the various devices and improvements elsewhere in the novel seem unimportant or useless; in addition, readers may identify more with imperfect humans left behind than with the new, transformed beings, further undermining their interest in more mundane scientific advances as a way to improve the human condition.

Similar conflicts emerge in the Gernsback work more strongly related to the tale of transcendence, *Ultimate World*. Here, aliens provide Earth's children with super-intelligence and new mental powers, by clandestine surgery and genetic engineering. In this way, they are creating a new and improved human race—a development that would seem to make the novel's other described innovations, like new methods of heating homes and communicating, seem trivial; as the narrator notes, 'humanity was undergoing the most fundamental change in its history' (p. 132).

However, just as he resisted the aura of the Gothic, Gernsback refuses to explore the full ramifications of this major transformation. The new intelligence of the children, in the novel, only presents one problem that is almost comical: 'What to do with these 188 millions of children who had completely outgrown all schools and seats of learning?' As a 'partial solution... In the mornings, children, accompanied by state guardians, were taken to various points of interest, to courts in session, to libraries, to museums, on various sightseeing trips, and so forth' (pp. 136–37). True, these transformed children 'mixed in *all* the affairs of their elders... originated their own inventions and labor-saving gadgets' (p. 138); they also have an inborn revulsion to war, which seems to be leading the world to permanent peace as the novel ends. Still, in no other way is it suggested that super-intelligent children will have any major impact on future human society, and throughout the novel, the mood remains strictly one of business-as-usual, thus avoiding either the celebration of, or revulsion toward, the transformation of human children that is seen at the end of Arthur C. Clarke's *Childhood's End*.

In listing these major generic models proposed by Gernsback and problematically embedded in *Ralph*, I do not mean to imply that these are the only generic influences present in the novel. To mention briefly two other examples, Gernsback was well aware of the detective story and later promoted a scientific version of the form with his *Scientific Detective Monthly*; and there are moments in his novel where Ralph seems momentarily to function as a detective, when he locates the invisibly abducted Alice or when he tracks down Fernand's spaceship. But a detective is manifestly devoted to restoring order to a temporarily disordered world (as Day's *In the Circles of Fear and Desire* points out), while the scientist in Gernsback's view is devoted to creating disorder in order to improve the world. *Ralph* might also be related to the modern romance novel, with Alice as the heroine forcefully rejecting the evil Fernand but seeming a bit torn between the mysterious stranger Ralph and the sympathetic Llysanorh'; but in revising the original version of the novel, Gernsback shortened and downplayed certain romantic passages, so that readers are incongruously asked to believe that their passion for each other grows solely by means of Ralph's science lectures. With more analysis, *Ralph* might emerge as a bewildering amalgam of any number of generic models—all of which fail to accord smoothly with Gernsback's theories and goals.

Overall, then, Gernsback's attempts in *Ralph* to combine disparate styles of writing, disparate goals, and disparate generic models consistently generate ruinous problems that contribute to the failure of the novel. And some evidence suggests Gernsback was aware of these problems, for in his next novel, *Baron Munchhausen's Scientific Adventures* (published in *Electrical Experimenter* in thirteen installments in 1915, 1916, and 1917; reprinted in *Amazing Stories* in 1927 and 1928), he tried an entirely different approach in an apparent effort to avoid the problems generated by the manner of *Ralph*. Unfortunately, the results were even less satisfactory.

The novel breaks into three parts. A frame story involves a man named I. M. Alier (Gernsback displaying his wit) who receives radio transmissions from space spoken by someone claiming to be the legendary Baron Munchhausen. The first chapters, when the Baron describes how he was revived in modern times and became involved in the First World War, have little science or prophecy in them, maintain a light atmosphere, and function successfully as satire. Consider the Baron's description of his brilliant plan to defeat Germany:

> I went to see General Joffre and said to him:
>
> 'My dear General, we must now resort to a more novel means than ever to crush the enemy. Here is my plan: The Allies are now spending untold millions each day and no headway is being made against the Germans. Why not take 20,000 picked men, who know how to dig and mine, and order them to build a few gigantic tunnels right under the German trenches, emerging in some forests miles behind the German lines?'... General Joffre's enthusiasm over my plan knew no bounds... [We built the tunnels and] pressed forward with great speed... when we were dealt a most terrible blow.
>
> We received the awful intelligence [that]... Some German had hit upon the same idea as I had, but instead of boring four tunnels they bored two. That was the only difference! While we thought we emerged behind their backs, they thought they were doing the same thing in reference to us. By a strange coincidence they marched out of their tunnels during the same night that we marched out of ours *and, while we captured Berlin, they captured Paris and then Bordeaux*!... A curious state of affairs had arisen in this terrible mix-up:
>
> *We held Germany and a part of Austria, while the Germans held nearly all of France!* Neither of us had gained any advantage, so we called a truce and agreed to trade back our present trenches for our former ones, while they agreed to take back theirs. (February 1928, pp. 1068–69)

These early episodes are at least occasionally amusing, and one can argue that they represent the very best of Gernsback's writings.

In the next part of the novel, Munchhausen reports that he then abandoned worldly affairs and travelled to the Moon, and the tone abruptly changes; now, instead of a playful strategist, Munchhausen presents himself as an earnest scientific investigator and goes to great length to explain the conditions on the Moon:

> At first we found it very difficult to walk on the Moon's surface, for the reason that we weighed so little there. The earth, being 50 times larger in bulk and 1.66 times denser than the moon, it naturally attracts all bodies with much greater force than does the moon.
>
> Thus, a stone weighing one pound on earth weighs 0.167 lb. on the moon, which is just one-sixth of earth weight. My own weight on earth being 170 lbs., it naturally follows that I could weigh only 28 lbs. on the moon. Buster [his dog], who weighs some 10 lbs. on earth, weighs but $1^1/2$ lbs. on the moon. He found this out when he began to jump about. On earth he would not have jumped higher than about 4 feet. On the moon his $1^1/2$ lbs. carried him six times higher, for he expended as much muscular energy in his jump as he was accustomed to do on earth. Consequently, he went up about 24 feet into the air... (March 1928, pp. 1154–155)

While the data about the Moon are accurate according to the science of its day, these chapters are rather lifeless—no pun intended—as there are few if any amusing events or incidents to report.

Finally, the Baron reports going to Mars, where he discovers an ideal society of humanoid Martians. Here, Munchhausen becomes a pupil learning about a superior civilization from its teachers:

> As the story of the evolution went on we could see how the Martian's small head and his small chest both kept on increasing with each subsequent generation. We were shown how big oceans and inland seas, as well as vast rivers, dried up gradually, and how the whole population turned into mechanics, electricians and chemists. No true happiness and contentment, however, seemed to exist on Mars until thought transference was established, till gravity was conquered and money was abolished. There had been wars and disorders up to that period, but it seems that these three achievements, apparently invented and originated at about the same time, emancipated the race completely...
>
> Beginning with that period only did the Martians really become great. We saw how in less than five generations speech had been

entirely abolished, it being possible to 'converse' over considerable distance by thought transference. We were shown the evils of too many languages and the race hatreds produced thereby, and how finally one universal language was adopted by all races and nations. We saw the abolition of presidents and rules of small and big nations, and the inauguration of a Universal Council and a Planet Ruler, both elected by popular votes.

We witnessed how the once dense air became thinner and thinner and how fertile valleys turned into deserts on account of lack of water. We saw the transmutation of the metals, as well as the transmutation of all other matter. Thus we were shown how iron or lead was turned into gold or copper, or into any other metal. Or else how marbel [sic] or stone was turned into steel or gold or other metals... (May 1928, p. 151)

And the Baron proceeds to describe more and more of the Martians' marvellous discoveries and ideal existence, making this part of the novel, not *Ralph*, Gernsback's true scientific utopia. The novel then ends abruptly, as the Baron's radio transmissions simply stop, with no indication of what happened to him afterwards.

Gernsback's strategy in this novel is obvious: if the effort to blend together various styles of writing, purposes, and generic models in *Ralph* did not succeed, perhaps the answer was to address those styles, purposes, and models *separately, one at a time*. Thus, the first part of the novel is primarily narrative, focuses on entertainment, and follows the model of satire; the second part is primarily factual exposition, focuses on scientific education, and follows the model of the travel tale or imaginary voyage; and the third part is primarily predictive exposition, focuses on stimulating scientific ideas, and follows the model of the utopia. No longer attempting to do everything at once, Gernsback discovers that he can successfully fulfil all aspects of his definition, defence, and history of science fiction: that is, he embeds his expository passages in those portions of the novel which follow the generic models—travel tale and utopia—which are best suited to such interruptions, eliminating the problems created by inserting such materials in an adventure story; by concentrating on one purpose at a time, Gernsback avoids the conflicts created by attempting to accomplish them simultaneously; and by employing one generic model at a time, Gernsback eliminates the difficulties caused by the effort to use several of them in combination. Apparently, then, Gernsback has solved all of the problems in science fiction which *Ralph* baldly demonstrated.

But is *Baron Munchhausen's Scientific Adventures* then a successful novel? Not at all: more so even than *Ralph*, this is a novel that simply does not cohere—the playful Baron of the first part seems a different person from the diligent explorer of the second part and inquisitive visitor of the third part. In addition, once the Baron leaves Earth for the generic confines of the travel tale and utopia, all conflict is eliminated from the novel, so there is almost none of the 'thrilling adventure' that Gernsback would later proclaim as a central element of science fiction. Overall, then, separating the purposes and models of science fiction essentially produces three separate works, and such a work additionally lacks the peculiar excitement that came from the intermingling of those purposes and models. Thus, *Baron Munchhausen's Scientific Adventures* is not a new kind of work; rather, it is three older kinds of work, crudely glued together. So this novel was not as popular as *Ralph*, and while Gernsback reprinted it once in *Amazing Stories*, it has never appeared in book form, or any form after 1928, and has essentially been forgotten.

One additional effort to solve the problems engendered by the approach of *Ralph* can be seen in pieces of lighthearted science fiction he continued to write after leaving the field in 1936. These were privately published as Christmas cards for his friends, though some of these generally dreadful exercises later surfaced in *Science-Fiction Plus*, the magazine that he and Sam Moskowitz briefly produced in 1953. Interestingly, these pieces usually took the form of imagined histories or articles about the future, written from the viewpoint of a narrator in the future, and lacking a traditional narrative structure; examples include his 'Exploration of Mars', 'World War III—In Retrospect', 'The Electronic Baby', and 'The World in 2046: The Next Hundred Years of Atomics'. The beginning of the first piece, originally written for his 1949 Christmas booklet, illustrates Gernsback's characteristic tone of scholarly discourse mixed with occasional juvenile humour:

> October 10, 1949, may well be referred to by historians as the most important date of the twentieth century! On that memorable day, at 4:56 p.m. Mountain Standard *Earth* Time, the intrepid explorer, Grego Banshuck [an anagram for Hugo Gernsback], landed his atom-powered space flyer on Mars, the fourth planet of the solar system.
>
> For obvious security reasons, I have only now been permitted to tell the full facts to the world.
>
> Financed by FAS, the Federation of American Scientists, the world-famed physicist-inventor, atomic pioneer, and explorer had labored for more than a year on his space flyer in the lonely fastness [*sic*] of Nevada's Ralston Desert. Here a crew of 22 FAS physicists and college professors toiled valiantly and efficiently in five air-conditioned Quonset huts... ('Exploration of Mars', p. 5)

This mock-essay format may have seemed to Gernsback to be the best way to avoid many of the problems that he faced in *Ralph* and his other more traditional works of fiction. Needless to say, though, eliminating the conventions of a narrative and protagonist renders these pieces rather uninteresting, and like *Baron Munchhausen's Scientific Adventures*, these have also been forgotten.

But *Ralph* has not been forgotten; it has remained a powerful presence in the genre and a strong influence on its development.

This is paradoxical, for I have taken some time to explain in more detail what everybody already knows: that *Ralph* is a dismal failure. The only added insight is that I explain its failure in the context of Gernsback's theory and history of science fiction. Specifically, *Ralph* fails to fruitfully combine its disparate elements of fiction, scientific explanation, and predictions; it fails to achieve the simultaneous goals of entertainment, education, and stimulating ideas; and it fails to satisfyingly fulfil the generic models— melodrama, travel literature, the Gothic novel, satire, utopia, dystopia, and tale of transcendence—that it draws upon, and it fails to combine them coherently.

Nevertheless, *Ralph* is an exciting book.

Certainly, readers of his time were excited by the many marvellous inventions and ideas that the novel threw off like a Roman candle, and the value of sheer novelty in science fiction, even in its surface effects, cannot be entirely discounted. More broadly, readers could sense that *Ralph* was something new, that Gernsback was attempting to combine features that had never been combined before and achieve goals that had never been attempted before. In fact, the novel was popular for a long period of time: its original publication in *Modern Electrics* in 1911 and 1912 made readers demand more of this 'scientific fiction'; it was published in book form in 1925, with apparent success, and was reprinted in *Amazing Stories Quarterly* in 1929; a second book edition appeared in 1950, an English edition in 1952, and a paperback edition published in 1958; and as late as 1968, one chapter from the novel was reprinted in Richard Curtis's anthology, *Future Tense*. All in all, this is a remarkable publishing history for a novel routinely denounced as one of the all-time worsts in its field.

Although it has now been out of print for almost forty years, *Ralph* still makes its presence felt in discussions of science fiction. In the 1960s, when Harlan Ellison needed a quick way to characterize—and criticize—the preferences of certain science fiction fans, he came up with a brief parody of Gernsback's novel:

> Now Al Lewis believes that stories of science fiction [should be like this:] the man of the future is standing on this slidewalk going

through future time and he looks around and says, 'look at this fantastic world that we live in, isn't it incredible, I say to you, Alice of the future 20432209, isn't this a grand world in which the buildings rise up a full screaming two hundred feet into the air, isn't this a marvelous slidewalk that's going at 25 miles an hour, and we have one over there that goes to 35 miles an hour, and another one right next to it at 45 miles an hour, to which we can leap, if we want to'. ('A Time for Daring', pp. 106–07)

In 1973, John Sladek published a parody of the novel, 'Ralph 4F...' And in 1982, William Gibson's 'The Gernsback Continuum' ends with a vision of an alternate world very much derived from Gernsback, with a woman in futuristic dress telling her companion, 'John... we've forgotten to take our food pills' (p. 33). At the same time, Bruce Sterling, attempting to describe the innovative nature of cyberpunk fiction, repeatedly contrasts the attitude of those modern writers to Gernsback's alleged picture of the scientist—implicitly, Ralph himself—as someone in his 'ivory tower, who showers the blessings of superscience upon the hoi polloi' ('Preface', *Burning Chrome*, p. xi; a similar reference to an 'ivory tower' is in his 'Preface', *Mirrorshades*, p. xiii). While many of these comments on *Ralph* are implicitly or explicitly critical, the fact that people still feel obliged to refer to *Ralph*—even if only to argue against it—demonstrates its continuing influence.

If this novel has failed to remain popular in recent decades, this is because modern readers of science fiction can easily find works that are better written, more modern in style, and more up-to-date in their science. But there is no excuse for critical neglect of *Ralph*, a work that represents the first conscious effort to write science fiction, and a work that is endlessly fascinating for that reason; indeed, the inability of critics to recognize the importance of Gernsback's seminal novel constitutes the single most crucial failure in all previous treatments of the genre.

One can, that is, list all the defects in *Ralph* and observe similar problems throughout modern science fiction. Looking at the later and better texts of science fiction, one first observes continuing problems in working necessary scientific explanations into the story. Consider Gibson's *Neuromancer*. Despite its overall polish, there are moments of awkwardly added exposition in passages rarely cited by critics; for example:

'The matrix has its roots in primitive arcade games,' said the voice-over, 'in early graphics programs and military experimentation with cranial jacks.' On the Sony, a two-dimensional space war faded behind a forest of mathematically generated ferns, demonstrating the spacial possibilities of logarithmic spirals; cold blue military footage burned through, lab animals wired into test systems, helmets feeding into fire control circuits of tanks and war planes. 'Cyberspace. A consensual hallucination experienced daily with billions of legitimate operators, in every nation, by children being taught mathematical concepts... A graphic representation of data abstracted from the banks of every computer in the human system. Unthinkable complexity. Lines of light ranged in the nonspace of the mind, clusters and constellations of data. Like city lights, receding...'

'What's that?' Molly asked, as he flipped the channel selector.

'Kid's show.' A discontinuous flood of images as the selector cycled. (pp. 51–52)

We see here the clumsy and illogical interpolation into the text of scientific information—exactly the sin for which Gernsback is criticized. Here, it is hard to believe that a skilled computer operator like Case would linger so long on an accidentally discovered instructional tape. Clearly, Case waits a while before shutting off the tape so that readers can pick up some needed data.

Second, the problem of reconciling scientific accuracy with the urge to offer entertaining visions can be observed in many later works of science fiction. A prominent example is Aldiss's *The Long Afternoon of Earth*, originally published in magazines as the 'Hothouse' series. In the first stories, Aldiss offered the brilliant poetic image of a far-future Earth where the Moon has stopped moving around the Earth, so that fantastically evolved spiders can spin immense webs from the Earth to the stationary Moon. However, scientifically aware readers quickly pointed out that the Moon could never remain stable in a position so close to the Earth. In response, the book version of the stories moved the Moon to the Trojan position in Earth's orbit, where it could in fact remain stationary relative to the Earth. But this did not solve the problem: there was first the question of what series of events could move the Moon so far without taking it entirely out of Earth's orbit, and the idea of spider webs stretching such an immense distance seemed rather improbable. More broadly, if the Moon were that far from Earth, it would appear as only a pinprick of light in the sky, entirely spoiling Aldiss's imagery. In a deeper way, then, the novel again reveals a conflict between providing entertainment and providing education.

Third, later works of science fiction reveal similar problems in trying to adapt the various generic models Gernsback proposed. In their use of melodrama, later creators of science fiction first devised a solution to Gernsback's problem which I call the *counterhero*: the hero, stripped of scientific knowledge and abilities, reverts to his traditional character, while a new hero with villainous traits is created to be his companion. Examples of this pattern include Flash Gordon and Dr Zharkov of the *Flash Gordon* serials, Kirk and Spock of *Star Trek*, and Luke Skywalker and Obi Wan Kenobi of *Star Wars*. With this device, a coherent and satisfying structure can be set up for science fiction melodrama because the undivided main hero may dominate the action, shifting attention away from the divided, potentially tragic double hero.

Also, like heroes and counterheroes, villains and *countervillains* appear in many works of modern science fiction: the two evil races of *Star Trek*, Klingons and Romulans; the two opponents—one crassly opportunistic, the other more sympathetic—who threaten the space dancers in Spider and Jeanne Robinson's *Stardance*; and the now-sympathetic Darth Vader and thoroughly evil Emperor of the third *Star Wars* film, *Return of the Jedi*.

Next, a general lack of interest in travelling for its own sake is often manifest in modern science fiction. For example, in his novels *Methusaleh's Children* and *Time for the Stars*, Robert A. Heinlein elaborately mounts two grand expeditions into deep space to explore and possibly colonize various new worlds; each time, however, the journey is aborted by new scientific developments and the ship returns home after visiting only a few planets. More recently, William Forstchen's *Into the Sea of Stars* launches a similar expedition to reestablish contact with the 700 space habitats who left the Solar System; but the discovery of an old penal colony now plotting against Earth requires the crew to abandon their explorations and tend to this impending crisis. Science fiction, it seems, never sits back and watches the scenery; instead, other matters arise which become the centre of attention.

There are also efforts to employ the imagery and mood of the Gothic novel, but the results are generally compromised. Consider Heinlein's *The Puppet Masters* and Richard Matheson's *I Am Legend*. Both authors seize upon traditional horrific themes—demonic possession and vampirism— but also provide a somewhat convincing scientific explanation for the phenomena: Heinlein offers alien parasites instead of devils, and Matheson painstakingly explains vampirism as the symptoms of a strange disease. As a result, the stories seem less and less like horror stories; instead, the heroes are presented with a comprehensible scientific problem which can be solved in a scientific manner. Heinlein in particular wastes no time quivering in fear or indulging in the typical emotions of a Gothic novel; his manner throughout is unemotional and analytical, exactly the opposite of the awestruck posture of the Gothic. Thus, the story's tone ultimately is closer to *Ralph* than to *Dracula*.

In reference to utopia and science fiction, I argue that the pointillistic utopia remains the standard depiction of future human civilizations in science fiction: marvellous machines and scientific advances have in some ways made life easier and have in some ways made life harder; but the basic problems of human nature and human society remain more or less as they always have been, and no writer proposes that marvellous inventions in themselves will provide the answer. This description would apply to works like Isaac Asimov's *The Caves of Steel*, Philip José Farmer's 'Riders of the Purple Wage', James Blish and Norman L. Knight's *A Torrent of Faces*, John Brunner's *Stand on Zanzibar*, and Sterling's *Islands in the Net*.

Of course, the continuing imperfections of these societies may be a bit more conspicuous than those of Gernsback's world of 2660—which may create the impression that these works are actually dystopias. But such a characterization simply cannot be supported. Just as Gernsback did not argue that technological progress would in itself create a perfect world, these authors cannot bring themselves to argue that such progress in itself would create a nightmare world. Indeed, both Farmer and Brunner display delight in, as well as dissatisfaction with, their future societies, and neither work can be accurately read as a call to abandon scientific advances as a way to return to a simpler and happier existence. It seems misleading, therefore, to interpret works like *Ralph* which lean toward optimism as utopias and works like *Stand on Zanzibar* which lean toward pessimism as dystopias, for this distinction is too fine, considering that both types essentially depict societies fundamentally unaffected by scientific progress, with problems that are identical to those of present-day society.

Next, despite the prominence of satirical science fiction in the 1950s, and despite Kingsley Amis's view that this is the characteristic genre of science fiction, one can observe continuing problems in adopting the approach of satire in science fiction. Even when they initially construct a future world simply as a means of attacking aspects of contemporary society, science fiction writers are driven by the priorities of their genre to start taking their future world seriously, to turn their cartoons into realistic drawings. Such a transformation occurs in the most prominent science fiction satire of the 1950s, Pohl and C. M. Kornbluth's *The Space Merchants*. The opening chapters of the novel clearly serve as a commentary on the modern influence of advertising by envisioning a future society that is almost entirely controlled and manipulated by advertising; the ultimate joke is that one company is presenting an insidious advertising campaign to persuade people to emigrate to Venus, a planet that is a virtual hellhole. However, the tone of the novel begins to change when the smug and satisfied hero is captured and forced to work as a laborer cutting off slices of an artificial protein source—an immense blob called Chicken Little. It is difficult to detect any particular satiric intent in this creation, since the children's story referred to has no clear relevance to the situation in the novel. Rather, it seems simply like an interesting detail in this future world. And the scenes with Chicken Little may have suggested to their authors that the world they were creating was in fact worth taking seriously. So the novel loses its satiric aura and begins to sound more like a serious adventure novel, and we are asked to identify strongly with the hero as he struggles to escape from his imprisonment and triumph over his twisted society. At the end of the novel, he and his girlfriend decide to emigrate to Venus, as a way to escape from the madness of their society and establish a new and better life; thus, what was once a joke—emigrating to Venus— is now presented as a serious and worthwhile alternative. Another novel which gradually loses its satirical tone is Sladek's *Mechasm* (also known as *The Reproductive System*). In fact, the most successful examples of science fiction satire take the form of short stories, which end before problems in the combination emerge, or novels structured as a series of short stories, like Robert Sheckley's *Journey beyond Tomorrow* and *Dimension of Miracles.*

Finally, there are several later works, ranging from Arthur C. Clarke's *Childhood's End* to Spider and Jeanne Robinson's *Stardance*, which present the double theme of a doomed and imperfect humanity and a promising new form of a humanity. The form, however, remains problematic, perhaps for the same reason that Gernsback avoided it: that the solution seems to abandon present-day people like the reader in favour of people who are very much unlike the reader.

While far from the best, *Ralph 124C 41+* can be defended as the most important science fiction novel ever written: the novel that launched, anticipated, and encapsulated the entire genre, and one that Aldiss and Lundwall should bother to read more carefully.

Notes

1 There is a Martian in the novel, but he is unambiguously humanoid— humanoid enough to fall in love with Ralph's girl friend.

2 Though one earlier piece by Gernsback might qualify for that distinction: 'Wireless on Mars', published in the February 1909 issue of *Modern Electrics*, was a short satirical essay from the magazine's 'Martian correspondent' which described the development of matter transmission by radio on that planet.

3 Chris Morgan also notes the incongruity: Ralph 'shows [Alice] the wonders of New York, most of which she seems ignorant of despite the fact that she is well educated and that there is perfect availability of information for all. (This is known as idiot plotting.)' (*The Shape of Futures Past*, p. 109).

4 The story is also related in Gernsback's 'Preface' to the 1925 edition of Ralph, reprinted as the blurb to *Ralph* in *Amazing Stories Quarterly*, Winter 1929, and in the 1950 edition.

5 This analysis of the relationship between *Ralph* and melodrama is adapted from 'Man against Man, Brain against Brain'.

6 One might protest that Ralph simply undergoes a character transformation like other melodramatic characters who initially seem cold and uncaring but are converted to heroism by the love of a beautiful woman; but no such pattern can be imposed on the novel. After every passionate outburst Ralph reverts to coldness: after taking direct action to rescue Alice from Fernand, he returns to indirect action in the second rescue; and after he returns from his forbidden mission to space, all is forgiven and he is restored to his high position. It is also possible that displaying conflicting impulses might make Ralph a divided and, in Heilman's terms, tragic character, moving away from melodrama; this does not occur because Ralph, as Heilman says of Bosola in Webster's *The Duchess of Malfi*, 'is one thing at one moment and another thing at another moment; rarely... a human totality in which rival urgencies are operative at the same time' (p. 293). That is, in alternating and contradictory modes, Ralph fails to emerge as a complete character—a minor problem with a secondary figure like Bosola, but a crucial flaw in a melodramatic hero with whom audiences must identify.

7 To convey some novelty in Martian pronunciation, Gernsback spells the name with a final apostrophe; to make the possessive form, I simply add an s: Llysanorh', Llysanorh's.

8 Of course, nineteenth-century American melodrama grew from earlier dramatic adaptations of Gothic novels, so one might rescue Aldiss's argument on those grounds; still, the melodramatic pattern that Gernsback inherited had long ago lost any sense of forces transcending nature or an incomprehensible universe, key elements in Gothic novels like *Frankenstein* which Aldiss discusses.

9 The following analysis of *Ralph* and utopia includes some material which originally appeared in 'The Gernsback Continuum' and incorporates portions of an expanded version of that argument which was included in 'Gadgetry, Government, Genetics, and God'.

10 Gernsback includes a letter from Llysanorh' in which he explains his plight and discusses plans to commit suicide—clearly designed to contrast him favourably with the other villain, Fernand, whose own letter reveals less noble motives (pp. 141–42); even when Alice is kidnapped by Llysanorh', she thinks he was 'very pathetic' (p. 190) and displayed 'genuine, and fervent love for her' (p. 193).

11 Incidentally, 'The Killing Flash' may be the first science fiction story which incorporates correspondence between an aspiring science fiction author and a science fiction magazine editor—a type of 'recursive' science fiction that would later be popular, exemplified by stories like Jack Lewis's 'Who's Cribbing?' and Arthur C. Clarke's 'The Longest Science Fiction Story Ever Told'.

12 The sense of human science achieving something beyond the human also explains a puzzle in Gernsback's novel; while the meaning of '124C 41' is obvious, Ralph's last name includes that '+' which does not seem to fit the pun. Accepting that science fiction sees mankind's role as creating successors to mankind, one could read the name as 'one to foresee for one-plus'—*one* meaning man, and *one-plus* meaning a superior type of man (as in the title of Pohl's novel about one such transformed human, *Man Plus*). The idea that Gernsback saw 'plus' as an announcement of superiority is reinforced by the name of his last magazine—*Science-Fiction Plus*.

'A Lot of Rays and Bloodshed': Hugo Gernsback's Career as a Science Fiction Editor

The story of Hugo Gernsback's life is reasonably well known and has been told elsewhere,[1] so there is no need to provide a complete biography; but two aspects of his youthful development should be noted, as they explain the priorities which Gernsback brought to his science fiction activities and events in his career.

First, there is the 'charming story [of Gernsback's childhood] that ought to be true', as James Gunn puts it (*Alternate Worlds*, p. 122), best related in Sam Moskowitz's mythopoeic prose:

> At the age of nine, Gernsback came across a German translation of *Mars as the Abode of Life*, by the renowned American astronomer Percival Lowell. Though he was highly imaginative, the concept that intelligent life might exist on other worlds had never occurred to young Hugo. He slept restlessly that night, and the next day, on the way to school, his mind wrestled with the idea, unable to resolve the enormity of its implications.
>
> Straining for comprehension he *literally* developed a fever, which may have been psychosomatic in nature. He was immediately sent home, where he lapsed into delirium, raving about strange creatures, fantastic cities, and masterly engineered canals of Mars for two full days and nights while a doctor remained in almost constant attendance… The direction of Hugo Gernsback's future thinking was greatly conditioned by that experience. He was never to be content with the accumulated scientific knowledge of his day. Now he was to search the libraries for books that opened up imaginative vistas beyond the scientific knowledge of the period. Though he was to become an expert technician, scientist, and inventor, such pursuits could never satisfy him.
>
> His mind took wings where his work left off. He almost memorized the works of Jules Verne and H. G. Wells, and wrote excursions of

his own, which, despite their juvenility, displayed a sure facility for the use of words. (*Explorers of the Infinite*, pp. 228–229)

It matters little that the story is probably a complete fabrication; that *Mars as the Abode of Life* was published in 1908, when Gernsback was 23 years old and living in America; that even Lowell's earlier book *Mars* was not published until 1895, when Gernsback was eleven; that I have found no records of any German translations of Lowell published before 1900; or that later, when editing *Amazing Stories*, Gernsback had to rely on his associate editor Charles Brandt, not his own allegedly voluminous literary knowledge, to locate older stories to reprint. What matters about the story is that Gernsback felt compelled to tell it, as a way to establish himself as someone with a long knowledge of and interest in literature, someone who could casually boast that he had 'made scientifiction a hobby since I was 8 years old' ('Idle Thoughts of a Busy Editor', p. 1085), someone with expertise in literary matters—an area where he conspicuously lacked credentials—so that he could enhance both his own reputation and that of his genre.

Still, Moskowitz provides more evidence about Gernsback's early literary leanings in 'The Ultimate Hugo Gernsback', his 1971 introduction to *Ultimate World*, though they do not directly relate to an early interest in science fiction. Gernsback first used the name 'Huck Gernsback' (as in his 1905 item in *Scientific American*) because he loved Mark Twain's *The Adventures of Huckleberry Finn*; and in 1901, he wrote an unpublished novel, *Ein Pechvogel* ('The Schlemiel'), about the misadventures of a maladroit youth who occasionally does scientific tinkering. Certainly, Gernsback did read, and attempt to write, literature as a youth, but the extent of his interest in science fiction remains questionable.

While one can remain sceptical about Gernsback's early literary pursuits, the other major activities of his youth are better documented and seem more credible. As Moskowitz relates:

> The telephone and electrical communications systems were fledgling sciences in Gernsback's youth, yet he taught himself their intricacies. At the age of thirteen he was already accepting contracting jobs for such installations in Europe. A memorable instance in that connection was the day the mother superior of the Carmelite convent in Luxembourg City obtained a special dispensation from Pope Leo XIII, so that young Hugo could equip that institution with call bells.
>
> Among the projects that Hugo occupied himself with was the invention of a battery similar to the layer battery produced by Ever-Ready in the United States today. When both France and Germany

refused him patents, he decided that there was no opportunity for a young inventor in Europe and, taking the accumulated savings from his electrical installation work, he packed up his battery and booked passage, first class, for the United States. (*Explorers of the Infinite*, p. 229)

Here a different picture of young Gernsback emerges: someone fascinated by science and its practical applications, who learns enough about the subject on his own to make a living at it, who comes to America to make his mark in the 'fledgling sciences' of electronics and communications. This Gernsback apparently wishes to be recognized as an inventor and a scientist—though this is also a field where he lacks formal training and credentials.[2]

These twin urges to achieve status in the realms of literature and science would define and shape the direction of Gernsback's career in science fiction. Clearly, the genre was the best vehicle for his own literary aspirations, and being the editor of a fiction magazine gave him a certain status. I have noted his desire to achieve literary respectability, and science fiction was also a good way to establish Gernsback's status in the field of science; while his science magazines could not compete with professional journals in terms of erudition, science fiction in a peculiar way could serve as a better way to attract the company of scientists intrigued by the novelty of scientific ideas in the form of fiction. Indeed, by gathering a team of scientific experts to review stories in the 1930s, Gernsback developed a way to regularly correspond with scientists; in *The Creation of Tomorrow*, Paul Carter reports that this system was more than 'window dressing': 'Donald H. Menzel of the Lick Observatory', the listed astrophysicist, 'informed me that Gernsback regularly sent him story manuscripts and took due account of his criticisms' (p. 11).

Overall, after launching *Amazing Stories* in the 1920s, it seemed as if Gernsback was destined to be a remarkable success. He had announced the existence of a new form of fiction, given it a name, and described its characteristics; both the stories he published and ideas he promulgated proved popular with large numbers of readers; and he seemed to be gradually developing the aura of literary and scientific respectability that he sought.

He had given his new genre added dignity and a sense of tradition by describing its literary history. In his own novel *Ralph 124C 41+*, he had revealed, however ineptly, the possibilities created by this new genre, and that novel was also well liked despite its manifest flaws. And yet, only a few years after he got started, Hugo Gernsback emerged as a conspicuous, spectacular failure.

He more or less abandoned efforts to publish his own science fiction, so he lost the small reputation he had as a writer. In 1929, he went bankrupt and lost control of *Amazing Stories*, and the magazines he published later never achieved the same level of success. He had a knack for making enemies of writers (as shall be discussed) and was not energetic in establishing strong personal relationships with science fiction writers or readers. After he sold *Wonder Stories* in 1936, he virtually vanished from the field, reappearing only sporadically and with little impact. Even Gernsback himself, commenting on the field in the 1960s, appeared to indicate that his own influence on the genre was no longer visible, that most 'science fiction' was not in fact fulfilling his initial vision. Thus, one could argue, Gernsback was a failure as a writer, businessman, editor, and critic.

Certainly, this is not the whole story; but the reasons for Gernsback's apparent failures are worth exploring.

To account for the eventual collapse of Gernsback's own science fiction magazines in the 1930s, and subsequent withdrawal from the field, there is first a practical explanation to explore: the way that Gernsback habitually mistreated his authors.

On the one hand, there is some evidence, especially in the early years of *Amazing Stories*, of Gernsback displaying an active interest in writers and their problems. As Eric Leif Davin notes in 'Gernsback, his Editors, and Women Writers', Moskowitz and Michael Ashley discuss correspondence from Gernsback where he seemed to be helping and encouraging writers, and the suggestions in 'How to Write "Science" Stories' indicate that he was sometimes capable of offering good advice for writers: 'A story is a good story when the reader can imagine himself threatened by the same peril as the characters in the tale'; 'avoid hackneyed characterization. Keep clear of fair-haired, blue-eyed Irishmen; long, lanky, keen-eyed, dark complexioned clean-cut Americans'; 'Break up your story into action, dialogue, and description. So many lines of one, so many lines of another. If you have a long descriptive passage to write, interlope some action'; and 'When you have finished the first draft of your manuscript, hold it for a few days. Then read it over carefully and see if you have left any points unexplained, and threads tangled' (pp. 28–29).

More remarkable, given Gernsback's general image as an inactive editor, is David H. Keller's 'Foreword' to *The Human Termites*, which offers an anecdote about an evening with Gernsback showing him as a genial host and a stimulating source for ideas:

> Mr. Gernsback laughed at me as he said:
>   'But you should come to see us more frequently. Everytime you come you secure ideas for several stories.'

'I admit that,' I replied… 'The hard thing is to get a new idea. Just one absolutely original idea makes a story possible.'

My host pondered for a moment and then walked over to his library and picked up a book.

'Here,' he said, 'is an idea for a story. This book is "THE WHITE ANT" by Maurice Maeterlinck. He tells about the termite and suggests that the conduct of the individual ant may be controlled by a central intelligence, and that the termitary is really one large individual animal'. Mr. Gernsback half-seriously then suggested that all life may be that way and that the human being may be controlled by a central intelligence. He felt that this may account for the fact that individuals in different parts of the world often do the same thing at almost the same time… 'You take this book with you and read it. There is a big story in it. I give you *one* idea. *All you have to do is to work out the details.*' ('Foreword', *The Human Termites*, p. 295)

Here Gernsback does what John W. Campbell, Jr would later be noted for: talking to writers, giving them ideas, prodding them to write in a particular way; and while one cannot know how often this sort of contact occurred, it is a revelation that it occurred at all.

In the 1930s, Frederik Pohl recalls that Gernsback's *Wonder Stories* was more considerate than other magazines in responding to stories submitted by unknown writers:

The other thing that made *Wonder* attractive was that they had mighty nice rejection slips… I usually wrote very short stories, hardly having the confidence to tackle anything much over two thousand words, and so it seemed to me more than once that *Wonder's* rejections were longer than the stories concerned. There was a form letter signed by Hugo himself, benignly explaining how strict his standards were. There was a printed check-off sheet, listing thirty or so reasons for rejection:
- Plot stale
- Errors in science
- Material offensive to moral standards

and lots more. And, to take the sting out of it, there was a jolly little 'translation' of a 'Chinese rejection slip'. ('Your honorable contribution is so breathtakingly excellent that we do not dare publish it, since it would set a standard no other writer would be able to reach.') It was almost fun to be rejected by *Wonder*. Impersonal fun, though. Hugo Gernsback was by no means as gregarious a personality as F. Orlon Tremaine. (*The Way the Future Was*, pp. 42–43)

And there is uncharacteristic testimony from writer Frank K. Kelly:

> One winter day in December, 1930, when I was sixteen, I wrote a story... and sent it to Hugo Gernsback, who had begun to publish *Wonder Stories*... Four months went by. I thought my story had been lost in the mail. The world for me was dark and dreary. Then I got a letter from Gernsback. He had accepted my story and sent me a check. The world for me was bathed in light again.
>
> 'The Light Bender' appeared in the June, 1931 issue of *Wonder Stories*... I was delighted to find myself described as 'a brilliant young author'—and Gernsback offered me a contract to write six stories a year for his magazines. ('Foreword', *Starship Invincible*, pp. 8–9)

Perhaps Gernsback truly thought Kelly was an extraordinary young talent and decided to treat him with special kindness. Unfortunately, however, this may be the only anecdote on record of Gernsback paying an author *before* his story was published.

That is, balanced against these data suggesting Gernsback was occasionally thoughtful in dealing with writers is an overall picture of a distant, uninterested editor who simply read and published stories without building relationships with writers, and who—most damningly—was regularly negligent about paying them. Indeed, in this respect Gernsback had a positive gift for *alienating* writers—as numerous examples demonstrate.

Gernsback's abortive relationship with H. G. Wells provides one example of his problems in this area. As two letters suggest, Gernsback badly wanted Wells to offer a response to, or gesture of support for, his efforts to promote and publish 'scientifiction'. His letter of 4 May 1926 said:

> AMAZING STORIES is a new magazine, facing an uphill fight for recognition by the reading public, and there can be no question about your interest in a magazine of this kind, which is the first to come out with scientifiction. It really deserves your best cooperation to help put this publication on its feet... We have arranged for you to receive a complimentary copy of this magazine each month.

A year later, he again sought some substantive comment from Wells:

> The readers of AMAZING STORIES are all very much interested in your writings, as you probably have noted from the discussions appearing in the columns of our magazine... we should like to publish a letter from you on any subject you may choose—preferably scientifiction. This would lend a personal touch for our readers. Perhaps a few

words as to your impression of this magazine might not be amiss...
May not we hear from you? (5 May 1927)

Apparently, Wells never responded personally to these letters and never said anything at all about 'scientifiction'. To be sure, since he was at that time busily cementing his reputation as a serious writer and world statesman, the last thing Wells would have been interested in was a new image as a writer of 'scientifiction'. However, Gernsback spoiled what slim chance he had to get Wells's attention or support when he slipped into bad habits—failing to obtain prior permission for reprinting stories, making late payments, not making full payments—all documented in the later letters to Gernsback from Wells's associates.

Similar habits poisoned possible relationships with other writers. After selling Gernsback *The Master Mind of Mars* for $1250, Edgar Rice Burroughs was appalled to receive payments in the form of 'trade acceptances'—not cash—and though he eventually accepted this arrangement, he avoided further contact with Gernsback by demanding the exorbitant price of $800 when Gernsback asked to reprint *Beyond Thirty* (Porges, *Edgar Rice Burroughs*, p. 756). H. P. Lovecraft's experiences are described by L. Sprague de Camp:

> Lovecraft sent ['The Colour Out of Space'] to A*mazing Stories*. In June, 1927, he learned that it had been accepted. Getting paid for it, however, presented a problem. After Lovecraft wrote many dunning letters, the magazine sent him a check for $25 the following May. This was a fifth of a cent a word—a ridiculous price. Thereafter, Lovecraft referred to Gernsback as 'Hugo the rat'. (*H. P. Lovecraft: A Biography*, p. 298)

Jack Williamson said that Gernsback 'bought perhaps a quarter-million words of my fiction, and he paid for it rather reluctantly. After he paid for the first few stories at half a cent a word (sometimes less), he stopped paying me altogether. Finally, I got an attorney associated with the American Fiction Guild to force Gernsback to send me payment. I gather other writers had similar experiences with him' (Interview, *Science-Fiction Studies*, p. 238).

After sympathetically explaining why editors like Gernsback might be driven to such practices, Pohl concludes, 'It's interesting to try to calculate just how much money Gernsback traded the good will of his writers for. It probably was not very much' (*The Way the Future Was*, p. 34). One can reasonably ask: while Gernsback was promoting science fiction in other ways, why was he so thoughtless about the other necessary aspect of any effort to establish the genre—developing and supporting talented writers?

Gernsback implicitly defended his penny-pinching as a matter of financial need, but one can question his sincerity. In August 1927, Gernsback announced that *Amazing Stories* was 'not yet on a paying basis' and 'Only by having additional readers can the magazine hope to be put on a profitable basis' ('A Different Story', p. 421)—as he also maintained in a letter to Wells where he noted that 'In another year the magazine should be on a paying basis' (Gernsback to Wells, 5 May 1927). But a sceptical response to these claims of financial hardship comes from James Gunn: 'From a good businessman, the statement was hard to believe; the editorial costs were low—he used many reprints which must have cost almost nothing, and he paid only one-half cent a word or less for new stories—and the price of the magazine was relatively high for its period' (*Alternate Worlds*, p. 125). Perhaps Gernsback secretly enjoyed taking advantage of writers; perhaps, with no experience of producing a fiction magazine, he did not realize such a project demanded treating writers with fairness and civility.[3] The best judgement may be that of Isaac Asimov: 'He had a constitutional aversion, it would seem, to paying his authors. Heaven knows he paid tiny sums and keeping them could not improve his financial situation, but he kept them anyway as long as he could.' Asimov's conclusion is simply that 'It was his quirk' (*Asimov on Science Fiction*, p. 95).

Regardless of his motives, Gernsback's policies undermined both his immediate position in the science fiction field and his eventual reputation in that field. His stingy habits with *Wonder Stories* drove major writers to *Amazing Stories* and *Astounding Stories*, contributing to the demise of his own magazines; his failure to endure in the field almost defined him as peripheral; and historians often rely on the testimony of writers, so Gernsback gave them no reason to remember him fondly, adding to the impression that he was an unimportant and unpleasant person.

Consider Gernsback's relationship with Williamson. As noted, he contributed two 'Guest Editorials' to Gernsback's magazines that essentially parroted Gernsback's argument for science fiction as a stimulus to scientific progress and basically repeated Gernsback's version of science fiction history. Also, the definition of science fiction he offered in 1947— 'a specialized type of fantasy, in which the prime assumption usually is a new scientific discovery or invention' ('The Logic of Fantasy', p. 42)— seems to reflect Gernsback's priorities. Clearly, young Williamson was significantly influenced by Gernsback. Yet in an interview sixty years later, he is dismissive about Gernsback's impact: 'his main influence in the field was simply to start *Amazing* and *Wonder Stories* and get SF out to the public newsstands' (Interview, p. 38). One must suspect that Williamson's judgement has been clouded by bitterness regarding Gernsback's failure to pay for his work.

However, beyond Gernsback's acknowledged personal failings, there were broader problems manifest in his magazines involving elements in his science fiction theories which were problematic to his authors, and which produced difficulties that those authors were unwilling or unable to confront. This is only to be expected: when new ideas about fiction are aired by an editor, working writers, already set in their ways, are most likely to respond by continuing to write in their accustomed fashion while paying lip service to whatever new demands emerge—and that was how most of Gernsback's writers responded to his theories.

In the stories published in the early years of Gernsback's magazines, one observes authors simultaneously adapting to, and evading, his requirements. The stories are generally melodramatic and exciting, the focus is generally on scientists and scientific inventions, and the action generally stops at times to provide scientific facts and explanations of inventions—just as Gernsback demanded. Yet a number of stories have peculiar lacunae: the story leads right up to the detailed explanation, the informed character seems poised to provide that explanation, but there comes at some point an abrupt and unnatural halt to the explanation.

Characters in the stories provide a number of lame excuses for these omissions. It is too difficult for me to explain further—'I shall not attempt to explain the process by which the electrical impressions are generated, amplified, translated again into light and finally projected to the screen below' (Charles C. Winn, 'The Infinite Vision', pp. 138–39); it is too complicated to explain—the invention involves 'other factors too complicated for the lay mind' (Kaw, 'The Time Eliminator', p. 805); it is too boring to explain—'I won't bore you with any explanation of the inner workings of the machine' (Samuel J. Sargent, Jr, 'The Telepathic Pickup', p. 829); I wish to keep it a secret—'"But how," I interrupted, "do you do it [invisibility]?" Dr. Unsinn smiled knowingly. "That is a secret I do not care to divulge"' (A. Hyatt Verrill, 'The Man Who Could Vanish', p. 904); I do not remember the explanation—'It is thousands, perhaps millions of years since Sir John explained to me. What little I understood at the time I may have forgotten' (G. Peyton Wertenbaker, 'The Coming of the Ice', p. 55); and I do not comprehend it myself—'By the end of that century I had been left behind by all the students of the world… Other men came with other theories… But I could not understand them' (also 'The Coming of the Ice', p. 62). Paul Carter's *The Creation of Tomorrow*, discussing the situation about a decade later, notes similar strategies:

> Such writers [without a scientific background] quickly found ways
> of finessing the science fiction editors' and readers' requirements. As

one successful practitioner pointed out (Ross Rocklynne, 'Science Fiction Simplified', *Writer's Digest*: 21, October, 1941), you could always fake it, either by telling your story from the uncomprehending layman's point of view ('I don't recall everything he said—it was way over my head') or by having the learned professor's explanation interrupted by action such as a woman's scream. At the story's climax, the pulp canons of rugged adventure commonly pushed the gadgets offstage anyhow. (p. 19)

In these devices, we see what might be termed *the strategy of avoidance*: the story is structured to provide a scientific explanation, but all or part of that explanation is left out.

In some cases, as Carter indicates, the omission may simply reflect the author's lack of scientific knowledge. Kaw's 'The Time Eliminator', for example, is as pure a homage to *Ralph 124C 41+* as one might wish, and in fact reads like a Classic Comics version of that novel: a brilliant young inventor creates a remarkable long-range seeing device, the inventor shows his device to a general, and the general is so impressed by the military potential of the machine that he agrees to allow the inventor to marry his daughter. Certainly, for 'factors too complicated for the lay mind', one might simply read, 'Factors too complicated for the author's mind'.

However, these omissions may in other cases be motivated by the desire to avoid potentially ruinous story problems. 'The Coming of the Ice' sounds similar to the legends of the Golem and Wandering Jew, a helpless figure condemned to immortality—here, a man of the present who is made immortal and forced to live through the future rise and fall of the human race. By having the narrator forget the process that made him immortal, and by making him incapable of understanding future science, Wertenbaker can comfortably fit his protagonist into the familiar pattern of the immortal as a paradoxically powerless victim. However, if the hero could have remembered exactly how he became immortal, he might have been able to reverse or otherwise make use of the process; and if he could have understood the progress of future science, he might have been able to do something to reverse the decline of humanity. And in these ways, the man could have become the master of the situation, not its victim. Thus, the absence of scientific explanations enables Wertenbaker to adhere to the standard formula for such stories, whereas the inclusion of such explanations may have diverted the story into new and unfamiliar territory.

Another reaction to Gernsback's theories might be termed *the strategy of distraction*: here, authors scrupulously fulfilled Gernsback's demand for long scientific explanations, but inserted them in stories filled to the brim with exciting adventures in outer space, massive new inventions, and strange alien beings. Maintained by such marvellous effects, the story stays alive. In a sense, such stories were anticipated by an editor's 1930 response to a letter which said, 'If there is any change in the stories, it will be to make them more interesting. We have never believed in, or allowed, long, dreary, windy scientific discussions to intrude themselves at the wrong point. In other words, the stories will have the same high level of scientific accuracy and truth; but if they are changed, it will be to make them more interesting' ('The Reader Speaks', *Science Wonder Stories*, May 1930, p. 1139). The most successful stories displaying the strategy were E. E. 'Doc' Smith's space epics, which offered sufficient grandeur and excitement to hold readers' interest despite convoluted scientific explanations.

Despite short-term gains, there are eventual costs in pursuing a strategy that emphasizes spectacular effects: a general sense of monotony sets in, and the writer is driven to outdo himself—if one spaceship is a thousand miles long, the next must be a million miles long; if one weapon destroys planets, the next must destroy suns—and so on, to the point of exhaustion.

The progress of the Arcot, Wade and Morey series written by John W. Campbell, Jr—who first emerged as Smith's most prominent imitator—illustrates how adventures sustained by the strategy of distraction inexorably expand to the point of collapse. The first adventure, 'Piracy Preferred', only involves action in the upper atmosphere of Earth; in the next stories in the series—'Solarite', *The Black Star Passes* and *Islands of Space*—Campbell's heroes venture out to the planet Venus, to another solar system, and to other worlds throughout the galaxy. Finally, in *Invaders from the Infinite*, they go beyond the galaxy. Of course, each successive step beyond is accompanied by an amazing leap in technology, with the ultimate accomplishment in *Invaders from the Infinite* being 'cosmic power'—literally, the ability to accomplish anything with a single thought. This new power both eliminates any possibility of real conflict and introduces a disquieting element of anguish in its discoverer Arcot, as he now pauses in his efforts to defeat evil aliens to worry about the awesome effects of such unlimited power. In this way, the straightforward melodrama of the earlier stories is now complicated, undermining their generic identity. Overall, once Arcot, Wade, and Morey have explored and effectively conquered the entire universe, and once they have achieved the incredible ability to overcome all opponents, and once they are left with nothing to do but contemplate the burdens of their limitless power, where can the series go? Absolutely nowhere; Lester del Rey said, 'The story left readers gasping—science fiction could go no further' (*The World of Science Fiction*, p. 49), and George Turner agreed that 'He had in those five Arcot, Wade and Morey tales taken technological sf as far as it could possibly go, given the physical knowledge of the time. And he killed the genre stone dead' ('John W. Campbell: A Symposium', p. 49). *Invaders from the Infinite* was thus the last adventure in the series.

If the strategy of avoidance enabled authors to omit scientific explanations, and if the strategy of distraction led them to emphasize spectacular effects, the logical result of both strategies would be stories which offered little more than presentations of marvellous places and machines, without scientific information or stimulating ideas for inventors. This was exactly the sort of story that Gernsback increasingly received.

Several forces were driving the science fiction of Gernsback's era in this direction. First, from the very beginning readers made it clear that they preferred 'interplanetary stories'; in October 1927, for example, a description of a seven-year-old reader noted that 'he unhesitatingly stated that he preferred stories of space and of interplanetarian travel' ('Amazing Youth', p. 625). And this was also the kind of story supported and favoured by the new magazine *Astounding Stories of Super-Science* (discussed in the next chapter), as an editor obliquely indicated while responding to a letter that complained about weak science in recent stories: 'we have been carrying on a campaign against these very things that Mr. Race so soundly complains of. The difficulty has been that a new element entered the field of science fiction, magazines of "wild west fiction" in which science was of little or no consequence' ('The Reader Speaks', *Wonder Stories Quarterly*, Summer 1932, p. 576).

It should be noted, though, that these stories may have seemed like new developments, but they actually represented a return to an older style of writing, the approach seen in popular imaginative fiction before Gernsback: fast-paced adventure stories with lots of colour and little scientific substance, exemplified by Burroughs and others. Since stories of this kind were so common in the 1920s and 1930s, when Gernsback was a dominant figure, it is common to blame him for them; but they actually reflect not the influence of his theories, but resistance to them—the desire of writers and readers to return to an easier and more familiar approach.

To see the problem in criticizing the fiction of the Gernsback era, consider Brian W. Aldiss, who speaks of Gernsback as 'one of the worst disasters ever to hit the science fiction field' who had 'the effect of introducing a deadening literalism into the fiction' (*Trillion Year Spree*, pp. 202, 204), projecting a picture of a thriving, imaginative tradition of science fiction suddenly dampened and destroyed by Gernsback's ideas. But this is simply not true.

The problem here is that if one invents a tradition of, say, Shelley, Poe, Verne, Wells, and Doyle, and then picks up an early issue of *Science Wonder Stories*, a natural reaction would be that yes, something has gone horribly wrong. But this framework is, as I have noted, illusory, insupportable, and based on an extremely selective look at the available literature. If critics go beyond the masterpieces and look at the vast majority of works which now pass for 'science fiction' written between 1870 and 1920, they will find an awful lot of junk—dull imitations of Haggard's lost race adventures transplanted to other planets (like Garrett P. Serviss's *A Columbus of Space*), trivial cautionary tales of foolish inventors (like Ellis Parker Butler's 'An Experiment in Gyro-Hats'), and routine horror stories dressed up with a little scientific jargon (like George Allan England's 'The Thing from— Outside'). The fact that Gernsback reprinted stories like these, and later published similar new stories, is hardly his fault; he had to make use of what was available, and stories written in the manner of earlier eras— with, perhaps, some nods in the direction of Gernsback's desires for scientific explanations and predictions—were generally what was being produced. A comprehensive look at 'science fiction' before Gernsback reveals, then, a literature that is already dead, far beyond Gernsback's power to 'deaden' it.[4]

As an indication that Aldiss knows little about this era, it is fascinating to examine his final condemnation of Gernsback:

> As long as the stories were built like diagrams, and made clear like diagrams, and stripped of atmosphere and sensibility, then it did not seem to matter how silly the 'science' or the psychology was.
>
> A typical story might relate how a scientist experimenting in his private laboratory found a new way to break up atoms so as to release their explosive power. In so doing, he sets up a self-perpetuating vortex of energy which kills either the scientist or his assistant, or else threatens the career of his beautiful daughter, before the vortex rolls out of the window and creates great havoc against which the local fire brigade is powerless. Soon it is destroying New York (or Berlin or London or Moscow) and causing great panic. Tens of thousands of lunatics roam the open countryside, destroying everything in its path. The CID (or the militia or the Grenadier Guards or the Red Army) is helpless.
>
> Fortunately, the scientist's favorite assistant, or the reporter on the local paper, or the boyfriend of the beautiful daughter, has a great idea, which is immediately taken up by the President (or the Chancellor or the King or Stalin). Huge tractors with gigantic electromagnets are built in every country, and these move in on the vortex, which is now very large indeed, having just consumed San Francisco Bridge (or Krupps' works or Buckingham Palace or the Kremlin). Either everything goes well, with the hero and the

beautiful daughter riding on the footplate of one of the giant machines as the energy vortex is repulsed into space—or else things go wrong at the last minute, until a volcanic eruption of unprecedented violence takes place, and shoots the energy vortex into space.

The hero and the beautiful daughter get engaged (or receive medals or bury Daddy or are purged) by the light of a beautiful new moon. (pp. 204–205)

And in a footnote, Aldiss coyly reveals exactly which story he is paraphrasing: 'A story suspiciously similar to this apocryphal one appears in the April 1929 issue of *Amazing Stories*' (p. 461).

The story that Aldiss describes is Vladimir Orlovsky's 'The Revolt of the Atoms', originally written in the 1920s in Russia by an author who knew nothing about Gernsback or his theories! Thus, Aldiss demonstrates not that Gernsback's science fiction was dull and stagnant, but rather that science fiction in the 1920s and 1930s *outside* the American tradition was dull and stagnant; and that dull and stagnant tradition was not created in Gernsback's magazines, but rather lingered on in them. The only real novelty in the science fiction of the 1930s was that the typical story did not, like 'The Revolt of the Atoms', involve a scientist on Earth, but rather emphasized interplanetary and interstellar settings; otherwise, the mood and approach remained very similar to those of stories published before Gernsback launched *Amazing Stories*.

The irony is that the period usually called the 'Gernsback Era'—1926 to 1938—featured, and became associated with, a style of science fiction which Gernsback did not originate and did not champion; in fact, he campaigned *against* this kind of story.

In the 1930s, though he was no longer deeply involved in the day-to-day decisions of his magazines, Gernsback was aware that certain stories he was publishing fell conspicuously short of his announced ideals of polished literature incorporating scientific explanation and prediction. A first response was conciliatory, as he attempted to deal with scientifically suspect stories in what could be termed a policy of classification. Stories with strong scientific content—previously described simply as science fiction—could be called a special and separate category of the genre and given a new name, while stories outside this category were granted more freedom to avoid or violate science. Gernsback unveiled this approach in his editorial 'Science Fiction vs. Science Faction':

> In time to come, also, our authors will make a marked distinction between science fiction and science *faction*, if I may coin such a term...
> In science fiction the author may fairly let his imagination run wild

and, as long as he does not turn the story into an obvious fairy tale, he will still remain within the bounds of pure science fiction. Science fiction may be prophetic fiction, in that the things imagined by the author may come true some time; even if this 'some time' may mean a hundred thousand years hence. Then, of course, there are a number of degrees to the fantastic in science fiction itself. It may run the entire gamut between the probable, possible and near-impossible predictions.

In sharp counter-distinction to science fiction, we also have science *faction*. By this term I mean science fiction in which there are so many scientific facts that the story, as far as the scientific part is concerned, is no longer fiction but becomes more or less a recounting of fact.

For instance, if one spoke of rocket-propelled fliers a few years ago, such machines obviously would have come under the heading of science fiction. Today such fliers properly come under the term science *faction*; because the rocket is a fact today... the few experimenters who have worked with rocket-propelled machines have had sufficient encouragement to enable us to predict quite safely that during the next twenty-five years, rocket flying will become the order of the day. (p. 5)

In a sense, this editorial can be read as the first manifesto on behalf of 'hard science fiction'.[5] That is, Gernsback is trying to isolate, define, and defend a type of science fiction where scientific accuracy is most central.

A bit later, Gernsback responded differently to science fiction which was not strong in its science with a his policy of condemnation: having separated the less scientific fiction from the truly scientific fiction, Gernsback begins to attack the former as an inferior and degenerate form of writing. The issue emerged most clearly when Gernsback printed a story by John W. Campbell, Jr called 'Space Rays' while introducing it with a special signed editorial entitled 'Reasonableness in Science Fiction':

When science fiction first came into being, it was taken most seriously by all authors. In practically all instances, authors laid the basis of their stories upon a solid scientific foundation. If an author made a statement as to certain future instrumentalities, he usually found it advisable to adhere closely to the possibilities of science as it was then known.

Many modern science fiction authors have no such scruples. They do not hesitate to throw scientific plausibility overboard, and embark on a policy of what I might call scientific magic, in other words, science that is neither plausible, nor possible. Indeed, it overlaps the fairy tale, and often goes the fairy tale one better... In the present offering, Mr. John W. Campbell, Jr., has no doubt realized this state of affairs and has proceeded in an earnest way to burlesque some of our rash authors to whom plausibility and possible science mean nothing. He pulls, magician-like, all sorts of impossible rays from his silk hat, much as a magician extracts rabbits... I have gone to this length to preach a sermon in the hope that misguided authors will see the light, and hereafter stick to science as it is known, or as it may reasonably develop in the future. (p. 585)[6]

Certainly, Gernsback can be accused of inconsistency in coyly criticizing Campbell's story; after all, its miraculous rays seem to be no less scientific than 'The Shining One' of A. Merritt's *The Moon Pool*—which Gernsback had defended in 'Amazing Creations'—and Gernsback had conceded that 'In science fiction the author may fairly let his imagination run wild'—a fair description of Campbell's methods in 'Space Rays'. Now, however, Gernsback seemed to be fed up with stories like these; an occasional extravagant idea, or occasionally suspect science, was one thing, but a regular stream of such stories was hard to stomach.

Gernsback was upset because publishing stories of this kind could contribute neither to the literary, nor to the scientific, respectability of science fiction; rather, they seemed to establish the genre as nothing more than another variety of inferior pulp fiction. And Gernsback had consistently sought to avoid that milieu: he published *Amazing Stories* and *Wonder Stories* in a large format to eliminate any association, and some suggested that he began to lose interest in science fiction when he was finally obliged to publish *Wonder Stories* in the size of a pulp magazine. In sum, the genre that Gernsback had hoped would be 'a tremendous new force' transforming the world was instead offering only 'a lot of rays and bloodshed' ('Wanted: Still More Plots', p. 437).

Facing the problem of science fiction that did not reflect his critical preferences, Gernsback in the 1930s not only criticized stories, but worked to improve the situation in a number of ways.

One possible answer was that the genre lacked new ideas; so he began to sponsor contests for new 'Interplanetary Plots', and winning entries were given to established authors who turned them into stories. His instructions warned contestants that 'A plot submitted that simply relates a war between two planets, with a lot of rays and bloodshed, will receive little consideration'. What was wanted instead was 'some original "slant" on interplanetary travel, or of the conditions on other worlds' ('Wanted: Still More Plots', p. 437). Perhaps readers would come up with ideas to improve science fiction, a hope expressed in an editorial announcement: 'We firmly believe that this contest has been the means to stir up something entirely new in science fiction literature, and to advance the art of science fiction' ('Wanted: More Plots', p. 5).

Despite that optimistic note, however, the stories resulting from these contests did not represent any dramatic improvement. Looking over the science fiction of the 1930s, in fact, one finds the problem was not that authors lacked good ideas, for the stories are filled with them; however, writers were simply not thinking about or developing those ideas in a scientific or logical manner.

As examples, consider the scattered stories of the 1930s that featured space stations or structures in space.[7] One story based on a winning idea in the 'Interplanetary Plots' contest, Everett C. Smith and R. F. Starzl's 'The Metal Moon' (*Wonder Stories Quarterly*, Winter 1932), offered an intriguing picture of an immense space station with an Earthlike landscape on its upper level; but that station functions only as the setting for a tale of oppressed underground workers rebelling against arrogant masters that is more than a little reminiscent of the novel and film *Metropolis*. In other magazines, H. Thompson Rich's 'The Flying City' (*Astounding Stories of Super-Science*, August 1930) presented the powerful image of people forced by their dying planet to construct and inhabit an immense city in space— an idea later used with great effectiveness in James Blish's *Cities in Flight* novels; but that city serves only as the vehicle that brings evil aliens who attempt to invade and conquer the Earth. And Williamson's 'The Prince of Space' (*Amazing Stories*, January 1931) astonishingly depicts the first true space habitat in science fiction—an immense cylinder with parks and houses on its inner surface; but that habitat is only briefly seen as the home of a space pirate who is persuaded to help Earth battle against a Martian race of vampire plants.

If the writers had stopped to think about these structures—what they would be like, how people who lived in them would act, what sorts of problems they would face—original and exciting stories might have resulted; but no one had explained to these writers how to think about such ideas. Instead, they were relying on time-tested formulas of action and adventure, and concepts that would later serve as bases for innovative science fiction merely function as decorative embellishments to routine stories.

In a second effort to improve the genre, to maintain and strengthen its focus on scientific accuracy, Gernsback gradually introduced purely factual materials into his magazines. From the beginning of *Amazing Stories*, readers had expressed an interest in having articles about science published alongside the stories; but Gernsback first resisted their suggestions, and in the February 1927 'Discussions' column an editor was obliged to respond, 'AMAZING STORIES is purely a fiction magazine, and for the present we intend to keep it as such. AMAZING STORIES' sister magazine, *Science and Invention*, every month brings all amazing new inventions... This moon rocket, by the way, has been described in *Science and Invention* several times, and while such items are of interest, we believe for the present they should not take up valuable space in AMAZING STORIES' (p. 1079). Still, *Amazing Stories* did introduce the science quiz 'What Do You Know?' to emphasize the scientific facts in the stories, a feature reintroduced in *Wonder Stories* as 'What Is Your Scientific Knowledge?' And when Gernsback launched *Science Wonder Stories*, he immediately published Hermann von Noordung's nonfiction book about the possibilities of space travel, *The Problems of Space Flying*, and soon included monthly columns of 'Science News' and 'Science Questions and Answers'. These materials might inspire writers to tackle different kinds of scientific subjects—Noordung's book, for example, inspired a space station in J. M. Walsh's *Vandals of the Void*—and could also continue to provide the mandated scientific education and inspiration that the stories were now not always providing.

As a third way to improve science fiction, Gernsback consistently sought to expand the genre beyond the milieu of the pulp magazines into other media. In *Amazing Stories*, he published some science fiction poetry by Leland S. Copeland and a science play, Raymond Knight's 'Just Around the Corner', perhaps hoping to inspire others to produce science fiction in these forms. In the 1930s, he campaigned for more science fiction movies: an advertisement in the December 1931 issue of *Wonder Stories* asked 'Do You Want Science Fiction Movies?' and said:

> despite the success of science fiction in this country, and the rapidly growing reading public, the number of science fiction movies that have appeared in America have been pitifully few... We are organizing a gigantic petition signed by all those who want science fiction movies and will present this petition to the large motion picture companies... Sign this petition yourself, get four other signatures of your friends and relatives and return them to us. We will do the rest! ('Do You Want Science Fiction Movies?', p. 904)

Much later, in a 1953 editorial for *Science-Fiction Plus*, Gernsback noted with approval not only growing numbers of science fiction films, radio and television programmes, and comic strips, but also 'a new form' of the genre *'the third dimensional world of science-fiction... consist[ing] of toys, games, gadgets, scientific instruments of all kinds, wearing apparel for youngsters, and countless other constantly-evolving, ingenious devices'* ('The Science

Fiction Industry', p. 2; author's italics). Expanding to other media, science fiction could become more prominent and popular.

As a fourth effort to improve science fiction, in 1934 Hugo Gernsback founded the Science Fiction League, the first large-scale organization of science fiction fans. To be sure, there is some truth in Pohl's charge that the League was 'a plain buck-hustle', as he explained in mock-biblical prose: 'And Hugo looked upon the sales figures of *Wonder Stories* and pondered mightily that they were so low. Whereupon a Voice spake unto him, saying, "Hugo, nail those readers down", so that he begat the Science Fiction League, and thus was Fandom born' (*The Way the Future Was*, pp. 18, 17). Still, Gernsback's fervour for science fiction was genuine, and announcing the formation of the League, he repeatedly returned to the theme that the organization could serve as a way to improve science fiction. 'The SCIENCE FICTION LEAGUE', he announced, 'is purely a literary, scientific organization for the betterment and promotion of scientific literature in all languages' ('The Science Fiction League: An Announcement', p. 933); and it was designed to continue the work of 'a number of scattered clubs and organizations... which exchange information on Science Fiction and otherwise further the art' ('The Science Fiction League', p. 1061). In the later editorial—one of his last sustained arguments for the genre—he stressed once again the educational value and serious purpose of science fiction:

> Science Fiction is highly educational and gives you a scientific education, in easy doses... The founders of the SCIENCE FICTION LEAGUE sincerely believe that they have a great mission to fulfill. They believe in the seriousness of Science Fiction. *They believe that there is nothing greater than human imagination, and the diverting of such imagination into constructive channels.* They believe that Science Fiction is something more than literature. They sincerely believe that it can become a world-force of unparalleled magnitude in time to come. ('The Science Fiction League', p. 1062)

In gathering together dedicated readers who shared those beliefs, then, the League might function to promote the kind of science fiction that Gernsback wanted to see.

Inadvertently, the League also served as a fifth way to improve science fiction. In the 1930s, Gernsback was no longer reprinting older stories in his magazines, because, he said:

> I have, as yet, to see one old time science fiction novel which, in the light of today's advance in science fiction, is readable.
> Take, for instance, the majority of Jules Verne's books. Quite a

number of them read so tamely today that the average reader would yawn. The incredible wonders in Jules Verne's day are commonplaces today. The same is the case with a number of other older science fiction books. Time has caught up with them, and progress has been such that the authors' predictions have mostly been fulfilled, leaving the present-day reader with a very ordinary story on his hands... ('On Reprints', p. 101)

Thus, it seems, readers and writers were now being deprived of the salutary and literary examples of superior past works. However, members of the Science Fiction League, inspired by Gernsback's initial emphasis on the subject, soon made explorations of science fiction history one of their priorities, and in response to P. Schuyler Miller's call for a science fiction bibliography, there came not only J. O. Bailey's letter (already mentioned), but a number of bibliographies from members. Thus, the August 1935 column of 'The Science Fiction League' mentioned a bibliography submitted by Walter Dennis of Chicago (p. 371); the September 1935 column lists bibliographies received from LeRoy Chapman Bashore, Oswald Train, and the Leeds, England Chapter of the League (p. 497); and the November-December 1935 issue mentions contributions from Paul Valansky and Carl Adams (p. 753). Even if Gernsback no longer highlighted the history of science fiction, others were continuing to investigate older works as possible inspirations and models.

In the monthly news columns about the League after this announcement, there are signs of many efforts to promote and improve science fiction—though the League can also be observed moving away from Gernsback's focus on science to a general enthusiasm for science fiction of all kinds. The fans attracted to the League did not always share Gernsback's desire to emphasize scientific content and education (as noted in the next chapter), but such fan organizations would eventually have a major impact on the field.

The final way Gernsback attempted to improve science fiction had begun long ago—by getting other people to talk about science fiction. His letter columns featured regular commentaries from scores of interested readers; and in the last issues of *Amazing Stories Quarterly* that he controlled, he sponsored a contest for 'Guest Editorials', and winning entries were published in the space usually reserved for Gernsback's editorials. Intentionally or not, the symbolism of the gesture was powerful: Gernsback was training people to replace him as commentators on science fiction.

Overall, the science fiction magazines Gernsback published in 1936 were notably different from those he published in 1926, even if the stories were not always better. Early issues of *Amazing Stories* only included stories, blurbs, and an editorial; the 1936 issues of *Wonder Stories* also included a column of science news, a science quiz, a large number of letters from readers and editorial responses, and a column discussing the activities of the Science Fiction League. And these were only the public signs of a vast amount of other activities on behalf of science fiction being carried out by various amateur organizations and publications.

Science fiction had developed a support system; and, in part because of the ideas Gernsback promulgated and the activities he launched, the genre was showing signs of significant improvement.

To be sure, the 1930s produced more than enough stories of the 'Lizard-Men from Pluto' variety; but science fiction in the 1930s did not consist entirely of undistinguished space opera. There were stories—like Raymond Z. Gallun's 'Old Faithful' and Lester del Rey's 'The Faithful'—which worked to achieve a solemn elegiac mood; Alva Rogers mentions 'the remote future, dead-or-dying-Earth theme that was so popular in the thirties' (*A Requiem for Astounding*, p. 56). While these works may project the air of an over-serious juvenile—like teenagers talking about True Love—they nonetheless represent a sincere effort to rise above 'thrilling adventure'. Other stories manifest an oddly appealing, surrealistic craziness, like Williamson's 'Born of the Sun', which theorizes that moons and planets are actually the gigantic eggs of immense space dragons. Nat Schachner's stories started to explore social and political themes (as discussed by Carter in *The Creation of Tomorrow*). And two authors in particular seemed to be providing what everybody was looking for—a new 'slant' on science fiction. One of these—Campbell writing as 'Don A. Stuart'—will be discussed later; the other is Stanley G. Weinbaum, whose 'A Martian Odyssey' and subsequent stories had a tremendous impact on the field.

The innovative aspects of Weinbaum's stories were both obvious and subtle. As Rogers reports, 'Weinbaum, who studied chemical engineering at the University of Wisconsin, took particular pains with the science content of his stories and they are all models of accuracy in fact and logic and reason in extrapolation' (*A Requiem for Astounding*, p. 34). Here is a new element: attentiveness not only to scientific 'fact' but to 'logic and reason in extrapolation'—anticipating the concerns in science fiction writing to be articulated by Campbell. Weinbaum was consistently inclined to think through imagined possibilities in a scientific manner. For example, while previous stories simply presented animal-like aliens (hawk-men, lobster-men, and so on) and imbued them with purely human qualities, Weinbaum's 'The Lotus Eaters' pondered how a plant with intelligence would really think. And while previous tales of alien contact solved communications problems with 'translation discs' or the like, 'A Martian Odyssey' explores how an alien might have to struggle to communicate with humans. Gernsback's blurb to 'A Martian Odyssey' noted just how innovative the story was:

> practically all authors have an idea that future explorers will step into another world and find conditions like they are on earth. They picture human beings with two feet and two legs, two eyes, etc., just as we have them here, although the chances are not one in a million that such conditions will even remotely prevail. Biologists are pretty much unanimous on this point, and feel that if there is such a thing as intelligent life on Mars or Venus, it certainly will be radically different from the human life that we know here.
>
> On our own earth, we find the most grotesque animals and the most grotesque insects, some of which, like the ants, are endowed with extraordinary intelligence. Imagine a human being, reduced to the size of an ant, being brought into an ant hill and what his chances would be to really understand what was going on... Our present author, fully conscious of this thought, has written a science-fiction tale so new, so breezy, that it stands out head and shoulders over similar interplanetarian stories. (p. 175)[8]

Gernsback's blurb also mentioned 'the lighter vein in which it is written' (p. 175), and Weinbaum's smooth dialogue was clearly a stylistic improvement. However, his dialogue also illustrated the process of scientific analysis: the couple in 'The Lotus Eaters' talk about the plant-being named Oscar to figure it out, and the hero of 'A Martian Odyssey' recounts his adventures to his companions to better understand them. The use of dialogue as a discovery process, of course, would later be perfected by Isaac Asimov[9]—one reason why he once offered this tribute to Weinbaum: 'what would have happened if Weinbaum had lived?... What if he had stayed in magazine science fiction over the years... In that case, there would never had been a Campbell revolution... All that Campbell could have done would have been to reinforce what would have undoubtedly come to be called the "Weinbaum revolution"' (pp. 194–95). Asimov's comment is interesting, for in arguing that Weinbaum 'was a Campbell author before Campbell' (194), he acknowledges that it was in fact possible to become a Campbell author without Campbell; that is, simply by combining his background in science with the ideas he found in the science fiction magazines, Weinbaum was able to develop an approach to writing science fiction that prefigured in some ways what Campbell would later announce.

Thus, as I will argue, the noteworthy improvements in science fiction stories of the 1940s should not be regarded solely as the result of Campbell's work; rather, they were a natural culmination of an evolutionary process originally inspired by Gernsback. Lester del Rey accurately describes this process in scattered comments from pages 83 and 85 of *The World of Science Fiction*:

> Somehow, bit by bit, methods were discovered for dealing with the problems of background and development necessary for a story laid in some alien culture or strange future... As some of the crudity of too many early stories was abandoned, the fiction became more accessible to readers who appreciated better writing... Many of the more critical readers began to read and like science fiction, and some began writing it, bringing a further improvement in style. Characterization improved considerably, too... The improvement was also partly due to the fact that the literature became popular enough to be taken up by regular publishers and turned over to editors who had experiences with other fiction. (pp. 83, 85)

Irritatingly, del Rey documents these developments as a magical, agentless process which happened 'Somehow' and is best described in the passive voice ('methods *were discovered*', 'crudity... *was abandoned*', 'popular enough *to be taken up*'); in fact, writers were inspired by, and working within, the framework established by Gernsback as they strove to improve their science fiction.

However, the process was gradual, and the improvements did not come quickly enough to save Gernsback's increasingly troubled magazine. *Wonder Stories* suffered from declining sales and distribution problems, and in 1936 Gernsback finally gave up and sold *Wonder Stories* to another company—which renamed it *Thrilling Wonder Stories*. In its first editorial, new editor Mort Weisinger promised to maintain the Science Fiction League and Gernsback's commitment to scientific accuracy; but these were empty promises, as the true agenda of the new publishers was to emphasize juvenile adventure stories with little scientific substance. Two years later, Gernsback's old magazine, *Amazing Stories*, was also sold and underwent a similar transformation under a new editor.[10]

The Gernsback era of science fiction, it appeared, was over.

While the failure of *Wonder Stories* was disappointing, I suspect that Gernsback was not gravely upset when he was forced out of the science fiction field: he was interested in science fiction, but it was not his only interest. He always had other ideas and other projects to pursue, other vehicles for his literary and scientific aspirations. While he might have worked through personal contact to maintain some influence over science fiction, this was not his style; Pohl noted that he was not 'gregarious', and James Gunn reported that after meeting Gernsback, he 'thought him a strange mixture of personal reserve and aggressive salesmanship' (*Alternate*

Worlds, p. 123). A naturally retiring man, Gernsback naturally retired from an arena where he had not enjoyed success; and it became easy to forget his contributions to science fiction.

Still, Gernsback never completely abandoned the genre he had established. He kept writing science fiction, and whenever there was an opportune moment, he returned to the field: when comic books became popular in the late 1930s, he launched a science fiction comic book, *Superworld Comics*, which promptly failed; and when many new magazines appeared in the 'boom' period of the early 1950s, Gernsback started a new magazine, *Science-Fiction Plus*, which died after seven issues. He kept reading science fiction, though, as suggested by his letter to P. Schuyler Miller in 1961, and whenever he was asked, Gernsback would talk about science fiction—in his 1952 pamphlet 'Evolution of Modern Science Fiction', his speech at the 1952 World Science Fiction Convention, in his 'Guest Editorial' for the April 1961 issue of *Amazing Stories*, and in his unpublished talk for the MIT Science Fiction Society in 1963.

While Gernsback tried to maintain a characteristically upbeat and supportive tone, these later discussions are sometimes bitter. Apparently, Gernsback saw his influence on the genre as minimal, and comments in the 1950s and 1960s suggest that he was adding a fourth era of science fiction to his history—a period of decline—which began in the 1950s and is marked by two developments.

First, while Gernsback had wanted science fiction to be more 'literary', he later felt the genre was becoming *too* literary:

> *Modern science-fiction today tends to gravitate more and more into the realm of the esoteric and sophisticated literature, to the exclusion of all other types.* It is as if music were to go entirely symphonic to the exclusion of all popular and other types. The great danger for science-fiction is that its generative source—its supply of authors—is so meager. Good S-F authors are few, extremely few. Most of them have become esoteric—'high brow'. They and their confrères disdain the 'popular' story —they call it 'corny', 'dated', 'passé'... If the young and budding S-F author—unspoiled by the prevailing snob-appeal—will look around carefully, he will note that all S-F media—with the exception of science-fiction magazines—*always* cater to the masses. They rarely have snob-appeal, the story is nearly always simple, understandable to the masses, young and old... At present, science-fiction literature is in its decline—deservedly so. The masses are revolting against the snob dictum 'Let "em eat cake!' They're ravenous for vitalizing plain bread! ('Status of Science-Fiction: Snob Appeal or Mass Appeal?', p. 2)

Second, Gernsback saw a growing inclination to avoid science; he said in his 1952 speech to the World Science Fiction Convention, 'Let me clarify the term Science-Fiction. When I speak of it I mean the truly, scientific, prophetic *Science*-Fiction with the full accent on SCIENCE. I emphatically do not mean the fairy tale brand, the weird or fantastic type of what mistakenly masquerades under the name of Science-Fiction today' ('The Impact of Science-Fiction on World Progress', p. 2). In 1963, he also protested against:

> the parading of pure fantasy stories as science fiction and their sale
> as such to gullible readers. I consider this an out-and-out fraud. It
> was particularly humiliating to me when I read the 1962 volume of
> the *Hugo Winners* which the publishers, on the cover, lightheartedly
> labeled '*Nine prize-winning science fiction stories*'. Well, in my book it
> should have read, 'Eight fantasy tales, plus one science fiction story'.
> (cited in Panshin, 'The Short History of Science Fiction', p. 19)

In such remarks, Gernsback seems to accept the argument often made against him: that later science fiction shows little signs of his influence. And by employing such remarks, Alexei Panshin built his case in 'The Short History of Science Fiction' that Gernsback's impact on the field was brief and unimportant. There is another sad irony here: the only time that Gernsback's comments are taken seriously is when he seems to argue against his own influence.

Still, as noted, Gernsback's theories had both an immediate and lasting impact on the field; and if the later Gernsback was not perceptive enough to recognize the clear signs of his own continuing influence, he shared that problem with many critics.

However, while the spirit of Gernsback continued to haunt the genre from 1936 to the present, the ongoing story of the idea of science fiction must now shift away from him. Gernsback had essentially taken the idea of science fiction as far as he could; now, other commentators would have to carry on its development.

The trouble was that the first successors to Gernsback who emerged did not seem to be up to the task.

Notes

1 A capsule biography: born in Luxembourg in 1884, Gernsback learned about electronics at an early age and was already working on several projects as a teenager; looking for better opportunities, he immigrated to America in 1903 and quickly became involved in several business ventures; one of these, a catalogue of radio parts, led to a magazine, variously called *Modern Electrics*, *Electrical Experimenter*, and *Science and Invention*, to other scientific magazines like *Radio News* and *Practical Electrics*, and eventually to an exclusive focus on

a publishing career. After publishing his own novel *Ralph 124C 41+* in *Modern Electrics*, Gernsback began to feature 'scientific fiction' stories by himself and others in all his science magazines; and their popularity eventually inspired Gernsback to publish *Amazing Stories*, the first American magazine devoted to science fiction and the principal forum for his theories of the genre. The best biography is 'Hugo Gernsback: Father of Science Fiction' in Moskowitz's *Explorers of the Infinite*; Daniel Stashower's 'A Dreamer Who Made Us Fall in Love with the Future' offers a charming picture of Gernsback's life based on the recollections of Gernsback's cousin; and more data are available in the otherwise undistinguished *Hugo Gernsback: Father of Modern Science Fiction* by Mark Richard Siegel. In this, the only book-length study of Gernsback, Siegel neglects Gernsback as a critic except to mention his belief that science fiction should be educational; instead, he offers a standard list of Gernsback's accomplishments and attempts, hopelessly, to rehabilitate Gernsback as a major science fiction writer, even as an anticipation of the New Wave. The ultimate indictment of the book is that Siegel thought there was so little to say about Gernsback that he padded out the book with essays on Frank Herbert and Bram Stoker.

2 It is worth noting, then, that Gernsback's first publication, as by 'Huck Gernsback', was a brief 1905 article in *Scientific American* describing his proposed mechanical improvement.

3 Gernsback's thinking may have been coloured by his experience with Clement Fezandié, the author he published most frequently (over 40 stories between 1920 and 1926). As Gernsback noted in his 1961 'Guest Editorial', Fezandié 'wrote for fun only and religiously sent back all checks in payment of his stories!' (p. 141). Not knowing many professional writers, Gernsback may have imagined that Fezandié was representative—that all writers mainly worked for the joy of writing and pleasure of seeing their stories in print; so he may have been surprised to find writers getting upset about small and tardy payments. Of course, this hardly excuses Gernsback's behaviour; an editor who is regularly getting sued should have the sense to change his policies, but Gernsback never did, at least while editing *Amazing Stories* and *Wonder Stories*. Yet there are no recorded complaints from writers for his 1953 magazine *Science-Fiction Plus*; perhaps Gernsback had finally learned his lesson.

4 Indeed, with depressing regularity, science fiction criticism often enacts the cycle of discovering a lost 'classic' of 'science fiction' from this period, describing and celebrating it, and then forgetting it as completely uninteresting.

5 More information on Gernsback's relationship to hard science fiction is in my *Cosmic Engineers: A Study of Hard Science Fiction*, including a longer analysis of this editorial.

6 Of course Campbell had no such satiric intent, and his anger at Gernsback for so labelling his work evidently led him to never submit a story to a Gernsback magazine again, and may be one reason why Campbell only mentioned Gernsback once in his decades of writing editorials, articles, and letters about science fiction.

7 A subject explored in the second chapter of my *Islands in the Sky*, which surveys a number of works from the 1930s; these are also summarized and discussed in *The Other Side of the Sky*.

8 While unsigned materials in Gernsback's magazines of the 1930s are

attributed to an 'editor'—since Gernsback was less involved in editing those magazines—I attribute this blurb to Gernsback because Eric Leif Davin's 'Gernsback, his Editors, and Women Writers' cites a report that Gernsback was excited enough about 'A Martian Odyssey' to write the blurb himself (p. 148).

9 Asimov's use of dialogue in this way is discussed by Orson Scott Card in his 'Afterword' to 'The Originist'.

10 Weisinger and Ray Palmer of the new *Amazing Stories* are discussed more thoroughly in the next chapter.

'Carefully Projected Scientific Thought': Critical Voices between Hugo Gernsback and John W. Campbell, Jr

In the 1930s, while Gernsback's magazines declined and his personal influence diminished, his ideas continued to dominate all discussions of science fiction. Different editorial voices may have offered different emphases and may have cautiously contracted or extended Gernsback's theories, but there were no major innovations in the idea of science fiction. Thus the situation that developed in Gernsback's magazine—a proclaimed dedication to literary quality and scientific accuracy, an actual surrender to juvenile adventures with 'a lot of rays and bloodshed'—is duplicated elsewhere. There were signs of improvement, but little evidence of an overall transformation in the field.

The original rival to Gernsback's magazines in the 1930s was *Amazing Stories*, which under new ownership was now edited by Gernsback's former associate T. O'Conor Sloane. Sloane had little to contribute in the way of new approaches for the genre; still, as shown by the first editorial he wrote for the magazine, Sloane did present a slightly different picture of science fiction:

> The basic idea of the magazine was the publication of fiction, founded on, or embodying always some touch of natural science… We have published many stories on interplanetary travel. The subject remains a great favorite with our readers. Though it appears an impossible achievement, our authors make it a vehicle for much science, astronomical and in other branches. The Fourth Dimension, which is after all to be regarded as a mathematical conception, has been very ingeniously used by some of our writers. From archaeology, the science in our stories runs through geology, chemistry, biology, psychology, and others, for the entire field of science is covered in the various stories published in these pages. And it is no wonder. Among our authors we number chemists, physicians, astronomers, psychiatrists, and other leaders of thought in their scientific fields. To these it is a pleasure

we are sure, to enter the realm of fiction, and use their knowledge there, for the instruction, as well as amusement of their readers.

Sloane went on to promise 'various improvements' resulting from the change in editorship, though none were specified and, indeed, no significant improvements followed ('Amazing Stories', p. 103).[1]

In Sloane's manifesto, his basic definition of the genre—'fiction, founded on, or embodying always some touch of natural science'—mentioned only two of Gernsback's three elements, fiction and science, with no mention of prophecy or prediction. While references to 'Interplanetary travel' and 'The Fourth Dimension' established that science fiction includes imaginative materials, they seemed to have no particular purpose; rather, they were only another way to provide entertainment, and another 'vehicle' for scientific education. Thus, Sloane refused to argue that science fiction stories are in any way predictions of, or inspirations for, future scientific developments. Gernsback, at least in published comments, believed that almost anything was possible, and defended stories on the grounds that their inventions and events, no matter how implausible, might someday be realized. Sloane, more conservative than Gernsback, refused to present some developments like space travel as real possibilities, and defended such predictions only as 'vehicles' to offer entertainment or education.

In a sense, one could argue, Sloane improved upon Gernsback's theories, since the argument that science fiction was inspiring, or could inspire, actual inventions was always a questionable aspect of his theories. With a PhD in science, Sloane may have cringed when he read Gernsback's claims that science fiction stories might be useful to working scientists, and once he took over the magazine, he may have been happy indeed to abandon such claims.

But this truncation of Gernsback's theories had unfortunate consequences. Eliminating the pretence that science fiction could give scientists ideas, Sloane could offer no reason why scientists should read science fiction—since they presumably could find other forms of entertainment and had no need for further scientific education. And if science fiction could not transform the world with its imaginative ideas, the genre became less valuable, less significant, since it now could only offer entertainment and education that was already available elsewhere. The general air of lassitude that came to permeate *Amazing Stories* under Sloane, then, may reflect not only Sloane's age and leisurely work habits, but also his implicit admission that science fiction, after all, was really not that important—the same attitude which, as noted, helped to doom Gernsback's *Scientific Detective Monthly*. Of course, science fiction prophecy might be defended on new grounds which downplayed the possibility of inspiring inventions while making predictions valuable to scientists and the world in other ways; but Sloane did not, or could not, devise such an argument.

In other large and small ways, Sloane seemed to turn back the clock. Gernsback's editorials had always focused on speculations about future scientific developments, as a way to stimulate readers' and writers' imagination; Sloane's editorials increasingly talked only about present-day technology—his last two editorials for *Amazing Stories*, for example, simply described the modern printing methods used to produce *Amazing Stories*, something highly unlikely to stimulate anyone's imagination. Sloane also stopped using Gernsback's term 'scientifiction', which he had long despised—a response to a reader's letter called it a 'made-up word' ('Discussions', *Amazing Stories*, November 1929, p. 762)—and returned to Gernsback's old 'scientific fiction'. Even in small ways, Sloane was retreating from the positions Gernsback had taken.

Behind the scenes, Sloane's major innovation came in finding new ways to irritate science fiction writers. Gernsback usually rejected, or accepted and published, stories with reasonable promptness, though he was negligent about paying for them. Sloane, however, became notorious for losing manuscripts, holding stories for years before responding, and even publishing stories that had already been published in other magazines. Some writers who had initially stayed with Sloane and *Amazing Stories* started to drift back to Gernsback, whose new magazines at least projected a more businesslike air in every area except remuneration. Sloane was also more inclined to tinker with and revise stories than Gernsback. In September 1929, he produced a curious editorial, 'The Editor and the Reader', which included these remarks:

> Many authors are unduly sensitive. In pre-Victorian days authors were very willing to submit their writings to critics for emendation. But the author of today often objects to even minor changes... Any printer who has had extensive experience with authors can tell strange stories about the way they act with regard to corrections of their copy. They are a very sensitive class of people... Then comes the question of authors. There is no need to recapitulate their names. There are a number of them that have done much for us in past years—they are all at our service and are so highly appreciated by our readers that there is danger of a lack of variety. But it will not do for a magazine to have too small a staff of authors. It is essential that its pages should be open to newly discovered merit, not only to the personality of the writer. (p. 485)

Sloane seemed to circumspectly acknowledge that a number of major authors have stopped appearing in *Amazing Stories*—though he claims that is because of a desire for new voices—and he implied that they are leaving because they unreasonably object to his helpful corrections. As evidence for the theory that Sloane was indeed an overactive reviser, Alva Rogers reports that E. E. Smith once sent a novel to *Astounding Stories* because 'he was thoroughly sick of *Amazing's* rewriting his material' (*A Requiem for Astounding*, p. 14).

Still, despite his lapses, the image of Sloane as a doddering incompetent may be a reflection of ageism—as all accounts note, he was eighty years old when he took over the magazine. Descriptions of his career tend to dwell upon, for example, how incongruous it was that Sloane regularly declared space travel was 'impossible' while publishing many stories about it; clearly, they conclude, Sloane was out of touch with the times. But Sloane was genial and undogmatic in making his arguments; in one editorial, he said, 'we are inclined to think that interplanetary travel may never be attained. On the other hand, in science, "never" has proved to be a very dangerous word to employ' ('Acceleration in Interplanetary Travel', p. 677). In regards to his work habits, while Sloane allowed *Amazing Stories Quarterly* to drift into irregular publication and finally expire, he kept producing *Amazing Stories* on a regular basis until 1938, when the magazine was sold to another company; and his magazine still printed a number of worthwhile stories.

And Sloane, unlike Gernsback, was respected and well liked by his contemporaries: Frederik Pohl, in *The Way the Future Was*, says he was 'amiable and cordial enough' (p. 43). When Ray Palmer took over *Amazing Stories*, he said, 'we stepped into a mighty big pair of shoes when we stepped into those of Dr. T. O'Conor Sloane… it is with humble hope that we can fill them to as satisfying a degree as he did. It was in his able hands that the magazine earned the enviable title of "The Aristocrat of Science Fiction"' ('The Observatory by the Editor', *Amazing Stories*, June 1938, p. 8). When he died in 1940, he was eulogized by his former competitor, F. Orlon Tremaine: 'Dr. Thomas O'Connor [*sic*] Sloane, scientist, editor, and author—and one of the greatest figures ever to touch the field of science-fiction—has set forth on his last great adventure' ('Editor's Note Book', pp. 127–28). And another competitor—John W. Campbell, Jr—at least praised his energy: 'My model science-fiction editor was T. O'Conner [*sic*] Sloane, who was doing fine in his late 70's!' (letter to Ted White, 30 October 1969). While Sloane can receive little credit as an innovator in a history of the idea of science fiction, he may deserve more credit as an editor in a history of the science fiction magazines.

In any event, caught between the Scylla of Gernsback's reluctance to pay and the Charybdis of Sloane's languid pace, writers were surely pleased to see a new science fiction magazine, *Astounding Stories of Super-Science*, appear in 1930. Because it did not copy the large bedsheet size of *Amazing Stories* and *Wonder Stories*, it qualifies as the first science fiction pulp magazine. In the first issue, editor Harry Bates announced:

> ASTOUNDING STORIES... is a magazine whose stories will anticipate the scientific achievements of To-morrow—whose stories will not only be strictly accurate in their science but will be vividly, dramatically, and thrillingly told. Already we have secured stories by some of the finest writers of fantasy in the world—men such as Ray Cummings, Murray Leinster, Captain S. P. Meek, Harl Vincent, R. F. Starzl and Victor Rousseau. (cited in Clarke, *Astounding Days*, pp. 8–9)

While Bates later claimed to be only mildly familiar with other science fiction magazines (in 'Editorial Number One: To Begin'), he exactly restated the three elements in Gernsback's definition: 'stories', 'accurate in their science', that 'will anticipate the scientific achievements of To-morrow'. However, Bates introduced some different emphases to the equation.

First, while he listed a number of previous science fiction predictions that were later realized, stressing more strongly than Sloane the element of prophecy in science fiction, Bates, like Sloane, did not argue that the present-day predictions of science fiction might inspire or lead to future inventions. Here, science fiction prophecies seemed to have no purpose whatsoever.

Second, Bates often paid lip service to Gernsback's ideals of scientific education and accuracy: when a letter advised, 'Since this magazine is about science every story must be examined to discover any false statements by the author concerning present-day science', the brief editorial reply was, 'We Examine All Science Very Carefully' ('The Readers' Corner', *Astounding Stories of Super-Science*, May 1930, p. 279). However, his hidden agenda made science a low priority: as Jack Williamson notes, 'Bates was professional... [he] wanted well-constructed action stories about strong, successful heroes. The "super-science" had to be exciting and more-or-less plausible, but it couldn't take much space' (cited in Edwards, 'Harry Bates' 61). Or, as Bates put it, while *Amazing Stories* was 'awful stuff... Cluttered with trivia! Packed with puerility. Written by unimaginables!', *Astounding Stories of Super-Science* would instead emphasize 'story elements of action and adventure' ('Editorial Number One: To Begin', pp. x, xiii).

An emphasis on fiction, not science, was often announced in early issues of the magazine: one statement quoted a reader's letter saying that 'The

Editor seems to know that such stories should have real story interest, besides a scientific idea', and Bates continued, 'Every story that appears in *Astounding Stories* not only must contain some of the forecasted scientific achievements of To-morrow, but must be told vividly, excitingly, with all the human interest that goes to make any story enjoyable today' ('Our Thanks', p. 127). While the promised combination of science and 'story interest' sounded promising, the stories that he actually published conspicuously failed to fulfil these ideals—thrill-packed space adventures, with an occasional 'weird tale'.

Still, Bates later protested that 'I welcomed stories with more refined or scientific values... when I had the rare luck to receive an uncrippled one' ('Editorial Number One', p. xv) and in one of his last issues, he announced a new feature—a 'Science Forum'—and said the magazine would be placing more emphasis on scientific accuracy; perhaps, then, Bates's magazine might have eventually moved in the direction of more mature and scientific stories, like F. Orlon Tremaine's *Astounding Stories*, if Bates had remained in charge. In fact, Alva Rogers's *A Requiem for Astounding* defends Bates's editorial skill, noting that 'Bates has come to be regarded over the years—quite unjustly—as an incompetent, lowbrow editor', but arguing that the low quality of his stories was solely due to the fact that 'Bates had literally nothing to work with in the way of a reservoir of skilled, knowledgeable science fiction writers, nor a body of tradition going before on which to build' (p. 182).

The other innovation of *Astounding Stories* was a firm policy twice announced in early letter columns: 'We're Avoiding Reprints' ('The Readers' Corner', *Astounding Stories of Super-Science*, April 1930, p. 129; 'The Readers' Corner', June 1930, p. 422). In an editorial response, 'About Reprints', Bates gave two reasons for this policy: first, 'some splendid Science Fiction stories have been published in the past—but... Aren't even *better* ones being written today?' Second, 'And how about our authors?... how will they eat, and lead respectable lives, and keep out of jail, if we keep reprinting their old stories and turning down their new ones?' (pp. 134–35). These explanations cannot be taken seriously: none of the new stories in the magazine could be described as '*better*' than Verne or Wells, and it was surely the desire to attract readers, not to subsidize authors, that inspired the policy of no reprints. That is, as a new magazine entering a field dominated by two older magazines which regularly featured reprints, *Astounding Stories of Super-Science* could make itself seem more novel and attractive by printing original stories only. However, beyond their marketing value, such comments could also be read as an attempt to de-emphasize the importance of the science fiction history previously established by Gernsback, and to maintain instead that its really great and noteworthy works were those of the 1920s and 1930s.

Still, there was one element of truth in the second claim: *Astounding Stories of Super-Science* paid better, and more promptly, than either *Amazing Stories* or Gernsback's magazines, and many authors who had previously written for those magazines probably profited by sending their work to this new magazine. Bates also offered an interesting contrast to Gernsback, who announced a policy of fewer reprints (in 'On Reprints') largely on the grounds that their science has become out-of-date (of course, given his habit of not paying authors, Gernsback could hardly claim he was emphasizing new stories as a way to support those authors).

While *Astounding Stories of Super-Science* was reasonably successful, the financial problems of its parent company led to its demise in 1933; the magazine was then sold to Street & Smith, which soon started publishing again with a new editor, F. Orlon Tremaine, who, as will be discussed, established a rather different editorial policy. But the formula Bates developed would later be imitated, ironically, by both of Gernsback's former magazines—*Wonder Stories* and *Amazing Stories*—when they were sold to other publishers.

When *Wonder Stories* became *Thrilling Wonder Stories* in 1936, new editor Mort Weisinger announced the magazine would be:

> Bound to no tradition but the high standard of quality in imaginative fiction set by Jules Verne, H. G. Wells, Lord Dunsany and other masters... Man has made the fields of the air his park—the depths of the sea his pleasure-ground. Long before these things came to pass, they were foreseen in the clear vision of early prophetic writers... Our objective will always be to provide the most thrilling and entertaining fiction possible—while never ignoring basic scientific truths. ('The New Thrilling Wonder Stories', p. 10)

Two years later, when Ray Palmer took over *Amazing Stories*, his first editorial column promised 'tales based on true scientific facts. Insofar as the basic subject matter is founded upon scientific research, it will be essentially a true story magazine although thrilling tenseness of adventure will still form a part of the many features yet to come' ('The Observatory by the Editor', p. 8).

In Bates, Weisinger, and Palmer, one observes a different truncation of Gernsback's theory of science fiction: while Sloane de-emphasized prophecy and the value of inspiring scientific inventions, these editors de-emphasized science and the value of providing scientific education. There was a vestigial insistence that the stories should have 'a scientific idea', should not 'ignor[e] basic scientific truths', or should be 'based on true scientific facts'. But these editors never claimed that scientific principles were actually being explained in these stories or that one could obtain a scientific education by reading them. Lester del Rey describes this change in emphasis bluntly; in Palmer's *Amazing Stories*, 'all claims for scientific accuracy were abandoned' (*The World of Science Fiction*, p. 115). Another new element in their policies was an inclination to blur the distinction between science fiction and fantasy. Bates casually referred to the coming writers in *Astounding Stories of Super-Science* as 'writers of fantasy'; and Weisinger included Lord Dunsany—a pure fantasy writer—in a short list of distinguished predecessors to the modern genre of science fiction. Furthermore, the prophecies in science fiction, while remaining an essential part of the stories, now had no value other than to provide entertainment; Weisinger did note that many actual inventions had been previously predicted in science fiction, but like Bates he did not explain why it is valuable to read about new inventions before they occur.

Whatever lapses they had as science fiction commentators, Weisinger and Palmer have been praised for their talent and energy as editors: Ashley says that in 1937, '*Thrilling Wonder* increased in strength and vitality... Due credit must be given to *Wonder's* editor, Mort Weisinger', and in 1938, 'Under Palmer *Amazing* underwent a considerable transformation... it was now lively and rejuvenated' ('SF Bandwaggon', pp. 21, 18, 28). However, Weisinger eventually left science fiction to take charge of the Superman comic books, while Palmer's later magazines reflected a significant—but undesirable—shift in focus: beginning in the March 1945 issue, *Amazing Stories* published a series of articles, purporting to be factual, about 'the Shaver hypothesis', involving a supposed race of robots invisibly influencing human history from below the surface of the Earth; Palmer also enthusiastically exploited popular interest in flying saucers at that time. Thus, Campbell's new argument of the 1950s, discussed later, that there existed a natural alliance between science fiction and various forms of pseudo-science was to an extent anticipated by Palmer.

While other editors were abandoning or downplaying aspects of Gernsback's theories, F. Orlon Tremaine, who took over the revived *Astounding Stories* (with that shortened title), enthusiastically embraced Gernsback's original approach to the genre, though he presented those ideas in a significantly different style.

Tremaine accepted Gernsback's three components of science fiction, as shown by a reference to a 'story that... those of you who like carefully projected scientific thought will like' ('Ad Astra', p. 7). Here are the three elements: a 'story' with 'scientific thought' that is 'carefully projected'. He agreed that these should be 'intermingled' in a science fiction story, for he asked rhetorically, 'Do we mingle too much of love and adventure with these projections? I think not' ('The Growing Consciousness', p. 123). He defended science fiction on Gernsback's grounds—entertainment, education, and stimulating ideas for inventors—in comments like these: 'There is no more interesting or educational reading anywhere' ('Star Dust', p. 65); 'we build the finest interest that any group could possibly have— the future science—sugar-coated, to be sure, in story form, but sound and true as an arrow speeding to its destined objective' ('About Brass Tacks', p. 149); '*Astounding Stories* holds a unique and important place in scientific achievement... Perhaps we dream—but we do so logically, and science follows in the footsteps of our dreams' ('Blazing New Trails' 153); and 'Our imaginative tales of the future pictured advance after advance before it came' ('The Door to Tomorrow', p. 123).

Also, although Tremaine rarely discussed science fiction history— appropriately enough, since *Astounding Stories* continued to include no reprints—his later comments on the subject recalled Gernsback's, with a few additions: 'And leading with a dream, ahead of the whole parade, down through the years, science fiction has shown the way. Jules Verne, Ryder Haggard [*sic*], Conan Doyle, Wells—and then, like a swelling tide, the writers of modern stories' ('Signposts in Space', p. 17). And he asked Sam Moskowitz, 'Why do you think the scientific romances of Edgar Rice Burroughs were so popular? Why do you think people took the utopias of More, Bellamy and Butler so seriously? They provided not only food for thought, but a mode of escape' (cited in Introduction to 'The Way Back', p. 189). While he omitted Poe, and added Thomas More and Samuel Butler, the general picture—a little early activity, important nineteenth-century pioneers, and a flowering of the genre in the twentieth century—recalls Gernsback's history of science fiction.

While the ideas he expressed were not that innovative, there is one key difference between Gernsback's rhetoric and Tremaine's: Gernsback's discussions of science fiction as education and prophecy were clear and concrete, and his points were usually followed by a specific example or two, even if only the hoary tales of Verne's submarine and Chief Radio Man Finney. Tremaine's discussions of science fiction were vague and abstract, and they never offered any examples. This is not surprising since, as Pohl points out, Tremaine was 'no scientist' and 'he knew nothing at all about science fiction when he took [the editorship of *Astounding Stories*] on; Street & Smith bought it and handed it to him as a chore, and that was that' (*The Way the Future Was*, p. 41). Thus, while he absorbed Gernsback's arguments, he could not present them with Gernsback's scientific knowledge, and thus he could not make any significant improvements in Gernsback's ideas.

Oddly, though he lacked a scientific background, Tremaine developed a remarkable interest in the subject: he began publishing science articles, renamed the letter column 'Science Discussions' to encourage comments on scientific ideas, and in general displayed what Paul Carter describes as 'an enthusiasm [for science] that out-Gernsbacked Gernsback' (*The Creation of Tomorrow*, p. 16).

Still, Tremaine made a few contributions to the theory of science fiction. First, like his predecessor Bates, Tremaine announced increased attention to literary qualities and boasted that 'I have worked with new writers as well as old for three years… it has meant that I have worked at night to help redress a story style because it carried an idea' ('Ad Astra', p. 7). However, the overall quality and maturity of the stories he published suggest that his claims, unlike those of Bates, had some substance behind them; as Alva Rogers later said, Tremaine 'most certainly had literary taste' (*A Requiem for Astounding*, p. 38). While *Wonder Stories* published the first story by Stanley G. Weinbaum, Tremaine then attracted Weinbaum to *Astounding Stories*, where most of his other stories appeared. and while all the other magazines rejected John W. Campbell, Jr's 'Twilight', Tremaine was perceptive enough to publish it promptly. Perhaps his experience with other magazines gave him a better idea of what readers wanted in their fiction; and as his magazine improved, he could boast in 1935 that 'We've awakened the whole field of science-fiction from the coma in which it rested in 1932 and early 1933' (cited in Rogers, *A Requiem for Astounding*, p. 32) and in 1936 that 'Astounding has bought the best science-fiction available for three years' ('Science Discussions', p. 123) and 'we are gradually building what will one day be called the greatest group of science-fiction writers of all time' ('Ad Astra', p. 7).

As with Gernsback, the question arises: but did Tremaine really work with writers to improve their stories? Moskowitz, apparently relying on an extraordinary memory, offers one anecdote involving Tremaine's later position as editor of *Comet Stories*:

> I had written a short story titled *The Way Back* which I personally submitted, and instead of a rejection I got a request to come up and see [Tremaine].
>
> 'You have an acceptable story,' Tremaine said reassuringly, 'but I want you to make it much more than that. I don't care how much wordage you add—double the length if you wish but I want you to answer the questions that every reader will want to know. Those questions are: what kind of world is your story taking place on, what are its topographical characteristics, its climate, its life forms, if any. I want you to tell readers about the customs of the people who live there, including their occupations, entertainments, architecture, philosophy, and temperament… What makes science fiction unique

is not merely the plot of the story, but the sense of awe and wonder
it inspires in the reader... It is up to you to take the reader literally
out of this world, into a place where things are astonishingly novel
and different. There is just as much entertainment in describing how
much and what varieties of food an alien eats as to the results of a
hand-to-hand battle with one of them. The effect of inadvertently
breaking a social code of another world may provide more fascinating
situations than a dozen mind-staggering theories'. (Introduction to
'The Way Back', pp. 188–89)

Here is Tremaine prodding Moskowitz to write in the manner that
Campbell would later espouse: to develop a fully worked-out background
for stories, and to explore social as well as scientific issues. Of course, since
this conversation occurred two years after Campbell took over *Astounding*,
Tremaine at this point may simply be borrowing some of his former
assistant's ideas.

Another new element in Tremaine's commentaries was a different
picture of the characteristic audience of science fiction. While *Amazing
Stories* had been reasonably successful, it never achieved a mass audience—
though Gernsback never stopped hoping that science fiction might some
day attain such an audience. Thus, one of his editors in 1930 commented
that 'The select group of science-fiction readers which now exists is a
marvelous nucleus for a far greater mass of readers that are yet to come'
('What I Have Done to Spread Science Fiction', p. 278). However, Tremaine
introduced the argument, later expanded and emphasized by Campbell,
that science fiction readers were by nature a small, elite group. In 1936,
he said:

> Is it strange, then, that the reading audience of *Astounding Stories*
> seems somehow akin? Is it strange that I can sit down and talk as if
> I know you all? I feel as if we were all members of that inner circle
> who see and understand a vision that is beyond the ken of the vast
> multitude. We have something in common binding us together...
> An outsider would not understand. He would have to seek this vision
> and grow for a while to become one of us. ('Looking Ahead', p. 155)

He again argued in a later editorial for *Astounding Stories* that 'ours is an
exclusive reading circle... We cannot expect every one to recognize or
understanding the impelling interest which grips us' ('The Growing
Consciousness', p. 123). And he contrasted 'we who comprehend and love
the spirit of Science Fiction' with 'the creepers of a workaday world' ('In
Tune with the Infinite', p. 81).[2]

Still, despite his greater attention to literary values, his espousal of

Gernsback's theories, and his innovative sense of the audience of science fiction, Tremaine was hardly perfect. In addition to noteworthy stories, he also presented a few poor ones—Pohl says he 'published some incredible rot' (p. 41). Second, while he seemed to feel, like Gernsback, a need for new directions in science fiction, he also proved unable to articulate exactly what those new directions should be. His strategy, not unlike Gernsback's 'Interplanetary Plots' contests, was to call for new things and celebrate them when he found them. So Tremaine inaugurated the policy of publishing what he termed 'Thought-Variant' stories: each issue would feature 'one story carrying a new and unexplored "thought-variant" in the field of scientific fiction' which would 'speak its mind frankly... without regard to the restrictions formerly placed upon this type of fiction' (cited in Carter, *The Creation of Tomorrow*, pp. 117–18). Yet the typical 'Thought-Variant' story was disappointing, described by Carter as 'a dreamily written tale in which space, time, matter, energy, and thought all were scrambled together into an unsavory omelet' (p. 118). Even the supportive Rogers conceded that by 1936, 'the thought-variant was rapidly becoming a dead end' (*A Requiem for Astounding*, p. 41). The policy, by the way, was soon imitated by *Wonder Stories*, which started to designate any unusual tale as a 'New Story'.

The problem was that Tremaine lacked the scientific background that might have enabled him to describe exactly what he wanted in a 'Thought-Variant' tale was or how an author might go about writing one. Thus, writers simply imitated other stories, each trying to get a little more 'cosmic' than the last effort, setting in motion another one of the tired cycles of imitation that distinguished much of the science fiction of the 1930s.

Certainly, one can argue that Tremaine was an important figure in the development of science fiction, who continued the Gernsback tradition while anticipating some of Campbell's reforms; but, like Gernsback's, Tremaine's science fiction career had an unhappy ending. In 1937, he moved to an administrative position and hired John W. Campbell, Jr to replace him—which may have been his most important contribution to the field; then, he developed a yen to return to the genre and began editing a new magazine, *Comet Stories*, which was a complete failure and ceased publication after five issues. He could not compete with his one-time protégé Campbell, who by that time was outclassing all the competition.

To summarize: Sloane downplayed Gernsback's element of science fiction prediction and the argument that those predictions could inspire actual inventions; Bates, Weisinger and Palmer downplayed scientific explanations and the argument that those explanations could be educational; Tremaine accepted all of Gernsback's theories but could not add any substance to them; and Tremaine offered a modified vision of the audience of science fiction and some genuine improvement in literary quality. In no way did any of these men significantly challenge Gernsback's theories, and in no way did they significantly improve upon them. Everybody from Gernsback and Tremaine seemed to be searching for something new in science fiction, but no one was really sure how to go about achieving it.

While these editors remained the most influential voices in defining and defending science fiction, they were not the only people discussing science fiction in the 1930s; increasingly, readers and fans were having their say. Letter columns featured energetic debates and commentaries, and fanzines were extending those discussions. At the time, these voices had no wide audience or impact, but they were starting to make their presence felt.

One major new theme emerged from the growing community of science fiction fans: science fiction as a projection of a 'sense of wonder'. I have searched many science fiction magazines to locate the first use of the term, and the one early instance I can cite does not clearly link the phrase with science fiction: an editor's blurb to Dennis McDermott's 'The Red Spot of Jupiter' which begins, '[To] Those who have been privileged to travel into remote corners of the earth and see new forms of life, *a sense of the wonder* and diversity of nature has come with years. But the sights that these explorers have seen will be commonplace as compared to what explorers to other planets will see' (p. 215; my italics). Years later, as noted, Moskowitz attributes the phrase 'sense of awe and wonder' to Tremaine. Regardless of its origins, the phrase came to describe the feeling of awe that a reader should obtain from reading some breathtakingly new or expansive story; however, while Gernsback's use of the word 'wonder' in connection with science fiction might be seen as the ultimate source of the phrase, the concept was not exactly his. To Gernsback, the goal of science fiction is to make readers understand the facts and possibilities of science, not simply to gape at wondrous visions with amazement and astonishment. The phrase, then, became another device for decoupling science fiction from the strong attachment to scientific explanation which Gernsback worked so hard to achieve.

In fact, while some early fans like the New York Scienceers were strongly interested in scientific projects, one distinguishing characteristic of the emerging fan movement was a growing willingness, already seen in Bates and Weisinger, to see no strong distinction between science fiction and fantasy—since fantasy could, after all, also provide a 'sense of wonder'. As noted in Harry Warner, Jr's *All Our Yesterdays*, many fan organizations and projects took the title 'Fantasy', and early bibliographies freely mingled science fiction and fantasy works. Thus, fans readily accepted an essential kinship between the two forms, which further weakened Gernsback's insistence on scientific content and ideas.

It should also be noted that some fans were not particularly committed to or involved in efforts to study or cultivate science fiction but instead became focused on the activities of other fans: Harry Warner, Jr's *All Our Yesterdays* explains that such a person was known as a 'faan'—'a fan who has lost most of his interest in science fiction and is now mainly interested in other fans and faans' (p. xx). Clearly, Moskowitz's history of fandom, *The Immortal Storm*, shows that many fans were more interested in fighting with each other than fighting to understand or improve science fiction; and Lester del Rey admits that 'Much [fan activity] had no direct effect on science fiction' (*The World of Science Fiction*, p. 73).

Still, in some ways the fans were beneficial to the genre. Writers usually appreciated the attention they received, and fans were instrumental in early efforts to publish the best magazine science fiction in book form: first Arkham House focused on the works of H. P. Lovecraft, then companies like Prime Press, Shasta Publishers, Fantasy Press, and Advent Publishers. Fans devoted much energy to bibliographical work, which would culminate in important reference works like Everett F. Bleiler's *The Checklist of Fantastic Literature* (1948), Bradford M. Day's *The Complete Checklist of Science-Fiction Magazines*, and Donald H. Tuck's *The Encyclopedia of Science Fiction and Fantasy* (first volume 1974). One fan, Moskowitz, became for a while what James Blish called 'the nearest thing to a scholar that science fiction has produced' (*More Issues at Hand*, p. 25), and his biographies of science fiction authors in *Explorers of the Infinite* and *Seekers of Tomorrow* remain in some cases the definitive studies of the writers.

In addition, many fans were, like Gernsback, unhappy with the trend toward thoughtless space adventures, and they developed critical terminology that could function as a mechanism for improving the genre. In 1939, as reported by Warner, Martin Alger sarcastically announced the formation of the 'Society for the Prevention of Bug Eyed Monsters on the Covers of Science Fiction Publications', thus adding 'BEM' to the language; and in 1941, Wilson Tucker coined 'space opera' to describe what he called the 'hacky, grinding, stinking, outworn spaceship yarn' (cited in *All Our Yesterdays*, pp. 234, 41).[3] Such reactions may have been one factor which fuelled John W. Campbell, Jr's drive to make science fiction a more adult form of literature in the 1940s.

Overall, the ideas and writings of science fiction fans remain a vast unexplored territory for scholars, since existing studies focus on their politics or sociology, not their criticism. Many concepts and themes that later became common no doubt originated in the fanzines, and many persons who wrote for fanzines—like Damon Knight, Blish, Forrest J.

Ackerman and Moskowitz—would become prominent as science fiction editors or critics. And three studies I examined—William Bainbridge's *Dimensions of Science Fiction*, Paul Carter's 'You Can Write Science Fiction If You Want to', and Patricia Monk's '"Not Just Cosmic Skullduggery": A Partial Reconsideration of Space Opera'—show that modern critics can make effective use of fan commentaries from science fiction magazines.

Overall, however, the contributions of these editors and enthusiasts still await detailed analysis—largely for one reason: in the 1940s, a man who would be the greatest of all Gernsback's successors emerged as a prominent presence, and it would prove difficult to take the spotlight away from John W. Campbell, Jr.

Notes

1 All Sloane quotations are from signed editorials.

2 Tremaine's belief in the unique élite audience of science fiction was evidently sincere, for years after he left the magazine he again said, 'The kinship of interest among science fiction fans is a bond like a common language. Nowhere, outside of our own particular group, can we talk as freely about the things which will happen tomorrow' ('Editorial Number Two: In Absentia', p. xviii).

3 Though on page 41, Warner dates Alger's use of the term to the 'early forties'.

'A Convenient Analog System': John W. Campbell, Jr's Theory of Science Fiction

Because John W. Campbell, Jr's abilities as a writer and an editor have been overpraised—as will be argued—his contributions as a critic have been neglected or minimized. Introducing *Collected Editorials from Analog*, for example, Harry Harrison claims that 'Non-Escape Literature' was 'the only Campbell editorial ever written about science fiction itself' (p. ix), but this is not true. In his early career, Campbell wrote several editorials about the genre, such as 'Science-Fiction', 'Future Tense', 'The Old Navy Game', 'History to Come', 'Too Good at Guessing', and 'Science-Fiction Prophecy', and many later editorials and features of his magazines, while mostly devoted to other subjects, include comments about science fiction. Further, Campbell wrote enthusiastically about science fiction in other forums: introductions to his and others' anthologies, long letters (some later collected in *The John W. Campbell, Jr. Letters, Volume I*), speeches at science fiction conventions, and articles like 'The Science of Science Fiction Writing', 'The Science of Science-Fiction', 'The Place of Science Fiction', 'Science Fiction and the Opinion of the Universe', and 'Science Fiction We Can Buy'.

In his writings, Campbell retained and restated the essential elements in Hugo Gernsback's theory of science fiction, reformed and added to some of those elements, and incorporated ideas and improvements from other sources. In essence, he repaired Gernsback's ideas; and I maintain that it was primarily by means of his critical work—not his writing or editing— that Campbell had a major impact on the genre and became, after Gernsback, the second most important figure in the development of science fiction.

In calling Campbell a critic who built on Gernsback's ideas, I contradict what Campbell himself had to say; for late in his life, he told Alexei Panshin, 'Now you ask me if I disagreed with Gernsback's theories. Why hell, man, I didn't know he *had* theories—and I'll bet he didn't know it either, until he thought about it months or years later... I do not trust theories; I don't have theories, at least I don't let my theories "have" me to the extent that I can't try something that violates said theories' (letter to Alexei Panshin, 8 September 1970, pp. 587–88).

However, as I argued in a letter to *Foundation* (No. 52), one need not claim that Gernsback and Campbell were *aware* that they were propounding literary theories to demonstrate that they *were* propounding such theories; and as in the case of Gernsback, one need not demonstrate that Campbell was a *good* science fiction critic to show that he *was* a science fiction critic.

Granted, the totality of Campbell's statements on science fiction do not display the clear repetition of basic principles that distinguished Gernsback's pronouncements; instead, Campbell seemed to drift from subject to subject over the years. However, this does not mean that he was changing his mind; rather, having expounded one principle to his satisfaction, and having no desire to repeat himself, Campbell's restless, active mind simply moved on to another area of concern. Little in Campbell's later statements *contradicts* his earlier theories;[1] they simply add to them.

Another factor might be Campbell's different perception of the science fiction audience. Since Gernsback thought science fiction should be read by everyone, his tendency to keep reiterating key concepts may reflect a low opinion of the perceptiveness of common people. In contrast, as will be noted, Campbell thought science fiction naturally had an intelligent, well-educated audience, so repeating established principles would be unnecessary.[2]

Regarding Campbell's dismissal of Gernsback's influence, I note that Campbell was never inclined to acknowledge any debts to other editors: for example, I believe that he never once talked about F. Orlon Tremaine, the man who hired and trained him, to edit *Astounding Stories*, and never talked about later editors like H. L. Gold or Frederik Pohl who surely had some impact on his later policies. Campbell may have been particularly disinclined to praise Gernsback because of lingering anger over the way Gernsback introduced his 1932 story 'Space Rays'; and Gernsback was also an occasional rival of Campbell, another reason Campbell might fail to praise him. Finally, also as previously indicated, Campbell may have been unaware that he was actually responding to ideas originated by Gernsback, because by the time he became an editor those ideas were being promulgated in many places.

Still, the evidence of Campbell's statements is unambiguous: Campbell definitely had 'theories' of science fiction, and they definitely built upon and modified Gernsback's theories.

Late in his career, Campbell once claimed he was fundamentally unable to define science fiction:

How do you describe the taste of a green pepper to someone who's never tasted one—even though you have tasted it and do know the very definite, unmistakable flavor?

Could you describe the difference between the flavor of a tangerine and a grapefruit to an Eskimo who'd never tasted either?

You know what they taste like and what the difference is—but you can't define it in terms he can understand. Moreover, if you could give him only six drops of tangerine juice, and six of grapefruit juice, that wouldn't help much; in that small quantity they're not really distinguishable.

In much the same way, *I can not tell you what science fiction is*. And I can't tell you the difference between science fiction and fantasy. ('Science Fiction We Can Buy', p. 27)

Despite this moment of reticence, Campbell previously offered many definitions of science fiction. One can be chosen as typical: 'Basically, science fiction is an effort to predict the future on the basis of known facts, culled largely from present-day laboratories. Within that broad field—and it is exceedingly broad, indeed, far more so, in fact, that even modern science-fiction readers fully realize—there are many species, types, and families of story material' ('Introduction', *Who Goes There?*, p. 5). Here again are the three elements of science fiction that Gernsback identified: 'story material' (fiction) based on 'known facts' (science) which aims to 'predict the future' (prophecy). However, Campbell did not simply accept these concepts as Gernsback characterized them, but rather expanded and developed them.

Referring to 'story material', Campbell, unlike Gernsback, did not identify a characteristic form such as 'charming romance' or 'thrilling adventure': 'there are many species, types, and families of story material'. He claimed that 'science-fiction is the freest, least formalized of any literary medium' ('Introduction', *Who Goes There?*, p. 5) and that '*Astounding's* policy is free and easy—anything in science fiction that is a good yarn is fine by us' ('The Science of Science Fiction Writing', p. 100). He even declared that 'That group of writings which is usually referred to as "mainstream literature" is, actually, a special subgroup of the field of science fiction—for science fiction deals with all places in the Universe, and all times in Eternity, so the literature of here-and-now is, truly, a subset of science fiction' ('Introduction', *Analog I*, p. xv). Science fiction encompasses all literature and, as a result, incorporates all of its possibilities.

On occasion, with no great conviction, Campbell would list the types of science fiction narratives. In 1946, he divided the genre into 'Prophecy stories', 'Philosophical stories', and 'Adventure science fiction' ('Concerning

Science Fiction', p. vi), noting Gernsback's generic model as only one of three possibilities; in 1948, he listed 'the gadget story, the concept story, and the character story' ('Introduction', *Who Goes There?*, p. 3); and in 1968, he added 'sociological science fiction' ('Introduction', *Analog 6*, p. xii). But Campbell acknowledged that such categories were not fixed—there was much 'cross-over between types' ('Introduction', *Who Goes There?*, p. 3)— and his purpose in listing them was clearly not to establish a taxonomy, but simply to illustrate the broad range of options available. And Campbell, unlike Gernsback, did not see 'thrilling adventure' as the central or most important form of science fiction: in 'Concerning Science Fiction', he said, 'to most people, SF seemed lurid, fantastic, and nonsensical trash... Science fiction has, definitely, been a misunderstood type of material. In the public mind, "Buck Rogers" is the standard science-fiction character; the comic strip has tended to be accepted as representative of the field. It is—to precisely the extent that Dick Tracy is representative of detective fiction' (p. v).

Campbell also announced an increased degree of attention to the literary quality of science fiction. In 1968, he placed an emphasis on effective story-telling: 'Science-fictioneers want stories—entertainment... Poor characterization, poor style, even poor plotting will be willingly forgiven, if the author produces a real yarn, if he's a wing-ding story-teller... What can't be forgiven is a poor story' ('Science Fiction We Can Buy', p. 28). Realistic characterization was also important: 'In older science fiction, the Machine and the Great Idea predominated. Modern readers—and hence editors!—don't want that; they want stories of people living in a world where a Great Idea, or a series of them, and a Machine, or machines, form the background. But it is the man, not the idea or machine that is the essence' ('The Science of Science Fiction Writing', p. 92). Lester del Rey once paraphrased the 'gist' of Campbell's directives in a 1938 issue of *Writer's Digest*: 'I want reactions, not mere actions. Even if your character is a robot, human readers need human reactions from him' (*The World of Science Fiction*, p. 153–54). Campbell also stressed the importance of 'style', which 'makes the difference between a "nice idea, too bad he can't write" story and a bell-ringing, smash-hit yarn' ('The Science of Science Fiction Writing' 98); and in a letter to Terry Carr, he said, 'You can forgive a weak writer for the sake of a gorgeous idea—but not simply awful writing' (17 June 1968, p. 541).

The second defining characteristic of science fiction became that it was built 'on the basis of known facts'—but these facts would now have a very different role in science fiction. Specifically, Campbell dropped Gernsback's insistence that science fiction incorporate lengthy scientific explanations and urged authors to provide information in more subtle ways: 'The best modern writers of science fiction have worked out some truly remarkable techniques for presenting a great deal of background and associated material without intruding into the flow of the story' ('Concerning Science Fiction', p. ix). He praised Robert A. Heinlein's 'The Roads Must Roll' by saying, 'notice how much of the cultural-technological pattern he has put over, without impressing you, at any point, with a two-minute lecture on the pattern of the time' ('Introduction', *The Man Who Sold the Moon*, p. 14), and he repeatedly stressed that all the necessary scientific information must be 'worked into the story without interrupting' ('Brass Tacks', *Astounding Science-Fiction*, November 1942, p. 109).[3] Science fiction now does not *lack* the long scientific and prophetic descriptions that Gernsback cherished; rather, these materials *precede and inform* the story while not fully presented in it. Later, Campbell agreed that Heinlein had originated this approach while criticizing him for abandoning it: rejecting *Starship Troopers*, he said, 'Bob's departing from the principles he himself introduced in science-fiction—"Don't *tell* the reader about the background; let him gather it from what happens"' (letter to Lurton Blassingame, 4 March 1959, p. 362). So the second defining characteristic of science fiction is not lengthy explanations of scientific data but signs of such data, evidenced only by hints and passing references.[4]

Campbell also redefined 'science', offering writers a wider range of subjects than Gernsback, who focused on 'hard' sciences. Campbell included social sciences in the range of science fiction—'Sociology, psychology, and parapsychology are, today, not true sciences; therefore, instead of forecasting future results of applications of sociological science of today, we must forecast the *development of a science* of sociology. From there, the story can take off' ('The Science of Science Fiction Writing', p. 91). Campbell also embraced subjects deemed unscientific or pseudo-scientific: 'Ghosts can enter science fiction—if they're logically explained' ('The Science of Science Fiction Writing', p. 91), and 'those areas where there is data, observational facts, which Science stubbornly rejects, and labels as "folklore" or "fantastic nonsense" and refuses to examine... [are] fair game for a science-fictioneer. He has a perfect right to accept the data, propose an integrated explanation for the observational material, and use that as a basis for a story' ('Introduction', *Analog 6*, pp. xii–xiii). Among others, Judith Merril noted Campbell's 'broader concept of the scope of "science" (technology and *engineering*); he wanted to explore the effects of the new technological world on people. Cultural anthropology, social psychology, cybernetics, communications, sociology, education, psycho-metrics—all these, and a dozen intermediate points, were thrown open for examination' ('What Do You Mean: Science? Fiction?', p. 67).

In his omission of detailed explanation, and phrases like 'forecast the *development of a science* of sociology' and 'propose an integrated explanation for the observational material', one detects another element in Campbell's characterization of science: it is not simply a body of data, but rather an attitude, a way of looking at the world, and fiction based on this attitude can be accepted as science fiction even if it is not based on 'science of today'. That is, 'Science-fiction, being largely an attempt to forecast the future, on the basis of the present, represents a type of extrapolation' ('The Perfect Machine', p. 5)—a form of scientific thinking. In 'The Science of Science Fiction Writing', he again said that 'To be science fiction, not fantasy, an honest effort at prophetic extrapolation of the known must be made' (p. 91); and in his 'Introduction' to *14 Great Tales about ESP*, he argued that science fiction 'takes a known fact and extends it; or it introduces one new postulate and studies the resultant world' (p. 13).

Third, science fiction included prophecy, but of a special and rigorous type. Science fiction writers could not simply predict inventions, but must also consider 'what the results look like when applied not only to machines, but to human societies as well' ('Introduction', *Venus Equilateral*, p. 5) and must do so in the manner of scientists. Science fiction needed to examine 'This complexity of interaction of technology and social custom' along with 'the third factor: the reaction of human nature to the resultant mixture' ('Introduction', *The Man Who Sold the Moon*, p. 14). Thus, prediction became more taxing and thoroughgoing, 'mental research into possible futures' ('History to Come', p. 5): 'Mapping out a civilization of the future is an essential background to a convincing story of the future... you've got to have that carefully mapped outline in mind to get consistency of minor details' ('The Old Navy Game', p. 6); and he told Dean McLaughlin that 'science fiction tries to present the incidents in the life of, and the consequent development of, a whole culture—instead of an individual person' (letter to Dean McLaughlin, 4 June 1953, p. 175). Many have discussed this desire for developed and realistic futures: Pohl quotes Campbell as saying, 'I want the kind of story that could be printed in a magazine of the year two thousand A.D. as a contemporary adventure story. No gee-whiz, just take the technology for granted' (*The Way the Future Was*, p. 82); James Gunn cites a similar statement—'I want a story that would be published in a magazine of the twenty-fifth century' ('John Wood Campbell', p. 18); and del Rey says that Campbell 'wanted [his writers] to live in their futures. And he wanted those futures to be livable. The time to visit futures that were only stage fronts was over' (*The World of Science Fiction*, p. 149). And separate passages of expository 'prophecy' are not needed; like scientific information, predictions can be smoothly integrated into the narrative.

Again, Heinlein was a key reason why Campbell advocated this sort of detailed development, and early in his career Campbell published

Heinlein's 'Future History' chart (in 'Brass Tacks', *Astounding Science-Fiction*, May 1941, pp. 124–25) specifically to illustrate the benefits of this approach.[5] However, the later work of Hal Clement was also an influence: and Campbell displayed and celebrated Clement's skills in this area by publishing Clement's 1953 article, 'Whirligig World', on the scientific thinking and development that went into his *Mission of Gravity*.[6]

In redefining and expanding the concepts of fiction, science, and prophecy, Campbell also explained the method of writing science fiction involving these three elements as stages in a process. He outlined the steps in describing Norman L. Knight's 'Crisis in Utopia': 'He's got an idea that definitely makes background for a story with potent, near-dynamite emotional reactions' ('In Times to Come', *Astounding Science-Fiction*, June 1940, p. 50). First, an author has a scientific—or pseudo-scientific—'idea' which he then develops, by employing scientific thinking, into a complete 'background'. At this point, the complexity of the task requires that some of this material be written down. Then he can create a 'story' based on that background, consulting and making use of, but not necessarily incorporating, his expository materials.

Campbell thus makes writing science fiction a sort of thought-experiment, in which the author carefully creates a set of hypotheses regarding future events and lets the story grow out of those hypotheses; as Stableford says, 'the Campbellian school of thought is inclined to compare the attitude of the sf writer and his method to the attitude and method of the scientist' ('Anthropology', p. 38). Under these circumstances, the story may to an extent develop on its own, beyond the conscious control of the author; in historical fiction, Campbell observed, 'Frequently a study of the period leads directly to the story—the plot and action are logical outgrowths of the conflicts inherent in the times... all those things should apply to science fiction' ('History to Come', p. 5). If a science fiction author follows this procedure, then, the story that emerges may be quite unexpected and strange, even to its author. As a result, Campbell claimed:

> the fun of science-fiction writing [is that] the plotting is as nearly 100% uninhibited as anything imaginable... In this field, the reader can never be sure just how the author may wind up—and because the author feels that freedom, he can let the story have its head, let it develop in any direction that the logic of the developing situation may dictate. Many times a story actually winds up entirely different from the idea with which the author started. And, very rarely, an author can simply start a story, and let it work its own way out to a conclusion! ('Introduction', *Who Goes There?*, p. 5)

The concept of a story that essentially writes itself is nothing new: long ago, Samuel Taylor Coleridge offered the theory of 'organic form', and in practice, many authors outside the field have had the experience of a story that moves in its own direction—L. Frank Baum once complained that 'My characters just won't do what I want them to' (cited in Hearn, *The Annotated Wizard of Oz*, p. 64). But 'organic form' is generally seen as unpredictable and somewhat mysterious; Campbell claims that by beginning with concepts that are scientifically sound, and pondering them in a scientific manner, authors might regularly achieve this result.[7]

As he expanded and altered Gernsback's notions of 'fiction', 'science', and 'prophecy', Campbell also projected a different view of who the proper readers and writers of science fiction should be. He rejected Gernsback's concept of a mass readership and, like his predecessor Tremaine, insisted that it could only reach an educated audience: 'No average mind can either understand or enjoy science-fiction' ('Science-Fiction', p. 37), he said in 1938, and twenty-one years later repeated that 'Science fiction is not, and never will be a mass-appeal type of material' ('Non-Escape Literature', p. 231). While the man on the street could not appreciate science fiction, Campbell specifically stated who should properly read and write science fiction: 'Science-fiction is written by technically-minded people, about technically-minded people, for the satisfaction of technically-minded people' ('Science Fiction and the Opinion of the Universe', p. 10). This was also Campbell's private opinion: in one letter, he called 'the science-fiction readership' 'the most thoughtful, speculative, and philosophical group of mankind' (letter to Poul Anderson, 25 October, 1952), and he told Pohl 'in science fiction, we're trying to please technologists and philosophically inclined adults of the very highest level' (letter to Frederik Pohl, 2 February 1953, p. 134). Campbell went so far as to say that the 'ability' to appreciate science fiction and its unique perspective on reality (discussed below) 'is, I am fairly sure (probability about .95, in my estimation) apt to be based on a *genetic* difference' (letter to Tony Boucher, 18 May 1956, p. 314). Science fiction readers were an elite not simply because of their background and education, but because of their genetic make-up.

Just as he had no desire to appeal to the masses, Campbell did not want uneducated amateurs to write science fiction; L. Ron Hubbard, introducing *Battlefield Earth: A Saga of the Year 3000*, says that Campbell had to be pressured by his publishers to use writers like Hubbard with no background in science (p. viii).

Like Gernsback, Campbell accepted the importance of youthful readers, but with a qualification: science fiction could only attract 'young adults who were acutely interested in the middle-distance future' ('Introduction', *Prologue to Analog*, p. 10); in general, he advised writers, 'do *not* make the egregious error of thinking science fiction is for kids' ('Science Fiction We Can Buy', p. 28). He boasted in one letter that 'The students of major universities read [my magazine]—and so do their instructors' (letter to J. B. Rhine, 23 November 1953, p. 225). And as one early indication of his belief that science fiction should only appeal to particularly bright youngsters, Campbell, when he took over *Astounding Stories*, dropped one promotional gimmick—a free baseball to subscribers ('Over the Fence', p. 146)—and substituted 'The Argon Glow Lamp and the Fluorescence Kit... a wonderful opportunity for science fans to experiment with ultraviolet light' ('Ultra-Violet Fluorescence', p. 126). Science fiction, it seemed, did not want young readers who were more interested in playing baseball than carrying out scientific experiments.

Also, as shown by the way that he worked with the young Isaac Asimov, he considered such youngsters good candidates to become science fiction writers; he once even asserted that '*Astounding* is, characteristically, authored by *young men*, with engineering training' ('In Times to Come', *Astounding Science-Fiction*, August 1942, p. 98; my italics).

Campbell was proud that science fiction could attract readers with scientific training—Gernsback's third audience, which he accepted enthusiastically. Campbell presented readership surveys in his magazine to prove science fiction had such an educated audience: 'Over thirty percent of *Astounding's* readers are *practicing technicians*—chemists, physicists, astronomers, mechanical engineers, radio men—technicians of every sort' ('In Times to Come', *Astounding Science-Fiction*, October 1938, p. 11).

Scientifically trained, Campbell was an appropriate science fiction writer, and he preferred authors with similar credentials, claiming that 'Science-fiction authors almost always have a good bit of scientific background' ('In Times to Come', *Astounding Science-Fiction*, November 1942, p. 42). And in 1946, he asserted that 'The top authors of science fiction are, in general, professional technicians of one sort or another... In recent years, the professional scientists have, more and more, taken over the pages of the magazines' ('Concerning Science Fiction', p. x). But a 'scientific background' was a necessary, but not sufficient, requirement to write 'the best type of science-fiction', which demands not only 'a technically inclined mind', but 'Imagination' and 'An understanding of how political and social set-ups react to technological changes' ('Introduction', *Venus Equilateral*, p. 9).

In defending science fiction, Campbell sometimes parroted the three arguments of Gernsback: its stories provided entertainment, scientific education, and useful and stimulating scientific ideas.

First, he called science fiction 'a form of entertainment that has attracted tens and hundreds of thousands of readers' ('Future Tense', p. 6) and said 'Science fiction is for fun—for those who enjoy stretching, reaching beyond the daily limits' ('Introduction', *Analog 1*, p. xviii). And he described his own story 'Twilight' as a special kind of entertainment: '["Twilight"] predicts no particular scientific advance, nor does it study a character as an individual—it's simply an effort to share a conception, a pure feeling. It's an effort to do, with words, what certain melodies and songs can do in evoking pure emotions. "Stardust" or "Memories" do it for some; "Finlandia" has the same emotion-stirring power on a different order, for others' ('Introduction', *Who Goes There?*, pp. 3–4). Thus he accepted the argument that science fiction was valuable because it offered pure entertainment.

Second, he noted that 'the good science-fiction author takes the same sort of care with his background science that the good detective-fiction writer does with his local color. A reasonably quick-minded reader of science fiction can readily pick up an astonishing fund of scientific fact from reading the stories' ('Concerning Science Fiction', p. ix). And when the radio broadcast of *War of the Worlds* inspired panic, he commented that 'we might have recognized in science-fiction's spread a means of teaching those members of the American Public with an excess of imagination with respect to radio dramas, and a lack of understanding of things interplanetary, just what chances the Martian invaders would have' ('A Variety of Things', p. 6). Thus, he accepted the argument that science fiction could offer scientific education.

Finally, a 1942 editorial warned about the possible effects of science fiction prophecies: 'The periscope was and is an important military instrument; if one of our current writers made an equally acute guess as to what was coming up in our immediate future, he would be doing a very real disservice to the nation in publishing his guess' ('Too Good at Guessing', p. 6). Thus, he accepted the argument that science fiction could provide useful ideas for working scientists and inventors.

However, Campbell had no patience with Gernsback's notion that science fiction stories might qualify for patents, and he offered a clear contrast between science fiction predictions and patentable concepts: 'if we science-fiction authors had known exactly what twist to put on [the idea of hardened glass] we wouldn't have made a suggestion; we'd have gotten a patent' ('Invention and Imagination', p. 6). And when a reader asked a technical question about one of E. E. Smith's imagined devices, Campbell joked, 'Might be he'd write for the Patent Office instead of for *Astounding* if he had a complete answer!' ('Brass Tacks', *Astounding Science-Fiction*, December 1941, p. 158). One problem was that science fiction writers, by nature unable to develop detailed, step-by-step predictions, and now crafting works with a greater focus on literary value, could not provide the necessary exactness in prediction: 'Science-fiction, to be dramatic, must be interesting. It skips the details—and arrives at flexible glass or completely self-controlling airplanes or thinking robots' ('Invention and Imagination', p. 6).

One more point of similarity was that Campbell embraced Gernsback's argument that the imaginative ideas in science fiction were needed because scientists are 'unbelieving' and 'intolerant of projected scientific progress' ('Surprising Facts', p. 317). The damaging conservatism of scientists was due in part, Campbell first argued, to their occupation:

> if an ordinary science-fiction writer can dream up the gadget, is there any reason to consider it as something secret? If the science-fiction author can think of it, surely a research scientists would think of it sooner, and in a more practical form, wouldn't he?
>
> Nothing to date shows that it is necessarily true. If anything, there's excellent reason for the reverse to hold—the science-fiction author is paid specifically to imagine devices even if he can't think of a way to make them. The industrial research scientist isn't paid to dream up super-doopers… ('Too Good at Guessing', pp. 6–7)

Second, there was an institutional conservatism that hindered creative scientists, a point Campbell made in a letter to Carl Sagan: in 'professional scientific journals… scientists are not adequately free to speculate on possible systems in public… That is one very real service that science-fiction magazines such as *Analog* can serve, and which I try to make it serve' (letter to Carl Sagan, 10 October 1967, p. 513). Finally, in later years, Campbell argued that scientists were by nature unable or unwilling to envision certain possibilities—a point most emphatically made in the title of one *Analog* anthology introduction, 'Scientists Are Stupid', and in the statement that 'There is a great list of resounding Authoritative Scientific Statements on the books that were spectacularly wrong' ('Introduction', *14 Great Tales about ESP*, p. 13). He said, 'One of my largest gripes about Science and the attitude of modern Scientists is that they forget, deny, reject, and refuse the simple fact that we're ignorant. Our science is about three centuries old, and to equate "we don't understand how such a thing could be" with "it is impossible" is decidedly arrogant stupidity' (letter to George O. Smith, 10 July 1965, p. 447).

While Campbell accepted these arguments from Gernsback, he also went beyond Gernsback to offer three rather different defences that challenged and extended Gernsback's original arguments.

First, in his other critical writings he made no effort to build on the 'emotion-stirring' concept of 'Twilight' as a defence of science fiction;

incongruously, despite his attention to 'mood' in that story, he once told Pohl, 'I *hate* a story that begins with *atmosphere*. Get right into the story, never mind the *atmosphere*' (*The Way the Future Was*, p. 82). Instead, he maintained that the 'entertainment' offered by science fiction was of an especially stimulating and demanding form, appropriate to a more educated and imaginative audience: 'it's not the summer-vacation-snooze type of fun. More like the roller-coaster or mountain-climbing type, it presents a real mental challenge. It demands active participation—not spectator type watch-what-those-characters-are-doing' ('Introduction', *Analog 1*, p. xvi). And when Sputnik provided dramatic evidence that science fiction was indeed serious business, Campbell explained why science fiction could not provide simple 'escape':

> Imagine a man who came across an old, Fifteenth Century *Grimmoire*, full of magical formulas and incantations, and directions for summoning demons. Intrigued and amused by the old superstitions, the pompous ridiculousness of the things the old boys believed, he shows it to a number of friends. They decide it'll be a wonderful stunt for a Halloween party, and go through the ancient rigmarole for summoning a Demon.
>
> And there is the Demon.
>
> Only because it was just a lot of ridiculous flubdubbery, the amateur magicians didn't bother to draw the protective spell of the pentacle. They thought the old boys were kidding... I think the people of the United States thought we were kidding too... That nuclear weapons and space flight were amusing ideas to play with... nonsense, of course, but amusing nonsense... Apparently, they thought that science fiction *was* an escape literature, and read it as such.
>
> It happens that science fiction's core is just about the only *non-*escape literature available to the general public today...

Far from providing entertainment for the masses, science fiction was entertaining only to those 'who have the unusual characteristic of being able to enjoy non-escape literature—who can look at a problem that hasn't slugged them over the head yet, and like thinking about it' ('Non-Escape Literature', pp. 227–28, 231).

While Gernsback emphatically separated science fiction from other forms of pulp literature, Campbell, in discussing the issue of entertainment, established a distinction between science fiction and fantasy. In his fantasy magazine *Unknown* (later *Unknown Worlds*), he freely identified its stories as 'pure entertainment' ('Unknown', p. 5; 'Of Things Beyond', p. 6); but science fiction was different. He explained the difference in 1946:

Some while ago, I was trying to figure out why it was that a friend who very much likes fantasy—(as distinct from science fiction, fantasy embraces only the 'ghoulies and ghosties and things that go boomp i' the night')—could not abide science fiction... In fantasy, the author knows it isn't true, the reader knows it isn't true, knows it didn't happen, and can't ever happen, and everybody is agreed. But in a science fiction, this man felt an overwhelming pressure on the part of the author to convince him that the story was possible, and could happen, a driving sincerity that oppressed and repelled him. ('Concerning Science Fiction', p. x)[8]

Therefore, science fiction, given its inherent seriousness of purpose, could not possibly function as 'pure entertainment'.

In offering a 'mental challenge' to its readers, science fiction might simply present an unusual idea and scientific possibility worth pondering, but the challenge could also often take the form of a scientific problem or puzzle to be solved, as claimed in Campbell's introduction to a Jack Williamson 'contra-terrene matter' story: 'can you figure out a mechanism which will make a completely rigid support between two kinds of matter that *must not touch*?' ('In Times to Come', *Astounding Science-Fiction*, December 1942, p. 74). And he introduced Hal Clement's 'Technical Error' as a similar puzzle: 'You try figuring out how to turn an oval object in a close-fitting oval hole!' ('In Times to Come', *Astounding Science-Fiction*, December 1943, p. 32). As Sam Moskowitz noted, Campbell 'favored the scientific problem story' (*Seekers of Tomorrow*, p. 416) and printed many stories of this type by contributors like Williamson, George O. Smith, and Ross Rocklynne.

However, he also used the language of 'problem' and 'solution' to celebrate other stories that did not take that particular form, including Anthony Boucher's 'Barrier', Heinlein's *The Day after Tomorrow* (*Sixth Column*) and *Beyond This Horizon*, and Asimov's 'Nightfall' and *Foundation* stories.[9] By reading a wide variety of science fiction stories, the emerging scientific élite sought by Campbell could find stimulating puzzles and problems to ponder and could get something more than the scientific information celebrated by Gernsback: practice in scientific thinking—enhancing the conventional scientific education that they receive elsewhere, and possibly influencing them to be imaginative in other ways.

Such practice could be seen as a form of scientific education, a needed accompaniment to traditional scientific training, which Campbell regarded as rather limited: a scientist 'has been trained to consider purely, solely, and exclusively physical facts' ('The Place of Science Fiction', p. 19). Science fiction thus offered a more exciting, involving type of scientific education.

A good analogy to explain how Campbell differed from Gernsback in this area is the contrast between scientific education in high school, which primarily involves absorbing and memorizing facts, and scientific education in college, which, while still including important information to learn, focuses more on laboratory work and scientific problem-solving. Gernsback, who lacked a college education, essentially envisioned science fiction as a kind of high-school education: here are the facts in the stories that you should learn, and here is the quiz—literally, in the monthly 'What Do You Know?' feature. Campbell, with a BA in physics, saw science fiction as similar to college education: here is a problem you should be able to solve, and submit your answers to me.

There is an interesting contrast, then, in Gernsback's and Campbell's use of science fiction stories as bases for contests. As noted, Gernsback employed Geoffrey Hewelcke's 'Ten Million Miles Sunward' as a contest in spotting a factual error in science. Campbell employed Heinlein's 'Solution Unsatisfactory' as a contest in thinking through a scientific problem: 'this story presents a problem mankind must solve, soon or late. The problem can be generalized to cover any irresistible weapon: *how can it be controlled...* The solution [in this story] is unsatisfactory from start to finish. But—is there a better one? Can you suggest one?' ('Editor's Note' to 'Solution Unsatisfactory', p. 86).[10]

At this point, a contradiction of sorts in Campbell's thinking emerges. Having accepted and celebrated the power of science fiction to pose challenging 'scientific problems' for its readers, Campbell should naturally have accepted the logical possibilities of stories which combined science fiction and detective fiction—the other established genre that regularly involved a focus on problem-solving. However, Campbell publicly and repeatedly argued that the combination was impossible, that 'Detective stories in science-fiction are decidedly unsatisfying' for this reason:

> they're supposed to be a challenge for the reader to solve the case before the explanation is given. In science-fiction, they're fundamentally unfair. The locked-door mystery, for instance, might be solved by (a) the villain's possession of an invisibility suit, (b) a fourth-dimensional penetration, (c) time-travelling, or, (d) radio transmission of the murderer into and out of the locked room. Neat, nice, but not fair to the reader; the author can pull anything he wants out of the hat. ('In Times To Come', *Astounding Science-Fiction*, May 1941, p. 87)

However, that comment came while previewing a story, Ross Rocklynne's 'Time Wants a Skeleton', which Campbell acknowledged was something of an exception; and years later, in a letter to Clement, he admitted he had been wrong: 'Once upon a time I told you "Science fiction detective stories don't work—you can't write a good one". So you proved I was wrong in that, and wrote "Needle"' (letter to Hal Clement, 12 April 1953, p. 142).

Still, Campbell never publicly changed his position, creating a paradox: nothing in Gernsback's theories justified a science fiction detective story, yet Gernsback promoted the form and even published a magazine devoted to such stories. Campbell's theories provided a perfect justification for science fiction detective stories, yet Campbell denied that the form was legitimate.

Referring to science fiction prophecies, Campbell added a number of new defences.

First, in the infancy of the modern genre, Gernsback had celebrated individual science fiction authors for their creativity and possible insight; Campbell, speaking after the writers and readers of science fiction had grown into a genuine community, saw the entire genre debating, developing and presenting useful ideas:

> Science-fiction has the interesting characteristic of causing its own predictions to come true. Since the stories are frequently written as a spare-time hobby by professional engineers—and thoroughly competent ones—they frequently contain sound engineering suggestions... The Manhattan Project scientists read science-fiction, so did the Nazi scientists working on V-2 at Peenemunde... Genuine engineering minds have considered the problems [of rocket spaceships], mulled them over, argued them back and forth in stories, and worked out the basic principles that will most certainly appear in the first ships built—partly because their builders will have read the magazines, seen the stories, and recognized the validity of the science-fiction engineering! ('The Science of Science-Fiction', pp. 5–6)

Science fiction is thus a kind of gigantic, continuing scientific brainstorming session, where worthwhile ideas are 'argued... back and forth in stories', and the concepts which finally emerge are worth considering and possibly valuable because they represent not only the conclusions of isolated individuals, but the reasoned conclusions of a group of qualified individuals who 'started going into detail', so 'This type of suggestion becomes prophecy' ('Science-Fiction Prophecy', p. 4—where the argument is restated).

While celebrating the collective scientific acumen of science fiction writers, Campbell also argued that science fiction could go beyond creating new scientific ideas to consider thoughtfully the implications, and possible effects on society, of those ideas. In this way, science fiction performed duties that were unlike those of science. Science fiction writers required 'An understanding of how political and social set-ups react to technological changes' so that they could examine both 'new and still undiscovered phenomena' and 'what the results look like when applied... to human society' ('Introduction', *Venus Equilateral*, pp. 9, 10). As he once explained:

> For a long time... if men tried a new idea, and it proved to be an exceedingly sour one, the result was disastrous to a relatively small group. Unfortunately, a small group, today, may be able to try out some interesting idea that happens to involve the annihilation of the planet Earth. The old method of trial and error comes to a point where it is no longer usable—the point where one more error means no more trials... Science fiction can provide for a science-based culture—which ours is, willy-nilly, and must be, since science is inherently available by the nature of the universe—a means of practicing out in the no-practice area. We can safely practice anything in imagination—suicide, murder, anything whatever... the important aspect of imaginative exploration of areas of no practice is that the basic outlines of the consequences of a particular course of action can be worked out. ('The Place of Science Fiction', pp. 16, 17, 20)[11]

This significantly augments Gernsback's defence of science fiction prophecy: Gernsback praised science fiction for because it could inspire new inventions, while Campbell praises science fiction because it can prepare society for the *effects* of new inventions.

In exploring the 'consequences' of scientific innovations in human society, science fiction writers did what scientists were not capable of doing: 'in his professional life', Campbell claimed, 'the physical scientist must *not* consider human wishes' ('The Place of Science Fiction', p. 19). The commentaries in science fiction would thus be interesting both to scientists who create new inventions and those who make decisions about new inventions. Specifically, science fiction, unlike other offshoots of science, could be a critic of the scientific community—work Campbell believed would be welcome and useful: 'Science is *not* a sacred cow—but there are a large number of would-be sacred cowherds busily devoting quantities of time, energy and effort to the task of making it one, so they can be sacred cowherds' ('Introduction', *Prologue to Analog*, p. 13). With their valuable independent outlook, science fiction writers thus became an important factor in improving—and controlling—scientific progress. In two letters, Campbell described this purpose more succinctly: 'science fiction needs to fulfill its job of stimulating people to try for something better than we have, or have had' (letter to Lurton Blassingame, 4 March 1959, p. 364), and

'The function of science-fiction is to indicate wrong answers, and why they're wrong, as well as suggesting right answers and possibilities!' (letter to Howard Myers, 17 May 1968, p. 536).

As another argument, Campbell in expansive moments would envision science fiction predictions as effective commentary on a variety of conditions and problems—not just the impact of future scientific discoveries. Science fiction was 'a way of considering the past, present, and future from a different viewpoint, and taking a look at how else we *might* do things... a convenient analog system for thinking about new scientific, social, and economic ideas—and for re-examining old ideas' ('Introduction', *Prologue to Analog*, p. 13). In this way, science fiction was similar to, but better than, other forms of literature: 'science-fiction is the ideal medium for doing that sort of examining. It's so much easier to recognize the foolishness of the fanatical fights of the Liliputians [*sic*] over Big-Endianism and Little-Endianism than to consider some of our own political squabbles' ('Introduction', *Cloak of Aesir*, p. 13–14). This theme sometimes came up in Campbell's letters: he told Philip José Farmer that 'the essence of good science-fiction is the introduction and development of a new and different idea, or viewpoint... science-fiction begins when you take a divergent viewpoint, and make the reader gradually understand that that cockeyed viewpoint... is a sound, wise, and rational way of life... [Tom Godwin's] 'The Cold Equations' was a test of that idea' (letter to Philip José Farmer, 30 July 1955, pp. 290, 293). Thus, science fiction is not simply designed to comment on scientific advances and possibilities; rather, it is a mechanism for examining virtually any accepted idea or philosophy.

While this purpose is often ascribed to literary works of all kinds, Campbell added a final defence of science fiction prophecy that cast the genre as fulfilling a function that no other form of literature could fulfil: science fiction, also as prominently illustrated by Godwin's 'The Cold Equations', could present an entirely different perspective on the universe—a scientific perspective—which was more valuable, and more relevant to modern conditions, than older literary perspectives:

> Where classical values hold that human nature is enduring, unchanging, and uniform, science-fiction holds that it is mutable, complex, and differentiated. David Riesman... has suggested that there are three basic personality types: the Tradition-Directed man, the Inner-Directed, and the Other-Directed. But there's a fourth type that only *appears* to be Inner-Directed. Let's call it the Universe-Directed type... The Universe-Directed type isn't ruled by opinions—he's dominated by the facts of the Universe.

With this attitude, science fiction writers are led to prophecies which transcend personal biases and inclinations:

> There's a human tendency to assume that what the prophet predicts is what he *wants* to have happen. The pilot... [of Godwin's] 'The Cold Equations' predicted accurately what *would* happen—but that had no relationship whatever to what he *wanted* to happen. A mother can tell her child exactly what will happen if he sticks his hand in the fire; that doesn't mean she *wants* it to happen. ('Science Fiction and the Opinion of the Universe', pp. 10, 43)

In starting with a fundamental attention to cold scientific fact, then, and in its willingness to anticipate coming changes because of scientific fact, science fiction was easily superior, as he once maintained, to other forms of literature:

> The essence of 'main stream literature' is that There Are Eternal Truths And Nothing Really Changes.
> Sure, the Fundamental Things Remain... but their value changes. Instincts several hundred million years old remain in Man... but they no longer constitute the dominant force in Man... The Ancient Fundamentals make the entire body of mainstream literature— which is, today, almost one hundred per cent purely escape literature. The soft, almost formless, nearly pointless stories found in the mass-circulation magazines are a wonderful retreat from the reality that is somewhat more fundamental than the ones they choose to consider. ('Non-Escape Literature', p. 228)

And he told Boucher that 'The great crime of science-fiction that produces acute uneasiness in the normal, well-adjusted individual is that it proposes... that the Eternal Verities are neither eternal nor verities', so 'Trying to get true, opinion-oriented people to read and understand and enjoy sf is inherently impossible; it requires the emotional courage to accept slavery to the "merely mechanical" level of fact' (letter to Tony Boucher, 18 May 1956, pp. 319, 315).

Overall, then, Campbell sees science fiction not as a corrective adjunct to the scientific community—Gernsback's plan—but as a new, autonomous power in society, offering stimulating education to future scientists, valuable conclusions about proposed scientific ideas to scientists and other authorities, useful commentaries on a wide variety of social issues and problems, and a uniquely scientific perspective on all matters of human concern.

In a sense, Campbell's vision of science fiction was less subversive than Gernsback's in claiming no effort to elevate the uneducated or address the masses; instead, science fiction was written by and written for those already in the elite. However, these features actually intensified the genre's power to change the scientific community and society. First, science fiction sought as readers young people planning to be scientists; by making those readers more imaginative and creative, the genre might make them scientists less inclined to accept orthodox opinions. Arguably, it is more effective to encourage those already about to be members of the scientific community to change their minds instead of, in Gernsback's way, trying to recruit and insert outsiders into that community. Second, science fiction, as a separate forum for commentary concerning scientific research, might achieve even more authority than the scientific community, in that its alternative attitudes might influence decisions involving scientific research; while researchers might seek permission—and support—to develop a certain device, science fiction, by pointing out the implications and dangers of that device, might persuade authorities to reject the proposal. Finally, in going beyond scientific issues to discuss other important matters, science fiction might achieve the broad social impact of other successful forms of literature.

Like Gernsback, Campbell shaped his magazine to reflect his goals. Not wishing to attract general readers, he eliminated the outlandish illustrations of aliens and spaceships previously seen on the covers of science fiction magazines, substituted more subdued paintings, like astronomically accurate scenes of planetary surfaces, and announced, '*Astounding* has taken the word *garish* from the description vocabulary of its covers' ('In Times to Come', *Astounding Science-Fiction*, October 1938, p. 11). Thinking the title *Astounding* rather juvenile, he progressively reduced the size of that word on the cover and increased the size of *Science-Fiction*; and Alva Rogers's *A Requiem for Astounding* and other sources report that he planned to rename the magazine *Science-Fiction* but could not do so because another short-lived magazine appeared with that name. He finally found a way to get rid of the word 'astounding' in 1961 by renaming the magazine *Analog: Science Fact/Science Fiction* (quickly switched to *Analog: Science Fiction/Science Fact*). Yet while making the magazine more dignified, and regularly printing scientific articles, Campbell did not imitate the features of a scientific journal—he felt no need to, for in his view science fiction had a unique dignity and purpose of its own.

Instead of footnotes and diagrams, Campbell expressed the importance of science fiction by repeatedly conducting and reporting on readership surveys, which to him demonstrated that the genre was having an impact:

> The remaining question is, obviously, whether science-fiction magazines are actually doing anything having a detectable influence on society.

In the case of my own magazine, *Astounding* Science Fiction, the readership represents only about 0.2 per cent of the population of the United States. This minute fraction would appear to be completely unimportant...

However, reader surveys show the following general data: that the readers are largely young men between twenty and thirty-five, with a scattering of younger college students, and older professional technical men; and that nearly all the readers are technically trained and employed... the readership... represents a good one third of the young technical personnel of the nation... nearly all the creative work of mankind has been done by young men between twenty and thirty-five; the older man specializes in executive management of the enterprise created during his younger years.

We can say, then, that the magazine is reaching about one third of the men in the most creative age levels... Science-fiction magazines are not entirely without effect, despite their relatively small circulation. ('The Place of Science Fiction', pp. 21–22)

Thus, Campbell argued his readers were uniquely influential, and that science fiction was uniquely influential for that reason.

Overall, one readily sees the smoothing-out, the amelioration, the improvement of Gernsback's theories in the hands of Campbell. Indeed, while one anticipated reaction to my explanations of the theories of Hugo Gernsback was—So what?—the most common reaction to explanations of the theories of Campbell will be—Of course. In fact, the ideas about science fiction first promulgated by Campbell have effectively permeated modern critical commentary of all kinds, although Campbell is rarely if ever acknowledged as their source.

First, the idea that science fiction was no longer purely 'thrilling adventure' surfaces in Robert Scholes and Eric S. Rabkin's denunciation of A. E. van Vogt's *Slan* as 'not fiction for adults' (*Science Fiction*, p. 52); and the argument that science fiction can take many different forms is evident in efforts to identify the genre with forms such as satire (Kingsley Amis), utopia (Darko Suvin), and the Gothic novel (Brian W. Aldiss).

Second, the idea that science fiction must pay more attention to people, and less attention to machines, was promulgated by Damon Knight, who insisted that works in the genre be judged by 'ordinary critical standards' such as 'originality, sincerity, style, construction, logic, coherence, sanity, garden-variety grammar' (*In Search of Wonder*, p. 1); and virtually all academic critics have evaluated science fiction stories by such standards.

Third, the idea that science fiction should not incorporate lengthy explanations, but should provide data in a more subtle manner, is routinely accepted without much emphasis; for example, Isaac Asimov, after saying that science fiction must display 'some indication that the writer knows science', immediately adds that 'This does not mean that the science has to be detailed and stultifying; there need only be casual references—but the references must be correct' (*Asimov on Science Fiction*, p. 241).

Fourth, the idea that science fiction should not be limited to the hard sciences, but should fruitfully explore the social sciences and pseudo-sciences as well, is often advanced by critics; for example, Willis McNeely concludes in a 1968 essay that 'It may be that the inclusion of theology—and the other "soft" sciences—as viable subject matter is one step toward the restoration of SF's human element' (*Nebula Award Stories Four*, p. xviii).

Fifth, the idea that science fiction demands a thoroughly detailed and consistent background for its predicted future worlds has long been a standard criterion for judging science fiction works; as early as 1945, Knight criticized van Vogt's *The World of Null-A* because it 'abounds in contradictions', is filled with 'loose ends and inconsistencies', and has a generally illogical background that 'is as bad as no background at all' *(In Search of Wonder*, pp. 48, 51, 55). Scholes and Rabkin similarly criticize van Vogt's Slan as 'riddled with internal inconsistencies' (*Science Fiction*, p. 52). And Suvin argues that:

> If the suggested alternative world, or the alternative formal framework, is not suggested *consistently*—if, that is, the discrete syntagmatic novelties are not sufficiently numerous and sufficiently compatible to induce a coherent 'absent paradigm', or indeed if the novelty is, without regard for its logically to be expected consequences, co-opted and neutralized into the current ideological paradigm—then the reader's specific SF pleasure will be mutilated or destroyed. (*Positions and Presuppositions in Science Fiction*, p. 67)

Yet Suvin's statement is little more than an elaboration on Campbell's 'Mapping out a civilization of the future is an essential background to a convincing story of the future... you've got to have that carefully mapped outline in mind to get consistency of minor details' ('The Old Navy Game', p. 6).[12]

Sixth, the idea that science fiction should provide thought-provoking puzzles to solve or problems to ponder, while less prominent in recent considerations of the genre, occasionally surfaces, as in Everett F. Bleiler and T. E. Dikty's 1950 statement that 'Science-fiction is... intellectually aimed; often it is just as much a riddle or puzzle tale as the whodunit' (*The Best Science Fiction 1950*, p. 19), and in Asimov's defence of the science fiction detective story at the beginning of *Asimov's Mysteries*.

Seventh, the notion that science fiction represents a process of consensually creating and discussing scientific ideas has long been recognized within the science fiction community; as Donald A. Wollheim notes in *The Universe Makers*, 'Somewhere in the early days of the literature someone invented a premise, argued it out with scientific (or more likely pseudoscientific) logic and convinced the readers. Once the argument is made, the premise is at once accepted on its own word, enters the tool shed of the science-fiction writer, and may be utilized thereafter by any craftsman without further repetition of the operational manual' (p. 14).

Eighth, the argument that science fiction could help society anticipate the possible effects of future scientific developments dates back to the first academic study of science fiction, J. O. Bailey's *Pilgrims through Time and Space*, which says that:

> Some of this fiction has dealt thoughtfully with concrete instances of startling new discoveries in science, their impact upon man's life, and the various possible readjustments to them. It is only fiction, but it may have graphic value now that we have got to anticipate a course of events in what is essentially a realm of sheer, unpredictable fiction, the future. Insofar as statesmen today need facts, fiction has nothing to offer, but insofar as we all need to bring to the consideration of certain new facts, such as atomic power, every scrap of foresight we can find, many pieces of this fiction are worth review. (p. 2)

Ninth, the idea that science fiction should be employed to consider and comment on political and social problems now is almost a truism; thus, Fredric Jameson casually refers to 'the various logical worlds of science fiction, in which our own universe is reduplicated at an experimental level' (*Marxism and Form*, p. 11).

Finally, the argument that science fiction provides a unique, and a uniquely scientific, viewpoint on certain issues sometimes occurs in others' defences of the genre; consider, for example, Gunn's characterization of 'The Cold Equations' as 'a touchstone story because if readers don't understand it they don't understand science fiction. The intellectual point made by the story is that sentimentality divorced from knowledge and rationality is deadly... Perhaps the point of the story is science-fictional after all; where else would such a point be made; by what other audience would it be understood? And considered satisfying?' ('The Readers of Hard Science Fiction', pp. 72–73).

As I hope is clear, I am not arguing that Campbell necessarily originated all these descriptions of or arguments for science fiction; however, by bringing these ideas together and forcefully articulating them, he undoubtedly has had a powerful impact on modern perceptions of science fiction, and it is tempting for that reason to maintain that Campbell in essence originated the modern genre. However, as already argued, the principles of Gernsback have also remained as a strong influence on the genre, so it is necessary to sort out the different roles Gernsback and Campbell have played in describing and defending science fiction.

Essentially, Gernsback established the hidden agenda of science fiction; while Campbell established its public agenda.

That is, despite what one might call their inner logic, Gernsback's theories unquestionably display some outer stupidity. Writers and readers of science fiction could not hold their heads up high and defend their genre by arguing that it was juvenile adventure designed to give young readers a scientific education while tossing out ideas that might inspire a scientist to build something or serve as the basis for a patent. A more intelligent characterization and defence of science fiction—as a matter of public relations, if nothing else—was clearly necessary.

And that is where Campbell stepped in, to soothe those alarmed by Gernsback's pronouncements and murmur reassuringly about the genre's true nature and value. Of course, Campbell said, science fiction was not merely 'thrilling adventure' for children, but rather could take many—and more mature—forms; of course it was not simply fiction about machines and ideas, but rather about people and their interactions with machines and ideas; of course it need not include long explanatory passages about science, but could convey its data in more subtle and acceptable ways; of course it was not simply concerned with rays and machines, but rather reflected a broad preoccupation with all aspects of science; of course it did not simply offer isolated ideas, but rather presented logical and fully developed imaginary worlds; of course it was not designed simply to teach scientific facts, but rather to stimulate one's imagination and thinking; of course it was not a collection of individual writers' wild ideas, but reflected a broad range of thoughtful opinion; and of course it was not simply a source of ideas for inventions, but rather was intended to thoughtfully explore all sorts of possible developments and their consequences, in fact to offer observations on all aspects of human civilization, and possibly to illustrate harsh truths that other forms of literature evade. With these arguments, writers were free from the naïve and restrictive demands of Gernsback and could thus produce better fiction; and readers could more convincingly argue for the literary and social value of science fiction.

Writers and readers responded to Campbell's new and improved arguments, and the arguments surely influenced them; but they did not forget Gernsback's arguments, even if they were not so energetic in announcing and defending them.

However, there was one problematic effect of Campbell's reforms: while Gernsback's focus on scientific education and scientific prediction applied only to science fiction, and kept writers focused on science fiction, some of Campbell's principles could apply to other forms of writing and could inspire writers to leave the field of science fiction. Thus, if writers, readers, and critics do not detect the presence of Gernsback, and try to build an approach to science fiction solely on Campbell, they discover a paradox: Gernsback's theories are divisive and contradictory, yet they serve to keep the genre together, because they steer writers to produce science fiction and only science fiction; Campbell's theories are more unified and consistent, yet some of their elements have constantly threatened to tear the genre apart, because they steer writers to produce other types of literature.

Thus, observing science fiction from 1950 onwards, one sees the unity of the Gernsback era weakened, as various writers in various ways are driven away from writing in the tradition of science fiction and instead evade the demands of science fiction, borrow the standards or conventions of other genres, or leave the field to write in other genres. And while Campbell cannot be entirely blamed for these tendencies—since he often reflected developments rather than initiating them—it is surely true that in bringing together and celebrating these new principles, Campbell contributed to the phenomenon, so the ideas of Gernsback, not Campbell, have enabled the genre to endure as a distinct entity.

To describe the nature of modern science fiction, then, one could employ the imagery of Carl Sagan's *The Dragons of Eden*, which pictures human intelligence as the combination of an advanced mammalian brain which has embedded in it a more primitive reptilian brain. That is, the theories of Campbell represent the mammalian brain of science fiction—thoughtful, intelligent, probing and exploratory, altogether admirable and respectable. However, lurking within this attractive cluster of motives is the reptilian brain of Gernsback—simple-minded, naïve, childlike, rather less than admirable and less than respectable. Yet both sets of thought patterns can be detected in science fiction. That is, modern writers may well set out to ponder the implications of some new scientific ideas, examine human reactions, or offer profound commentary on human society—the priorities of the Campbell mammalian brain; but lurking within their consciousness, they will still feel the urge to simultaneously meet high literary standards and entertain twelve-year-olds, to adhere strictly to scientific laws and perhaps slip in an explanation or two, or to present an interesting idea that might inspire an actual invention—the priorities of the Gernsback reptilian brain.

As an explanatory model for the critical heritage of modern science fiction, this will do.

Notes

1 Two exceptions would be his divergent views on science fiction history, discussed in the next chapter, and his changing opinion of science fiction detective stories, discussed below.

2 As an example, several of Campbell's statements in the 1940s stressed that science fiction writers must work expository material into their fiction without long interruptions; later, he was publicly silent on the subject. Had he changed his mind? No, for in a 1959 letter to Luther Blassingame, he again made that point. Rather, Campbell felt that by the 1950s, writers and readers understood the principle, so there was no need to mention it again.

3. I attribute all editorial writings in Campbell's magazines—editorials, responses to letters, blurbs, and the monthly columns 'In Times to Come' and 'The Analytical Laboratory'—to Campbell, who by all accounts wrote all such materials himself.

4 Like Gernsback, Campbell did not insist on complete scientific accuracy: 'Minor goofs in science—provided they're not crucial to the theme of the story—can be forgiven' ('Science Fiction We Can Buy', p. 28).

5 Though Alva Rogers notes earlier precedents for Heinlein's approach: 'The idea of a working outline of background events to be used from story to story was not, of course, entirely new (Neil R. Jones, several years earlier, had a plan of the future into which he fitted most of his stories; Manly Wade Wellman and Eando Binder also used connected backgrounds for a number of their stories), but all of these were mere skeltal [*sic*] outlines compared to Heinlein's comprehensive future' (*A Requiem for Astounding*, p. 91).

6 James Blish noted this aspect of Campbell's approach: 'most of us are aware of his admiration for elaborately worked-out story backgrounds'. And he saw Campbell's publication of Clement's essay on writing *Mission of Gravity*, 'Whirligig World', as 'addressed primarily to *Astounding's* writers' to demonstrate how a science fiction story should be written (*The Issues at Hand*, pp. 45, 47).

7 Years later, it should be noted, Campbell indicated that his own approach to writing science fiction was both similar to and different from his recommended method:

> Writing, so far as I have been able to make it out, is just about a 100% subconscious function, with the conscious mind sort of reading over your shoulder, interestedly watching what the story says. 'I' doesn't do it—something else does the job.
>
> When I was writing, I'd start, usually, with a very general idea, and figure out an ending. Then the hardest thing was figuring out where to begin the story. (Letter to Gordon R. Dickson, 25 September 1967, p. 508)

While Campbell claimed to rely on his subconscious, he acknowledged that he knew how the story would end before he began writing it.

8 Years later, he made the same point that fantasy 'inherently... says, "I know you don't believe this, and I don't believe it either, but we can have fun pretending". Science-fiction—to be good science-fiction—must not have that approach' (letter to E. J. Carnell, 16 June 1964, p. 433). The same argument surfaces again in his 'Introduction' to *14 Great Tales about ESP*.

9 Boucher's 'Barrier', Campbell said, is 'An ingenious explanation of one

of the old and well-known problems of time travel' ('In Times to Come', *Astounding Science-Fiction*, August 1942, p. 98); Heinlein's '"Sixth Column"... poses a rather lovely problem, and, finally, an even more fascinating answer' ('In Times to Come', *Astounding Science-Fiction*, December 1940, p. 112); he praised Asimov's 'Nightfall' because it 'discusses... How would men believe— and what—if the stars appeared but once in a millennium or two?... Asimov has an idea, and a story' ('In Times to Come', *Astounding Science-Fiction*, August 1941, p. 36); and of Asimov's 'Bridle and Saddle' (later incorporated into *Foundation*), he said, 'Given: a Foundation with much knowledge, much skill, and no military resources... How can the few, the weak—but the wise—men of the Foundation rule, as they must if they would not die?' (introduction to 'Bridle and Saddle', p. 9). Of course, since Campbell provided the story lines of *Sixth Column* and 'Nightfall', Campbell in those cases was essentially celebrating his own ingenuity.

10 A similar invitation to readers to think scientifically accompanied L. Sprague de Camp's article, 'Design for Life', about 'the engineering of life forms', challenging 'any reader or readers to think up a method of locomotion that hasn't been tried by some form of life here on Earth that is possible to life's necessities' ('In Times to Come', *Astounding Science-Fiction*, May 1938, p. 92).

11 He makes the same point in his 'Introduction' to *Venus Equilateral*, quoted in the next chapter, and his 'Introduction' to *14 Great Tales about ESP*: 'Good science fiction seeks to work out, in fiction, the meanings and probable consequences of new ideas—before the same new ideas slap us in the face as reality. It gives one a chance to duck a little—or at least be prepared' (p. 13).

12 Yet Suvin, unaware that Campbell was probably the first person to apply the adjective 'consistent' to science fiction, attempts to derive the principle from an obscure Wells lecture.

'A Characteristic Symptom of this Stage of Evolution': John W. Campbell, Jr's History of Science Fiction

There are several reasons why Hugo Gernsback examined the history of science fiction. He had a genuine interest in some older writers, especially Verne; attempting to explain a new category of literature to the public, he had to find and present a number of notable and familiar examples to illustrate what type of story he was describing; and since his magazines often reprinted older works, Gernsback needed to establish an extended history of science fiction to justify the practice.

In contrast, John W. Campbell, Jr had every reason to ignore the history of science fiction. While Reginald Bretnor reports that he read Verne and Wells as a child (*Modern Science Fiction*, p. 3), he seems to have developed no strong fondness for these or other older writers; when he became editor of *Astounding Science-Fiction*, the idea of science fiction was fairly common and well-accepted, so that there was no need to offer a number of older examples of the genre; and he had inherited a magazine which proudly proclaimed and maintained a 'No Reprints' policy, so he had no practical incentive for a thoroughgoing look at previous literature.

Nevertheless, in various editorials, articles, introductions and letters, Campbell occasionally discussed the history of science fiction in a general way, emphasizing certain authors and certain themes; and while he does not merit the status of a science fiction historian, he is interesting as a commentator on that history. In particular, Campbell offers two distinct and irreconcilable visions of science fiction history, which together provide one indication of the entire genre's divided view of itself.

In his first discussion of science fiction history, Campbell argued that science fiction actually did not have any history; instead, it was a new and unprecedented form of literature:

> Any form of entertainment that finds a considerable audience of patrons must grow out of some fundamental characteristic of the civilization which it serves. Most basic of all characteristics in any of

Man's civilizations must be the nature of Man—which doesn't change appreciably in any such brief span as the ten millennia of recorded history.

It's not surprising, in view of this, that the recorder of happenings—the reporter—existed in Babylon and exists today. The historian, the playwright, the dancer—all existed... Save for one thing. Science-fiction finds no counterpart in the entertainment of history. They had fantasy—but science-fiction isn't pure fantasy. They had prophecy—but it wasn't entertainment; it was protection, necessary defense against the blank terror of the unknown future.

For the first time in all Man's climb, science-fiction has appeared. As a form of entertainment that has attracted tens and hundreds of thousands of readers, it must represent some totally new characteristic of our civilization... It arises, I think, in this: for the first time in all the history of Man's climb, he looks *forward* to better things, and not backward to a forgotten 'Golden Age'.

Science-fiction rose when men reached that stage of civilization that looked forward gladly... science-fiction is not a happenstance, a fad that comes and goes by chance listing of public interest, but a characteristic symptom of this stage of evolution, a type of entertainment that would, inevitably, arise in any civilization that reached this particular level of advance. ('Future Tense', p. 6)

In this account, science fiction emerged only when technological developments inspired a true sense of optimism about the future; previous writings about the future, lacking this feeling, are not really science fiction. Thus, the emergence of science fiction was destined to happen—'It's as inevitable an outgrowth of our time as is the vacuum tube and the rocket plane' ('Introduction', *The Astounding Science Fiction Anthology*, p. x)—and in the conclusion of 'Future Tense' Campbell announced that any technological civilization will 'inevitably' develop science fiction.

In 1952, Campbell was more specific about when science fiction appeared and offered a rather different explanation of its origins:

No extensive development of a literary form, the work of many keen and highly trained minds, can take place without some powerful social force behind it. Normally, such a development starts uncertainly, in a loose, uncertain and self-conscious manner; only with passing years and interacting development does it begin to find itself, and its agents of expression—the authors... by 1890... the Technological Revolution started... Science fiction is the literature of the Technological Era. It, unlike other literatures, assumes that change is the natural order of things, that there are goals ahead larger than those we know. ('Introduction', *The Astounding Science Fiction Anthology*, pp. ix, xi, xiii)

Here, the necessary condition for science fiction is not optimism about future changes but simply the new realization that future changes will be constant and far-reaching. This became a major theme in Campbell's discussions of science fiction: again and again, he argued that science fiction was a unique modern form of literature because it accepted and understood the importance of 'change'. In 1950, for example, he claimed that Robert A. Heinlein '"invented"... the use of that fact' that 'cultural patterns change', and while 'human nature doesn't change over the years... human nature is a reaction to group mores and the cultural pattern' ('Introduction', *The Man Who Sold the Moon*, pp. 13, 12).[1]

In such comments, Campbell offered a chronology of events in the early history of science fiction. The first important date was 1890, when 'the Technological Revolution' began—an interesting choice, since it coincides with the appearance of the 'scientific romance' in England, and since it indicates that H. G. Wells could be seen as the first major writer of science fiction. And in fact, Campbell displayed a certain amount of respect for Wells. After praising Heinlein for his ability to provide readers with 'an understanding of the cultural pattern', he noted that 'H. G. Wells did something of the sort in some of his novels' ('Introduction', *The Man Who Sold the Moon*, p. 13). In 1971, he said that three of Wells's novels 'were the "hard" science-fiction of their day' (letter to Jack Williamson, 7 January 1971, p. 592). And he praised Wells's *The Invisible Man* as a 'science-fiction story that explores what happens to an individual's character when he is suddenly possessed of absolute immunity to restraint by law, force, or society... This story was *not* a story of technology alone—though it was based on the Wonderful Invention theme' ('Introduction', *A World by the Tale*, p. 10). However, since Campbell advanced the time that science fiction emerged from the early nineteenth century—Gernsback's choice—to the late nineteenth century and Wells, one must ask: what about Poe and Verne, the other major writers that Gernsback identified as pioneers of science fiction?

To my knowledge, Campbell only mentioned a Poe story once, in a 1952 letter to Robert Moore Williams suggesting only that the mood and writing style of Gothic stories, while formerly legitimate in science fiction, were no longer appropriate in the modern genre:

A good many years back, you started selling yarns that had a lot of 'mood', and they went pretty well. They were in a way, rather like the Gothic horror story the 'Fall of the House of Usher' sort of thing, built up with *Roget's Theasaurus* [*sic*] and various sources of adjectives. Lovecraft did the same kind. I did some of them myself. As of the time and the slant of the field, they were right.

That was a dozen years ago, and the field's changed far and fast since then. We're older, too, you and I, and we've got to change with the change... In this story... some of the older style still lingers—and to the extent the adjectivies [*sic*], or *Roget's* Disease, lingers, the work is weakened.

The best writing is simple, clear, highly definite, and has the general characteristics of a fishnet. (Letter to Robert Moore Williams, 14 August 1952, pp. 66–67)

One might also recall his argument that science fiction existed to eliminate, not exploit, fear of the unknown,[2] further suggesting that stories like Poe's were not good examples for science fiction writers. Once he even suggested that traditional horror stories were not even good models for modern fantasy writers: 'Horror injected with a sharp and poisoned needle is just as effective as when applied with the blunt-instrument technique of the so-called Gothic Horror tale' ('Foreword', *From Unknown Worlds*, p. 3).

While Campbell talked about Verne more often, he usually mentioned Gernsback's 'favorite author' only to criticize or ridicule him: he pointed out the inadequacies of his device for a breathable spaceship atmosphere in *From the Earth to the Moon* ('The Science of Science-Fiction', p. 6), once described him as 'a hide-bound reactionary' ('Not Simply More', p. 6), and further argued that Verne's 'bright new dreams look rather silly now—his air machine in "Robur the Conqueror" is, as every twelve-year-old now knows, aerodynamically impossible. Most of his wild inventions are old stuff, and he's got 'em all wrong. There's no dream left in his stories, and, since they were built around those dreams, they seem silly' ('We Can't Keep Up!', p. 6). Campbell rejected Verne not only because his visions are now outdated—as Gernsback conceded in 'On Reprints'—but because Verne's ideas were 'all wrong' in the first place. Perhaps Verne lacked both the broader vision and technical expertise to write good science fiction by Campbell's standards.

The next crucial date in Campbell's history of science fiction was 1926—or thereabouts—when Gernsback provided the world with the idea of science fiction, although Campbell never mentions his name. Still, he wrote in 1953 that 'Science fiction is, at the present time, only about twenty-five years old as a self-aware system of literature' ('The Place of Science Fiction', p. 12)—making its birth date about 1928, or about the time when Gernsback was first publishing *Amazing Stories*. A year earlier, he had indicated that 'science fiction is young' and 'isn't yet the mature literature it should be' ('Introduction', *The Astounding Science Fiction Anthology*, pp. xiii, xv), further suggesting its recent origins. And while he devoted most of his energies to praising the modern authors in his stable, Campbell was willing to single out one of Gernsback's writers for special recognition: hearing of Philip Francis Nowlan's death in 1940, he announced that 'The quality of Nowlan's written science-fiction was certainly exceptionally high—even ten years ago, when magazine science-fiction was just starting' ('In Times to Come', April 1940, p. 71). Also, in 1946, he noted that Nowlan's original Buck Rogers stories 'were well and thoughtfully done... Phil Nowlan's first story of Rogers had an excellent dissertation on the military qualities and advantages of bazookas... ' ('Concerning Science Fiction', p. v).[3]

The third major date, variously indicated as 1935 or 1940, coincided with the emergence of Campbell as a science fiction editor; as he announced in 1953:

> The early science-fiction stories, about 1925 to 1935, were largely concentrated on technical devices per se. The development of means of releasing the vast energies known to be present in the atom. Methods of developing television, or space flights. Speculations as to what might be on the moon or Mars.
>
> But, beginning about 1935, the emphasis gradually shifted from technical to over-all cultural considerations. 'Yes, we could release atomic energy... but what would its effect on the culture be? If we had a free source of energy, would it mean the end of the coal, oil, and electric power industries... and if so, would that be advantageous to the culture as a whole?' ('The Place of Science Fiction', p. 12)

A year earlier, he had said that science fiction 'has, in the past decade, passed through its period of adolescence from the childhood form of self-consciousness and rambunctious play to a sincere self-searching. The decade from 1941 to 1951 is probably the most significant' ('Introduction', *The Astounding Science Fiction Anthology*, pp. ix–x). And in that piece, Campbell listed the 'strongest influences' and 'great shapers' of this era as Heinlein, Isaac Asimov, Lewis Padgett (Henry Kuttner and C. L. Moore), Jack Williamson, A. E. van Vogt, and Eric Frank Russell (p. xiv).

This change to the modern period involved at least two major developments that Campbell could take some credit for. First, the subject matter of science fiction expanded beyond engineering and technology to focus more on human and social issues: 'In older science fiction, the Machine and the Great Idea predominated. Modern readers—and hence editors!—don't want that; they want stories of people living in a world

where a Great Idea, or a series of them, and a Machine, or machines, form
the background. But it is the man, not the idea or machine that is the
essence' ('The Science of Science Fiction Writing', p. 92). Second, as noted,
there occurred improvements in the technique of writing science fiction:

> Wells's method was to spend two chapters or so describing, for the
> reader, the cultural pattern he wanted to operate against. In the
> leisurely '90's and early twentieth century, that was permissible. The
> reader accepted it. Long descriptive passages were common. But the
> development of literary technique in the last third of a century has
> changed that; stage techniques, where long character-descriptions
> are ruled out, have moved into the novel field. To-day, a reader won't
> stand for pages of description of what the author thinks the character
> is like; let the character act, and show his character... Heinlein was
> one of the first to develop techniques of story-telling that do it. Like
> the highly skilled acrobat, he makes his feats seem the natural, easy,
> simple way—but after you've finished and enjoyed one of his
> stories—'The Roads Must Roll', for example—notice how much of
> the cultural-technological pattern he has put over, without
> impressing you, at any point, with a two-minute lecture on the
> pattern of the time. It's a fine action yarn—with an almost incredible
> mass of discussion somehow slipped in between without interrupting
> the flow of action. ('Introduction', *The Man Who Sold the Moon*, pp.
> 13–14)

Although Campbell explicitly credited some of his own stories of the
1930s (collected in, and extolled in the introductions to, *Who Goes There?*
and *Cloak of Aesir*) for inspiring the first development, and suggested that
Heinlein largely inspired the second development, there was also implicit
praise for his own editorial acumen in recognizing and demanding this
new approach to science fiction. But Campbell also identified another
cause: increasingly sophisticated readers, whose expectations have grown
beyond mechanistic stories and who are now conditioned by their other
reading to expect improved writing techniques.

Because of the improvements in the 1940s, earlier science fiction now
seemed hopelessly outclassed, and Campbell was later critical of stories
published before he became an editor:

> Could [E. E. Smith's] 'Skylark of Space' be published, as a *brand-new
> work, today*? No, it could not. The present readers, *without previous
> indoctrination that* Skylark *is a classic*, would see that the love interest
> was poured from the syrup bottle, the science was nonsense, and, as
> E. E. Smith said, the whole thing is indefensible. You think 'Hawk

Carse' [a series of stories by Harry Bates in *Astounding Stories of Super-Science*] could get published today? Why not? Well, the science stunk [*sic*], the whole thing was wildly improbable, it was made up of clichés, it had no characterizations, and it was all black-white-good-evil-yes-no-without-evaluation nonsense. Totally unacceptable after [A. E. van Vogt's] 'The World of Null-A'. ('Editorial Number Three', p. xx)

Finally, in comments after 1950, Campbell identified a fourth era of science fiction, marked by a shift in its focus:

Up to about 1945, science fiction concentrated largely on physical science; this, actually, is a far less dangerous field than the field of the humanic sciences, because the available forces in the physical field are less powerful... Human thought, not atomic energy, is the most powerful force for either construction or destruction in the known universe. It is this aspect that science fiction is exploring today—the most dangerous and most magnificent of all *terra incognita* still lies a half inch back of your own forehead. Naturally, that is the next great area of exploration for science fiction! ('The Place of Science Fiction', pp. 20–21)

Similarly, he noted that:

With the development of science into engineering proceeding at the pace it has, by 1950 the major developments that science fiction had been forecasting were definitely under engineering—not theoretical—study. It was time for us to move on, if we were to fulfill our function as a frontier literature. To some extent, science fiction moved on into the social sciences—sociology, anthropology, and psychology. ('We *Must* Study Psi', p. 217)

Finally, while Campbell, unlike Gernsback, rarely made glowing predictions of science fiction's coming prominence, one letter did, as an analogy, offer this vision of the genre's future:

There'll come a time when science-fiction will be an orthodox literature, and only properly trained professionals will be considered fit contributors... because it will be recognized for what it is—a major cultural tool for reshaping the thinking of the more imaginative and creative citizens, from which group the future leaders inevitably arise. (Letter to Harry Stine, 16 May 1956, p. 309)

Thus, more than Gernsback, who tended to emphasize individual geniuses, Campbell saw the emergence and development of science fiction as a consequence of larger outside events. First, the Technological Revolution made it possible to write science fiction by establishing that change is the natural order of human existence and creating the need for a genre devoted to examining technological and other coming changes. Next, increasing numbers of works of this type led to an awareness of science fiction as a genre—which occurred around 1926—followed by improvements in other areas of literature and an increasingly sophisticated audience which inspired an improved approach to science fiction in the 1940s. Then, the realization of earlier science fiction predictions in the physical sciences around 1950 inspired a shift into the social sciences; and in the future, people will understand the importance of science fiction, which will make it a more prominent form of literature. In such a context, the contributions of particular individuals—even Campbell—emerge as less important.

If these were the only comments that Campbell had ever offered regarding science fiction history, one would have from him a reasonably consistent and logical picture of the subject which is not that dissimilar from more scholarly treatments: that is, there is at least one science fiction historian, Brian Stableford, who would agree that science fiction essentially originated in the 1890s ('Marriage of Science and Fiction'); most critics would agree that Gernsback's magazines significantly increased the visibility and popularity of science fiction; the noteworthy improvements in the science fiction of the 1940s which Campbell described are usually acknowledged as Campbell's contribution to the development of the genre, as in Brian W. Aldiss's *Trillion Year Spree*, James Gunn's *Alternate Worlds*, and countless other studies; and the shift into the social sciences in the 1950s is also repeatedly noted, though it is usually attributed to the influence of H. L. Gold's *Galaxy* and other new publications, not to Campbell.

However, particularly in later writings, Campbell made some remarks indicating that science fiction was far vaster, and far older, than the above chronology would suggest. In doing so, he may have been inspired by contemporary works like Bailey's *Pilgrims through Time and Space* (1947) and L. Sprague de Camp's *Science Fiction Handbook* (1953), both part of a general trend in the 1940s and 1950s to expand science fiction history; but certain aspects of his own theories also tended to lead him in this direction.

The contrast between Campbell's two views is illustrated by his two comments on Plato's *Republic*. In 1953, he noted that 'In the sense that science fiction is the literature of speculation about changes to come, Plato's *Republic* is science fiction of the sociological level. But it misses being true science fiction because it is presented simply as a logical argument' ('The Place of Science Fiction', p. 13). But fifteen years later, in 1968, he was not so equivocal: 'science fiction is... a great way to study social concepts—

to consider the logical human consequences of various cultural propositions, from absolute dictatorship to absolute anarchy. Which is, of course, why so many utopian, and negative-utopian novels, ranging from Plato's *Republic*, through *Utopia* itself, to Orwell's *1984*, have been science fiction' ('Introduction', *Analog 6*, p. xv). Even earlier, he had said in 1961 that 'Utopias have always been in the legitimate field of interest of science fiction' ('Constitution for Utopia', p. 181).

The key date of the change is 1952; for at the time Campbell was establishing the basic chronology of his earlier version of science fiction history in his 'Introduction' to *The Astounding Science-Fiction Anthology*, he elsewhere began to identify older writers like Aesop and Jonathan Swift as science fiction writers:

> While most people tend to think of [science fiction] as being Jules Verne and H. G. Wells up-to-date, perhaps we might better remember that the tradition goes back earlier to Gulliver's Travels and even to Aesop's Fables. Aesop, of necessity, talked to his contemporaries in terms of Foxes and Lions and Donkeys; in our more enlightened age we call those same characters Robots and Martians or Sarn. ('Introduction', *Cloak of Aesir*, pp. 13–14)

In a 1953 letter, he observed that 'Science-fiction is somewhat falsely identified as spaceships and BEM stuff. True, it can be. But its essential core is wide-open philosophical speculation—*Gulliver's Travels*, *Pilgrim's Progress*, and *Aesop's Fables* all belong in the same field' (letter to J. B. Rhine, 23 November 1953, p. 222). Another letter compared three plays by Aristophanes to Edgar Rice Burroughs's *Tarzan of the Apes*, suggesting they were similar works.[4] Finally, in discussing the nature of 'truth' in science fiction predictions, Campbell seemed prepared to accept the parables of Jesus as at least analogous to science fiction:

> But what a science-fiction prophet can say is, in essence, 'I don't know just how to do it—but there must be some way to accomplish this. And there is a good reason for trying to, because if we could, these highly desirable ends could be accomplished'—and then tell his story.
>
> There is, in other words, a great difference between a factually accurate and true statement—and a philosophically true statement. Were Jesus' parables 'true', for instance? Do you believe that there actually was a certain Samaritan, as a specific individual, who did the precise actions described in the parable of the good Samaritan? Few do, but nearly all recognize the philosophical truth of the point Jesus was making.

In that sense, Truth is not a matter that can be checked by consulting factual records—nor can truth in science-fiction's parables be determined by consulting the statements of modern scientific textbooks. ('These Stories May Upset You', p. 12).[5]

While he was now willing to acknowledge certain earlier works as science fiction, Campbell never claimed that anything resembling an *awareness* of science fiction as a genre existed at those times. Thus, on another occasion when he discussed *Gulliver's Travels* as an example of science fiction, he added that 'it wasn't knowingly written as such' ('The Place of Science Fiction', p. 12). Still, there remained another major inconsistency: none of these new 'science fiction' writers—Aesop, Plato, Aristophanes, Jesus, More, Bunyan, and Swift—fit within the parameters of science fiction history which Campbell previously had established and proclaimed.

One explanation would be that as Campbell changed the essential background of science fiction from a general optimism about change to simple recognition of the inevitability of change, he was obliged to accept as part of the genre a number of earlier works which inarguably envisioned major changes in human society. Thus, in discussing *Gulliver's Travels* as science fiction, he explicitly offered a rather expansive definition of the genre: 'science fiction is the literature of speculation as to what changes may come, and which changes will be improvements, which destructive, which merely pointless. Because our culture has now accepted change as the normal, instead of the abnormal, state of things, science fiction has become a regular instead of a sporadic phenomenon' ('The Place of Science Fiction', p. 13). Here, Campbell recalls Gernsback in seeing a contrast not between an older era of no science fiction and a modern era of science fiction—his original argument—but between an older era of 'sporadic' science fiction and a modern era of 'regular' science fiction.

Second, in later comments broadening his other ideas about science fiction to see the genre simply as a way to 'study social concepts', Campbell eliminated the link between science fiction and the modern scientific attitude towards change. Thus, almost any non-mimetic narrative—*Aesop's Fables, Pilgrim's Progress*, and the parables of Jesus—could be regarded as a kind of science fiction. The logical conclusion of this line of thinking is to declare, as Campbell did, that 'Science fiction is the perfectly logical offspring of the basic nature of man' ('The Place of Science Fiction', p. 5)— a far cry from his earlier statement that 'Science-fiction finds no counterpart in the entertainment of history'.

From this perspective, the modernity of science fiction was once explained by Campbell as an essentially superficial change, a matter of new and different settings for an old form of fiction: 'a Wonderful Invention type story... is, in many instances, simply a variation of the Utopian novel, which is at least as old as Plato's *Republic*. Gulliver found strange cultures via shipwreck; now that Earth is mapped, Utopian novelists and satirists have to use spaceshipwrecks' ('Introduction', *A World by the Tale*, p. 10).

As another aspect of his science fiction history, Campbell both accepted, and modified a bit, Gernsback's implicit list of the suitable generic models for science fiction; indeed, Campbell appears to know more about the subject of literary genres than Gernsback, since he actually employed terms like 'Gothic Horror tale' and 'utopia'. At various times, he accepted four of the five basic genres offered by Gernsback: in listing types of science fiction, he once mentioned 'Adventure science fiction' ('Concerning Science Fiction', p. vi), endorsing—while not celebrating—the model of juvenile adventure fiction; his discussions of Verne—however disparaging—suggested the model of the travel tale; as noted, he explicitly embraced utopia as a form of science fiction; and repeated references to Swift endorsed the model of satire for science fiction. Only Gothic horror, it seems, is completely excluded, as indicated by his critical comments regarding Poe.

However, Campbell added one major genre to Gernsback's list—the fable, and the related forms of parable and allegory. In making these additions, Campbell effectively opened the door for a whole new category of literature to enter the history of science fiction—namely, myths, legends, and folklore, all of which share the atmosphere of the fable.[6] And science fiction emphatically became not something that is closely connected to the rise of modern science, but rather a characteristic narrative form that has existed since the dawn of time, and the twentieth century was simply to contribute some new devices—like Martians and spaceships—to re-enact the ancient patterns.

Furthermore, in examining Campbell's choices of representative earlier science fiction works, one observes an effort to achieve a general gentrification of the genre's literary history. In assembling his own history, Gernsback displayed no particular aesthetic concerns, as he included writers with excellent reputations (Poe, Verne, Wells), writers with fading reputations (Fitz-James O'Brien, Garrett P. Serviss), and writers who never had any reputations at all (Richard Henry Locke, Luis Senarens). And, while he rarely named names, Campbell's first argument implicitly embraced all of modern science fiction—good and bad—as superior to older and modern works which did not accept the inevitability of change. He was thus willing to extravagantly praise modern writers like Nowlan and L. Ron Hubbard, claiming, for example, that 'H. G. Wells... never wrote anything more powerful than [Hubbard's] "Final Blackout"' ('In Times to Come', March 1940, p. 49).

However, in his later comments, Campbell focused on more elevated exemplars: Aesop, Plato, Aristophanes, and the Bible, representing classical literature; Thomas More, John Bunyan, and Jonathan Swift, representing the English literary tradition; and George Orwell, representing the best of modern 'mainstream' fiction. Campbell thus seems prepared to accept the notion that science fiction has a long and glorious literary history and to read out of that history those writers who do not seem sufficiently distinguished. Particularly significant, perhaps, are writers of the late nineteenth and early twentieth century that Campbell never mentioned, such as Garrett P. Serviss, A. A. Merritt, and Murray Leinster.[7] Since Campbell was surely well aware of their work from reading Gernsback's *Amazing Stories*, his apparent refusal to ever discuss them may stem in part from his perception that these were not really presentable literary ancestors for modern science fiction.[8]

Overall, the contradictions in Campbell's accounts of science fiction history, and the differences between his and Gernsback's history, reflect three basic tensions in discussion of the subject which, I argue, still surface in modern commentaries.

First, there is on the one hand a desire to maintain that science fiction is new and special, a unique reaction to modern scientific and social developments; on the other hand, there is an urge to link the genre to older traditions—in Campbell's case, those of satire, utopia, and fable— and to see science fiction as a continuation of traditional and respectable forms of writing.

Of course, Campbell's ongoing tendency to embrace more and more ancient works as science fiction is a pattern that is seen elsewhere: Gernsback himself first drew the line at the start of the nineteenth century and declared Poe was the first science fiction writer (in 'A New Sort of Magazine'); two months later, though, he tentatively embraced Roger Bacon and Leonardo da Vinci as possible ancestors of science fiction (in 'The Lure of Scientifiction'). Three years later, one of Gernsback's readers, James T. Brady, Jr, simultaneously accepted Poe as the father of science fiction and contrived to drag Aristophanes, *The Arabian Nights*, Cyrano de Bergerac and Swift into the fold ('History of Scientific Fiction'). Campbell began by drawing the line at the end of the nineteenth century and effectively made Wells the first science fiction writer; then he went on to add a number of earlier writers to the canon. In a sense, then, the history of science fiction emerges alternately as very short and as very long; and Campbell himself is noteworthy not because he resolved the dilemma—indeed, it may be fundamentally irresolvable—but because he expressed this contradiction with unusual force and clarity.

Second, there is a recurring conflict involving whether modern science fiction originated around the beginning of the nineteenth century—Gernsback's view—or around the end of that century—Campbell's view—an argument that persists in modern claims for either Mary Shelley or Wells as the true founder of the genre.

Finally, there is a dichotomy between science fiction as High Literature and science fiction as Popular Literature—an issue not unrelated to the above question of chronology. Beginning at the start of the nineteenth century, a historian takes in Gothic novels, the 'invention stories' of dime novels, and Verne's 'imaginary voyages', and all of these might tend to support the position that science fiction's origins were popular in nature. Beginning at the end of the nineteenth century, with Wells and the 'scientific romance', the genres that emerge as prominent are the utopia, dystopia, and satire, and science fiction's origins now appear to be more elevated in nature.

Thus Campbell to some extent reinforced Gernsback's vision of science fiction history, to some extent expanded upon it, and to some extent contradicted it altogether. This is not surprising, since all academic histories of science fiction also tend to be somewhat similar to each other and somewhat contradictory.

For commentators who argue that science fiction has a real history and truly existed as a tradition well before Gernsback, and thus that examinations of science fiction history represent investigations and discoveries of that tradition, the differences between Gernsback's and Campbell's history, and between many other histories of science fiction, must be seen as a problem: how can people examining the same subject reach such different conclusions concerning the origins and central texts of science fiction?

However, for commentators who see Gernsback, Campbell, and others as engaged in the construction, not the discovery, of histories of science fiction, their differences are not problematic, but can be seen as insightful reflections of their authors' attitudes towards science fiction and can be appreciated for that reason. That is, to illustrate their own ideas, and to locate models which validate their own concerns, Gernsback, Campbell, and anyone else who examines and explicates the subject of science fiction history will tend to focus on those time frames and those texts which are best suited to fulfil their purposes. In this way, therefore, a new and valuable subject for study emerges—the history of histories of science fiction—one which runs parallel to and illuminates the history of theories of science fiction; and Gernsback and Campbell can be seen as the first major figures in both of these ongoing processes.

Notes

1 The most extensive development of this point is probably in Campbell's editorial 'Non-Escape Literature'.

2 As he said in his 'Introduction' to *Venus Equilateral*:

> science-fiction can be not only fun, but an extremely valuable experience. If a friend steps out of a dimly lighted doorway it may provoke a 'Yipe!' of momentary fear, or a casual 'Hi', depending entirely on whether or not you expected to meet him there.
>
> The science-fiction reader is a lot less apt to jump in senseless fear and alarm when a new process comes from some unexpected doorway— he'll have been expecting it, and recognize a friend or an enemy—which can be very helpful to survival. (p. 12)

Thus, it seems, science fiction exists to dispel fear—not to inspire it, which is the traditional goal of the Gothic novel.

3 Of course, one reason Campbell mentioned Nowlan at this time was that after concentrating on the comic strip *Buck Rogers* for a while, Nowlan had just started a new series of stories for *Astounding Science-Fiction* at the time of his sudden death.

4 He told Poul Anderson:

> Ever read Aristophanes' plays 'The Birds', 'Lysestrata' [sic], or 'The Clouds'?... They're no more philosophical—less so, probably, than *Tarzan of the Apes*. Give me 100 high-power philosophers, though, and I'll find 100,000 deep comments of philosophical understanding in Tarzan! Burroughs may not have put it in there—but the philosophers can! (Letter to Poul Anderson, 6 December 1952)

5 Campbell briefly employed the same analogy in his earlier 'Introduction' to *A World by the Tale* (p. 7).

6 Years later, though, Campbell was less sanguine about Aesop as a model for science fiction writers; writing to Harry C. Crosby, Jr (Christopher Anvil) about a story, Campbell commented, 'Aesop used to get away with this sort of thing... but in a somewhat simpler day' (letter to H. C. Crosby, Jr, 26 May 1958, p. 344).

7 I am grateful to an editorial consultant for *Science Fiction Studies* who first raised the issue of significant omissions in Campbell's discussions of science fiction history.

8 It might be noted that Campbell, unlike Gernsback, briefly published a fantasy magazine, and a comment in a letter to L. Ron Hubbard shows some awareness of the history of fantasy: 'every human being likes fantasy fundamentally. All we need is fantasy material expressed in truly adult terms. Every author who honestly and lovingly does that makes a name on it. Lord Dunsany, Washington Irving, Stephen Vincent Benet' (letter to L. Ron Hubbard, 23 January 1939, p. 45). While Campbell never incorporated such writers into science fiction, he saw their work as valuable and as worthwhile models for modern writers of fantasy. However, when his fantasy magazine collapsed in 1943, Campbell seemed to lose interest in the subject and rarely discussed it again, except in disparaging comparisons to science fiction; for example, he declared that 'The movie-TV brand of "science-fiction" *isn't* science-fiction; it's fantasy, because neither the author nor the audience expects it to be believed' ('These Stories May Upset You', p. 11).

'A Full-View Picture of the World that would Result': Robert A. Heinlein's *Beyond This Horizon*

For purposes of parallelism, this chapter should examine the earlier fiction of John W. Campbell, Jr, which would illustrate the possibilities and problems in his theories just as Gernsback's *Ralph 124C 41+* had illustrated the possibilities and problems in Gernsback's theories. However, this cannot be done because, despite popular opinion, Campbell's writing career was not especially distinguished, and his reputation, I believe, has been sustained largely by people who have not actually read his works.

Simply put, Campbell himself was not a Campbell writer.

As is commonly noted, Campbell began his writing career enthusiastically imitating the scientific space adventures of E. E. Smith; what is not commonly noted is that Campbell, more so than Smith—or Gernsback, for that matter—was inclined to include lengthy, intrusive, and complicated scientific explanations. Consider this passage of dialogue from the magazine version of 'Piracy Preferred', the first Arcot, Wade and Morey story:

> As to the gas, Dick found out but little more than what we had already known. It is a typical organic compound, one of the metal radical type, and contains one atom of thorium. This is a bit radioactive, as you know, and Dick thinks that this may account in part for its ability to suspend animation. Thorium has a valence of four, as have many of the semi-organic metal radicals. It is thus able to replace carbon in some structures. However, since it was impossible to determine the molecular weight, he could not say what the gas was, save that the empirical formula was $C_{62} ThH_{39} O_{27} N_5$. You can see it is a very complex molecule. It broke down at a temperature of only 89° centigrade. The gases left consisted largely of methane, nitrogen, and methyl ether. Dick is still in the dark as to what the gas is. (p. 237)

Even the normally supportive Moskowitz describes a later work in this series, *The Black Star Passes*, as 'thousands of words of thrilling action (and many thousand dull words of scientific gobbldygook)' (*Seekers of Tomorrow*, p. 35); and in later years, Campbell was equally critical of his original style: 'this ain't a story—it's a treatise! This is the kind of stuff I used to write way back yonder in 1933' (letter to Walt and Leigh Richmond, 12 June 1963, p. 414); and 'My early stories... were loaded with 500 words of action, 2,000 words of hypothetical technology, 500 words of action, 1,000 words of science, 500 words of action, 2,000 words of hypothesis' (letter to H. Beam Piper, 15 June 1964, p. 431).

In 1934, though, Campbell produced an entirely different kind of story—the famous 'Twilight' as by 'Don A. Stuart'. To the modern reader, what is distinctive about this story is not its picture of a decadent humanity in the far future—a commonplace theme previously seen in stories ranging from H. G. Wells's *The Time Machine* to G. Peyton Wertenbaker's 'The Coming of the Ice'—but rather its use of two simple-minded rustics as viewpoint characters. With this device, Campbell could offer a scientifically-grounded vision of the future with persuasive characterization, and without accompanying scientific lectures.

However, Campbell himself did not seem to understand this crucial element in 'Twilight'; instead, the only new element in the story which continued to be prominent in Campbell's later Stuart stories was its elegiac 'mood'. When he wrote a sequel to 'Twilight', for example, the everyday viewpoint characters were eliminated, so that 'Night' simply related the adventures of a scientist hurled into the same future world at a later time. In fact, everything about Stuart's career after 'Twilight' suggests a return to earlier modes of writing: a return to scientists as main characters, a return to extended scientific exposition, and a return to a focus on scientific matters. Thus, despite their 'mood', and despite their intermittently interesting ideas, Stuart's stories otherwise fail to fulfil some of the goals Campbell would later announce as important in science fiction.

In a typical Stuart story, the major activity consists of characters making long speeches, expounding Campbell's scientific or political ideas, with no effort to provide background by means of indirect reference. This is how Campbell begins 'Out of Night':

> The Sarn Mother looked down at Grayth with unblinking, golden eyes. 'You administer the laws under the Sarn', she clicked waspishly. 'The Sarn make the laws. Men obey them. That was settled once and for all time four thousand years ago. The Sarn Mother has determined that this thing is the way of progress that is most desirable. Is that clear?'
>
> Grayth looked up at her, his slow-moving eyes following from the

toe pads, up the strange, rope-flexible legs, up the rounded, golden body to the four twined arms, his lips silent. His steel-gray eyes alone conveyed his thought complete. The Sarn Mother, on her inlaid throne of State, clicked softly in annoyance.

'Aye, different races we are; the Sarn are the ruling race. The Sarn Mother will be obeyed by the slaves of her people no less than by her people. For many centuries the crazy patchwork has persisted— that the men have had freedoms that the masters have denied themselves. Henceforth men shall be ruled as the Sarn. The Sarn have been just masters; this is no more than justice. But be warned, you will see that this thing is administered at once—or the Sarn will administer it themselves.'

Grayth spoke for the first time, his voice deep and powerful. 'Four thousand years ago your people came to Earth and conquered our people, enslaved them, destroyed all our leaders, setting up a rabble of unintelligent slaves. Since your atomic energy, your synthetic foods, your automatic production machinery, and the enormous decrease in human population you had brought about made more of goods for each man, it worked no great hardship.

'Before ever the Sarn came to this world, your race was ruled by a matriarchy, as it is today, and must always be. To your people it is natural, for among you the females born in a generation outnumber the males five to one. You stand near seven feet tall, while the Sarn Father—as the other males of your race—is but four feet tall, but a quarter as powerful physically. Matriarchy is the inevitable heritage of your race.

'You differ from us in this fundamental of sex distribution. By pure chance our races resemble each other superficially—two eyes, two ears, rounded heads. Your race has two, wide-separated nostrils, four arms in place of two. But internally there is no resemblance... ' (and so on for another two pages; pp. 151–52)

The tone and content may be distinctive, but Campbell's manner of presenting information is, if anything, more awkward than Gernsback's, and here he is committing a fundamental writer's blunder that even Gernsback usually managed to avoid: namely, having characters tell each other at length what they already know.[1] In retrospect, F. Orlon Tremaine's suggestion that Campbell write a series of science articles for *Astounding Stories* may have represented his shrewd judgement that Campbell, as a writer, was more interested in delivering lectures than in telling stories.

In addition, as both passages suggest, Campbell was never much of a prose stylist, and his characters tended to be flat—another way in which his own writings failed to meet the standards he would later announce. As in other stories of the 1930s, the focus in both Campbell and Stuart stories is always the scientific ideas.

Finally, Campbell never mastered—or even considered—the process of working out a detailed background for science fiction stories in the manner of Heinlein and Clement; his stories are all foreground, without interesting detail or convincing development. Campbell admitted as much in a letter to Hal Clement: 'Precise, jig-saw-puzzle interlocking of details wasn't a forte of mine; the highly pleasing results you've produced by doing so has taught me that it's a satisfying thing to do, instead of being merely a damn nuisance' (letter to Harry Clement Stubbs, 12 April 1953, p. 151).

Campbell's stories from 1935 to 1937 demonstrate, in fact, that he was failing to become a major author even before he became the editor of *Astounding Stories*—the factor usually cited to explain his decline. Eventually, Campbell was reduced to writing terrible imitations of Stanley G. Weinbaum like 'The Brain Stealers of Mars' for *Thrilling Wonder Stories*. And while Campbell did produced one more masterpiece—'Who Goes There?'—two good stories do not make someone a great writer.[2] Overall, examining Campbell's fiction, scholars who are tracing the history of the *content* of science fiction may indeed note provocative and innovative ideas in those stories; but little in them relates to the history of the *idea* of science fiction, as Campbell displays no noteworthy improvements in the form or process of writing science fiction. As a writer, Campbell seems comparable to his contemporary Raymond Z. Gallun, another writer who provided moments of insight and power ('Old Faithful', *People minus X*) amidst scores of derivative and inferior texts; and if Campbell had not become a major editor, it is possible that he would today be forgotten as a writer.[3]

To illustrate Campbell's theories, then, one must turn to the work of his most distinguished writer, Robert A. Heinlein, to see Campbell's theories in practice. For my purposes, *Beyond This Horizon*, originally published in *Astounding Science-Fiction* in 1943, is the most appropriate choice since it can be seen in many ways as a reworking of Gernsback's *Ralph 124C 41+*— Heinlein's attempt to describe a scientifically and socially advanced future society in a more artistic and thoughtful manner than Gernsback ever achieved. And, in that novel one can observe virtually all of the reforms and new ideas which Campbell implanted into science fiction. At times, though, it will be useful to examine an earlier Heinlein novel, '"If This Goes On—"', which represents the flip side of *Beyond This Horizon*—a dystopian future society where scientific and social progress has been stunted—and which therefore provides further information on the broad range of possibilities opened up by Campbell's new approach; and other Heinlein stories will occasionally be relevant to aspects of Campbell's theories.

By focusing on Heinlein's fiction, I do not wish to minimize the importance of Campbell's critical pronouncements or imply that Heinlein was the true driving force behind the Golden Age. On his own, Heinlein could only have inspired imitations of Heinlein; it was Campbell's ability to notice and promote the innovative aspects of his fiction that was to eventually have a much greater impact.

The first observation to make about *Beyond This Horizon* is this: while there are many signs of a new approach here, the novel also perfectly fulfils Gernsback's theories of science fiction.

To be sure, Heinlein's stories often begin with a spectacular display of indirectly presented information, as can be seen in the first few sentences of *Beyond This Horizon*:

> Hamilton Felix let himself off at the thirteenth level of the Department of Finance, mounted a slideway to the left, and stepped off a strip at a door marked:
>
> BUREAU OF ECONOMIC STATISTICS
> Office of Analysis and Prediction
> Director
>
> PRIVATE
>
> He punched the door with a code combination and awaited face check. It came promptly; the door dilated, and a voice within said, 'Come in, Felix.' (p. 5)

Here, small, casually mentioned details—like 'a slideway', 'punched the door with a code combination', and 'awaited face check'—immediately convey to the reader that this is a future world permeated with advanced scientific technology. The phrase 'The door dilated' has often been particularly celebrated for its understated impact, as in these comments from Harlan Ellison:

> I am reminded… of the way in which Heinlein has always managed to indicate the greater strangeness of a culture with the most casually dropped in reference: the first time in a novel, I believe it was in *Beyond This Horizon*, that a character came through a door that… dilated. And no discussion. Just: 'The door dilated'. I read across it, and was two lines down before I realized what the image had been that the words had urged forth. A *dilating* door. It didn't open, it *irised*! Dear God, how I knew I was in a future world. ('A Voice from the Styx', pp. 133–34)

More recently, a version of the same sentence was employed—casually, of course—in Arthur Byron Cover's *Stationfall*: 'Suddenly the door to the bridge dilated' (p. 5).

To see how this approach could quickly convey information, one can also examine the opening of 'If This Goes On—', a novel in the 'Future History' series where the background information was given in the chart Campbell published in *Astounding Science-Fiction*. For the era of 'If This Goes On—' the chart said the following: 'Religious dictatorship in U.S. Little research and only minor technical advances during this period. Extreme puritanism. Certain aspects of psychodynamics and psychometrics, mass psychology and social control developed by the priest class' ('Brass Tacks', May 1941, pp. 124–25). In the novel, all this information is smoothly integrated into the first three paragraphs:

> It was cold on the rampart. I slapped my numbed hands together, then stopped hastily for fear of disturbing the Prophet. My post that night was just outside his personal apartments—a post that I had won by taking more than usual care to be neat and smart at guard mount... but I had no wish to call attention to myself now.
>
> I was young then and not too bright—a legate fresh out of West Point, and a guardsman of the Angels of the Lord, the personal guard of the Prophet Incarnate. At birth my mother had consecrated me to the Church and at eighteen my Uncle Absalom, a senior lay censor, had prayed an appointment to the Military Academy for me from the Council of the Elders.
>
> West Point had suited me. Oh, I had joined in the usual griping among classmates, the almost ritualistic complaining common to all military life, but truthfully I enjoyed the monastic routine—up at five, two hours of prayer and meditation, then classes and lectures in the endless subjects of a military education, strategy and tactics, theology, mob psychology, basic miracles. In the afternoons we practiced with vortex guns and blasters, drilled with tanks, and hardened our bodies with exercise. (p. 11)

The references to West Point, in connection with the 'Prophet' and 'the Angels of the Lord', establish that there is a 'religious dictatorship in U.S.'; that fact, and the mention of 'a senior lay censor', suggests an atmosphere of 'extreme puritanism'; the courses in 'mob psychology' and 'basic miracles' reveal that 'psychodynamics, psychometrics, mass psychology and social control' are perfected skills; and the mention of 'vortex guns and blasters', still used with 'tanks', shows that there have been only 'minor technical advances'. Thus, Heinlein indeed seems to illustrate the basic premise of Campbell's theories—that the necessary scientific and prophetic information sometimes can be 'worked into the story without interrupting'.

However, continuing to read *Beyond This Horizon*, one starts to encounter exactly the sorts of long expository passages that this method was supposed to avoid. Indeed, some discussions and explanations in the early part of the novel make for heavy reading:

> 'You know the history of the First Genetic War.'
>
> 'I know the usual things about it, I suppose.'
>
> 'It won't do any harm to recapitulate. The problem those early planners were up against is typical—'
>
> The problems of the earliest experiments are typical of all planned genetics. Natural selection automatically preserves survival values in a race simply by killing off those strains poor in survival characteristics. But natural selection is slow, a statistical process. A weak strain may persist—for a time—under favorable conditions. A desirable mutation may be lost—for a time—because of exceptionally unfavorable conditions. Or it may be lost through the blind wastefulness of the reproductive method. Each individual animal represents exactly half of the characteristics potential in its parents.
>
> The half which is thrown away may be more desirable than the half which is perpetuated. Sheer chance.
>
> Natural selection is slow—it took eight hundred thousand generations to produce a new genus of horse. But artificial selection is fast, *if* we have the wisdom to know *what* to select for.
>
> But we do not have the wisdom... (followed by five more paragraphs before the conversation resumes; pp. 25–26)

Here, Heinlein has the narrator paraphrase the contents of an extended conversation which, as suggested by the statement 'It won't do any harm to recapitulate', largely involves information that residents of this society should already know—the awkward expository approach of 'Out of Night', though handled with a little more skill. Further, to make sure that his readers understand genetics, Heinlein later introduces an even more explicit lecture from the narrator which occupies all of the third chapter;[4] and since the explanation is far more thorough than needed to advance the story, Heinlein seems to be fulfilling Gernsback's goal of using science fiction to provide a scientific education.

'If This Goes On—' has similar expository passages: for example, Lyle must explain to the reader exactly how he was transformed into a duplicate of another man:

> A simple operation made my ears stand out a little more than nature intended; at the same time they trimmed my ear lobes. Reeves' nose was slightly aquiline; a little wax under the skin at the bridge caused

mine to match. It was necessary to cap several of my teeth to make mine match his dental repair work... My complexion had to be bleached a shade or two; Reeves' work did not take him out into the sun much.

But the most difficult part of the physical match was artificial fingerprints. An opaque, flesh-colored flexible plastic was painted on my finger pads, then my fingers were sealed into molds made from Reeves' fingertips. It was touchy work; one finger was done over seven times before Dr. Mueller would pass it. (p. 56)

Of course, such passages are not as frequent or intrusive as they are in Gernsback's or Campbell's stories; still, they do occur. Thus, the revolution Campbell urged was not really one of overall writing technique, since expository passages remained necessary in science fiction; rather, it represented a better way to *begin* a story, to get the action going and readers interested before offering more detailed information in lecture form.[5]

This meant that Heinlein and later writers would face the same problem Gernsback faced: namely, how to insert lengthy explanations into a narrative. One recurring solution is to have a naïve hero, who constantly needs to have someone older and wiser explain matters to him; and 'If This Goes On—' in fact focuses on one, incredibly naïve hero, John Lyle, who is constantly befuddled by new developments. There is at least some variety, though, in that there are two older and wiser voices, Zebadiah Jones and Sister Magdalene, who take the time to explain the situations to him.

Beyond This Horizon represents a further advance in technique in that Heinlein does not employ one knowledgeable explicator and one ignorant listener; rather, he establishes hierarchies of such relationships. The low man on the totem pole is a recently awakened man from the twentieth century, J. Darlington Smith, who listens to explanations from Monroe-Alpha Clifford, the friend of protagonist Hamilton Felix. By the standards of his time, however, Clifford is rather dense, so Felix repeatedly must explain things to him. While Felix is highly intelligent, there remain aspects of his own society that he does not understand, so a government official called a Planner, Mordan, appears on the scene to explain things to Hamilton. And Mordan himself, meeting the powerful and mysterious members of the Board of Policy which governs the world, is obliged to listen to their explanations. As an added complexity, the novel does not linearly progress upward from the ignorant to the knowledgeable: it begins in the middle, with Hamilton knowledgeably explaining some things to Clifford, and then simultaneously moves upward—Mordan explaining to Hamilton, Planners explaining to Mordan—and downward—Clifford explaining to Smith. Still, all these machinations are only variations of the old Gernsback formula of Ralph the expert explainer and Alice the unaware listener, and at some points in *Beyond This Horizon*, as noted, Heinlein completely abandons the effort to work explanations into the dialogue and simply has the narrator provide them. Still, Heinlein's skill in writing and incorporating explanatory passages shows that Gernsback's approach does not in itself lead to inferior fiction; rather, it was Gernsback's clumsiness in following that approach that makes his fiction seem so 'unreadable'.

If *Beyond This Horizon* and other Heinlein stories thus mimic the format of Gernsback in their basic emphasis on and style of providing information, they are also similar in that they often refer to new inventions—such as the dilating door. Another invention briefly appears during a description of Felix's shower: 'The air blast dried him with a full minute to spare for massage. He rolled and stretched against the insistent yielding pressure of a thousand mechanical fingers and decided that it was worthwhile to get up, after all. The pseudo-dactyls retreated from him' (p. 20). In another story, 'Waldo', Heinlein spent some time describing more elaborate mechanical equivalents to human hands:

> Even the ubiquitous and grotesquely humanoid gadgets known universally as 'waldoes'—Waldo F. Jones's Synchronous Reduplic-ating Pantograph, Pat. #296,001,437, new series, *et al*—passed through several generations of development and private use in Waldo's machine shop before he redesigned them for mass production... Near the man, mounted on the usual stand, were a pair of primary waldoes, elbow length and human digited. They were floating on the line, in parallel with a similar pair in front of Waldo. The secondary waldoes, whose actions could be controlled by Waldo himself by means of his primaries, were mounted in front of the power tool in the position of the operator... (pp. 24, 26)

Later, when such artificial arms were actually built, they were named 'waldoes'. Obviously, their inventors were aware of Heinlein's story and were possibly inspired by it in exactly the manner that Gernsback proposed.[6] Thus, even though Heinlein rarely celebrates or describes his proposed inventions in detail, his works might still lead to the creation of actual inventions.

Therefore, while Heinlein's purpose in providing explanations and describing inventions was certainly not primarily to provide scientific education or stimulate inventors, his stories can still have that effect; so in its format and possible effects, *Beyond This Horizon* fits comfortably into Gernsback's parameters.

However, there is much that is new about Heinlein's novel, all features that were noted and announced by Campbell as important in modern science fiction. To recapitulate: along with the principle that science fiction no longer needed to incorporate lengthy explanations, but could provide data in a more subtle manner—discussed as the third item in Chapter 7—Campbell added these ideas and modifications to Gernsback's basic theory: first, science fiction was no longer purely 'thrilling adventure' but could take many forms; second, there was more emphasis on people and their problems and less emphasis on machines; fourth, science fiction was no longer limited to the hard sciences but could fruitfully explore the social sciences and pseudo-sciences as well; fifth, science fiction now demanded a thoroughly detailed background for its predicted future events; sixth, science fiction could provide thought-provoking puzzles for readers to solve or problems for readers to ponder; seventh, science fiction could provide collective informed opinions about possible scientific innovations; eighth, science fiction could explore the possible effects of future scientific developments; ninth, science fiction could be used to consider and comment on a broad range of political and social problems; and tenth, science fiction might be the vehicle for a unique scientific viewpoint, as in Godwin's 'The Cold Equations'. All of these features are evident to varying extents in *Beyond This Horizon* and Heinlein's other works.

First, one sees Heinlein consciously striving to go beyond the parameters of juvenile 'thrilling adventure'. True, there are episodes of melodramatic derring-do in *Beyond This Horizon* (as will be noted), but a more sombre mood is more prominent. Overall, Heinlein's basic attitude is revealed in comments in two letters to Campbell: 'I will not attempt to pep up my stories by introducing a greater degree of action-adventure'; speaking of *Beyond This Horizon*, he said, 'I wanted it to be fully mature, adult, dramatic in its possibility'; and he even brags at one point that he has 'completely abandoned the hero-and-villain formula' (*Grumbles from the Grave*, pp. 13, 19, 13). Heinlein also goes beyond that formula in the expressed attitude of 'If This Goes On—' that a successful revolution will require more than heroics. That is, the latter parts of 'If This Goes On—' describe the huge bureaucracy and meticulous planning that are needed to overthrow the dictatorial government, and Heinlein's hero John Lyle spends most of his time doing paperwork. Heinlein's later and longer version of the novel also includes some modest appeals to prurient interest, like a skinny-dipping escapade involving Lyle, Zebediah and two women, and some careful discussion of religion, further evidence that he was attempting to transcend the juvenile and reach an adult audience—exactly as Campbell wished. Finally, Heinlein obviously approached writing *Beyond This Horizon* in an exploratory manner, clearly feeling his way through his developing future society and narrative in a way that would become characteristic of his writing, and in another way freeing himself from the conventions of genre.

Second, readers could quickly see that Heinlein's focus was on his people and their interactions with a technologically advanced future society, and not merely on inventions, which are often mentioned in passing and not described; and Heinlein is much more successful than Gernsback in creating realistic and sympathetic characters. True, it is often remarked that many of his characters are variations on a single character—the Heinlein hero—but Heinlein can at least bring this kind of person to life on the page, something that Gernsback could not accomplish with Ralph, and something that Campbell could rarely accomplish in his stories.

Next, both *Beyond This Horizon* and 'If This Goes On—' are manifestly dedicated to exploring fields in the social sciences and pseudo-sciences. *Beyond This Horizon* is filled with neologisms that convey Heinlein's interest in government and psychology, including *socio-economics, psychologics, neo-nationalistic, pseudo-capitalism,* and a*spirant stock.* And 'If This Goes On—' includes a long discussion of the emerging future science of propaganda:

> 'Johnnie, you savvy how to use connotation indices, don't you?'
> 'Well, yes and no. I know what they are; they are supposed to measure the emotional effects of words.'
> 'That's true, as far as it goes. But the index of a word isn't fixed like the twelve inches in a foot; it is a complex variable function depending on context, age and sex and occupation of the listener, the locale, and a dozen other things. An index is a particular solution of the variable that tells you whether a particular word used in a particular fashion to a particular reader or type of reader will affect that person favorably, unfavorably, or simply leave him cold. Given proper measurement of the group addressed it can be as mathematically exact as any branch of engineering.' (pp. 81–82)

Certainly, this qualifies as an intelligent speculation about future developments in the art of verbal persuasion; nevertheless, there is a drawback of sorts. However contaminated with magical substances, Gernsback's predictions had substance, and some of them—like his descriptions of the Actinoscope which anticipated radar or the Hypnobioscope which anticipated sleep learning—might actually give inventors some ideas. But Heinlein's description of 'connotation indices' provides no suggestions as to how someone might actually set up such a system—a trait apt to be generally true of any speculation which is based on an imagined science, not an actual science. Thus, in expanding the concept of science, some of the practical utility of Gernsback's plans is compromised—though the literary value of the work may be enhanced.

It need hardly be stated, in illustrating the fifth innovation in Campbell's theories, that Heinlein was striving to develop a convincingly detailed and thoroughly developed future world, both in the novels and stories of his Future History like 'If This Goes On—' and stories outside the series like *Beyond This Horizon*. In this respect, Campbell's introductory description of the novel is accurate: 'The theme is old—controlled heredity. But in a way only McDonald [Anson McDonald, Heinlein's pseudonym] could achieve, this two-part novel presents a full-view picture of the world that would result from such a change in human life' (blurb to *Beyond This Horizon*, *Astounding Science-Fiction*, April 1942, p. 9).

It should be noted, though, that Heinlein was not always as methodical as he seemed in developing and providing such a 'full-view picture'. Alexei and Cory Panshin claim in *The World beyond the Hill* that Heinlein first decided to link together some of his early stories in the near future and 'If This Goes On—' while driving to Washington, DC; thus, the Future History may have been to an extent jerry-built rather than planned. Possibly as a result of this, or of simple inattentiveness, there are some conspicuous inconsistencies. For example, Heinlein for years included 'We Also Walk Dogs' as part of the Future History even though much of the story's background did not match the other stories in the series; and while one early story, 'Blowups Happen', established the existence of an orbiting power plant in the near future, all later stories fail to mention it, and it was not until his very last novel, *To Sail Beyond the Sunset*, that Heinlein finally offered the explanation that the power plant had been destroyed by an explosion soon after its construction.

In addition, *Beyond This Horizon* and 'If This Goes On—' both display a troubling trait that would appear in other Heinlein novels: the future world is established in a satisfying manner; the action is set in motion; then Heinlein loses interest in his environment and story and hastily and clumsily brings the work to a close. In 'If This Goes On—', after Heinlein depicts in great detail the growing conspiracy to overthrow the Prophet, the final scenes in which the totalitarian government is defeated are surprisingly brief and anticlimactic; while *Beyond This Horizon* employs another characteristic Heinlein device—a penultimate and rushed summary of events over a long period—to end the novel.

Similar problems crop up in later Heinlein works; as already noted, both *Methuselah's Children* and *Time for the Stars* devote much energy to mounting a massive expedition to the stars, then abort that mission after a few planetary landings and hurry the starship back to Earth. *The Number of the Beast* imagines an elaborate multiplicity of parallel universes and establishes mysterious evil beings dubbed the Black Hats as the villains who must be tracked down and defeated; but after visiting a few of these new worlds, Heinlein's heroes apparently forget all about the Black Hats and decide to throw a massive party, where a brief appearance by one Black Hat is almost a comical interlude. And, as Panshin complains in *Heinlein in Dimension*, a rushed summary concludes the action in his novella, 'Common Sense'.

The lesson might be that an author who sets out to create an elaborate future world as a backdrop to a story may become more interested in the background than in the narrative; what is intended as decoration then becomes the central focus of the author's energies; and once the imagined world is fully developed, the author can lose interest in his story, so that the traditional values of strong and well-paced narrative are neglected.

Sixth, one finds in 'If This Goes On—' evidence of an occasional desire to pose a scientific problem of some kind and invite readers to think about solutions. In a larger sense, of course, 'Solution Unsatisfactory' invited readers to ponder a puzzle that Heinlein himself could not solve, as Campbell noted; but there are also passages that present smaller problems that Heinlein solves. One episode involves Lyle's strangely fortuitous escape from agents of the dictatorship. Once he is flying in a commandeered aircraft, Lyle ponders his predicament: 'If a cat escapes up a tree, he must stay there until the dog goes away. That was the fix I was in and in my case the dog would not go away, nor could I stay up indefinitely… I was being tracked, that was sure… After that—well, it was land on command or be shot down' (p. 65). Lyle eventually devises a plan involving a dangerous dive near the ground so he can parachute away while the ship's automatic pilot returns to the programmed course to lead pursuers astray. Of course, the trick depends on Lyle's knowledge of the capabilities of future aircraft, which readers could not anticipate, so the problem does not pose a fair challenge to the reader. And Campbell, while praising 'scientific problem' stories, recognized that stories of that kind could 'cheat' in these ways. Heinlein's episode similarly demonstrates that the author of these stories can, as Campbell said, 'pull anything he wants out of the hat' ('In Times To Come', *Astounding Science-Fiction*, May 1941, p. 87).

Seventh, Heinlein clearly draws upon and adds to the opinions of other writers as he presents his future societies, reflecting and improving a consensus of views. That is, Heinlein was well aware of what other writers were saying about atomic energy in the 1930s, and in two stories he builds on their work to add two new ideas: in 'Solution Unsatisfactory', the proposal that radioactive materials in themselves, not actual bombs, would be effective weapons; and in 'Blowups Happen', a suggestion that the dangers of atomic power plants exploding and causing tremendous damage could be avoided by locating them in Earth orbit. And following the use of atomic bombs in 1945, Heinlein then applied what he and other writers had concluded to produce three articles aimed at general readers discussing the implications and effects of atomic weaponry—'The Last Days of the

United States', 'How to Be a Survivor', and 'Pie from the Sky'—all later included in *Expanded Universe*.

Eighth, Heinlein is clearly interested in using both novels as a way to consider the possible effects of future scientific progress. One matter considered in *Beyond This Horizon*, for example, is the integration of genetic engineering techniques and a civilized future society. In the case of 'If This Goes On—', a major concern is the possible effects and problems of an advanced science of mind control and manipulation. Combined with other technologies, such powers apparently could be used to maintain a horrible dictatorship, as in Heinlein's novel; similarly, they might be used to overthrow that dictatorship—which is how Heinlein's rebels succeed. Still, the issue remains, and emerges near the end of the novel, when the now-dominant rebels propose to use a carefully crafted propaganda film to inculcate the new values of secularism and democracy; but 'an elderly man' named Winters who 'looked like the pictures of Mark Twain' stands up in opposition:

> 'Free men aren't "conditioned!" Free men are free because they are ornery and cussed and prefer to arrive at their own prejudices in their own way—not to have them spoonfed by a self-appointed mind tinkerer! We haven't fought, our brethren haven't bled and died, just to change bosses, no matter how sweet their motives. I tell you, we got into the mess we are in through the efforts of those same mind tinkerers. They've studied for years how to saddle a man and ride him. They started with advertising and propaganda and things like that, and they perfected it to the point where what used to be simple, honest swindling such as any salesman might use became a mathematical science that left the ordinary man helpless.' He pointed his finger at Stokes. 'I tell you that the American citizen needs no protection from anything—except the likes of him.' (pp. 118–19)

Thus, a message about the dangers of mind control is driven home, and after heated debate and Winters's abrupt death, the rebels decide not to use the film.

However, the episode is visibly contrived. It is awkward to introduce a character solely to deliver a necessary speech, and the emotion of this scene is, as Panshin observes, forced:

> When Heinlein wants us to approve a character or a position, or to feel moved, instead of giving us a natural emotional reason growing out of the story or, alternatively, underplaying, he is all too likely to try to find a button in us to push... First, we are told that [Winter] looks like Mark Twain. That's a button. Then, we are told that the

end of his speech is punctuated by him dropping dead. That's another button. (*Heinlein in Dimension*, p. 112)

To enhance the scene, Heinlein even violates that careful 'consistency of minor detail' which he was often noted for—how would people in the late twenty-first century, in a society of rigid censorship which would surely not celebrate the works of Mark Twain, happen to know exactly what Twain looked like?

The point is that in employing science fiction to deliver a message—of any kind—the writer encounters the same problem that Gernsback encountered in trying to deliver scientific lectures: the story must stop, and the story may be contorted, to incorporate the message. It is a flaw which surfaces conspicuously in Heinlein's later fiction, beginning with *Stranger in a Strange Land*, where Jubal Harshaw's extended monologues on a variety of subjects only tangentially related to the plot became an irritant to many readers (and the posthumously published 'Complete and Uncut' version of that novel includes even more of such material).

Ninth, some passages in *Beyond This Horizon* provide general commentary on human nature and human problems. Consider the remarks of Mordan and Felix concerning the failed revolutionaries:

> 'I doubt if any one of them had sufficient imagination to conceive logically the complexities of running a society, even the cut-to-measure society they dreamed of.'
>
> 'They talked as if they did.'
>
> Mordan nodded. 'No doubt. It's a common failing, and it's been with the race as long as it has had social organization. A little businessman thinks his tiny business is as complex and difficult as the whole government. By inversion, he conceives himself as competent to plan the government as the chief executive. Going further back in history, I've no doubt that many a peasant thought the job of the king was a simple one and that he could do it better if he only had a chance. What it boils down to is lack of imagination and overwhelming conceit... I venture to predict that... we will find that the rebels were almost all—all, perhaps—men who had never been outstandingly successful at anything. Their only prominence was among themselves.'
>
> Hamilton thought this over to himself. He had noticed something of the sort. They had seemed like thwarted men... Pipsqueaks, the lot of 'em. (p. 104)

Heinlein's analysis has little to do with predicting or examining the effects of future development; rather he employs his narrative to explicitly describe and denounce an ancient human trait, a point that might have been brought out in other forms of narrative.

Finally, there are elements in *Beyond This Horizon* of a cold, scientific attitude displacing traditional human values. After all, what sets the story in motion is Mordan's desire to have Felix produce children with a carefully chosen woman—part of an overall system of genetic engineering:

> 'We simply enable each couple to have the best children of which they were potentially capable by combining their gametes through selection instead of blind chance.'
>
> 'You didn't do that in my case,' Hamilton said bitterly. 'I'm a breeding experiment.'
>
> 'That's true. But yours is a special case, Felix. *Yours is a star line.* Every one of your last thirty ancestors entered voluntarily into the creation of your line, not because Cupid had been out with his bow and arrow, but because they had a vision of a race better than they were. Every cell in your body contains in its chromosomes the blueprint of a stronger, sounder, more adaptable, resistant race. I'm asking you not to waste it... I want you to perpetuate your line... '
>
> 'My answer is "No"—'
>
> 'But—'
>
> 'My turn—Claude. I'll tell you why. Conceding that I am a superior survival type... Even so, I know of no reason why the human race *should* survive... other than the fact that their make-up insures that they will. But there's no sense to the whole bloody show. There's no point to being alive at all. I'm damned if I'll contribute to continuing the comedy.' (pp. 29, 31)

Note that Felix does not resist the idea of mating with a pre-selected woman or wax eloquent about the virtues of free, romantic love; his objection to Mordan's proposal is based on other reasons. Indeed, the novel supports 'controlled heredity'—an approach that might strike many people as cold and inhuman.

The next question is the relationship between Heinlein's work as an illustration of Campbell's revised theories and the various generic models Gernsback first posed for science fiction, and the model of the fable which Campbell added. The result seems to be that Campbell's announced new approaches in fact alleviate many of the generic tensions created by Gernsback's theories and manifested in *Ralph 124C 41+*; however, new tensions also emerge.

First, because the new approach to science fiction illustrated by Heinlein did not strongly mandate presentations of scientific information and ideas, writers are no longer obligated to take the side of intellect over emotion, indirect action over direct action, and the elite over the common man, so they are free to indulge in pure, uncomplicated melodramatic adventure. In fact, while it is not a dominant approach, there are often such episodes in Heinlein's works. In *Beyond This Horizon*, the placid future society is disrupted by a secret conspiracy to overthrow the government which Felix infiltrates to thwart it; however, because Mordan and other officials do not take the rebellion seriously, the effort is allowed to proceed, and the rebels mount a serious attack on the valuable 'plasm bank' which requires Felix and Mordan to engage in a furious armed battle to protect the facility.

Still, there is a curious dénouement to the adventure: afterwards, Mordan announces that 'the issue was never in doubt' (p. 104); even if the rebels had managed to capture the plasm bank, the rebellion still would have been an utter failure. Thus, the reader is told that the whole affair really did not matter at all.

'If This Goes On—' includes a similar passage of exciting action: an extended account of Lyle's perilous journey to the secret headquarters of the rebellion, including the aforementioned daring escape from a moving aircraft. However, the conclusion is similar; after his adventures, Lyle learns that his successful arrival with his important message was actually not important:

> 'I don't mind telling you, in a general way, what you were carrying—just routine reports, confirming stuff we already had by sensitive circuits mostly… '
>
> 'Just routine stuff? Why, the Lodge Master told me I was carrying a message of vital importance. That fat old joker!'
>
> The technician grudged a smile. 'I'm afraid he was pulling—Oh!'
>
> 'Eh?'
>
> 'I know what he meant. You were carrying a message of vital importance—to you. You carried your own credentials hypnotically. If you had not been, you would never have been allowed to wake up.' (p. 80)

Thus, the whole episode is trivialized; and more broadly, this novel trivializes the conventions of melodrama. The early parts of 'If This Goes On—' have several exciting episodes: midnight assignations, daring rescue of the beautiful Judith from the Palace prison, and desperate escape from the Palace; one might imagine that the rest of the novel would proceed in a similar fashion. However, after getting to General Headquarters, Lyle is assigned as an officer's aide, keeping track of paperwork; and while he participates in the final battle, Lyle is not exactly on the scene, but instead issues orders to those doing the actual fighting.

What is happening here can be analysed. In proclaiming that science fiction was not a 'mass-appeal' literature, and announcing its serious purposes and adult audience, Campbell effectively declared that adventure and excitement were no longer appropriate priorities in writing science fiction. In matters of revolution, Heinlein asserts, action and violence are not key elements; from a mature perspective, a revolution is simply a matter of setting up an efficient bureaucracy and carefully planning and arranging events. And rebels who fail to take this approach, as in *Beyond This Horizon*, are doomed to failure. Yet despite this grey and logical perspective, writers still felt impelled to include elements of melodrama and excitement in their writing—a lingering effect of Gernsback's pronouncements. Thus, driven to both avoid and provide 'thrilling adventure', Heinlein develops the solution which can be noted in both *Beyond This Horizon* and 'If This Goes On—': he presents and exploits such events, then follows the escapade by winking knowingly to the audience and explaining that such juvenile exploits are of course of no real consequence.

However reasonable it seems, this solution does not work all that well, for readers are astute enough to realize that the author is using the devices of melodrama, regardless of ironic distancing; and the effect of these after-the-fact deflations is more or less to make the reader feel cheated, to ask: if it did not matter whether Lyle made it to headquarters or not, or if it did not matter whether Felix successfully fought off the rebels or not, then why was I made to feel so strongly that it mattered?

Overall, Campbell's revision of Gernsback's theories allows for full-throttle, uncomplicated melodrama; but his insistence on literary maturity makes writers uncomfortable with the form, introducing an element of contrived apology in the melodrama.

Second, lacking Gernsback's preoccupations with laboratory science, the workings of machines, and 'thrilling adventure', Heinlein would at times include a little sight-seeing in the manner of a travel tale. An example in 'If This Goes On—' is a description of the cave used by rebels as their headquarters:

> It was a limestone cavern so big that one felt outdoors rather than underground and so magnificently lavish in its formations as to make one think of Fairyland, or the Gnome King's palace... They led me down a path which meandered between stalagmites, from baby-sized to Egyptian pyramids, around black pools of water with lilypads of living stone growing on them, past dark wet domes that were old when man was new, under creamy translucent curtains of onyx and sharp rosy-red and dark green stalactites. My capacity to wonder began to be overloaded and presently I quit trying. (pp. 77–78)

Needless to say, there are not many passages like this in 'If This Goes On—', since Lyle quickly gets down to business in his new job assisting the general. Discussions of paperwork, meetings, and strategies soon replace any further descriptions of the cave.

In *Beyond This Horizon*, there are almost no extended descriptions of this kind at all. Consider, for example, this singularly anaemic description of the city of the future: 'The night life of the capital offered plenty of opportunity for a man to divest himself of surplus credit, but it was not new to him. He tried, in a desultory fashion, to find professional entertainment, then gave up and let the city itself amuse him. The corridors were thronged as always, the lifts packed; the Great Square under the port surged with people' (pp. 16–17). And Felix quickly becomes more interested in watching the people around him than the environment, so the appearance of the city remains elusive to readers.

Like Gernsback, but for different reasons, Heinlein has little concern for appearances. Gernsback was interested in how machines worked, not what they looked like; Heinlein is interested in how society and people work, not what they look like. Both writers seek to go beyond surface detail to probe inner workings—diminishing any impulse to spin travel tales and linger on descriptions.

A further key element is conveyed by one Heinlein statement: 'It was not new to him.' Gernsback focused on a main character, Alice, who was a European tourist, establishing a pretext for extended visual description; Heinlein, who 'takes the future for granted' (as is repeatedly noted), employs the viewpoint of people who are thoroughly familiar with their societies. Thus, there are no occasions for extended passages of description in the manner of the travel tale; residents of a future world will not pause to study or inquire about the features of their environment. In *Beyond This Horizon*, the convention of the visitor to the future emerges only as a vestigial element, in the subplot of Smith; however, he is introduced far too late in the novel to become a major character, or to make his introduction to the future society a major subject. Other characters in the novel may reflect varying degrees of naïveté, so as to provide a basis for exposition, but they are also not strangers to the society of the novel.

Again, Campbell's changes in Gernsback's theories, as seen in Heinlein's work, permit use of the travel tale model; but by adopting a style of indirect explanation most appropriate while focusing on characters who are already integrated into the imagined world, Heinlein makes the approach seem outdated and unfashionable.

Third, without Gernsback's strong commitment to the abilities of scientists to understand and control their world, Heinlein should be free to employ the conventions of the Gothic novel without complications; and there are moments in 'If This Goes On—' which recall the Gothic: the opening scenes in the dark, mysterious catacombs of the Prophet's Palace, the torture in the Inquisitor's chambers, the time where Lyle envisions himself as trapped in a doomed aircraft, and the enclosure of the cave itself.

However, Heinlein declines to dwell on these distressing minor touches of the Gothic in 'If This Goes On—'. For example, he abruptly cuts off his report of the Inquisitor's tortures: 'There is no point in describing what he meant by "the mechanicals" and no sense in making this account needlessly grisly.... let's skip the details' (p. 47). Thus, where a Poe would have lingered to consider at length the 'grisly' tortures, Heinlein prefers to 'skip' it.

Like Gernsback in his commitment to an understandable and controllable universe, Heinlein resists the blind fear and terror of the Gothic novel. Unpleasantries are to be endured and forgotten; they are not important in Heinlein's novel or in the general scheme of things in his future worlds.

In a broader sense, however, Heinlein's stories do sometimes present a vision of a mysterious realm lurking beyond and governing everyday reality; but Heinlein, like Gernsback in *Ultimate World*, quickly moves to rationalize and thus subdue this realm. A case in point is 'Waldo'. In the story, the deKalb receptors which provide energy are unaccountably breaking down, and the only person who is able to repair them is a strange 'back-country hex doctor' who tells Waldo about the 'Other World' that people mentally inhabit, and that actually governs the physical world (pp. 71, 65). As a trained scientist, Waldo is at first horrified and repulsed by these ideas, which run counter to everything he has believed: 'Magic loose in the world. It was as good an explanation as any, Waldo mused. Causation gone haywire; sacrosanct physical laws no longer operative. Magic' (p. 70). Nevertheless, Waldo begins to ponder this theory in a rational and scientific manner:

> What did [the phrase, 'Other World'] mean, literally? A 'world' was a space-time-energy continuum; an 'Other World' was, therefore, such a continuum, but a different one from the one in which he found himself. Physical theory found nothing repugnant in such a notion; the possibility of infinite numbers of continua was a familiar, orthodox speculation. It was even convenient in certain operations to make such an assumption... Schneider had said that the Other World was all around, here, there, and everywhere. Well, was not that a fair description of a space superposed and in one-to-one correspondence? Such a space might be so close to this one that the interval between them was an infinitesimal, yet unnoticed and unreachable, just as two planes may be considered as coextensive

and separated by an unimaginably short interval, yet be perfectly discrete, one from the other.

The Other Space was not entirely unreachable; Schneider had spoken of reaching into it. The idea was fantastic, yet he must accept it for the purposes of this investigation. (p. 71)

After further thought and research into old books of magic, he declares, 'Time to stop speculating and get down to a little solid research' (p. 76); and he learns how to reach and manipulate the Other World so that he can solve the problem of the deKalb receptors and cure his *myasthenia gravis*. He revealingly declares, 'He would *set* the style. He would impress his *own* concept of the Other World on the Cosmos!' (p. 76) In other worlds, confronted with a vision of reality that seems strange and unknowable in the Gothic manner, Waldo instead researches the phenomenon, masters it, and imposes his own priorities upon it—negating the Gothic mood.

While this is a characteristic Heinlein response to a developing Gothic universe—seen also, for example, in 'The Unpleasant Profession of Jonathan Hoag'—*Beyond This Horizon* is a noteworthy exception. While the novel also recalls the Gothic in the way that it steadily generates the feeling of an enveloping and mysterious realm beyond normal human experience, Heinlein fails to provide a final, rationalistic explanation. Felix begins, like Ralph, in a calm and rational future world, and the first chapter of the novel has the matter-of-fact attitude used by Gernsback in presenting the world of 2660. However, Felix's visit to Mordan in the next chapter introduces an awareness of a higher level of authority manipulating human relations. Later, readers eavesdrop on Mordan meeting with the Board of Policy, the people that govern the entire world, and they emerge as impersonal and enigmatic voices. Finally, the end of the novel suggests that Felix's daughter is in fact the reincarnation of one member of the Board of Policy, suddenly validating the existence of strange cosmic forces governing humanity and beyond their scientific control.

However, while the larger sense of the Gothic in *Beyond This Horizon*— a proposed introduction of a spiritual level in Heinlein's future world—is not undermined in the novel, the idea ultimately contradicts other announced aspects of his imagined society. Specifically, the concept of reincarnation undermines Heinlein's painstaking efforts to construct a legitimate utopia.

In fact, one may next discuss the generic models of utopia, dystopia, and the tale of transcendence together, since these related forms deal with either an almost completely perfect world, an almost completely imperfect world, or the juxtaposition of a relatively imperfect world for present-day humanity and a relatively perfect world for some successor race. Without Gernsback's limited emphasis on scientific projections, Heinlein is free to construct future worlds which conform to these generic models, and both 'If This Goes On—' and *Beyond This Horizon* have elements of these forms. However, while there are individual problems in adopting these forms to science fiction according to Campbell's model, it is the simultaneous combination of these forms in *Beyond This Horizon* that creates ruinous narrative difficulties.

'If This Goes On—' is overtly designed to be a dystopia about an oppressive and unattractive religious dictatorship; while *Beyond This Horizon* is overtly designed to be something of a utopia, with its generally benevolent and well-ordered world. What is lacking in both of these worlds, though, is a sense of anything resembling absolute imperfection or absolute perfection, even progress towards absolute imperfection or absolute perfection. As a dystopia, the future world of 'If This Goes On—' gradually emerges as not all that repressive: the cruel controlling forces are incompetent enough to allow the existence of an underground group in the guards of the Prophet himself; they cannot prevent subversive activities of all kinds; and while the capital city of New Jerusalem makes a desperate last stand, the rest of the government collapses quickly after the rebels manage a trick involving the broadcast of the Prophet's annual miracle. In contrast, the totalitarian world of George Orwell's *1984* was not so sloppy, so inept, or so fragile.

As for *Beyond This Horizon*, it offers, as indicated, a strange combination of types of utopia.[7] First of all, it is to an extent a pointillistic utopia in the manner of *Ralph 124C 41+*, in that it presents many small inventions and improvements that have made life easier for the human race. Unlike Gernsback, to be sure, Heinlein pays only cursory attention to these inventions, not focusing on and celebrating them, but readers still get periodic glimpses of a society where doors dilate, where hot air cleans and mechanical *pseudo-dactyls* massage people who take showers, and where water beds provide complete sleeping comfort—and, by means of a system for draining those beds, a uniquely effective alarm clock as well.

However, Heinlein also sets up his novel as a traditional utopia, more in keeping with Campbell's expanded vision of science fiction as a commentary on social problems. He describes, more fully than Gernsback, a humane world government, led by democratically elected Planners who are assisted by Moderators to monitor and assist individual citizens. An efficient and intelligent economic system ensures continuing prosperity for all, and jobs are provided primarily because people feel the need to work, not because their work is really necessary. Politeness and social harmony are maintained by the practice of wearing arms and duelling when a dispute arises. And Heinlein includes a specific reference to the genre when Felix says of a group of would-be revolutionaries that 'I can't see them building a Utopia' (p. 61).

Next, *Beyond This Horizon* functions as a transcendent vision of present humanity doomed while an improved version of humanity triumphantly emerged—what I call the tale of transcendence. It depicts a society obsessed with genetics, determined to improve the human race by encouraging marriages between well-matched partners and genetically engineering their offspring to be the best children possible. This programme has not only eliminated congenital defects but promises to create 'a stronger, sounder, more adaptable, more resistant race' (p. 29); and Mordan is particularly anxious for Felix to have children, because genetic charts indicate that they will be excellent specimens. And the final section of the novel, focused on Felix's unusually intelligent and apparently telepathic son, reinforces the theme of a coming superior humanity.

These three simultaneous approaches to perfecting the human race—through gadgets, government, and genetics, as it were—do not exactly harmonize, which creates tension involving the unsuccessful rebellion that occurs in the middle of the novel. In pointillistic utopia, evil and discontent are still rampant and one must be vigilant and energetic in fighting against them—which explains the many police officers in *Ralph* and the menace of the planned rebellion here. However, this spirit of melodramatic struggle must fade in a true utopia, because in that context all fundamental social problems are presumed to be solved, and an attempted revolution must be regarded as a dim, atavistic echo of earlier, imperfect days—something to be opposed, to be sure, but not a real matter of concern.[8] Hence, there is another reason that Mordan must claim, after the fact, that 'the issue was never in doubt' (p. 104). Finally, in a tale of transcendence, the new humanity is by definition superior and sure to win out over inferior predecessors; hence, there is no need to worry about a revolt by their opponents that will inevitably fail. Mordan expresses this view when he suggests fatalistically that the problem of the revolt does not involve appropriate action, but biological destiny: 'If the rebellion is successful, notwithstanding an armed citizenry, then it has justified itself—biologically' (p. 97). Thus, Heinlein is effectively torn between depicting the attempted revolution as a serious matter, a not-so-serious matter, and a matter of no consequence of all—an indication that the distancing from melodrama and generic freedom allowed by Campbell's theories can lead to complications in mixing generic models.

If these conflicting attitudes toward its central event somewhat muddle *Beyond This Horizon*, a more basic problem is that its protagonist firmly rejects all the approaches to perfecting humanity which its three models suggest, and the answers he finally accepts contradict the premises underlying all these approaches.

The source of Hamilton Felix's angst is that he can see no purpose in human existence; as he said, 'I know of no reason why the human race *should* survive... There's no point to being alive at all' (p. 25). His proposed resolution is to investigate the question of life after death: 'The one thing that could give us some real basis for our living is to know *for sure* whether or not anything happens after we die' (p. 100). At his behest, the Planners eventually initiate the Great Research, which seems to be moving into fruitful directions; at the end of the novel, Felix is particularly excited because his son Theobald, using his telepathic ability, deduces that his new sister is the reincarnation of a female member of the Board of Policy who recently died. And solid evidence of reincarnation, of course, would demonstrate beyond doubt the immortality of the soul. In this way, Heinlein moves away from other forms of science fiction utopia to suggest what might be termed a mystical utopia—an envisioned perfect society founded on some religious force; and, since the principles and dimensions of that enveloping spiritual world remain unexplained in the novel, this approach recalls the typical Gothic universe, though with a more positive— yet still mysterious—atmosphere.

In creating a story which validates such concerns, Heinlein effectively argues against all three quests for an ideal society. If human beings have an afterlife of some kind, then clearly any desire to improve civilization, either by gadgets or government, becomes less important. Heinlein seems to present an opposite position in a specious argument made by one member of the Board of Policy supporting the need to prove the existence of an afterlife: 'It would seem obvious to me... that the only rational personal philosophy based on a conviction that we die *dead*, never to rise again, is a philosophy of complete hedonism' (pp. 110–11). Yet earlier in the novel Mordan effectively refutes that argument when he tells Felix, 'You don't want children. From a biological standpoint that is as contra-survival as a compulsion to suicide' (p. 33). That is, the natural instinct and desire for species-preservation—not just self-preservation—in itself provides ample justification for a 'rational personal philosophy' based on altruism. Indeed, if that member's argument is accepted, then the society Heinlein depicts could never have evolved, since it does not offer its citizens any proof of life after death. Everything else in the novel instead suggests that it is this very lack of proof regarding an afterlife that has motivated Heinlein's society to work so hard to provide its helpful machines, to devise an ideal government, and to improve the race by genetic manipulation.

Furthermore, proof of reincarnation in particular would render the desire to improve humanity through genetics pointless as well—a mere matter of creating better bodies for the same old souls. Indeed, in belatedly raising this possibility, Heinlein completely ignores the strong belief in genetics that informed the rest of his story. Earlier, Mordan praised Felix because of his genes: 'I know your chart. I know you better than you know yourself. You are a survivor type.... I counted not only on your motor reactions, but your intelligence. Felix, your intelligence rating entitles you to the term genius even in these days' (pp. 30–31). But now, it appears, Felix's genes have nothing to do with his personality and traits, which would be, by the doctrine of reincarnation, simply the personality and traits of the soul that happened to enter his body.

In discussing the novel, H. Bruce Franklin papers over this basal contradiction: 'Several centuries of systematic genetic engineering have created a race of human beings superior in health, longevity, physique, and intelligence... We witness this dynamic utopian society passing through a series of crises to advance to what Heinlein often projects as the next stage of human evolution, the development of telepathic powers' (*Robert A. Heinlein*, p. 58). But Heinlein introduces not only telepathy but reincarnation—and that cannot logically be the genetically achieved 'next stage of human evolution'; rather, it can only be the final overt emergence of a supernatural mechanism which predated human civilization.

Thus, while Gernsback's theories led him to approach but back away from the Gothic, Heinlein freely enters the Gothic but in doing so contradicts the other premises of his science fiction novel. For as Day notes in *In the Circle of Fear and Desire*, the 'Gothic atmosphere subverts the physical world of science' (p. 35).

The only unifying factor in this novel's disparate approaches to achieving the betterment of humanity is the idea of progress, as indicated by Alexei Panshin's description of the story as 'a story about process' (*Heinlein in Dimension*, p. 38) and Franklin's comment on its 'dynamic utopian society' (*Robert A. Heinlein*, p. 58). Felix is persuaded to have children not because answers have been found, but because the process of finding them has begun; Felix becomes content with his life not because his doubts are quickly resolved, but because there are promising hints in the Great Research; and in harkening back to the concept of reincarnation, Heinlein seems to support the old Hindu belief in the gradual improvement of humanity by step-by-step progress through lifetime after lifetime. In short, Felix—and Heinlein—do not need perfection to be happy; they merely need to observe progress towards perfection to be happy. Thus, if the bad of 'If This Goes On—' is not so bad, the good of *Beyond This Horizon* is not so good—but it's getting better, and that seems to be enough for Heinlein.

Next, without the complications introduced by Gernsback's emphasis on scientific education and prediction, Heinlein may produce pure satire;

and there are elements in Heinlein's fiction which are clearly satirical: in 'If This Goes On—', the scene where Lyle professes to be unaffected by mere language, then starts to attack his friend when he deliberately uses an offensive expression; and in *Beyond This Horizon*, the celebrated scene where Felix and Monroe Alpha-Clifford compare their fingernail polish:

> 'Say—you've got a new nail tint. I like it.'
>
> Monroe-Alpha spread his fingers. 'It *is* smart, isn't it? *Mauve Iridescent* it's called. Care to try some?'
>
> 'No, thank you. I'm too dark for it, I'm afraid. But it goes well with your skin.' (p. 11)

Both Monroe-Alpha Clifford and the man from the twentieth century, Smith, are frequently ridiculed, and Heinlein sneaks in a little joke when Smith inspires the future society to adopt the game of 'feetball'. Heinlein is thus never afraid to make either his characters or his imagined societies look a bit ridiculous, and he is unemcumbered by Gernsback's particular set of serious purposes in doing so. However, Heinlein has other priorities that mute the atmosphere of the satirical.

In devising a thorough and logical background for his future society, and in evoking that society through carefully chosen details, Heinlein evidences a tremendous desire to make readers believe in the world he presents. Thus, he cannot intimate that the world is nothing more than 'a playfully critical distortion of the familiar', as Leonard Feinberg put it (*Introduction to Satire*, p. 19), a grotesque picture of present-day society which is presented to offer commentary on that society. As shown by the agonies of composition described in letters to Campbell in *Grumbles from the Grave*, Heinlein had many uncertainties about the developing story in *Beyond This Horizon*, suggesting that he was exploring his way through this world, and not constructing it only as a way to make some point about human nature and problems.

More broadly, while the principle that science fiction can offer commentary on social problems sanctions a satirical tone, the general tendency of the science fiction writer is to develop the imagined world, make it seem real, and thus diminish the pointedly opinionated atmosphere of satire. In Gernsback's theories, a preoccupation with suggesting scientific improvements leads to the neglect of any consistent authorial stance toward larger social issues as is typically found in the satire; in Campbell's theories, as exemplified by Heinlein, it is what Suvin termed 'the questioning or problematic "attitudinal field"' (*Positions and Presuppositions in Science Fiction*, p. 71) which the author brings to his writing that mitigates against such a stance, along with the author's desire to present the world as a realistic and possible alternative, not simply an altered portrait of current realities.

Finally, there is a definite element of the fabular permeating 'If This Goes On—', reflecting the new genre which Campbell, in his references to Aesop and the parables of Jesus, seems to add to the list of possible generic models for science fiction. In 'On the Writing of Speculative Fiction', Heinlein identified 'three main plots for the human interest story: boy-meets-girl, The Little Tailor, and the man-who-learned-better' (p. 14). All three (with the last two particularly suggesting the fabular) can be seen in 'If This Goes On—'. If anything, there is an emphasis on the third form, as the impossibly dense Lyle keeps learning more and more about the future world he thought he was already familiar with. The comparable figure in *Beyond This Horizon* is the naïve Monroe-Alpha Clifford, whose romantic illusions about pre-industrial life are bluntly contrasted with the real-life experiences of Smith:

> 'I was hoping that you would be able to tell me something of the brave simple life that was just dying out in your period.'
> 'What do you mean? Country life?'
> Monroe-Alpha sketched a short glowing account of his notion of rustic paradise. Smith looked exceedingly puzzled. 'Mr. Monroe,' he said, 'somebody has been feeding you a lot of cock-and-bull, or else I'm very much mistaken. I don't recognize anything familiar... I followed the harvest two summers, I've done a certain amount of camping, and I used to spend my summers and Christmases on a farm when I was a kid. If you think there is anything romantic, or desirable *per se*, in getting along without civilized comforts, well, you just ought to try tackling a two-holer on a frosty morning. Or try cooking a meal on a wood-burning range... you have your wires crossed. The simple life is all right for a few days' vacation, but day in and day out it's just so much dirty back-breaking drudgery... There never was and there never could be a noble simple creature such as you described. He'd be an ignorant savage, with dirt on his skin and lice in his hair. He would work sixteen hours a day to stay alive at all. He'd sleep in a filthy hut on a dirt floor. And his point of view and his mental processes would be just two jumps above an animal.'
> (pp. 73–74)

In the characters of Lyle and Monroe-Alpha, and in their sagas of disillusionment and re-education, Heinlein seems attracted to a mode of writing resembling the fable; however, this attraction creates problems in his narrative.

To understand why this is the case, one first notes that, as indicated by

Gilbert Highet's phrase 'simple little animal fable' (*The Anatomy of Satire*, p. 177), the fable is by nature a simple form, designed for an audience of children and simple folk. Second, the fable is intended to present 'lessons for human beings', to serve as 'proverbs made visible' (Highet, p. 177). And neither characteristic fits very well with the priorities of science fiction announced by Campbell and expressed by Heinlein.

In an apparent effort to conform to the dictates of the fabular, Heinlein seems to weaken his novels, as Lyle's and Monroe-Alpha's stupidity in a world and in positions that virtually require extensive knowledge becomes unbelievable. Even Hamilton is driven to comment on the incongruity: 'He wondered how a man could be as brilliant as Monroe-Alpha undoubtedly was—about figures—and be such a fool about human affairs' (p. 74). By encouraging readers to think in a scientific manner, science fiction must endorse and illustrate the act of thinking; a focus on a character who cannot think emerges as a major contradiction. Significantly, by the time he wrote *Beyond This Horizon*, Heinlein had learned not to make such a person a viewpoint character, so the more intelligent and plausible Felix becomes the focus, while the dense and implausible Monroe-Alpha is relegated to the sidelines.

Second, as indicated by the difficulties encountered by Monroe-Alpha in *Beyond This Horizon*, Heinlein does not believe in the applicability of simple lessons to human problems. If there is indeed any general 'lesson' in the novel, it is that things are always more complicated than they seem; hence, Monroe-Alpha, who accepts situations at face value, repeatedly seems like an idiot. Indeed, the specific point of the exchange between Monroe-Alpha and Smith—that modern scientific living is superior to the simple country life—runs directly counter to the traditional message of fables like 'The City Mouse and the Country Mouse'.

Indeed, what is more interesting about 'If This Goes On—' is not that Heinlein follows the form of the fable, but that he works to contradict the simple formulas he offered for successful fiction. That is, Lyle does meet and marry a girl, but it is not Sister Judith, the young woman who he initially fell in love with; instead, he is gradually drawn to another revolutionary conspirator, an older woman named Magdalene who earlier in the novel seemed more like a motherly companion. And while the effort to overthrow a powerful and entrenched dictatorship does initially seem like an example of the Little Tailor, Heinlein keeps expanding the extent and resources of the rebellion until it begins to seem more like a shadow government than a group of revolutionaries. To topple the Prophet, Heinlein indicates, requires more than a Little Tailor; and instead of assuming the character of a David-versus-Goliath story, 'If This Goes On—' finally argues that to defeat a powerful government, one has to build one's own government—in effect, David must become another Goliath. In his later novels, one of the consistently interesting features of Heinlein's fiction is the manner in which he confounds conventional expectations to move in unexpected directions—exactly the opposite of a writer who feels bound to follow in the footsteps of myths and fables.[9]

Overall, drawing upon the example of Heinlein's works, one can reach one general conclusion: Gernsback's ideas starkly conflict with all of the generic models he essays; given his concerns and priorities, Gernsback cannot produce a satisfying melodramatic adventure, travel tale, Gothic novel, utopia, or satire, and his pattern of drifting from model to model may reflect the fact that he is thwarted at every form he attempts. In contrast, the ideas followed by Heinlein and articulated by Campbell do not necessarily generate such tensions, but the attempt to combine all of those priorities and approaches creates problems. That is, Heinlein's desire to craft a serious and realistic utopia undermines his use of melodrama; his approach of providing information in a casual, indirect manner undermines his use of the travel tale; his emphasis on scientific thinking undermines his use of Gothic horror and the fable; his attempt to evoke a Gothic atmosphere undermines his use of utopia and the tale of transcendence; and his effort to create a fully realized future society undermines his use of satire. Thus, *Ralph 124C 41+* is an unsatisfactory combination of several unsuccessful novels; *Beyond This Horizon* is an unsatisfactory combination of several successful novels. And the novel therefore anticipates continuing improvements in science fiction, as Campbell's ideas stimulated the next generation of writers and gradually became standard features of the modern genre.

It is not necessary, I think, to list again all of Campbell's reforms and explain at length that they have permeated modern science fiction; almost everyone would accept without comment that numerous science fiction stories since 1950 have shown great variety in their forms and approaches, placed more emphasis on people, tried to avoid extended exposition, explored the social sciences, provided detailed backgrounds, presented interesting puzzles, offered a consensus of opinion on certain scientific issues, commented on the effects of possible scientific developments and on various social problems, and sometimes strived to present a scientific rather than humanistic viewpoint. And the continuing ubiquity in science fiction of the generic models of melodrama, travel tale, Gothic horror, utopia, satire, tale of transcendence, and fable also does not demand extensive support.

What should be noted, though, is that certain aspects of Campbell's reforms can lead writers away from science fiction, or into specialized forms of science fiction; and this visible splintering of the genre, along with its tremendous improvement, are the major developments in science fiction of the 1950s.

Campbell said, 'science-fiction is the freest, least formalized of any literary medium' ('Introduction', *Who Goes There?*, p. 5)—and writers increasingly felt the freedom to write in new and experimental manners. By the 1960s, J. G. Ballard, Philip K. Dick, Brian W. Aldiss, Harlan Ellison and others defined the New Wave in science fiction—what might be termed avant-garde science fiction.

Since many of these writers admired so-called 'mainstream' writers, there emerged an impulse to leave science fiction altogether and write mainstream fiction—a move also suggested by Campbell's emphasis on 'stories of people' with a certain amount of 'style', his inclusion of fields like 'Sociology' and 'psychology' as apt subjects for science fiction ('The Science of Science Fiction Writing', pp. 92, 98, 91), and his view of science fiction as 'a convenient analog system for thinking about new scientific, social, and economic ideas' ('Introduction', *Prologue to Analog*, p. 13). After all, if a writer is primarily focused on writing about people, exploring fields like psychology, and commenting on social and economic issues, there is no particular need for the scientific apparatus of science fiction. Thus, in the 1950s there began a slow but steady exodus of writers from science fiction to the mainstream—including Bernard Wolfe, Ray Bradbury, and Kurt Vonnegut, Jr. One also notes the increasing appearance of science fiction stories which simply transplant familiar plots into exotic environments; Sam J. Lundwall, for example, has criticized a Robert Silverberg story as nothing more than a western set on Venus (in *Science Fiction: What It's All About*). Another case in point might be Roger Zelazny's award-winning novelette, 'The Doors of His Face, the Lamps of His Mouth': certainly, its characters are involving and its writing impeccably polished, but all the story amounts to is *The Old Man and the Sea of Venus*, and one searches in vain for any other reason to consider it science fiction.

Another possible form of science fiction is created by eliminating Gernsback's demand that authors include scientific data and allowing for indirect explanation, for this may let writers to avoid completely science in science fiction, even while apparently writing in the genre. A. E. van Vogt is the best example here, and Damon Knight first realized what was going on in his stories:

> by a canny avoidance of detailed exposition, van Vogt has managed to convey the impression that he has a solid scientific background... It is his habit to introduce a monster, or a gadget, or an extraterrestrial culture, simply by naming it, without any explanation of its nature. It is easy to conclude from this that van Vogt is a good and a profound

writer, for two reasons: first, because van Vogt's taking the thing for granted is likely to induce a casual reader to do the same; and second, because this authorial device is used by many good writers who later supply the omitted explanations obliquely, as integral parts of the action. The fact that van Vogt does nothing of the sort may easily escape notice. (*In Search of Wonder*, pp. 60–61)

And since the time of Vogt, other writers have produced what might be termed hallucinogenic science fiction—mad adventures ostensibly based on an unstated logical background that actually do not make any sense; examples might include Charles L. Harness's *The Paradox Men*, Gordon R. Dickson's *The Pritcher Mass*, and Frederik Pohl and Jack Williamson's *Starchild* trilogy.

At the same time, other aspects of Campbell's theories, if dominant, would lead writers to an even more intense commitment to science in science fiction: the call for writers to develop a 'carefully mapped outline in mind to get consistency of minor details' ('The Old Navy Game', p. 6), offer 'a real mental challenge' in their stories ('Introduction', *Analog 1*, p. vi), join the 'Genuine engineering minds' that have 'argued [over ideas] back and forth in stories' ('The Science of Science-Fiction' 5–6), and produce tales that reflect 'the facts of the Universe' ('Science-Fiction and the Opinion of the Universe', p. 10). These impulses led to two forms of science fiction generally regarded as hard science fiction.[10]

First, some writers have resolved to set their stories in the near future and to devote themselves to working out practical possibilities for near-future technologies; examples include Ben Bova's *The Weathermakers*, Arthur C. Clarke's 'The Wind from the Sun', and Davin Brin's 'Tank Farm Dynamo'. Thus, these writers attempt to participate in the ongoing process of developing solutions to problems like weather control, spaceflight, and space station design. Other writers employ the same sort of setting to present an interesting puzzle for readers to solve, as in Hal Clement's 'Fireproof' and Isaac Asimov's 'The Talking Stone', clear descendants of the 'scientific problem' story.

However, other writers with an equally good grasp of science have applied the challenge of creating a 'carefully mapped outline' to a new task: designing not a future society but an entirely different environment. The first prominent example was *Mission of Gravity* by Hal Clement, who also contributed an article explaining how he had created the planet Mesklin. Other examples of this 'world-building' form of hard science fiction include Larry Niven's *Ringworld*, Arthur C. Clarke's *Rendezvous with Rama*, and John Varley's *Titan*. These stories also provide one way to adapt Campbell's priorities to the genre of the travel tale; for, by embedding their scientific ideas in a new environment instead of a new society, writers can freely use the model of the travel tale to tell the story of a knowledgeable adventurer travelling through and discovering the wonders of the imagined new world. Thus, all four of the listed examples are unproblematic examples of the travel tale.[11] And other far-ranging works of hard science fiction—like Clarke's *Childhood's End* and Charles Sheffield's *Between the Strokes of Night*—strive to project an odd and inhuman viewpoint, a large reflection of the message in 'The Cold Equations'.

Still, even these apparently scientific priorities can lead writers away from science fiction. If a writer finds she has a good scientific idea or new perspective, she might ask: why waste it in a story? Why not write an article about it? And in fact, another trend in the 1950s is for science fiction writers to become science-fact writers; Asimov is the most obvious example, but other writers like Poul Anderson, Otto Binder, Lester del Rey, and Clarke have also spent some time writing non-fiction.[12]

On the other hand, if writers find they are more interested in creating and solving puzzles than in developing scientific ideas, there is another option open to them: detective fiction, the traditional genre of puzzle-solving. John D. MacDonald abandoned science fiction altogether for detective fiction, and writers like Heinlein, Anderson and Asimov have dabbled in the form. One also observes, as James Blish noted, 'private eye yarns masquerading as science-fiction stories' (*The Issue at Hand*, p. 20).

As for the process of world-building, this need not be applied only to the writing of science fiction: J. R. R. Tolkien's *Lord of the Rings* trilogy—which first became popular in science fiction circles in the early 1950s—fortuitously demonstrated that a thorough attention to background development can also be a key element in crafting superior fantasy, and eventually helped to create new interest in this category of fiction. Indeed, the modern fantasy novel hardly seems complete without its maps, glossaries, and appendices. And since this process of creation could appeal even to a logical scientific mind, the Tolkien style of fantasy became another alternative for science fiction writers like Anderson, Ursula K. Le Guin, and Robert Silverberg.

There is also an impulse towards fantasy in two of the generic models which Heinlein adopted with mixed success: the Gothic novel and the fable. That is, if the scientific priorities of science fiction seem to conflict with the characteristic world-views of these forms, the obvious answer is to recast stories as fantasies. So the Gothic is now the dominant model for two fields adjacent to science fiction—the modern horror story, epitomized by Stephen King, and the 'dark fantasy' celebrated by Dennis Etchison and others, which can be seen as an attempt to create hard-edged adventure stories, not unlike science fiction, which simultaneously are firmly grounded in the mysterious and ominous world of the Gothic novel. And gentler, fabular fantasy became the trademark of some quite different writers like Clifford D. Simak (who named one of his *City* stories 'Aesop') and Thomas Burnett Swann.

Finally, while many science fiction writers continue to be drawn to the patterns of melodrama, they often seem embarrassed about doing so in works aimed at an adult audience. One sees, for example, Clarke using Heinlein's strategy of first exploiting, and then minimizing, that narrative element: in *Childhood's End*, for example, Clarke does toss in a bit of 'thrilling adventure'—some rebels seize the Secretary General of the United Nations who is cooperating with the Overlords—but later refers to the incident apologetically as 'This ridiculously melodramatic kidnapping, which in retrospect seemed like a third-rate TV drama' (p. 49).[13] Another approach is to employ melodrama while burying its patterns in levels of irony—a pattern observed in William Gibson's *Neuromancer*.[14] However, if science fiction writers are driven to trivialize or conceal their use of melodrama, there is one answer—to openly write a juvenile novel, another form of science fiction which became established in the 1950s. Many commentators have noted that Heinlein seemed most effective as a writer in producing his juvenile novels, where he could freely present 'thrilling adventure' without any of the troubling complications that arise in his adult novels. And other writers like Ben Bova and Richard A. Lupoff have arguably done their best work in juvenile fiction.

Therefore, the lessons learned from Heinlein's works suggest again the twofold impact of Campbell: to liberate writers to produce more diverse and interesting works; and encourage them to move out into specialized subgenres—such as avant-garde science fiction, hallucinogenic science fiction, hard science fiction, juvenile science fiction—or to move out of the field altogether—into detective fiction, fantasy, nonfiction, or 'mainstream' fiction. Thus, Campbell simultaneously strengthened and weakened the genre. By 1968, Harlan Ellison could observe the results: 'it now becomes clear that the fractioning of the genre has for ten years been in progress. We now have war novels of SF (*BIll, the Galactic Hero*; *Starship Troopers*), we have westerns of SF (*War of the Wing-Men*; *The Horse Barbarians*), we have religious allegories (*Thorns*; *Lord of Light*), and we have love stories, historicals, novels of manners' ('A Voice from the Styx', p. 127). Anderson similarly noted that 'As I see it, science fiction, ever since the Golden Age, when John W. Campbell, Jr. first took over *Astounding*, has never gone in any one direction. It's gone in all directions, which, I think, is a very good thing' (interview with Jeffrey M. Elliot, *Science Fiction Voices #2*, p. 49). To be sure, this freedom and diversity might be celebrated; but there are also advantages in a unified vision of a genre's nature and priorities, and since

Campbell's time, one notes continuing conflicts and divisions which regularly threatened to destroy that unified vision. Only Gernsback's principles have kept the genre together.

There remains one paradox to explore: though the improvements and potential conflicts illustrated by Heinlein and announced by Campbell indeed came to dominate science fiction of the 1950s, it was at this time, when his theories were having their greatest impact, that Campbell's own attentions seemed to be focused elsewhere; and to understand fully how Campbell influenced science fiction, one must discuss how Campbell came to function as both an incentive, and an impediment, to the progress of science fiction.

Notes

1 To appreciate the idiocy of this passage, imagine Martin Luther King, Jr meeting with John F. Kennedy in the early 1960s and telling him, 'People of your race typically have blonde or brown hair that is straight, pale pinkish skin, and green or blue eyes. Whereas people of my race typically have black hair that is curly, brown skin, and brown eyes. But though these differences are superficial, your ancestors from Europe, hundreds of years ago, took my ancestors from Africa and made them slaves... '

2 I might add 'Forgetfulness' as a third story by Campbell worth remembering—though it is twice as long as it needs to be.

3 Partial support for this bleak picture of Campbell's skills as a writer comes from George Turner, who said, 'Let's not pretend for a start that John W. Campbell as a writer was of any importance—as a writer. In his early days he was one of the worst writers who ever wrote science fiction. In his later days he became a comparatively good one, and actually managed to finish up with two memorable stories out of about forty or fifty' ('John W. Campbell: A Symposium', p. 47). For an opposing view of Campbell's skills, see George Hay's letter in *Foundation* No. 55 (pp. 81–82).

4 A sampling from this chapter:

> A life-producing cell in the gonads of a male is ready to divide to form gametes. The forty-eight chromosomes intertwine frantically, each with its opposite number. So close is this conjunction that genes or groups of genes may even trade places with their opposites from the other chromosomes. Presently this dance ceases. Each member of a pair of chromosomes withdraws from its partner as far as possible, until there is a cluster of twenty-four chromosomes at each end of the cell. The cell splits, forming two new cells, each with only twenty-four chromosomes, each containing exactly half of the potentialities of the parent cell and parent zygote... (p. 37)

5 As noted in 'Words of Wishdom', my study of neologisms in *Ralph 124C 41+*, Heinlein's *Beyond This Horizon*, and six other novels, suggests there is no stylistic difference in novels of the Gernsback era—which purportedly stressed exposition—and novels of Campbell's era—which purportedly avoided

exposition.

6 And, as noted in Chapter 2, Heinlein once claimed that one of his stories had indeed inspired an actual invention.

7 The following discussion is adapted from a portion of the essay 'Gadgetry, Government, Genetics, and God'.

8 One example would be the revolt that briefly disturbs the tranquillity of the utopian society in H. G. Wells's *Men Like Gods*.

9 See, for example, my discussion of Heinlein's *Job: A Comedy of Justice* in 'Wrangling Conversation'.

10 As noted in my *Cosmic Engineers*.

11 There can be one distracting side effect to this world building, however: an excessive concern for imagined future universes can yield not true science fiction but imaginary reference books, mimicking the format of nonfiction, explaining those worlds in detail. Thus, *Star Trek* has inspired not only several films, three additional series, and scores of original novels but a number of books like *Star Trek Spaceflight Chronology*, *Star Trek Maps*, and *Star Trek Engineer's Manual* which offer additional—and highly detailed—background information about the future universe of the *Enterprise*. Thus, one observes a growing body of writings whose sole purpose is to expand and elaborate on the background to a story without actually telling a story.

12 Another minor danger is that writers might be inspired to move away from writing science fiction to researching and promoting the areas of science where they have bright ideas. Thus, L. Ron Hubbard abandoned the field to establish the religion of Scientology, and he took writers like van Vogt with him. Raymond Palmer, the editor of *Amazing Stories*, increasingly devoted his energies to promoting the 'Shaver hypothesis' and exploiting interest in UFOs. More recently, Don Wilson began to research a science fiction novel presenting the idea that the Moon is an ancient alien spaceship, but became convinced that the theory was correct and instead wrote a purported work of nonfiction, *Secrets of Our Spaceship Earth*, explaining and defending the hypothesis.

13 Another example is *Islands in the Sky*, where Clarke repeatedly indicates that something exciting and 'melodramatic' is about to happen—a meteor crashes through a space station wall, an alien being is glimpsed, suspicious characters hanging about the station seem like space pirates—but then backs away with a prosaic explanation—the meteor is a training exercise, the alien is an enlarged hydra, and the space pirates are crewmen filming a space movie. This novel is discussed in my *Islands in the Sky*.

14 The final scenes of that novel enact a typical melodramatic adventure: a daring young hero and stalwart companion enter the lair of a despicable villain to rescue a fair maiden. However, Gibson first makes Case a reluctant hero who, when hearing of Molly's plight, announces 'I'm not going' (p. 184)—then inexplicably goes anyway. Gibson's tough-as-nails heroine, Molly, is of course a far cry from the traditional helpless heroine of melodrama. And at the climactic moment, the crucial action of rescue is performed not by Case, but by a confederate of the villains who experiences a change of heart. Still, no matter how much cynicism Gibson piles on to the incident, the spirit of melodrama endures.

'Can Openers, Clichés and Case Studies': John W. Campbell, Jr's Career as a Science Fiction Editor

As was the case with Gernsback, exploring the career of John W. Campbell, Jr first demands a few remarks on his life. Here, Sam Moskowitz's discussion of Campbell's upbringing provides an interesting contrast to his treatment of Gernsback. Moskowitz mentions Campbell's early interest in fantastic literature—'He discovered Edgar Rice Burroughs' Tarzan and John Carter of Mars at the age of $7^1/2$'—and Reginald Bretnor adds that 'His mother introduced him to science fiction, of the Jules Verne and H. G. Wells variety, when he was eight' (introduction to 'The Place of Science Fiction', p. 3). Regarding his relationship to science, Campbell said that 'I got into theoretical physics back in 1928, because science fiction had convinced me that that was the field wherein the great advances would be made in my lifetime—atomic energy and the like' ('Our Catalogue Number', p. 67), attesting to the later influence of science fiction on Campbell. Moskowitz also describes his early interest in practical science— 'He blew up the basement with his chemistry experiments. Manually dexterous, he repaired bicycles for other kids. For their parents he revitalized electrical appliances' (p. 30); while Bretnor says this scientific bent came even earlier: 'His father, an electrical engineer, aroused his interest in physical science at the age of three' (introduction to 'The Place of Science Fiction', p. 3).

However, as was not the case with Gernsback, Moskowitz focuses most of his attention on young Campbell's family situation:

> At home, his relationship with his parents was emotionally difficult... His father carried impersonality and theoretically objectivity in family matters to the brink of fetish... Not only was he an authoritarian in his own home but a self-righteous disciplinarian as well, who put obedience high on the list of filial duties. Affection was not in his make-up, and if he felt any for the boy he managed to repress it.
> The mother's changeability baffled and frustrated the youngster...

His mother had a twin sister who was literally identical… John's aunt treated him with such abruptness that he was convinced she thoroughly hated him. This created a bizarre situation. The boy would come running into the house to impart something breathlessly to a woman he thought was his mother. He would be jarred by a curt rebuff from her twin. Every time his aunt visited the home, this situation posed itself until it became a continuing and insoluble nightmare. (pp. 29–30)

One may discount Moskowitz's conclusion that 'More than is true of most writers, his early life and background shaped the direction he would take in specific plot ideas as well as in method' (p. 28); particularly fanciful, I think, is the idea that his experiences with his aunt led directly to the plot of 'Who Goes There?' But one general principle of human development may be relevant: more often than not, sons end up acting exactly like their fathers.

To temporarily employ simplistic psychohistory, assume—without evidence, to be sure—that Gernsback's father, like many of his time, was a distant figure who paid little attention to his son; so Gernsback became a distant, inattentive father to science fiction. Campbell had a father who was an 'authoritarian';[1] so Campbell became an authoritarian father to science fiction.

There emerge, for whatever reason, distinct differences between the aspirations of Gernsback and Campbell: Gernsback wanted to be a writer and scientist, he wanted recognition as a writer and scientist, and he correspondingly wanted science fiction to be recognized for its literary and scientific value. Campbell wanted more to have power over writers and scientists, and correspondingly wanted science fiction to have power over literature and science—a view of Campbell confirmed by Theodore Sturgeon, who said that he 'conveyed his preoccupation with power (all kinds), superiority (*our* kind), and scientific probability up and down and across the disciplines' (cited in 'John Wood Campbell', p. 33).

An obsession with being in control accounts for other aspects of Campbell's early life described by Moskowitz. Campbell had the habit of arguing with his instructors; Moskowitz accepts and restates Campbell's claim that he 'flunked out of MIT because I could not pass first-year German in three tries!' (letter to John Arnold, 21 April 1953, p. 159), but his less-than-conciliatory attitude may have had something to do with it. Though he earned a degree in physics from Duke University, he did not pursue a career in science—perhaps because he could not endure the long period of disciplined apprenticeship that such a career would involve.[2]

An obsession with power also accounts for one fact: Gernsback, generally regarded as a failure, was actually a success, while Campbell, generally regarded as a success, was actually a failure.

Of course, the conventional picture of Campbell's impact on science fiction is that as editor of *Astounding Science-Fiction*, he singlehandedly invented modern science fiction and carefully laid the foundation for its future greatness; indeed, I could fill several pages of this book with quotations of that kind.[3]

But, one can argue, this is mostly a myth.

A recent and forceful restatement of this myth appears in Alexei and Cory Panshin's *The World beyond the Hill*, which not only depicts Campbell's writing career as a consistent and conscious effort to wrestle with and resolve the fundamental problems of humanity's future in the universe, but also presents Campbell's early editorship of *Astounding Science-Fiction* as a vast, complex conspiracy to create an entirely new type of science fiction. Yet until they provide something resembling documentation for their intricate descriptions of Campbell's inner thought processes, the bulk of this account must be dismissed as imaginative fantasy.[4]

Based on available evidence, Campbell's editorial goals were, at first, unfocused. He reshaped his magazine to appeal visually to a more mature audience; he regularly announced he was looking for new writers with scientific backgrounds (as in 'Contest'); to call attention to noteworthy stories, he used the already hoary device of a special label (a 'Nova' story); he announced forthcoming publication of a special 'Mutant' issue; and so on. Yes, he was looking for new and better science fiction, but nothing suggests that he had any particular ideas about the nature of that new and better science fiction; and many early gestures could be dismissed as promotional gimmicks. The difference was that Campbell fulfilled his promise and did improve his fiction. However, he did not *create* the 'Golden Age of Science Fiction'; rather, he noticed it, responded to it, and helped it along.

The evidence to support these assertions is clear.

First, many talented writers became adults and began writing science fiction in the 1940s, meaning that they were all typically born about twenty years earlier. In the words of Frederik Pohl:

> James Blish once had a theory that science-fiction writing was the specific consequence of some historical event, as Parkinson's Syndrome was considered to be the late aftereffect of the world influenza epidemic of 1920. He could not identify that event, but he based his theory on the observation that, of all major science-fiction writers alive a decade or two ago, more than half had been born within a year or two of 1920. (*The Way the Future Was*, p. 16)

Donald M. Hassler also reports that 'I have heard the writers talk about how something must have happened around 1920 since so many of them were born within a year or two of that date—[Hal] Clement in 1922, Pohl in 1919' (*Comic Tones in Science Fiction*, p. 104).

I attempted a crude test of Blish's hypothesis. First, I needed a list of major science fiction writers before 1960; but since compiling such a list myself would involve subjective judgement, I used a list based on a broad consensus: authors whose stories or novellas were selected by the Science Fiction Writers of America to appear in the Volumes I, IIA, and IIB of *The Science Fiction Hall of Fame*. The list is not ideal, since it includes some minor writers who produced one noteworthy story (like Theodore S. Cogswell, Tom Godwin, and Wilmar Shiras) and excludes some major writers who never produced one especially noteworthy story (like Hal Clement, L. Sprague de Camp, and John Wyndham). Still, the list cannot be described

Table 2: Years of birth of authors with stories in *The Science Fiction Hall of Fame* (Volumes I, IIA, and IIB)

Poul Anderson	1926	Richard Matheson	1926
Isaac Asimov	1920	Judith Merril	1923
Alfred Bester	1913	C. L. Moore	1911
Jerome Bixby	1923	Frederik Pohl	1919
James Blish	1921	Eric Frank Russell	1905
Anthony Boucher	1911	James H. Schmitz	1911
Ray Bradbury	1920	T. L. Sherred	1915
Fredric Brown	1906	Wilmar Shiras	1908
Algis Budrys	1931	Clifford D. Simak	1904
John W. Campbell	1910	Cordwainer Smith	
Arthur C. Clarke	1917	[Paul Linebarger]	1913
Theodore R. Cogswell	1918	Theodore Sturgeon	1918
Lester del Rey	1915	Theodore L. Thomas	1920
E. M. Forster	1879	Jack Vance	1920
Tom Godwin	1915	A. E. van Vogt	1912
Robert A. Heinlein	1907	Stanley G. Weinbaum	1900
Daniel Keyes	1927	H. G. Wells	1866
Damon Knight	1922	Jack Williamson	1908
C. M. Kornbluth	1923	Roger Zelazny	1937
Henry Kuttner	1914		
Fritz Leiber	1910	AVERAGE YEAR OF BIRTH	
Murray Leinster		(excluding Wells and Forster)	1916
[Will Jenkins]	1896	Standard deviation	8.42

as pre-selected to achieve any particular results. Next, I looked up the years of birth of every author, with results presented as a list in Table 2 and a graph in Table 3. Finally, I computed average year of birth and standard deviation. The results were strikingly close to Blish's: the average year of birth was 1916, with a standard deviation of 8.42.

Table 3: Graph of years of birth of authors with stories in *The Science Fiction Hall of Fame* (excluding Wells and Forster)

1896	X	1910	XX	1924	
1897		1911	XXX	1925	
1898		1912	X	1926	XX
1899		1913	XX	1927	X
1900	X	1914	X	1928	
1901		1915	XX	1929	
1902		1916		1930	
1903		1917	X	1931	X
1904	X	1918	XX	1932	
1905	X	1919	X	1933	
1906	X	1920	XXXX	1934	
1907	X	1921	X	1935	
1908	XX	1922	X	1936	
1909		1923	XXX	1937	X

Excluding the possibility of some magical event, one must next look for some common factor to explain why so many talented writers were born around this time. And the common factor is *not* extended contact with, or the strong influence of, Campbell during their early years as writers. Arthur C. Clarke was in England, communicated sparingly with Campbell, and did not publish very much in *Astounding*; Ray Bradbury's stories were almost all rejected by Campbell; Pohl says in *The Way the Future Was* that Campbell helped him as an editor but is silent regarding his influence as a writer; Robert A. Heinlein said that *Sixth Column* (*The Day after Tomorrow*), based on a plot provided by Campbell, 'was the only story of mine ever influenced to any marked degree by John W. Campbell, Jr'. (*Expanded Universe*, p. 93); and writers like Damon Knight, Cordwainer Smith, Alfred Bester, and Jack Vance produced little fiction for Campbell. However, there is one common factor shared by almost every author on the list: *early exposure to Gernsback's magazines.*

Reading through the biographies of *Hall of Fame* writers in Sam Moskowitz's *Seekers of Tomorrow* (excluding Murray Leinster, who wrote professionally before *Amazing Stories* appeared), one notes this connection repeatedly: Campbell himself 'spotted the first issue of AMAZING STORIES when it appeared in April, 1926, and became a regular customer' (p. 31). 'Soon after AMAZING STORIES was started, [a friend of Jack Williamson] received the March, 1927, issue as a sample and turned it over to Jack... Appealing to his sister for aid, he scraped together enough funds to secure AMAZING STORIES regularly' (p. 87). 'The earliest science-fiction stories that appear to have made an impression on [Eric Frank Russell] are *The Gostak and the Doshes* by Miles J. Breuer, M.D. (AMAZING STORIES, March, 1930)... and Paul Ernst's *The Incredible Formula* (AMAZING STORIES, June, 1931)' (p. 136). Lester del Rey 'really went overboard on science fiction when a friend in St. Charles loaned him a copy of the Fall, 1929, SCIENCE WONDER QUARTERLY which featured Otto Willi Gail's *The Shot into Infinity*... When he picked up the August, 1932, AMAZING STORIES which included [John W.] Campbell's *The Last Evolution*, he resumed buying science fiction regularly' (pp. 171, 173). 'To a "classic" background in Wells, Verne, Haggard, and Burroughs [Heinlein] added regular purchase of ARGOSY ALL-STORY and Hugo Gernsback's ELECTRICAL EXPERIMENTER. When science-fiction magazines appeared, he bought and read them all. He was literally saturated in the popular periodical background of American science fiction' (p. 190). A. E. van Vogt 'became a regular reader of AMAZING STORIES when he chanced upon the November, 1926, issue with the first installment of Garrett P. Serviss' epic novel, *The Second Deluge*. He secured most back issues and read the magazines regularly until 1930' (p. 216). 'Since 1930 Sturgeon had intermittently read AMAZING STORIES, WONDER STORIES, ASTOUNDING STORIES, and WEIRD TALES' (p. 235). 1929 'was the year [Isaac Asimov] read his first science-fiction magazine [*Amazing Stories*, August 1929]... Young Asimov was enthralled and decided to supplement his education with AMAZING STORIES from then on' (p. 251). Clifford D. Simak 'picked up a copy of AMAZING STORIES in 1927 and became a regular reader' (p. 270). Fritz Leiber 'was religiously devoted to AMAZING STORIES, which he began reading with its first (April, 1926) number, and stayed with for the next four years' (p. 286). Moskowitz quotes C. L. Moore: 'in 1931... I succumbed to a lifelong temptation and bought a magazine called AMAZING STORIES whose cover portrayed six-armed men in a battle to the death [*Awlo of Ulm* by Capt. S. P. Meek, in the September, 1931, issue]. From that moment on I was a convert' (p. 306; Moskowitz's language in brackets). Henry Kuttner 'began with the Oz books, graduated to Edgar Rice Burroughs, and, at the age of 12, found himself "hooked" when the first AMAZING STORIES appeared in 1926' (pp. 320–21). Ray Bradbury's 'introduction to magazine science fiction is recorded with preciseness. It was the Fall, 1928, issue of AMAZING STORIES QUARTERLY, featuring A. Hyatt

Verrill's intriguing novel *The World of the Giant Ants*... [Four years later] he struck up a friendship with a youth who had a boxful of old AMAZING STORIES and WONDER STORIES, and he borrowed and read them all' (pp. 354–55). 'In 1927, Clarke discovered AMAZING STORIES, which served as a literary hypodermic, injecting him with an imaginative drug that required increasingly larger dosage as he grew older, until the day that he received an entire crate of WONDER STORIES for 5 cents a copy stood out with such memorableness that it was to be recorded unfailing in each autobiographical sketch he wrote' (p. 376). 'Already Edgar Rice Burroughs, H. Rider Haggard, A. Conan Doyle, Jules Verne, and Carl H. Claudy were at the top of his list, and when [Philip José Farmer] spotted the first (June, 1929) issue of SCIENCE WONDER STORIES it was as if Diogenes had found a reason to blow out his lamp' (p. 399).[5]

With a little research, one could not doubt locate similar reports for all the *Hall of Fame* writers who are not the subjects of Moskowitz biographies. Perhaps because of lingering animosity regarding old battles in fandom, Moskowitz gives little space to those writers involved with the Futurians, but two of them offer their own testimony: Pohl said, 'at some point in the year of 1930 I came across a magazine called *Science Wonder Stories Quarterly*, with a picture of a scaly green monster on the cover. I opened it up. The irremediable virus entered my veins... I found back-number magazine stores where I could pick up 1927 *Amazings* and 1930 *Astoundings* for the nickel or dime apiece that even my ten-year-old budget could afford' (*The Way the Future Was*, pp. 1–2, 6).[6] And Damon Knight said, 'I encountered science fiction in the August-September 1933 issue of *Amazing Stories*... I spent my hoarded allowance... on wonderful old bedsheet-sized *Amazings* and *Wonders*. Working my way back from the issues I already had, I discovered that magazine science fiction had been invented in 1926 by a man named Hugo Gernsback' ('Beauty, Stupidity, Injustice, and Science Fiction', pp. 67, 68). Also, Alfred Bester reported that 'Like every other chess-playing, telescope-loving, microscope-happy teenager of the twenties, I was racked up by the appearance of *Amazing Stories* magazine, Mr. Gernsback's lurid publication' ('Science Fiction and the Renaissance Man', p. 79). Undoubtedly other Futurians, such as C. M. Kornbluth and James Blish, and other young writers who became prominent in the 1940s and early 1950s, had the same experience.[7]

In short, there was a remarkable event around the 1920s which caused so many young people at that time to become science fiction writers, and it was Hugo Gernsback.

To be sure, the fact that all of these writers had an early encounter with science fiction in Gernsback's magazines has been noted; however, since these writers' stories were not like the stories in those magazines, the assumption was that the magazines had little influence on their writing careers, leading to the conclusion that their skills resulted from Campbell's magical powers. But those young people read not only the stories in those magazines but also the editorials and blurbs that repeatedly proclaimed that science fiction involved scientific content and scientific accuracy. And they read letter columns where readers debated serious scientific issues and took authors to task for apparent scientific errors in their stories. Without necessarily picking up all aspects of Gernsback's ideas, and certainly without consciously realizing that they were learning a theory of science fiction, they absorbed, accepted, and internalized the message that science fiction had a significant relationship to scientific accuracy and thinking; and when they reached the age when they were writing stories themselves, what they produced showed the influence of these ideas, even if they themselves were not aware of it.

Their solutions were different. Heinlein quickly developed a number of promising responses to the challenges posed by Gernsback's theories: a style of writing that relied more on indirect explanation, a logically thought-out background for his future societies, and a willingness to explore the life and social sciences, not just the physical sciences. Van Vogt mastered an entirely different approach: mad, surrealistic stories that threw off scientific ideas like a Chinese firecracker with little effort to impose an overall sense of logic or unity. Asimov built on the examples of detective fiction and the 'scientific problem' story to create scientific adventures of conversation, where heroes talked their way towards the solution of problems vaster than murders or escaping from a frictionless mirror. De Camp gravitated toward an approach that combined scientific ideas with the form and conventions of heroic fantasy, a style also followed by writers like Leiber and Vance. Bradbury, and to a degree Sturgeon, created stories drenched in emotion, rich in characterization and descriptive language, where the science, however, functioned more as a decorative element than anything else. A bit later, Clement applied Heinlein's detailed backgrounds to an entirely scientific matter—creating fascinating but plausible imaginary worlds.

The fact that their approaches were different makes it hard to argue that Campbell was responsible for their success; and though del Rey generally repeats the usual tributes to Campbell, he concedes that 'The field as a whole was improving [in the 1940s], and how much of that is due to Campbell is hard to say... Maybe the field would have evolved without Campbell (Personally, I doubt it...)' (*The World of Science Fiction*, pp. 156–57). Michael Ashley's 'SF Bandwaggon'—one of the few studies that gives equal attention to all magazines of the period—downplays Campbell's role:

Certainly in this year [1938] and the next a tremendous insurge of new talent made *Astounding* a most refreshing publication, with some of the greatest originality in story concept and treatment. This was not just the work of Campbell. Magazine SF was, after all, now twelve years old. Followers who had discovered the early Gernsback magazines in their teens were now in their mid-twenties. They had had time to evaluate the trend of the fiction, to work out new themes for hackneyed plots and to look at SF in a new light. (p. 23)

Other commentators suggest that Campbell's role in the 1940s was not as pivotal as is often supposed: George Turner, after discussing the work of Campbell's predecessors Bates and Tremaine, said: 'And there Campbell was in luck; the time was ripening and he was the one on the spot to direct the harvest' ('John W. Campbell: Writer, Editor, Legend', *John W. Campbell: An Australian Tribute*, p. 32). Barry Malzberg's *The Engines of the Night* notes, 'The second generation [of science fiction writers]—those identified with Campbell—was composed of people who had grown up reading the early science fiction and were prepared to build upon it' (p. 13). James Gunn's *Alternate Worlds*, after citing a similar downplaying of Campbell in Donald A. Wollheim's *The Universe Makers*, acknowledges, 'Surely Campbell did not *create* Asimov, Heinlein, Sturgeon and van Vogt... Obviously, though, other influences were at work' (p. 160). And Robert Scholes and Eric S. Rabkin's *Science Fiction*, discussing Campbell, says: 'in 1939 he published such new figures of A. E. van Vogt, Robert A. Heinlein, Isaac Asimov, and Theodore Sturgeon—names which soon eclipsed most of those that had appeared in the previous decade and a half of magazine fiction. How did it do it? It was partly luck, of course. The second generation of writers in this tradition was coming along anyway' (p. 41).

Interestingly, Campbell was candid enough—in letters—to admit that he was learning from his writers, not teaching them: he told Blish, 'If you can make a yarn out of that—by God you'll show me a new way of writing science-fiction, and I can promise you I'll steal that just as I've stolen every other new idea of how to write science-fiction that's come my way. And just as you have, too. We both learned a lot from Bob Heinlein, from Isaac Asimov, and the rest' (letter to James Blish, 2 February 1953, p. 118). And he said to Clement, 'I can quote back basic ideas from so many sources. I'm funneling ideas from Heinlein, de camp [sic], van Vogt, Ray Jones, Stein [G. Harry Stine/Lee Correy?], Stubbs [Hal Clement], Asimov—quite a collection of really sharp minds' (letter to Harry Clement Stubbs, 4 April 1953, p. 151).

If Campbell cannot be acclaimed for creating the styles of these writers, perhaps one might say that he was able to attract them and greatly improve their work; so that he still might deserve credit for the flowering of modern science fiction. But these claims are questionable as well.

It is true that Campbell had a reputation as an innovative writer, which in itself may have attracted writers to his magazine. Moskowitz reports that Simak returned to writing science fiction specifically because Campbell became an editor: '"I can write for Campbell,' he told his wife, Kay. 'He won't be satisfied with the kind of stuff that is being written. He'll want something new"' (*Seekers of Tomorrow*, p. 273). And del Rey says, 'The Faithful' 'would never have been written except for the writer's knowledge that Campbell was the editor' (*The World of Science Fiction*, p. 92).

However, the appeal of Campbell in the 1940s may relate more to his cheque book than to his brain. He inherited a magazine that already paid the highest rates in the field and established a policy of giving bonuses for stories he thought were especially good or proved to be especially popular in readers' polls. Thus, to account for the superiority of *Astounding Science-Fiction* in Campbell's first decade, one can develop an economic explanation. In the 1930s and 1940s, *Astounding* was the highest paying and most reliable market for science fiction; by nature, the best writers and the best stories would gravitate to it. Even before Campbell took over, the magazine was clearly the best; yet it is hard to say this was because Tremaine, Campbell's predecessor, was also a great editor, because Tremaine later became editor of a lesser magazine, *Comet Stories*, and, as noted, he had little success there. If Campbell had found himself editing, say, *Thrilling Wonder Stories*, he would have found it harder to attract talented writers and produce a memorable magazine. To continue the argument, in the 1950s and 1960s, when other, equally attractive markets opened up for science fiction, *Astounding* naturally lost its previous superiority. Pohl provides indirect support for this position in discussing why his *Galaxy* was able to compete with Campbell's *Analog* in the 1960s: after noting that 'John just wasn't very interested any more', he significantly adds, 'I could pay almost as much as he did' (*The Way the Future Was*, p. 85)—implicitly another reason why Pohl was then able to compete with him.

If Campbell was not responsible for the improved approaches of writers of the 1940s, and if he attracted them solely for economic reasons, there remains the argument that Campbell was an inspiring source of ideas, an insightful and demanding reader, and a stimulus to better science fiction writing. However, I don't think Campbell was really a particularly talented editor of this kind.

The howls of protest are almost audible. How can one say that about the man whose magazine, *Astounding Science-Fiction*, was the leader in publishing superior fiction for over a decade? The man who had the insight to articulate Asimov's Three Laws of Robotics, suggest the story line for

Asimov's 'Nightfall', change the ending of Tom Godwin's 'The Cold Equations'? The man whose editorial acumen has been praised so often by the writers who worked for him?

Nevertheless, the record on this point is clear as well.

First, while praising the *Astounding* of the 1940s, one cannot ignore the *Astounding* of the 1950s and its successor in the 1960s, *Analog Science Fiction/Science Fact*, which were consistently inferior to Campbell's earlier magazines. Apologists like Pohl say that Campbell was paying less attention to science fiction as he focused on various scientific and pseudo-scientific projects; but one might respond that an editor who is not paying attention to what he is doing is by definition not a good editor. In addition, the numerous letters in *The John W. Campbell Letters, Volume I* suggest that he was continuing to devote a considerable amount of energy and attention to the chores of editing; and until his death, he continued to read every manuscript submitted to his magazine. This is not a description of a man who has lost interest in editing.

To explain the numerous anecdotes about his great editorial skills, one must acknowledge that there is inevitable selectivity in such information. Critics are interested in great stories and investigate them, perhaps to discover that Campbell played a role in making them great. Critics are not interested in lousy stories and ignore them, perhaps failing to discover that Campbell played a role in making them lousy. Many times it is acknowledged that Campbell gave Asimov the story line for 'Nightfall'; it is less frequently noted that he also contributed the story line for Heinlein's *Sixth Column*, easily the worst novel of Heinlein's early career. Everyone knows that Campbell encouraged and molded the young Asimov; few realize that he ignored and rejected the young Bradbury. Everyone knows he welcomed the Asimov stories that became the Robot and Foundation series; few realize that he twice rejected Clarke's *Against the Fall of Night*, which has proved equally durable.[8] Everyone knows the key role Campbell played in shaping 'The Cold Equations'; no one talks about the equally key role he played in shaping Godwin's other, forgotten stories.

To be sure, Campbell's input and detailed suggestions surely improved many science fiction stories—but not necessarily because he was unusually insightful. Modern composition classes often involve a process of 'peer review' based on the principle that reactions from another reader, even an unlearned one, can help to improve a person's writing. And from my own experience writing criticism, I have learned that even unreasonable or absurd editorial demands can lead to noteworthy improvements. In this regard, it is interesting to examine the Panshins's account in *The World beyond the Hill* of the creation of Asimov's 'Reason'. (Since Asimov praised the book on its dusk jacket, it is probable that they consulted with him, so the story can be accepted as accurate.) As they tell the story, young Asimov was fed up with Campbell's stubborn insistence on his own beliefs; as a subtle message to Campbell that other beliefs might be equally valid, he wrote 'Reason', about a robot who refuses to accept that he was created by humans but nevertheless manages to do an effective job of running a solar power space station—demonstrating that different belief systems can have equally valuable results. Here, then, is a worthwhile story that did not emerge from Campbell's good ideas; rather, it emerged as a reaction to Campbell's bad ideas.

The opposite of a talented and stimulating editor is a silent editor; and Campbell was never silent. Simply by constantly talking to writers and responding to their work, Campbell could improve their work, and they were naturally grateful for the improvement, even if some aspects of the experience were grating.

Indeed, one mark of talented writers like Asimov is that they can successfully adjust to bad editorial input and even turn it to their advantage; untalented writers, on the other hand, will accept and incorporate editorial input, both good and bad, with less successful results. So Campbell helped the very good writers his magazine attracted in the 1940s; but he did not improve the lesser writers that he was left with in the 1950s and 1960s.

To account further for the accolades bestowed upon Campbell, one must consider three factors. While he was alive, Campbell solely controlled a major outlet for science fiction, which made it unwise to criticize him; recalling an argument he witnessed between John Brunner and Campbell, van Vogt obliquely makes this point:

> what happened to John Brunner, when he, in effect, contradicted [John W. Campbell, Jr] during a convention panel discussion, could never have happened to me.
>
> You might ask, what kind of caution was involved? Well, I once, without the slightest anxiety or fear, argued with a prowler and, in effect, persuaded him, now that he was discovered, to depart. That kind of incident had nothing to do with a possible threat to annual income in those early days. (cited in 'John Wood Campbell', pp. 24–25)

In fact, in light of his economic clout, the fact that there were a few free spirits like Blish and Harlan Ellison who repeatedly took him to task for publishing inferior and unreadable fiction increases in significance. Furthermore, Campbell at times could be a stimulating conversationalist, good companion, and staunch friend and supporter to many science fiction writers—grounds enough for effusive praise. Finally, when he died in 1971, there emerged a natural disinclination to speak ill of the dead.

It is appropriate, then, that another dead person—Heinlein—has stepped forward, in his posthumous collection of letters, *Grumbles from the Grave*, to offer a different perspective on Campbell's editorial talents. In the 1940s, while Heinlein tried to be friendly to Campbell, one letter reacted angrily and at length to a comment Campbell made about the American military:

> when it comes to matters outside your specialties you are consistently and brilliantly stupid. You come out with some of the goddamndest flat-footed opinions with respect to matters which you haven't studied and have had no experience, basing your opinions on casual gossip, newspaper stories, unrelated individual data out of matrix, armchair extrapolation, and plain misinformation—unsuspected because you haven't attempted to verify it... I don't expect such sloppy mental processes from you. Damn it! You've had the advantage of a rigorous training in scientific methodology. Why don't you apply it to everyday life? (p. 30)

And in 1963, while experiencing problems with *The Magazine of Fantasy and Science Fiction*, Heinlein commented that 'Still, it is pleasanter than offering copy to John Campbell, having it bounced (he bounced both of my last two Hugo Award winners)—and then have to wade through ten pages of his arrogant insults, explaining to me why my story is no good' (p. 152).[9]

If I am arguing that Campbell was not responsible for the improved science fiction in the 1940s, that he attracted and published talented new writers mainly because he could pay them well, and that he improved their writing only in the way that any talkative respondent might, then it seems that, after devoting considerable space to Campbell, I am turning around to argue that he was really not important. But in fact, Campbell did some highly important work during the 1940s—as a science fiction critic.

That is, while Campbell welcomed these new authors to his magazine in the 1940s, he noticed what they were doing, learned from what they were doing, and selected the most promising and powerful aspects of their approaches to praise as part of his new theory of science fiction. He saw Heinlein's approach as the most valuable and repeatedly extolled the principles of Heinlein's fiction in his editorials and articles. Though he quietly tolerated van Vogt's extravagances, he never described or celebrated his scattershot approach. He resisted at first, but gradually accepted, the detective story pattern of Asimov and Clement's *Needle*. He steered writers like de Camp and Leiber to his fantasy magazine, *Unknown*, and later was disinclined to publish their fantasy-oriented stories. And he had no patience with the lack of scientific thought in Bradbury and accepted only two of his early efforts. In these ways—through his advocacy of or silence regarding these various approaches—Campbell had a strong influence on the next generation of writers who appeared in the 1950s.

That is, the views that Campbell derived from the selected examples of his best writers can be directly linked to the science fiction written in the 1950s by the next generation of writers, the ones who grew up with and were shaped primarily by Campbell's statements, not Gernsback's statements. During that decade, as noted in the last chapter, signs of the influence of Campbell's ideas were everywhere. The paradox, though, is that most of the works that best reflected Campbell's ideas in the late 1940s and 1950s did *not* appear in Campbell's *Astounding Science-Fiction*.

The question is, then: during all these developments that he helped to instigate, what happened to Campbell himself?

Simply put, Campbell did not practise what he preached; or rather, Campbell was so preoccupied with establishing his personal power and the power of science fiction that he neglected almost every principle that he had articulated and helped to establish.

That is, to prepare an indictment of Campbell's last twenty-five years as editor of *Astounding/Analog*—a period when, by all accounts, his magazine declined in quality and influence—one can go back to most of the basic innovations in Campbell's theories, listed above, and present a parallel list noting their growing and conspicuous absence in Campbell's own magazine in the 1950s.

Campbell proclaimed that 'science-fiction is the freest, least formalized of any literary medium' ('Introduction', *Who Goes There?*, p. 5)—but in his own editorial practice, he insisted on certain rigid formulas. Stories had to be upbeat and optimistic, which is why Campbell did not care for, and rarely published, stories about Earth after a nuclear holocaust, for example. If stories involved conflict between humans and aliens, the humans had to win—every time; and it was this dictum which drove young Asimov, tired of arguing the point, to create a future universe for his *Foundation* stories where there were no aliens at all. As Asimov and Ben Bova put it, 'Campbell was sufficiently Earth-centered, in fact, to insist that human beings *must* win in the end and would not allow a human defeat. Unwilling to accept this limitation, Asimov evaded it by dealing with a Galaxy that had only a single intelligence, the human being' (*Asimov on Science Fiction*, p. 127).

Campbell proclaimed that 'Modern readers—and hence editors... want stories of people' which display a certain 'style' ('The Science of Science Fiction Writing', pp. 92, 98)—but his magazine offered stories with almost no characterization or style to speak of. In 'A Voice from the Styx', Ellison reacted to a novel published in the 1950s, Frank Herbert's *The Dragon in the Sea*:

One simply cannot *care* what happens to the stick-men who populate [the novel]. One cannot believe their war, cannot value their cause, cannot tense at their danger, in fact can involve oneself as a reader in only the most casual way.

It is this lack of the necessity for involvement on the part of a reader that typifies a type of writing John Campbell has championed in *Analog* (under its various logos and titles). What began as a New Wave in the Forties with Campbell's rejection of the Crustacean Period in speculative fiction... has come far past the end of its passage, and now represents something like a return to the T. O'Connor Sloane [*sic*] image of what a *good* science fiction story should be... The Campbell heavy-science story as typified by *Dragon in the Sea* is a sterile art-form to pursue... It is the usurpation of character and plot to the ends of the engineer... Campbell, as champion of hard science, has created an aura about *Analog* that... has produced novels of the *Dragon of the Sea* variety. Clanking, clattering, caliginous catastrophes containing can openers, clichés and case studies not characters. (pp. 122, 123, 125)

A particular problem noted by Blish was inferior works published in *Astounding* whose function is didactic: 'it has been clear that Campbell has been thinking of himself primarily as an educator, selecting stories for print primarily because they raise questions he wants to see put, make points with which he agrees, or otherwise act out his editorials in story form' (*The Issues at Hand*, p. 99); and this charge should be illustrated with an example. In June 1956, a Campbell editorial called 'Psionic Machine—Type One' enthusiastically described the 'Hieronymus Machine', a device which allegedly ran on psychic power alone. Two months later, a story appeared entitled 'There's No Fool... ', by Randall Garrett writing as David Gordon, describing a stage magician who dazzles audiences with his amazing 'psychocybernetic antigravitational levitator'. But as the 'magician' later explains, the machine is not a trick—it actually works by psychic power—and using it in a magic act is a strategy—so far unsuccessful—to convince the world to take the device seriously. His wife then laments, 'If only someone would see... would try to find out... how electronics and the human mind are linked. Or how a machine can act as an amplifier for telepath [*sic*], ESP, precognition, teleportation, and levitation' (p. 51). The story is transparently designed solely to convey that message; there is otherwise no narrative to speak of, no events, no characterization—no elements of fiction at all to speak of.

To be sure, Gernsback is often accused of instigating this trend, and in his talk of an earlier 'Crustacean period' in science fiction and mention of

Gernsback's colleague Sloane, Ellison indirectly makes this charge; however, one can question whether the type of fiction Ellison condemns should be attributed to Gernsback. True, the fiction that Gernsback and Sloane published leaned heavily on scientific explanations. Still, even if it was only boy-meets-girl or hero-versus-villain, Gernsback's science fiction always had a story of some kind; only in Campbell's magazines does one start to see works which seem to have no story to them at all.

Campbell proclaimed that all necessary scientific information in science fiction must be 'worked into the story without interrupting' ('Brass Tacks', November 1942, p. 109)—but he published stories like 'There's No Fool...' and Clement's 'Fireproof' that were little more than clumsy frameworks for lectures.

Campbell proclaimed that fields like 'sociology' and 'psychology' were apt subjects for science fiction ('The Science of Science Fiction Writing', p. 91)—but rather than involving a variety of disciplines, the stories he published, when not about psychic powers, increasingly focused on physics and engineering—which made *Analog*, as Ellison claimed, little more than a 'bull session' for 'other engineers and scientists' ('A Voice from the Styx', p. 124).

Campbell proclaimed that science fiction writers needed to develop a 'carefully mapped outline in mind to get consistency of minor details' ('The Old Navy Game', p. 6) in stories—but stories he published often had backgrounds that were dull and perfunctory, mere backdrops for discussion of an idea that appealed to Campbell.

Campbell proclaimed that science fiction should offer 'a real mental challenge' ('Introduction', *Analog 1*, p. vi)—but instead of stimulating puzzles, the stories he published tended to be static presentations of his own predictable ideas and positions. For example, Raymond F. Jones's 'Cry of the Wolf' attempts to present a puzzling situation: newly discovered aliens who seem to have amazing powers. But in the 1950s, Campbell's *Astounding* harped on the theme that the next major breakthrough in science would be the investigation and harnessing of 'psionic power'; in that context, then, Jones's story poses no real puzzle at all: the predictable answer is that the aliens have mastered 'psionic power'.

Campbell proclaimed that the ideas of science fiction regarding rocketry—and presumably, other subjects—are useful because 'Genuine engineering minds have considered the problems [of rocket spaceships], mulled them over, argued them back and forth in stories, and worked out the basic principles that will most certainly appear in the first ships built' ('The Science of Science-Fiction', pp. 5–6). However, during the 1950s, he ignored his own celebration of *collaborative thinking by scientifically trained people* to repeatedly support, as shall be described, the *isolated individual thinking of persons who lacked scientific training.*

Campbell proclaimed that 'Science fiction can provide for a science-based culture... a means of practicing anything in imagination... [so that] the basic outlines of the consequences of a particular course of action can be worked out' ('The Place of Science Fiction', p. 16) and can function as 'a convenient analog system for thinking about new scientific, social, and economic ideas—and for re-examining old ideas' ('Introduction', *Prologue to Analog*, p. 13); but rather than examining and exploring a broad range of coming developments and current problems, the stories he published in the 1950s came to obsessively focus on what he saw was the next major development—scientific exploitation of 'psionic power'. Scores of stories were dictated by this concern—yet to this date there has emerged no scientific proof of such phenomena and no method of making use of such phenomena. Under his direction, one might say, science fiction wasted a lot of time. And, as Blish noted, this obsession proved ruinous to the literary value of the stories he was publishing: 'when an editor becomes convinced that a concept like psi is more than just a device—that it is *real*—then he becomes more interested in the gimmick-thinking than he is in the fiction' (*The Issues at Hand*, p. 88).[10]

Finally, Campbell declared that science fiction could uniquely present the cold, harsh realities of 'the Opinion of the universe', instead of traditional stories centred on human opinions; but some of his 'psionic' stories are little more than whimsical exercises in wish-fulfillment, disguised fairy tales. Consider 'Aspirin Can't Help It', by Algis Budrys writing as John A. Gentry: a short-order cook gets a cold and, as a result, inexplicably develops telekinetic powers; when he is around, his bed rolls across the room and sheets fly through the air of their own accord. Eventually he learns to control his powers: 'I don't use it, except around the house to help Arlene, and maybe keep the neighborhood touched up a bit. It's no good to me at all, when I'm working, because I've got one to twenty people sitting in a row, watching me. About the best I can do, during a really bad rush, when everybody's yelling for service and everybody's intent on their own order, I can, if I'm careful, let the toast butter itself' (p. 59). This is no exploration of the harsh realities of the universe; it is the old fairy tale of the man who is granted magical abilities.

Like Gernsback, then, Campbell became increasingly associated with a style of writing completely antithetical to his own announced philosophy. But Gernsback at least actively resisted stories that did not meet his standards; Campbell, it seems, actively encouraged and happily published such stories.

One thus sees in Campbell's story, as in Gernsback's, an element of tragedy, though of a different sort. First, despite his prominence in science fiction, Campbell had unfulfilled aspirations outside the field: Gunn's *Alternate Worlds* reports his lifelong dream to edit a science magazine; after the Second World War, he tried to establish himself as an authority on atomic energy with his book *The Atomic Story*; and he wrote articles on science fiction for *The Atlantic Monthly* and *The Saturday Review*—yet he never made himself a figure of importance to the general public. Even within the field, Campbell grew marginalized, as readers and writers became alienated by Campbell and everything he represented.

Science fiction in the 1950s, then, presents a paradox: on the one hand, there was a new generation of writers who had listened to Campbell's ideas and were inspired to produce science fiction which exactly accorded with those ideas; on the other hand, the man who had articulated and announced those new ideas now seemed to be abandoning them. As one of those writers, Knight, put it:

> I was trying to explore other ways of organizing society, and to demonstrate other ways of writing science fiction, just as Campbell had done in the thirties. I had good company in this enterprise: Theodore Sturgeon, Fritz Leiber, Algis Budrys, and Cyril Kornbluth.
>
> I believe all of us had felt somehow betrayed by Campbell. With [H. L.] Gold's encouragement, we tried to revive the revolution Campbell had aborted a decade earlier—not just to make money in our profession, but to bring something beautiful and necessary into being. ('Beauty, Stupidity, Injustice, and Science Fiction', p. 88)

As was the case with Gernsback, there are two explanations for Campbell's later failures—involving his relationships with writers and aspects of his theories—both related to his desire for power.

First, one might account for the precipitous decline in the quality of the fiction Campbell was publishing in the 1950s and 1960s to one fact: almost all the writers Campbell made prominent who could find an equivalent or better market abandoned him in the 1950s. Only Asimov, who most energetically praised him, continued to write regularly for Campbell, and even he also published in other markets; others, like Heinlein, Sturgeon, and de Camp, avoided him. Writers may have voted with their mouths for Campbell, but they emphatically voted against him with their feet.[11]

Why did Campbell drive writers away? I have suggested that his input was not always helpful, and some later letters which outline story ideas were often dull and didactic.

Next, carefully examining the almost ritualized paeans to Campbell's editorial genius, one notes admissions of Campbell's numerous flaws, though these are often couched in apologetic or ameliorative language. Allow me to state those flaws plainly: to an extent that cannot be attributed solely to his upbringing and environment, Campbell was a racist, a bigot, a sexist, and an anti-Semite. He was incredibly gullible in believing what he wanted to believe, incredibly stubborn in refusing to believe what he did not want to believe. He played favourites and held grudges. Although he only had a BA in physics, he insisted that his own idiosyncratic research made him an expert in a large number of fields. None of this made him particularly pleasant company.

Descriptions of Campbell's powerful egotism and arrogance—recall Heinlein's reference to his 'arrogant insults'—are apparently contradicted by apparent modesty in claiming responsibility for the superior stories he published; for example, Asimov says that while Campbell 'was the brain of the superorganism that produced the "Golden Age" of science fiction in the 1940s and 1950s... He took no credit for himself' (*Asimov on Science Fiction*, p. 179). However, when a steady chorus of voices is praising one's editorial genius, even a proud man need not brag about it. Concerning aspects of his career where no celebratory consensus existed, Campbell was more than willing to brag about himself. Here is an edited version of his 'Introduction' to *Cloak of Aesir*:

> The straightforward science fiction story of the [1930s] 'proved' the wonderfulness of super-science, the super-machine, the straight-ahead progress of Man; and it assumed, as a matter of course, that thus, and only thus, would man progress.
>
> Originally, the stories *The Machine*, *The Invaders* and *Rebellion* were written as a series, titled *The Teachers*. Part One was the Machine—which taught laziness. Now this was not entirely according to the rules of science-fiction; this was saying that too darned good a machine can be a menace, not a help. The second 'Teacher' was the Invaders—which was also slightly askew on the then standard line of science-fiction... Again, *The Escape* is, quite forthrightly, in flat contradiction of science-fiction tradition, and also in flat contradiction of fiction tradition... Not cricket, doncha know—but fun.
>
> And *Forgetfulness* was another piece particularly calculated to be The Wrong Answer type of story for science-fictioneers... And *Forgetfulness* is quite an unfair story. Definitely the wrong answer... As a matter of fact, in many of the Don A. Stuart stories, there is the element of a dirty, underhanded crack at the pretensions of science-fiction... 'Don A. Stuart' was an uncomfortable sort of fellow for the dyed-in-the-wool, straight science-fictioneer. But the vistas that opened up when you started looking at the other side of the coin—considering whether an accepted tenet of The Eternal Fitness of

Things really *did* fit—made for a lot more fun. ('Introduction' to *Cloak of Aesir*, pp. 11–13)

The modest Mr Campbell, indeed![12]

Campbell's most obnoxious feature may have been his style of personal contact, which was bullying and obsessively self-focused. Pohl provides the following account of Campbell in action:

> I trotted up to the familiar decrepit office building... and was admitted to The Presence. As I came into the office John rolled down his desk top, swiveled around in his chair, pointed to a seat, fitted a cigarette into his holder, and said, 'Television will never replace radio in the home. I'll bet you don't know why.'
>
> That set the pattern. Over the next few years, and intermittently for much longer, I made the pilgrimage to John's office and was greeted with some such opening remark. The conversation always went the same way:
>
> Gee, no, Mr. Campbell, I never thought of that.
>
> Right, Pohl, and no one else did, either. But what is the audience for radio?
>
> Uh—
>
> (Rueful shake of the head.) The *primary* audience is bored housewives. They turn the radio on to keep them company while they do the dishes.
>
> Yeah, I guess that's right, all r—
>
> And the point (warming up, jabbing the cigarette toward me) is, you can't *ignore* television! You have to *look* at it!
>
> After a few such conversations, and after reading the editorials in *Astounding*, I figured out what was happening. That was how John Campbell wrote the editorials. On the first of every month he would choose a polemical notion. For three weeks he would spring it on everyone who walked in. Arguments were dealt with, objections overcome, weak points shored up—and by the end of each month he had a mighty blast proof-tested against a dozen critics. (*The Way the Future Was*, pp. 81–82)

In short, Campbell was not really interested in talking with other people, only in talking *at* them—using them as a sounding board for his own ideas. Based on my own experience, this becomes truly irritating after a while. *The John W. Campbell, Jr. Letters* is strangely unbalanced, with only a few letters from the 1930s and 1940s and many letters from the 1950s, 1960s, and 1970s, for many possible reasons, but perhaps in the 1940s, Campbell could maintain personal contact with most writers and get business done in that way; later, writers learned how to avoid personal contact with Campbell and he was obliged to write more and longer letters.

As his style of conversation with Pohl suggests, Campbell could show the desire to have personal control over writers. Asimov reports the following conversation with Campbell:

> curiosity finally got the better of me and I said, nervously, 'Mr. Campbell, how can you bear not to write?'
>
> 'I discovered something better, Asimov,' he said. 'I'm an editor.'
>
> I thought that over and then said, cautiously, 'How is that better, Mr. Campbell?'
>
> He said, enthusiastically, 'When I was a writer, I could only write one story at a time. Now I can write fifty stories at a time. There are fifty writers out there writing stories they've talked with me about. There are fifty stories I'm working on.'
>
> That was the way he saw us all. We were extensions of himself; we were his literary clones; each of us doing, in his or her own way, things Campbell felt needed doing; things that he could do but not quite the way we could; things that got done in fifty different varieties of ways. (*Asimov on Science Fiction*, pp. 177–78)

Notice how Asimov—Campbell's major apologist—treats this attitude as a charming quirk and softens the impact of his statements to emphasize the element of individual creativity—'each of us doing, in his or her own way', 'things he could do but not quite the way we would'. But Campbell's assertion is blunt and arrogant: he is actually 'writing' the stories of his authors. Heinlein, Sturgeon, van Vogt, and Kuttner were not puppets with strings being pulled by Campbell; yet Campbell wanted to see himself as their puppeteer.[13]

Giving writers ideas, trapping them in one-sided conversations, and writing extensive letters are all ways to maintain control over writers; but the ultimate power manoeuvre was to reject a story. And Campbell, displaying a mean streak, pulled this trick on all his writers—apparently, simply to remind them of his power over them. Consider these examples. For ten years, Campbell carefully and sympathetically nurtured the emerging talent of Asimov, and he obtained and published a number of excellent stories, including those that would later coalesce into his Robot and Foundation series. Yet when Asimov finally decided to try writing a novel, *Pebbles in the Sky*, Campbell rejected it. Heinlein made it clear that he would stop writing for *Astounding* the minute Campbell rejected one of his stories; yet in 1942, Campbell rejected 'Goldfish Bowl', and only reconsidered when Heinlein demonstrated that he intended to carry out his threat. Simak published the first seven stories in the City series in *Astounding*

Science-Fiction; yet when Simak sent him the eighth and final story, 'Trouble with Ants', Campbell rejected it.[14] Interestingly, when Simak reprinted the City stories in book form, the framing introduction to 'Trouble with Ants' (now called 'The Simple Way') has the future dog scholar say this: 'Structurally, it is an acceptable story, but the phraseology of it does not measure up to the narrative skill that goes into the others. Another thing is that it is too patently a story. It is too clever in its assembly of material, works the several angles from the other tales too patly together' (*City*, pp. 225–26). Since it is rare for authors to spontaneously criticize their own work, I suspect that Simak is paraphrasing Campbell's rejection letter— and that a year after the fact, Simak was still bitter about the rejection.

One could argue that *Pebble in the Sky*, 'Goldfish Bowl', and 'Trouble with Ants' did not represent their authors' best work; but that is not the point. Those works were clearly as good as or superior to the other fiction that Campbell was publishing at the time. And, to maintain a good working relationship with three talented writers, Campbell should have accepted their stories as a matter of course. But Campbell wanted to be in control of his writers and wanted them to know he was in control, and so, essentially to keep writers from getting too big for their britches, he periodically rejected one of their stories, just to tell them that despite their talent, they really were not that important to him.

In the 1940s, this policy might have worked, when Campbell headed one of the few markets for science fiction, and the market that paid the best rate. But by the 1950s, writers who chafed under Campbell's control had—or developed—other attractive options. Heinlein worked to sell stories to mass-market magazines, Hollywood, and juvenile publishers. Two new magazines, *The Magazine of Fantasy and Science Fiction* and *Galaxy*, became just as prominent—and just as profitable—as *Astounding*, and writers like Simak, Asimov and Sturgeon gravitated towards them. Science fiction novels and anthologies started appearing in hardcover, and the new field of paperback books offered exciting new opportunities for old and new writers. Successful writers didn't need to please Campbell any more, and most of them didn't bother to try; they just found other editors to accept their stories.[15]

So Campbell found a group of new writers who were malleable and amenable to his control—but they generally were not very good.[16] Clement significantly improved, Tom Godwin produced one memorable story, 'The Cold Equations', and Poul Anderson, Blish, and Robert Silverberg made some good early contributions, but the quality of the magazine in general greatly deteriorated.

Only once did Campbell explain why he was no longer publishing many major writers of the 1940s; and his explanation is remarkable:

So what about the Great Old Authors (please remember that 1940 was almost a quarter century ago)? Well, they're convinced that they already know how to write and aren't gonna be told what they should write by that dictatorial, authoritarian, uncooperative Campbell... Most of them got their scientific orientation back in the early thirties, and they've been running on it ever since. How many of them are in contact with actual research work being done today—and getting the feel for the major direction of science *now*?... Will somebody please tell me why the Great Old Authors will not get off their literary tails and consider something new? They hate me for shoving new concepts and ideas at them—and damn me for *their* lack of a Sense of Wonder! ('Editorial Number Three: Letter from the Editor', p. xxi)

I need not comment on the notion that Campbell in the 1960s was keeping himself up-to-date and open-minded in contrast to the stultified writers of the 1940s, and to say the least, Campbell displays a considerable amount of arrogance to imply that writers like Heinlein, Sturgeon, and Simak have stopped writing for Campbell because *they aren't good enough for Campbell any more*; they could not, one must suppose, meet the high standards then being set by Christopher Anvil, Walt and Leigh Richmond, Rick Raphael, and the other writers Campbell was then featuring in *Analog*. Still, the passage is interesting in that—though with intended irony—Campbell does provide what may be his most accurate self-description: 'dictatorial, authoritarian, uncooperative'.

As another possible explanation for the decline in *Astounding/Analog*, consider Campbell's claim in a letter to Terry Carr that as the man who read every single work ever submitted to the magazine, 'I have unquestionably read more lousy science-fiction than any other man in the world' (17 June 1968, p. 540). A person is not necessarily what he reads, and reading lousy books does not necessarily make one a lousy reader. Still, constantly reading so much 'lousy' prose might have deleterious effects—specifically, it might make it difficult to distinguish good prose from bad prose.

Another problem is suggested by a statement in a letter to Gunn: 'After I got started running *Astounding*, I was too damn busy reading for the magazine to keep up with what was going on in all the other magazines' (26 June 1970). Although it is hard to take this claim entirely seriously—surely Campbell occasionally looked at what the competition was doing—it may well be that to some extent Campbell was unaware that other magazines were regularly printing better stories than the ones he was selecting.

The most overt aspect of Campbell's decline—his obsessions with various areas of pseudo-science—is also related to his personality, but there is a connection to his theories as well.

Campbell sought power not only for himself but for science fiction. He retained Gernsback's idea that science fiction writers could suggest ideas that could lead to actual inventions, adding the point that this could be a collaborative process, not just an individual's inspiration. And this would make science fiction a major influence on the world. More broadly, Campbell saw science fiction as a way to consider the effects of future inventions, spot possible trends, envision certain problems, perhaps prevent disaster. And these unique abilities could make science fiction a mighty force in influencing society: scientists and policymakers would eagerly consult texts, looking for ideas and ramifications of ideas that could shape research strategies and policy decisions.

Of course, it didn't happen that way.

Gernsback no doubt realized that members of the scientific community were not consulting *Amazing Stories*, not attributing their inventions and discoveries to the stimulating ideas of science fiction, and apparently paying little or no attention to science fiction at all. But this didn't bother him. Science fiction was only one of Gernsback's interests; he always had other scientific schemes, magazines, and business to occupy himself with, so the failure of science fiction to live up to his dreams did not have a major effect on his life. And it did not bother him that science fiction was failing to have a major impact of society.

But Campbell was primarily—perhaps exclusively—concerned with science fiction; as Williamson observed, 'science fiction was his life' ('Foreword', p. ix). And, seeing its failure to change society, he confronted a question that had not been important to Gernsback: in theory, science fiction could do many wonderful things. But what if the theory didn't work? What if none of the things science fiction could do were actually happening?

Basically, Campbell came up with two answers. First, if the world was not paying attention to the random messages in science fiction, perhaps it was time to get organized—and to turn up the volume. Noting that the most spectacular success of previous science fiction involved its predictions about atomic energy, Campbell asked what other, entirely new form of energy might emerge in the future, and he decided that human mental energy, or 'psionics', was the likely answer. Accordingly, in the 1950s he repeatedly discussed this possibility in his editorials and repeatedly favoured stories of no great merit that happened to focus heavily on psychic powers. By choosing and emphasizing one theme, science fiction might be able to have some impact on the world.

Campbell's second answer was this: if members of the scientific community were not listening to the ideas of science fiction, if leaders were not listening to the advice of science fiction, then science fiction would have to do the work itself. Science fiction writers could do their own scientific research: in a comment attached to one of P. Schuyler Miller's book review columns in *Astounding*, he said, 'For genuine science-fiction, author, editor and reader alike must do research—and that means try the unknown, the uncertain, the unreliable, the untried' ('The Reference Library', September 1956, p. 153); and Campbell's letters of the 1950s report that he and his second wife conducted regular series of 'experiments' involving psychic powers. Along with such work, the science fiction community could gather to its bosom the talented scientists and inventors who were rejected by the scientific community because of their remarkable vision and heretical ideas. Science fiction magazines could publicize and promote their work, making the public aware of the scientific advances that were being denied them by a conservative power structure. Overall, then, the field of science fiction could make their new ideas work, demonstrate their effectiveness, and force the world to take them seriously, to accept their inventions and their implications.

To the extent to which there was any logic at all behind them, this is the logic behind Campbell's editorial embraces of various fantastic claims—the value of dowsing, the Hieronymus Machine, the Dean Drive, an anti-gravity machine, and so on. Campbell believed the people who talked of or apparently demonstrated these marvels, and he enthusiastically promoted them in his magazine.

However, as Campbell sought out, listened to, and embraced many of the ideas these scientific outcasts were promoting, he gradually learned one lesson: most of the ideas that the scientific community calls crazy really are crazy. And by promoting one unbelievable scientific device after another, Campbell simply made himself look ridiculous. Consider the testimony of Knight:

> In his restless urge to distance himself from the pack, he indulged in the fifties another persona, the credulous chela of pseudoscientists. One after another he trotted them out: Ehrenhaft, the discoverer of a nonexistent magnetic current; Dean, the inventor of an antigravity device which could not be produced for inspection; Hubbard, the founder of Dianetics and later the head of the Church of Scientology; Hieronymus, the inventor of a 'psionic' device that worked just as well when a wiring diagram was substituted for its electronic parts.
>
> What bothered me was that when one of these fantasies was exploded, as when a reader pointed out the flaws in Campbell's suggestion that a submarine powered by the Dean Drive could be flown to Mars tomorrow morning, he never admitted that he had

been wrong but simply went on to the next nutty idea. ('Beauty, Stupidity, Injustice, and Science Fiction', pp. 85–86)

In short, Campbell found it difficult to set up a shadow scientific community, and the materials he had to work with were quite feeble.

In the 1960s, Campbell abandoned his public obsessions with psionics and pseudo-science—though his letters from the 1960s continue to express interest and belief in psionics, dowsing, and the like—and tried one more strategy to make science fiction a powerful force in society. From the start of his career, Campbell wanted to publish speculative scientific articles— in April 1940, he declared, 'We want articles. We not only want them, we'll pay for them… The invitation is extended to any and all practicing technicians in any and all fields' ('Let's Make It Stronger', p. 6). After increasingly emphasizing articles, he finally made them the focus of his magazine: in 1961 he renamed the magazine *Analog: Science Fact/Science Fiction* and vowed to devote about half of its space to legitimate scientific nonfiction. (Later, though, the title would change to *Analog: Science Fiction/Science Fact.*)

This move to nonfiction reflected a decision that science fiction should re-align itself with the scientific community with articles by reputable scientists presenting reputable scientific discoveries and speculations. For example, *The John W. Campbell, Jr. Letters* contains a letter from Campbell to Carl Sagan requesting that he write an article for *Analog*. Campbell had found he couldn't beat the scientific community, so he tried to join it.

Coupled with this new drive for respectability came Campbell's efforts to make himself prominent as a political commentator, shamelessly devoting editorials to long opinionated tirades that had little to do with science or science fiction and occasionally contributing political articles to William F. Buckley's *National Review*. No doubt these diatribes were a refreshing change from long discussions of the Dean Drive and the like, but these political rumblings did little to repair Campbell's reputation or to enhance the quality of his magazine. Like Gernsback, then, Campbell increasingly found that science fiction was passing him by, increasingly found himself criticized and marginalized.

Still, there is one great difference between Gernsback and Campbell's fates: when Gernsback died quietly in 1967, his already-diminished reputation remained about the same. When Campbell died in 1971, his recent infelicities were forgotten, and his once-great reputation grew once again to enormous proportions. Thus, the power over science fiction that Campbell quickly lost during his life was paradoxically restored by his death.

The rehabilitation of Campbell began almost immediately. Consider this statement from Ellison, formerly one of his most vehement critics, on the day that he learned of Campbell's death:

> Sadly, as this is written, I learned that John W. Campbell, since 1937 editor of *Analog* (formerly *Astounding*), will never attend another convention; his death on July 11th, 1971, has thrown the entire field into shock and, whether he was loved, admired, tolerated or disliked, there is no denying he was the single most important formative force in modern sf, a man who was very much his own man, who lived by his own lights and by dint of enormous personal magnetism influenced everyone in the genre. The overwhelming sentiment is that he will be sorely missed and we will never be the same again. ('Introduction', '⬤', p. 9)

And Ellison's words of praise for Campbell would, in the years to come, be repeated again and again and again.

As discussed, histories of science fiction begin in many different places, choose different early authors to discuss, and say different things about them. When these histories talk about more recent science fiction, there is equal variety in the authors they choose to discuss and what they say about them. But when it comes time to talk about the 1940s, all histories of science fiction say exactly the same thing—that Campbell was 'the single most important formative force in modern sf'. From the grave, John W. Campbell, Jr summons all science fiction critics and scholars into his office, puts a cigarette in his holder, and forces them to listen to him, to examine his accomplishments, to ponder his idiosyncratic virtues and foibles.

In this way, allegedly independent critical voices are responding the way they have been told to respond: Gernsback did not demand attention, and he did not receive it; Campbell constantly demanded attention, and so he continues to receive it.

However, like science fiction writers during his lifetime, modern science fiction scholars confronting the 1940s must learn how to avoid The Presence.

The 1940s were indeed an important period in the history of science fiction—but that is because it was the time when the first generation of writers emerged who had grown up reading science fiction that was labelled as such, who knew something about what science fiction was, and who consciously tried to write science fiction. Their works were varied in quality but often remarkable. Some writers had extensive contact with him; some had very little contact with Campbell. And to tell their story through the lens of Campbell only limits and distorts the full picture.

Instead of casting him as the magician who transformed science fiction in the 1940s, therefore, Campbell should properly be credited with two achievements of incalculable importance. First, he established and promulgated the principles that have become universal in modern science fiction criticism; second, he inspired the tremendous outpouring of superior science fiction in the 1950s, perhaps the single most productive decade in the genre's history. For these accomplishments—and only for these accomplishments—everyone in the science fiction community should be grateful.

This book is not, and does not pretend to be, a history of science fiction. However, by explicating the critical history of science fiction, and by suggesting which commentators were most important and why they were important, this book can now suggest the structure of a history of science fiction.

There is nothing to say about the logical organization of histories of science fiction which extend back several centuries or to the dawn of literature; they cannot possibly have any logical organization. One observes the spirit of science fiction careening incoherently through literary history, skipping centuries, hopping from continent to continent, appearing and vanishing in the oddest places and at the oddest times. To the extent these histories have any structure at all, they are stories of disastrous decline, as a form of writing once occasionally practised by literary giants is gradually abandoned and left to wallow in the ghetto of pulp magazines—inexplicably at the same time that science finally became a prominent aspect of modern civilization—and since then only fitfully managing to regain its proper stature.

Histories focusing on the modern tradition may be more logically organized. This is the typical story: modern science fiction emerged in the 1920s and 1930s, but at first its stories were very poor. Then an editorial genius, Campbell, appeared, who single-handedly transformed science fiction into a mature genre. By the 1950s, the emergence of atomic energy and space programmes inspired an 'explosion', both in the amount and quality of science fiction produced. Then, actual space achievements seemed to deprive the genre of its most powerful subject, causing a sudden decline, though the genre was rescued by the New Wave movement, which brought new vigour to the field. After another decline, the popularity of the film *Star Wars* brought the genre new visibility and popularity, and feminist writers of the 1970s, and cyberpunk writers of the 1980s emerged to move science fiction in new directions.

There is some truth in this story, but it is unsatisfying, for it depicts science fiction as a genre at the mercy of unpredictable events. When conditions are favourable, or a Great Man or two comes along to provide guidance, the genre flourishes; when conditions are unfavourable, or there are no Great Men around, the genre deteriorates. Recognizing the importance of critical commentaries in creating and sustaining a genre, one can construct a different picture of science fiction history. While I have offered aspects of a general model, a full picture should be attempted.

The logic behind the model is this: when someone announces new principles and ideas regarding writing in a given genre, her ideas will, in the beginning, have little impact; established writers, and those just emerging, will already have fixed ideas about what they write and will at best grudgingly adapt their style to meet new demands. Some writers may eventually make a complete adjustment, but that will take some time. When the new ideas are promulgated, however, they also find a more receptive audience: young readers, who will enthusiastically read both the stories and commentaries surrounding those stories; and as they grow up, they will repeat, talk about, play with, and internalize those new ideas. And when some of them finally become writers, their works will reflect the impact of those new ideas. Once their stories appear, someone else will notice their novelty, and she will attempt to explain what they are doing, to codify and build on their approach. Again, these new ideas will have little immediate impact, but the coming generation of writers will be deeply influenced by them. Say that typical youngsters start reading the literature around the age of ten, and typical writers become full-time professionals in their mid-twenties; then one would expect about a fourteen-year gap between the promulgation of new critical ideas and their full effects.

Applying this model to the modern history of science fiction, then, one detects a recurring rhythm that I have explained in part. Gernsback announced his theories in 1926, but the literature of the time shows only superficial adjustment to those theories; in essence, writers kept writing the kind of fiction that was common before Gernsback. Young readers who accepted Gernsback's ideas became writers around 1940; Campbell noticed the novelty and higher quality of their work and commented on what they were doing. His ideas had no immediate effects, but young readers influenced by them became writers in the 1950s, demonstrating new approaches and styles. Various commentators of the 1950s like H. L. Gold, Damon Knight, and James Blish noticed the changes and presented new concepts, which had little immediate effect but eventually inspired the New Wave movement in the 1960s; and the voices of the New Wave did not immediately transform science fiction but eventually inspired the cyberpunk movement in the 1980s. Thus, the modern history of science fiction falls into these periods: 1926–1940, an era when older styles of writing imaginative fiction continued to dominate; 1940–1954, the era of the delayed impact of Gernsback's theories; 1954–1968, the era of the delayed impact of Campbell's theories; 1968–1982, the era of the delayed impact of the critical theories of the 1950s; and 1982–present, the era of the delayed impact of the New Wave theories.

The chronology is not perfect—by this model, both the 'boom' of the 1950s and the New Wave movement arrived a bit early, and the cyberpunk movement arrived a bit late. Also, of course, there are many writers whose careers and development do not match this or other patterns. In general, though, the model fits pretty well.[17]

Not only does this model impose a logical structure on the development of the genre, but it also contains a prediction: that some time around the new millennium, there will be another wave of new writings, when the cyberpunk commentaries finally have their full impact, and there will be another wave of new critical commentaries that will notice and respond to those new writings.

I also note that while all eras of commentary typically style themselves as efforts to replace previous approaches to science fiction, their actual effect is simply to impose a new layer of priorities on previous approaches, which remain important to the genre. Thus, to understand Gibson's *Neuromancer*, one first notices on the surface the announced concerns of the cyberpunks; beneath that, the priorities of the New Wave; beneath that, the approach of Campbell; and at the bottom, the theories of Gernsback.

While breaking the modern history of science fiction into these periods has advantages, one may also usefully speak of two larger eras. From the early 1920s to the early 1960s is the Age of Development, when the theories of Gernsback and Campbell were promulgated and absorbed, when authors discovered and worked with virtually all the themes and approaches that would characterize the genre; from the early 1960s to now is the Age of Refinement, when the theories of Gernsback and Campbell were further deepened or unsuccessfully challenged, when a new generation of more talented and literary writers returned to earlier themes and approaches to produce more sophisticated and aesthetically appealing stories and novels. And one of the faults of academic science fiction critics is a tendency to ignore the crucial Age of Development and attempt to make connections between early 'classics' of science fiction before Gernsback and recent works—a flawed vision which can only lead to flawed conclusions.[18]

While the eras of Gernsback and Campbell are most significant, full treatment of the history of science fiction will require at some point a thorough continuation of the critical history of the genre, discussing at length all of the important voices which emerged after Campbell; for now, however, having already produced a manuscript longer than any publisher would wish, I must leave that task for another time, or for another scholar.

Notes

1 Campbell once noted his abrasive relationship with his father: 'Dad and I used to have a running battle during my childhood, while I took extreme delight in doing *exactly* what he said every now and then to his acute discomfiture' (letter to Les Cole, 11 March 1953, p. 136).

2 Though Campbell told James Gunn (as reported in *Alternate Worlds*) that it was simply because there were not any jobs available for physicists when he graduated.

3 A long series of such laudatory quotations is offered in 'John Wood Campbell', in *The John W. Campbell Letters, Volume I*.

4 The Panshins often acknowledge that they have little real evidence for their extravagant claims, as, for example, in their statement that 'But nowhere did Campbell state the whole of his vision as explicitly as we have just tried to do' (p. 271). And their following assertion that the format of *Astounding Science-Fiction* implicitly announces this vision is not credible to someone who has actually examined those magazines. Ironically, the most powerful indictment of Panshin's treatment of Campbell comes from Campbell himself, who once advised Panshin to stay away from after-the-fact psychological explanations of what writers do: 'I'm afraid, though, that your quest for the motivations of it all will prove more than somewhat difficult. All you can get is somebody's explanation, long afterward, of something he did by the operation of unconscious mechanisms that his own conscious mind is inherently incapable of understanding!' (letter to Alexei Panshin, 8 September 1970, p. 588).

5 But are Moskowitz's claims accurate? In *The World of Science Fiction*, del Rey confirms that *Science Wonder Quarterly* 'was the first science fiction magazine I ever read' and that 'I didn't start reading the magazines regularly until 1931' (pp. 51, 77). Asimov tells the same story as Moskowitz in *Before the Golden Age*, though he says the magazine was *Science Wonder Stories*. Van Vogt agrees that 'in November, 1926, I saw this strange magazine with the fantastic cover, with the name *Amazing Stories*, on a newsstand. I bought that November issue and subsequent issues' (interview with Jeffrey M. Elliot, *Science Fiction Voices #2*, p. 32). Clarke says in *Astounding Days* that the first science fiction magazine he saw was the November 1928 issue of *Amazing Stories* (not a 1927 issue), though he claims that 'Curiously enough, I do not believe that Larry's 1928 *Amazing Stories* made such a great impression on me at the time' (p. 5), and his book's argument is that *Astounding Stories* actually had the greatest influence on him. Still, he acknowledges reading the other science fiction magazines—'Over the next few years, I acquired many of its brethren' (p. 12)—and at one point he 'started an index... for *Amazing, Wonder*, and their *Quarterlies*... At its peak, my collection of sf magazines must have totaled several hundred issues' (pp. 13–14), so he was familiar with the contents of many Gernsback magazines. So Moskowitz's statements seem generally accurate, though there may be some errors in detail.

6 In a later article, Pohl identified the science fiction magazine he saw as *Science Wonder Stories* ('Astounding Story', p. 42).

7 Another prominent Futurian, Judith Merril, is an exception to the rule, because she reports that 'It was in those bright days—in 1941, to be precise—that I discovered the science fiction magazines' ('What Do You Mean: Science? Fiction?', p. 68).

8 Clarke tells the story in *Astounding Days*: 'Campbell's chief objection [to

Against the Fall of Night] was that in my vision of the future the human race never amounted to anything much. As this was precisely the theme of "Twilight" and "Night", I felt this was a poor excuse' (p. 109).

9 The rejected stories Heinlein refers to are *Starship Troopers* and *Stranger in a Strange Land*.

10 Near the end of his career, Campbell candidly described his obsession with psionics: 'I let it be known, and known widely in the writing groups, that I wanted good stories using the ESP-psi theme. I got a remarkable collection of anti-psi propaganda!' ('Introduction', *14 Great Tales of ESP*, p. 14). Or, in other words, he got stories that did not agree with his own opinion of psionics.

11 In speaking of 'voting with their mouths', Harry Harrison makes much of 'the number of books that have been dedicated to [Campbell]... I would say there are at least thirty, a record that I am sure is unique in literature' ('Introduction', p. vi). However, there is again a prosaic explanation. Writers traditionally dedicate at least one book to someone who helped them at the beginning of their careers; the editor who published their early works is an obvious candidate for the honour; as a magazine editor for thirty-four years, Campbell was in a position to perform this service longer than any other editor; thus, he attracted many more dedications than other editors whose tenures were briefer.

12 Of course, these claims are preposterous—other writers in the 1930s explored the possible negative effects of scientific progress, and Stuart's stories, excepting 'Twilight', were not particularly unorthodox or discomfiting to science fiction readers.

13 Campbell repeatedly denied in his letters that he wanted to control what authors wrote: he told Sturgeon, 'Did I ever tell you, "Write me a story about this subject, in n-thousand words"? It's you I want in the magazine—not me in false whiskers' (letter to Theodore Sturgeon, 13 September 1954, p. 258); and he said to E. E. Smith, 'I do NOT want authors to write "my way", whatever various authors say' (letter to E. E. Smith, 26 May 1959). Still, it is interesting that he felt obliged to deny what 'various authors say'—suggesting there may have been some truth in what they said.

14 Asimov has often told the story of how Campbell rejected *Pebble in the Sky*, and Heinlein's experience with 'Goldfish Bowl' is documented in *Expanded Universe* and *Grumbles from the Grave*. It is only my theory that Campbell rejected 'Trouble with Ants', but that is the only logical conclusion: since Simak sent the first seven *City* stories to *Astounding*, it is hard to see why he would spontaneously decide to send the eighth and final story to *Amazing Stories* (where it was published); surely, Campbell saw it first.

15 Indeed, writers who praise Campbell should face two blunt questions: why did you stop sending stories to Campbell? How much time did you voluntarily spend in Campbell's company between 1950 and 1971? Only Asimov could have answered without awkwardness.

16 Knight sees the declining quality of writers for *Astounding* in the 1950s as Campbell's marketing ploy, a response to *Galaxy* and *The Magazine of Fantasy and Science Fiction*:

> he deliberately cultivated technically oriented writers with marginal writing skills, who could not hope to sell to more discriminating editors. Surveys had already shown that a large percentage of *Astounding's*

readers were technically or scientifically trained: they were interested in ideas, and didn't care if the stories were well or badly written. Although he continued to compete with Gold (and Boucher) for established writers, Campbell was building a new stable he knew he could keep. ('Beauty, Stupidity, Injustice, and Science Fiction', p. 77)

'Slow Sculpture': Conclusion

As I explained in 'Academic Criticism of Science Fiction', my entire approach to science fiction derives from lessons I learned as an English graduate student at Claremont Graduate School.

This particular project emerges directly from one lesson that was hammered in again and again: before scholars speak about a text or texts, they must first consult and codify previous scholarship regarding the text or texts. If that scholarship is inadequate or faulty, scholars can point out those omissions or flaws and present their work as a necessary correction; if that scholarship is worthwhile, scholars can acknowledge their debts to it and present their work as a helpful development of previous ideas.[1]

For the first time, this book thoroughly consults and codifies the commentaries concerning science fiction that existed prior to academic criticism of that field; so it could be argued that this book represents the true beginning of science fiction scholarship.

In a sense, though, the work of this book began long ago, with the publication of the first academic study of science fiction, J. O. Bailey's *Pilgrims through Time and Space* (1947). That is, we know from the modern stories he discusses, and from the letter he wrote to the Science Fiction League in 1934, that he was a regular reader of the science fiction magazines of the 1930s and 1940s, and I have discussed the possible influence of Gernsback's history of science fiction on his work. His term for the genre, 'scientific fiction', is the one first devised by Gernsback and later revived by Sloane, and his definition of science fiction—'a narrative of an imaginary invention or discovery in the natural sciences and consequent adventures and experiences' (p. 10)—is not unlike Gernsback's, especially in focusing on 'inventions', Gernsback's favourite subject, and conceding the importance of its 'adventures'. Bailey pauses to raise the question, 'It would be interesting to know whether any important invention has been inspired by an imaginary invention in fiction' (p. 261); and while his answer is noncommittal—'a direct influence of imaginary invention upon actual invention can hardly be demonstrated' (p. 261)—he was surely inspired to ask the question by recalling Gernsback's arguments about such possible results. His introductory argument for a study of science fiction, pointing to the emergence of atomic energy and the need for literature that will address coming scientific developments, is similar to Campbell's arguments for science fiction; later, striking a similar note in his conclusion, Bailey even quotes from Campbell's 1945 editorial, 'Atomic Age'.

There is ample evidence, therefore, to show that while his research involving the imaginative works of earlier centuries was entirely his, Bailey developed many ideas regarding science fiction by consulting and codifying the existing commentaries on that genre which were appearing in the early science fiction magazines.

But the names of Gernsback and Campbell do not appear in his book, and Bailey never suggests that his ideas are not original.

It is hard to get angry at Bailey for these omissions. In the scholarly climate of his day, it was miraculous enough to produce a dissertation and publish a book that even mentioned a few stories from pulp magazines; it might have been beyond the pale to further acknowledge that there were worthwhile critical ideas in those magazines. Thus, Bailey's failure to acknowledge Gernsback and Campbell is surely a matter more of discretion than of deceit.

Still, Bailey set a terrible pattern, since it appeared that he was inventing his own theory of science fiction and choosing his own texts to illustrate that definition; and later critics have assumed the same freedom. They approach science fiction as if no one else has ever talked about it before, and impose their own priorities on the genre, regardless of whether or not they relate to science fiction as perceived by its practitioners.[2]

So, in a way, I am going back in time to do more thoroughly and openly what Bailey did partially and covertly: to look at the theories of Gernsback and Campbell, consult and codify them, and build upon them, in the traditional manner of literary scholarship.

In my view, I am also doing more, because the commentaries I discuss are not belated scholarly ruminations on dead authors, but the ideas of the people who wrote, published, and read science fiction at the time the genre appeared and developed. Such commentaries, I argued, are literally part of the genre; so in thoroughly explicating what those people had to say, I provide the data that can complete our picture of science fiction history.

While there remains much work to be done on the critical history of science fiction (particularly regarding the later figures I omitted), one obvious next step would be an attempt to integrate the literary history of science fiction with its critical history, to see if those commentaries in fact can help critics to characterize and understand all the innumerable and variegated texts that have emerged from the modern tradition of science fiction. And, as a final suggestion for science fiction scholars, I will now make a tentative effort to outline exactly how such an integration might proceed.

*   *   *

First, I address what I see as the central question of science fiction scholarship: does science fiction warrant consideration as a separate category of literature? If there are good reasons to regard science fiction as intrinsically different from other forms of literature, there are logical grounds for discussing the genre in isolation as a group of texts and for developing theories and models of science fiction; but if there are no good reasons to regard science fiction as intrinsically different, there is no logic in discussing those texts separately or developing theories and models of science fiction. A defensible affirmative answer to that question, then, strikes me as a necessary precondition for any scholarly consideration of science fiction.

Throughout this book, I have discussed several critical claims for the uniqueness of science fiction that have been advanced by Gernsback, Campbell, and others: that works in the genre uniquely and rigorously adhere to known scientific facts, uniquely present realizable new scientific concepts, uniquely provide exercises in scientific thinking, or uniquely function to fruitfully anticipate new technologies and their effects. And academic critics have developed their own formulas to isolate certain texts as science fiction because of these or other features.

Yet all defences of the genre's special nature invariably falter in the face of numerous counter-examples: no matter how broadly or narrowly one establishes the parameters of science fiction, there are always left within its boundaries large numbers of texts which do not demonstrate these traits. John Huntington is one critic who likes to demonstrate how often science fiction works do not meet the genre's own announced criteria;[3] and one can mount similar objections to the criteria advanced by academic critics.

Even if it could be established beyond reasonable doubt that all texts of science fiction are in some ways uniquely 'scientific', there is another logical objection: why should those shared characteristics make those texts a separate category of literature? After all, there are many works which deal with religion, economics, or other disciplines, yet these are not regarded as separate literary forms; why should works with some special relationship to science demand that status?

There is, nevertheless, one characteristic of science fiction texts which is inarguably unique and which can be proven definitely and quantitatively: and that is the material I have described in this book. More so than any other form of modern literature, science fiction has generated an immense amount of accompanying commentary on science fiction from people who have not been employed to write about literature, who discuss science fiction only because they are intensely interested in the genre.

As an exercise, one can attempt a rough estimate of the volume of those commentaries. Let us say that science fiction has been recognized as a category of literature for about 70 years. It would be reasonable to assume the following: that during those 70 years, there have been published an average of five science fiction magazines per month, each containing an average of about 15 pages of science fiction commentaries in the forms of editorials, blurbs, letters, reviews, and articles; that during that time, there have been published an average of ten fanzines per month (probably many more), each containing about 50 pages of science fiction commentaries; that during that time there have been published an average of five fan-written books about science fiction per year, each containing about 200 pages; and that during that time there have been published an average of 100 science fiction books per year that each contain about 10 pages of commentaries in the forms of introductions and afterwords. These are all overall averages: during the first 15 years of the existence of science fiction as a genre, for example, there were few if any fanzines or books, but since that time these have multiplied well beyond the average numbers I suggest. (I omit the works of academic critics, since they are in a sense employed to write about literature, in as much as their publications lead to faculty positions, tenure, and promotions.)

These particular guesses yield this result: that in the last 70 years, approximately 650,000 pages have been written about science fiction by people who have not been employed to do so. And since this estimate does not include other, less voluminous bodies of science fiction commentaries —including science fiction articles written for publications outside the genre (like Campbell's articles for *The Atlantic Monthly* and *The Saturday Review*), science fiction convention programmes, transcriptions of panel discussions and interviews, and the relevant correspondence of science fiction fans—the actual figure must be significantly higher.

This is unique.

Without a doubt, no other form of literature has inspired such widespread devotion, such a fervent belief in its own special nature, such an immense volume of commentaries are discussions about that literature. Thus, there is one verifiable claim for the uniqueness of science fiction: *its texts have generated an intense shared belief that the genre is unique, an attitude documented in voluminous written commentaries of science fiction*. Here is another reason for making the focus of science fiction criticism the texts which have been regarded and labelled as science fiction: these are the texts that are unique. If one employs a phrase like 'literature of cognitive estrangement' or other subjective critical formulas, and recruits literary giants to represent the form, the resulting examination cannot generate a claim with similar weight.

Of course, one must investigate the issue of whether there is any substance to this widespread shared belief. A critic, after all, is not obliged to respect widespread false beliefs about literature; and if a widespread interest in science fiction and its accompanying commentaries is the *only* ground for considering science fiction to be unique, there may remain insufficient reason for regarding the genre as a separate category of literature.

In my second and seventh chapters, I argued that the theories of Gernsback and Campbell have had an enormous impact on modern *perceptions* of science fiction—a case that is relatively easy to prove. My fourth and ninth argued that those theories have had an enormous impact on the *writing* of science fiction—a more difficult case to prove. No matter how many suggestive examples I or other critics might provide, there remain too many texts to consider in detail, and large numbers of texts one can locate that do not seem to follow Gernsback's or Campbell's models to any significant extent.

This is not the end of the argument, however, because theories can influence a genre in ways other than universal and rigorous adherence to their dictates. Theories can inspire writers to elaborately avoid their dictates, modify or eliminate their dictates, even conspicuously flout their dictates. Given the pervasiveness of Gernsback's and Campbell's ideas, it seems logical to assume that those ideas have had some impact on the modern genre; and, if critics examine the science fiction tradition without preconceptions, they might better observe that impact.

Many have said that it is impossible to define science fiction, and that all such efforts are futile. If one considers the full connotations of the term 'definition', this view is correct: to offer a picture of modern science fiction which is *definite*, timelessly accurate, identifying all relevant texts without ambiguities or grey areas, is surely impossible. However, I believe it is possible to provide what might be called a *description* of science fiction: a reasonably comprehensive and succinct statement listing the shared characteristics of almost all texts to date which have been considered science fiction.

Such a description has not been attempted previously because of two problems: misguided priorities, and insufficient data.

The misguided priorities have been the desire to define *good* science fiction, or what science fiction *should be*—an impulse that produces definitions based primarily on personal opinions, and designed primarily to justify those opinions. A better priority for critics is to define what science fiction *is*; in other words, what are the shared characteristics of those texts which have been universally regarded and labelled as science fiction, those texts that were generated and influenced by accompanying commentaries. As a starting point, let us limit 'science fiction' to those works that emerged from the modern critical tradition of science fiction. One way to say this is: *'Science Fiction consists of those works which were written by authors, presented by editors and publishers, and sought out and read by readers who all share a thorough awareness of, and commitment to, the idea of science fiction'.*[4]

Of course, as indicated, if this is *all* one can say about those texts, a critic has not got very far; and some conclude that there are no other dominant or controlling features in the texts within this context. As Peter Nicholls put it, '"Science fiction" is a label applied to a publishing category and its application is subject to the whims of editors and publishers' ('Definitions of Science Fiction', p. 159). However, I believe the label has not been applied all that whimsically.

This brings up the other problem: insufficient data. Without information about the thoughts and ideas of the writers, editors, and readers who call certain works 'science fiction', critics cannot tell what standards, if any, are used to make such judgements and may decide there is no particular logic in those judgements. With access to that information, I propose to see if one can detect meaningful shared characteristics in the motley collections of texts that have been labelled science fiction. The process will be long, and messy, since genres that arise in and from historical circumstances do not always adhere to neat critical formulas.

To begin, one might return to Gernsback's first definition of science fiction—'a charming romance interwoven with scientific fact and prophetic vision' ('A New Sort of Magazine', p. 3). I argued that the priorities in that definition have had a lasting influence on the genre; thus, a version of that definition, recast with scholarly rigour and incorporating one idea from Campbell, might serve as a useful description of science fiction. One attempt at such a description might be:

> *Science fiction is a twentieth-century literary genre consisting of texts labelled 'science fiction' which are associated with explicit or implicit claims that each of its labelled texts has these three interrelated traits:*
> *A. It is a prose narrative;*
> *B. It includes language which either describes scientific facts, or explains or reflects the processes of scientific thought; and*
> *C. It describes or depicts some aspect or development which does not exist at the time of writing.*

In explaining this description, I note that there seems to be no critical problem in identifying a prose narrative or identifying a text whose presented world includes something that does not exist in the author's world. At the very least, other critics of science fiction seem to assume that these matters are not problematic.[5]

The difficult element in the list is the second one. Here, I necessarily soften Gernsback's claim that the language in science fiction is scientifically accurate, and Campbell's claim that science fiction is actually a product of the process of scientific thought. These are matters which demand scientific competence to resolve; but the genre has historically had many readers, writers, and editors who lacked scientific competence, and both accurate and inaccurate texts have been accepted as science fiction. The feature must only be identified, then, as an aspect of the way the story is told, not the story itself. That is, the stories of Smith's Lensman novels could proceed in the same way if their scientific jargon is removed, and the story of Ellison's 'Repent, Harlequin! Said the Ticktockman' could proceed in the same way if its extrapolative language was removed. To use the terminology found in Carl D. Malmgren's *Worlds Apart: Narratology of Science Fiction*—if not his thesis—science in science fiction is a matter of *discours*, rather than *histoire*, and as such is a feature separable from the issue of its non-realistic subject matter.

The term 'interrelated' is included to deal with anomalous examples which include all three traits while not relating them. An example (I long to think of a better one) is the television series *I Dream of Jeannie*. Its episodes are narratives; three of its main characters are astronauts or officials in the United States space programme, and there are sporadic discussions of lift-offs, orbital missions, splashdowns, and the like, so that the episodes arguably present scientific information; and the episodes feature a magical genie from a bottle, something that does not exist in the world of the programme's creators. Yet, since the scientific information is not connected to the unreal feature and is not employed to explain or justify that unreal feature, the series does not qualify as science fiction by Gernsback's criteria. (Still, it will later fit into the description of modern science fiction in one of two ways.)

If this description is accepted as reasonably rigorous (and if it has not really achieved a fully satisfying rigour for some, I am sure that additional scrutiny and thought could bring it to that status), it will be criticized for the reasons I have stated: that there have been in fact scores of texts published within the context of science fiction which do not meet these criteria. And of course this is true. However, in examining the texts that have been historically accepted as science fiction, one sees that all texts almost invariably meet *at least two of these three criteria*. So Gernsback's definition suggests the possible existence of three additional forms of science fiction, each meeting two of the three criteria, and these may be tentatively labelled and described.

I am not delineating, however, actual subgenres of science fiction, since these have not developed as historical realities. Rather, they are possibilities created by Gernsback's and Campbell's theories which have been realized in various texts, but those texts have never gelled into recognized categories.

The three additional forms suggested by Gernsback's definition could be described as follows:

> A. *A prose narrative which describes or depicts some aspect or development which does not exist at the time of writing, but does not include scientific language.*
>
> B. *A prose narrative which includes language which either describes scientific fact or explains or reflects the process of scientific thought, but does not depict any unrealistic phenomena.*
>
> C. *A piece of writing which includes language which either describes scientific fact or explains or reflects the process of scientific thought, and which describes or depicts some aspect or development which does not exist at the time of writing, but is not a narrative, falling rather into the category of nonfiction.*

Have works of these three types appeared within the context of science fiction?

Of course they have.

First, stories which are outright fantasies have always been published as science fiction or alongside science fiction. Gernsback himself printed works like H. G. Wells's 'The Man Who Could Work Miracles' and A. Merritt's *The Moon Pool*, and labored explanations could not conceal their absence of true scientific language and thought. Since then, pure fantasies have habitually crept into science fiction publications; some, like Robert Bloch's 'The Hell-Bound Train' and Fritz Leiber's 'Gonna Roll the Bones', even won Hugo Awards as Best Science Fiction Stories, though both are nothing more than traditional fantasies about men dealing with the Devil. I concede that these stories are not always labelled science fiction—in publications like *The Magazine of Fantasy and Science Fiction*, they are explicitly not labelled science fiction—but these stories regularly accompany the publication of science fiction stories, establishing at least their informal membership in the genre. Brian Stableford notes that 'There is and always has been a large overlap between the audience that attends to books published in the science fiction category and the audience for the purest kind of fantastic romance' ('Science Fiction between the Wars', p. 53); and in *Age of Wonders*, David Hartwell acknowledges that fantasy has effectively been absorbed into science fiction:

> There is an interesting investigation to be done someday on why the classical fantasy, a main tradition of Western literature for several millennia, is now part of the science fiction field. In the latter half of

the twentieth century, with certain best-selling exceptions, fantasy is produced by writers of science fiction and fantasy, edited by editors of science fiction, illustrated by SF and fantasy artists, read by omnivore fantasy and SF addicts who support the market. Fantasy is not SF but is part of the phenomenon that confronts us. (p. 20)

Similarly, Allen's *Science Fiction: An Introduction* blandly incorporates 'fantasy' as one of the four types of science fiction.

One could also include in this category the kinds of stories that Gernsback objected to in 'Reasonableness in Science Fiction'—those which feature all sorts of fantastic inventions and phenomena without offering any persuasive scientific explanations for them. Such works which take place in outer space have come to be described as 'space opera' and are generally held in little esteem, though they also are always accepted as a form of science fiction.

Second, Gernsback himself periodically attempted to present as science fiction works which involved little or no real speculation. Prominent examples include the Luther Trent 'scientific detective' stories by Edwin Balmer and William B. MacHarg. An editor could grandly say that one of them, 'The Man Higher Up', 'involv[ed] the reading of the mind by curves produced by means of a detecting apparatus' ('In Our Next Issue', *Amazing Stories*, November 1926, p. 673), but the story simply involved a lie detector, a machine already in evidence at the time. Similar stories were common in earlier science fiction magazines, as noted by Sam Moskowitz: 'The thinking of the science fiction editors of that day was that if a crime is committed or solved through the utilization of established scientific principles, it constituted a legitimate science fiction story, regardless of whether any element of fantasy was present' (*Strange Horizons*, p. 144). Gernsback also published in *Amazing Stories* a play by Raymond Knight, 'Just Around the Corner', which was not, he acknowledged, 'a scientifiction story proper; it is published for those who would like to produce a play, based on science in a sense' (blurb, 'Just Around the Corner', p. 358). Still, he did publish that play in a science fiction magazine.

More recently, Asimov placed a detective story—'What's in a Name?'—in his science fiction collection *Asimov's Mysteries*, arguing that even though the 'story is not, in the strictest sense of the word, a science fiction mystery… I include it. The reason is that science is closely and intimately involved with the mystery, and I hesitate to penalize it by non-inclusion merely because the science is of the present rather than of the future' ('Foreword', 'What's in a Name?', p. 55). And consider a story like Eric Vinicoff's 'Blue Sky', recently published in *Analog Science Fiction/Science Fact*: as I summarized its plot in *The Other Side of the Sky*, the director of NASA is

almost assassinated by a man working at one of its factories who shouts
that he has 'sold out' (p. 160). Investigating, he discovers that there is a
high-level conspiracy, including the President himself, to divert funds from
the popular space programme to work on other, less glamorous solutions
to pressing problems. When the President explains that this is the best way
to maintain the space program, he agrees to join the conspiracy. Here is a
story of the near future, involving actual agencies, predictable initiatives
in space travel, and an imagined conspiracy that might actually occur in a
modern American government. In what way is this story truly speculative
or prophetic? Yet stories like this are regularly seen in science fiction
magazines, especially *Analog: Science Fiction/Science Fact*.

Also, consider films like *Fail Safe* and *Marooned*, which are always
described in reference books as 'science fiction'. Why? Both films depict
events happening in the present involving only existing technology;
allowing for dramatic licence, both films depict events that might have
actually happened at the time they appeared. In no sense of the term do
they involve any element of 'prediction' or 'prophecy'; they are entirely
realistic works. One could maintain that such films are considered science
fiction as a matter of habit: because stories about space travel and atomic
bombs were once in the realm of science fiction, such stories continue to
be associated with that realm, even when their subject matter has become
reality. But that is not the entire story. For these films also involve scenes
of tense technicians facing boards of blinking lights, exchanges of technical
jargon, and men in spacesuits or advanced aircraft. They definitely have
the 'feel', or the language, of science fiction, even if there is nothing
speculative or imaginative in what they depict; and that is one reason, I
argue, that they have been accepted as science fiction.

Finally, there has existed since the 1950s a variety of science fiction
featuring space adventures set in the near future with devices and events
closely tied to existing plans and possibilities, and no startling leaps of the
imagination. Two common subjects at the time were the construction of
the first space station and the first flight to the Moon—both developments
that were then being planned and were later realized. Such stories of
realistic near-future adventures have continued to appear in science fiction
magazines and anthologies, but one has to question exactly how they truly
qualify as science fiction under Gernsback's guidelines. They involve
predictions, but thoroughly safe ones; their element of speculation is
minimal at best; and they seem another instance of the science fiction story
which does not really involve presentation of an unlikely or non-existing
element.

One subvariety of such science fiction is the near-future novel written
for general readers, a trend noted by Hartwell:

some of the major writers have been seduced by prosperity into expanding the scope of their SF novels to include large casts of engaging minor characters, panoramic disasters, obligatory sex romantically described, vast superficial detail, all the elements of the fat best-seller novel: Gregory Benford and William Rotsler's *Shiva Descending* (1979) and Larry Niven and Jerry Pournelle's *Lucifer's Hammer* (1977) are examples. (*Age of Wonders*, p. 183)

Third, from the very beginning of *Amazing Stories*, readers expressed an interest in having articles about science published alongside the stories—as noted; and Gernsback eventually responded with Hermann von Noordung's nonfiction book about the possibilities of space travel, *The Problems of Space Flying*, and a monthly column of 'Science News of the Month'. In *Astounding Stories*, Tremaine published a long series of Campbell essays about the Solar System, and when Campbell took over the magazine, he made speculative science articles a regular feature of *Astounding Science-Fiction* and eventually renamed the magazine *Analog Science Fact/Science Fiction* (later *Analog Science Fiction/Science Fact*) to make the articles more frequent and more prominent. Almost all science fiction magazines regularly featured science articles by writers like L. Sprague de Camp, Willy Ley, Robert S. Richardson, and Asimov. Launching the magazine with his name, Asimov listed many past science articles in science fiction magazines and concluded, 'are we going to have science articles? Of course! We've had them in the past, and we'll have them in the future. Thanks to Campbell and [Willy] Ley, science fiction readers have been educated into the virtue of science articles' (*Asimov on Science Fiction*, p. 233).

There have also been science fiction anthologies—including Brian Aldiss's *All about Venus* (*Farewell, Fantastic Venus!*), Jerry Pournelle and John F. Carr's *Endless Frontier* collections, and Jim Baen's *New Frontiers* collections, that nonchalantly combine science fiction stories with scientific essays and articles; and modern novels may include as separate features detailed discussions of the science featured in those novels; I recall the afterwords to Robert Forward's *The Flight of the Dragonfly* and Clarke's *The Ghost from the Grand Banks*, but there are no doubt many other examples.

Like fantasies, these articles are rarely if ever labeled science fiction—since they are manifestly not fiction at all—but again they regularly accompany science fiction stories and hence can claim some kinship with the genre. Indeed, in listing types of science fiction for his survey of science fiction fans, William Bainbridge's *Dimensions of Science Fiction* included 'factual reports on the space programme and spaceflight' and 'factual science articles' as categories, just as he included 'fantasy'.

Since these three types of writings are regularly published as science fiction, or published alongside science fiction, they must be included in any description of modern science fiction.

In addition, there is one other type of writing regularly found with science fiction—commentaries on science fiction; and the sheer volume and exuberance of these commentaries, already described, argue that they are more than decorative. Magazines—the only major exception I know of being *The Magazine of Fantasy and Science Fiction*—always have editorials discussing science fiction, occasional articles about the genre and its writers, lengthy letter columns with readers' comments, introductions or blurbs about individual stories, and other incidental material. Anthologies almost always have an introduction or afterword talking about science fiction and the featured stories, and it has become increasingly common to employ the style, pioneered by Asimov in *The Hugo Winners*, of also incorporating extended commentaries before and after each story. Prominent examples of the practice include Ellison's *Shatterday*, Heinlein's *Expanded Universe*, and Orson Scott Card's *Maps in the Mirror*—the latter featuring, as the dust cover boasts, commentaries as long as an entire novel. Truly, the phenomenon must be noted in a descriptive definition of the genre.

Therefore, the entire working description of science fiction that I propose is as follows:

> *Science fiction is a twentieth-century literary genre consisting of texts labelled 'science fiction' which manifest the following characteristics:*
>
> *1. In theory, the genre explicitly or implicitly claims that each of its texts has these three interrelated traits:*
>
> *A.It is a prose narrative;*
>
> *B. It includes language which either describes scientific facts, or explains or reflects the processes of scientific thought; and*
>
> *C. It describes or depicts some aspect or development which does not exist at the time of writing.*
>
> *2. In practice, the genre embraces, or is accompanied by, two types of texts: texts which have all three of the listed traits, or texts which have only two of the three listed traits. The four possible types of science fiction, then, are:*
>
> *A. A prose narrative which includes language which either describes scientific fact or explains or reflects the process of scientific thought, and which describes or depicts some aspect or development which does not exist at the time of writing;*
>
> *B. A prose narrative which describes or depicts some aspect or development which does not exist at the time of writing, but does not include scientific language;.*
>
> *C. A prose narrative which includes language which either describes scientific fact or explains or reflects the process of scientific thought, but does*

not depict any unrealistic phenomena;

    D. A piece of writing which includes language which either describes scientific fact or explains or reflects the process of scientific thought, and which describes or depicts some aspect or development which does not exist at the time of writing, but is not a narrative, falling rather into the category of nonfiction.

    3. In addition, the genre is characteristically accompanied by extensive critical commentaries on the genre and particular works.

If this description seems longwinded, an expedient shorter version is: *A work labelled science fiction has these three features—it is a prose narrative with scientific language and non-realistic subject matter—or any two of these three features.*

And, on the basis of this description, I would answer the question I first posed in this way: science fiction is unique because its texts have inspired or generated a widespread and fervent belief that they are unique, a belief documented in innumerable commentaries; those commentaries generally announce three important criteria which distinguish science fiction works; significant numbers of science fiction works demonstrate reasonable fidelity to those three criteria; and virtually all texts demonstrate a limited fidelity to two of those three criteria.

To some, despite my protestations, this description of the modern genre will sound like just another definition of science fiction, one that is in some respects not noticeably different from other definitions. Why should anyone regard mine as superior?

First, unlike previous efforts, my description is not my own invention, or the importation of ideas from other areas of literary study; instead, it is grounded on the ideas articulated by the persons who actually wrote, published, and read science fiction.

Second, unlike previous definitions, my description is purely and relentlessly descriptive, in that it simply attempts to account for all the forms of writing that have been regularly published under the aegis of science fiction. Pick up any science fiction magazine, book, or anthology, and what will you find? Stories with scientific language and prophetic content, stories with only prophetic content and little if any scientific language, stories with only scientific language and little if any prophetic content, nonfiction essays combining scientific language and prophetic content, and commentaries on science fiction. That is everything you will find; that is the totality of science fiction.[6] Amis, whose *New Maps of Hell* remains one of the few studies of science fiction to focus on magazines and related publications, captured well the full range of elements found in the average magazine:

> If the stage of actually beginning to read [a science fiction magazine]
> is attained, the material will be found to include a novella of perhaps
> fifteen thousand words, three or four short stories of between three
> and eight thousand words each, sometimes an installment of a three-
> or four-part serial running up to fifteen thousand (failing that,
> another novella or a couple of shorts), editorial matter often marked
> by a hectoring, opinionated tone, readers' letters covering a
> staggering range of IQs, a book-review section conducted with
> intelligence and a much greater readiness to be nasty than one finds,
> say, in the *Sunday Times*, in some cases a popular science article on
> atomic physics, sea serpents, telepathy, or the evaporation of the
> Caspian Sea, and an interesting department in which are tabulated
> the results of the readers' voting on the stories in the previous issue—
> these are arranged in order of popularity and, in at least one case,
> the author receiving the most votes regularly gets a cash bonus from
> the publisher. (p. 45)

While references to a 'hectoring, opinionated tone' and a 'department in
which are tabulated the results of the readers' voting' suggest Amis is
thinking primarily of Campbell's *Astounding Science-Fiction*, his description
is broadly true of the modern science fiction magazine—and many science
fiction anthologies.

Third, while my description may seem intolerably broad, it only reflects
the actual ameliorative tendencies in modern science fiction history.
However, not all texts which could possibly qualify as science fiction by
that description have actually crept into the genre. For example, pure
examples of myths, folktales, and fairy tales are rarely found, except in
self-conscious adaptations like Roger Zelazny's *Lord of Light* and Joan
Vinge's *The Snow Queen*; stories about modest advances in medicine are for
some reason usually not featured; and purportedly nonfactual discussions
of pseudo-science—subjects not generally accepted as fit for scientific
analysis, like ghosts, Unidentified Flying Objects, Bigfoot, and the like—
have only sporadically appeared. (Indeed, an ongoing question for
scholars—only partially addressed below—would be why certain texts
which qualify as science fiction by two of the three criteria have actually
entered the genre, while others which seem to qualify have not.) Thus,
the overarching limitation of inclusion in the context of science fiction
restricts the description to a manageable, somewhat coherent body of
works.

Fourth, my description—and here my language must be careful—does
not attempt to establish a 'taxonomy' of science fiction, does not insist that
its categories actually exist as subgenres, and does not claim that all works

of science fiction can be unambiguously placed into one category. All it states is this: the critical tradition of Gernsback and Campbell announces three traits, creating the possibility of four types of stories, one with all three traits and three with only two traits; examining a text, one invariably finds that its inclusion in science fiction can be justified because it can be fitted into one or more of these four categories. However, I accept that any given text may be difficult to exactly place in one and only one of the four categories, since subjective judgements—is there a sufficient amount of scientific language? is the prediction far-reaching enough?—inevitably enter into the decision. In fact, such decisions are not necessary.[7]

Fifth—another point I must emphasize—my description is not judgemental, does not establish a hierarchy of superior and inferior forms, and does not promulgate one type of science fiction as 'pure' and others as 'impure'. To be sure, the description could be the basis for an argument that works exhibiting all three traits are the most interesting and stimulating of all science fiction texts, while works with only two of the traits, whatever their other virtues, do not manifest the peculiar tension and excitement of works with the three traits. Certainly, Gernsback and Campbell would support that argument, and I might support it. However, the description itself does not; it notes that there are different types of science fiction without labelling any of them as better. Indeed, one could accept this description as a reasonably accurate picture of modern science fiction as it exists while at the same time maintaining that stories with only a prose narrative and non-mimetic content, for example, are actually the superior form.

As it happens, that is the best way to characterize the major thrust of the New Wave movement, and the major thrust of most academic criticism of science fiction.

In the writings of various New Wave figures, one notices first repeated campaigns for the term 'speculative fiction', a way of etymologically removing science as a major issue in the genre. Furthermore, when Ellison spoke of 'a need for new horizons, new forms, new styles, new challenges in the literature of our times' ('Introduction: Thirty-Two Soothsayers', p. 19), and when Moorcock called for 'fresh subject matters and techniques' (cited in Barron, *The Anatomy of Wonder*, p. 296), they clearly advocated, among other things, a move away from an emphasis on scientific language; and the call was sometimes explicit. Ellison once argued that:

> The time for science fiction is past... It seems to me that novels such as [Frank Herbert's] *Dragon in the Sea*, ponderous with the weight of its own science, sluggish with the accumulated gimcrackery of engineering persiflage, floundering under the burden of hardware that can

never substitute for story, is [*sic*] one of the reasons why we are today struggling toward a new definition—and a 'new thing', if I may be permitted—of the form. ('A Voice from the Styx', p. 122–23)

Yet when comments like this provoked vigorous disapproval from many in the science fiction community, Ellison softened his language: 'No one suggests that the more traditional forms of speculative fiction be denied; there is more than enough room for a full measure. And with craftsmen like Simak, Asimov, Niven, Clarke, Pohl and del Rey working we will continue to find new lessons to learn in the tradition. All we ask—no, the time for asking is well past; what we *demand*—is equal time for the new voices' ('Introduction: The Waves in Rio', pp. 12–13). So 'traditional' science fiction remains a valid possibility—though only one of many possibilities—in the hoped-for genre of 'speculative fiction'.

Academic science fiction critics have been more circumspect in removing science from the idea of science fiction, though Robert Scholes's *Speculative Fabulation* might be counted as one attempt to reshape the genre in that way. Rather, they have de-emphasized the importance of science, sometimes to an extreme extent, and they make no effort to stipulate the presence of scientific language. Aldiss's definition of the genre reduces science to a parenthetical term, part of the general environment that the modern writer is responding to; similarly, Franklin argues that science fiction is a literary response to science. Darko Suvin attempts to impose the notion that science fiction is somehow defined by its estranged, scientific perspective, though such concerns are alien to most of the genre's own texts and commentaries. Malmgren's *Worlds Apart* strives to maintain that scientific data are embedded in the imagined new element in the story. However, while all these formulations may drag scores of unrelated texts into the genre, they simultaneously affirm that those texts traditionally associated with the modern tradition are also part of the genre; Heinlein, Asimov, and Clarke are always discussed, even if only in brief condescending passages between Karel Capek and Stanislaw Lem.

To sum up all these attempts to re-define science fiction, one might see a consensus building around this sort of definition:

> *Science fiction is a prose narrative which describes or depicts some aspect or development which does not exist at the time of writing; one significant subgroup of science fiction additionally includes language which either describes scientific fact or explains or reflects the process of scientific thought.*

If this is accepted as a broadly accurate description of these critical efforts, an intriguing conclusion emerges: attempts to define science fiction without reference to, or without an emphasis on, science are often criticized because they are too expansive; they seem to take in too many works that are only tangentially relevant to the field as it is usually regarded. There is some merit in that viewpoint; still, my description enables us to see that the real problem with these attempts is not that they expand the genre too much, but that they *limit the genre too much*. Specifically, if one insists on narrative and prophetic content as the sole defining elements of science fiction, while accepting narratives with both scientific and prophetic content as one key subset of the genre, one must also exclude works of the other two types I have listed, since one of them lacks prophetic content and the other lacks narrative form. Thus, in terms of the actual body of works that traditionally appear under the aegis of science fiction, the New Wave was not an effort to broaden the genre; rather, it was an effort to truncate two of its existing branches.

To illustrate the point, one can abandon any effort to characterize New Wave science fiction in itself and consider the movement in terms of the company it kept. Looking at more conventional science fiction publications of the 1960s and 1970s, one still sees the full array of earlier science fiction, including scientific essays and near-future space adventures. In New Wave publications, one finds many things, but few if any essays on science, and few if any near-future space adventures.[8] Thus, one reason for resistance to the New Wave among many science fiction readers was not simply their objections to its works—and, except for some excesses in sexual content and style, the stories were rarely that provocative—but rather the implicit fear that the New Wave would remove from science fiction two forms of writing that had been traditionally linked to the genre. And one reason many science fiction readers dislike academic critics may be not so much the texts they discuss, but the texts that they conspicuously refuse to discuss and seek to disassociate from the genre.

Along with these efforts to make what might be loosely termed fantasy the genre's centre, there has emerged a similar challenge in the marketing of science fiction. Publishers have discovered that fantasy novels are easier to obtain, easier to evaluate, and easier to sell; and readers have complained that visiting the 'Science Fiction' section of a modern bookstore involves wading through scores of books about unicorns, dwarves, and wizards to find a few books about robots and spaceships. The bookstore racks, then, physically reflect modern critical formulas, making science fiction a subgroup of fantasy. The point is that even if this happens, science fiction as Gernsback and Campbell envisioned it can survive, even if it must jettison two of its related forms.

The model I propose also enables us to anticipate two other possible challenges to the centrality of fiction, science, and prophecy in characterizations of science fiction.

First, in my view, modern readers may be witnessing the birth of a significant new literary genre. Tom Clancy is its most prominent writer, though many others have produced similar works. The cover of one such novel, Dale Brown's *Silver Tower*, calls these works 'military novels', and another term sometimes seen is 'techno-thrillers'. However, neither seems entirely appropriate. Rather, these novels incorporate elements from several other genres—war novels, political thrillers, detective and espionage fiction, and science fiction. A typical story begins during a period of rising global tensions in the near future. Some item of new technology—most often an advanced aircraft, though one sees other types of hardware—is introduced into the equation, and that either precipitates or becomes involved in a growing world crisis. The action hops all over the globe—or even into outer space—as various politicians, soldiers, detectives, spies, astronauts, and scientists struggle to cope with the ramifications of the crisis.

Most of these works could qualify as new examples of the form I have previously described, a combination of narrative and science, in that they present scientific language in connection with a modest scientific advance that is either already on the drawing board or clearly feasible by current standards. And these works are often accepted by science fiction readers: I recall a group of science fiction fans leaving a conference because they wanted to see the new film version of Clancy's *The Hunt for Red October*—though the film did not really involve any element of prediction. Like *Fail Safe* and *Marooned*, the film had the language and feel of science fiction, which connected it to the genre.

Since works of this type seem popular, it is possible that some figure like Gernsback will coin a popular term for these works, describe their characteristics and virtues, and lead a movement to set up magazines, publications and separate sections in the bookstore exclusively devoted to those works. Such efforts would serve as another attack on the centrality of fiction, science, and prophecy, but this time to establish the limited form combining fiction and science as the new focus of the genre.

A definition of this new genre might take this form:

> *Science fiction is a prose narrative which either describes scientific fact or explains or reflects the process of scientific thought; One significant subgroup of science fiction describes or depicts some aspect or development which does not exist at the time of writing.*

A movement in support of this concept, if successful, would have two effects: first, two forms of science fiction would again be jettisoned, this time fantasy and nonfiction involving science and prophecy, since both fiction and scientific language would now be regarded as essential. Second, science fiction would survive as a subsidiary element in the new genre. That is, though the science in these novels is usually minimally prophetic, the form can be adapted to feature more spectacular advances: George Bishop's *The Shuttle People* features a new technique to achieve human immortality, and Edward M. Lerner's *Probe* involves apparent contact with alien beings. Indeed, some noteworthy science fiction writers have already been attracted to this type of novel—James P. Hogan (*Endgame Enigma*) and Dean Ing (*The Taking of Black Stealth One*).

Finally, one can envision a third effort to reshape the definition of science fiction, this time from the standpoint of nonfiction that combines science and prophecy.

As background, it can be noted first that 90% of all books published are nonfiction, meaning that works of nonfiction threaten at all times to overwhelm and dominate works of fiction in the marketplace. Furthermore, there have been predictions that prose fiction is becoming less important because of, and may eventually be supplanted by, other narrative forms that have appeared in the twentieth century—films, comic books, television, video games, interactive computer games, and presentations of 'virtual reality'. Even should this happen, though, prose nonfiction will surely survive as the most efficient mechanism for presenting information.

With these things in mind, one might first consider the fact that *Analog*—the science fiction magazine that explicitly devotes half of its contents to 'science fact'—has been one of the most consistently successful science fiction magazines in the last thirty years. More recently, the magazine has been overshadowed by the phenomenon of *Omni*, for many years the most successful science fiction magazine of all time, the only magazine that appeared on almost all newsstands, and one whose sales were larger than those of all other science fiction magazines combined. Though its recent retreat to electronic publishing and eventual demise— due not to declining sales, but failure to anticipate dramatic increases in the cost of paper—diminishes its aura of success. The pattern of *Omni*'s success would seem easy to duplicate by other publishers with greater foresight.

However, even though *Omni* was commonly accepted as a science fiction magazine, it was a most unusual one, for the vast majority of its contents fell into the category of nonfiction: reports of new scientific developments and speculations about their possible effects or future discoveries—a ratio much larger than the 50% or less of *Analog* and other science fiction magazines. In fact, each issue usually only had one or two science fiction stories. While there were, I must emphasize, no editorial pronouncements or manifestos on this matter, the very format of *Omni*, and its acceptance as a science fiction magazine, can be seen as an anticipation of a third way to re-define science fiction:

> *Science fiction is a piece of writing which includes language which either describes scientific fact or explains or reflects the process of scientific thought, and which describes or depicts some aspect or development which does not exist at the time of writing, typically in the form of nonfiction; one significant subgroup of science fiction is additionally structured as a prose narrative.*

Should a definition of this sort become dominant, of course, two forms traditionally accepted as science fiction will again have to be removed—in this case, fantasy and narratives which only involve science, since scientific language and speculation are now stated as essential elements. One could protest that these exclusions cannot be observed in *Omni* itself, since the magazine has published some fantasy stories and near-future space adventures. Again, I do not ascribe any promotion of this new definition of science fiction to the magazine; I merely argue that the contents of the magazine could be seen as an embodiment of that possible new definition. And, if that new definition ever becomes dominant, science fiction in the form of combined fiction, science, and prophecy will survive as one subsidiary form.

To some, it will seem absurd to imagine that the term 'science fiction' could evolve into a description of something that is not a narrative; yet to an extent, *such a definition has already been widely accepted.* That is, when the term 'science fiction' is used in the mass media, it often means 'an imaginable but impossible scientific development', in statements like: 'A household robot that could vacuum your house, cook dinner, and balance your cheque book? Sounds like science fiction. But researchers at Bell Laboratories... ' In such cases, 'science fiction' does not refers to a narrative about an advanced robot, but simply to the robot itself. Thus, some evidence suggests that 'science fiction' could come to mean descriptions of future scientific advances, not necessarily narratives about such advances.

Examining how the idea of science fiction has been challenged in the past, and anticipating how that idea might be challenged in the future, one begins to understand the true mechanics of wonder.

At first, Gernsback presented science fiction as a genre that combined three elements: narrative, scientific language, and non-mimetic content. But problems arose immediately: writers found all three elements were often hard to combine; some editors felt uncomfortable about one of its elements; and many readers reacted unfavourably to one of its elements.

At this point, Gernsback and other advocates of science fiction might have been rigid and dogmatic, insisting on all three elements in every story published, and firmly excluding all stories that did not meet all those criteria. Had that happened, the genre might have died, or might have remained a tiny and insignificant part of literature. But that did not happen. Instead, Gernsback and his successors were ameliorative and conciliatory. They created, developed, or drew into the genre three forms of writing which satisfied only two of their three criteria; and, to varying extents, they embraced those forms as science fiction. Gernsback himself first published A. Merritt, the Luther Trent detective stories, and von Noordung's *The Problems of Space Flying*—representing the additional possible forms I have described. And, now including types of writing that could satisfy all readers and writers attracted to the genre, science fiction survived and prospered; and despite the growing prominence of its added forms, the original combined form of fiction, science, and prophecy continues to serve as an important element in the genre.

And, by bringing in and accepting those other forms, the original form of science fiction benefited in a number of ways.

The genre of heroic fantasy has offered forms and conventions for narratives involving fantastic elements that some science fiction writers can usefully assimilate. Thus, Sheila Finch's *The Garden of the Shaped* employs a story that is in mood and structure a fantasy—a young princess must display her magical powers in order to win the throne—as a vehicle for solid scientific speculation involving an experiment in controlled human genetics.

Realistic, near-future adventures on Earth and space have functioned as a workshop of sorts, where technically inclined writers could work out in detail basic items of futuristic machinery—like the spaceship itself, solar-energy space stations, the lunar mass-driver, and the space elevator—which could then be usefully employed by other, more imaginative (and possibly more talented) writers, as noted in Wollheim's *The Universe Makers*.

Finally, the speculative scientific articles provide a continuing source of new ideas for writers to work out in their fiction; for example, a 1989 article in *Analog* by Douglas Cramer, 'Wormholes and Time Machines', discusses theoretical work suggesting that the theory of general relativity may allow for the construction of a time machine, and openly urges science fiction writers to make use of this work in their stories.

While these added forms thus contributed to science fiction, the genre, in accepting them, also created threats to its own existence, in that one of the newer forms might become the dominant form; but science fiction at the same time ensured its own continuing existence through a possible future revolution, for its original form could always survive as a subsidiary element in all three of its adopted forms, should any one ever become dominant.

While one can thus characterize science fiction as a shaky coalition of warring factions, this picture is to some extent mythological, since subgenres of the sort I describe have not actually come into existence, and advocates of various attitudes toward science fiction do not explicitly embrace such subgenres as their preference. It is also appropriate to see science fiction as a unified organism, different organs cooperating to perform different functions. Considered as a whole in this way, science fiction has in fact consistently fulfilled Gernsback's agenda. That is, while critics like John Huntington can justly point out that many individual science fiction stories fail to satisfy the genre's own announced concerns for scientific accuracy and logic, such stories are typically accompanied by other stories that do fulfil those criteria, and/or by scientific and speculative articles that fulfil those criteria even more explicitly. If someone consistently reads a wide variety of science fiction works, she will consistently read works of all types, and thus will consistently be exposed to narrative, scientific facts, and scientific prophecies. Thus, the entire genre remains committed to Gernsback's priorities—to entertain, provide scientific education, and offer new scientific ideas—even if many individual works in the genre do not address all of those priorities.[9]

The story of science fiction, then, involves factors that have never been fully examined by critics. There are first the many forms of writing that make up the genre, which have all co-existed with and influenced each other. There is the overarching element of science fiction commentaries, which have attempted to reconcile different forms of science fiction or to establish one particular form as superior. Thus, the texts traditionally isolated as 'science fiction' must instead be seen as only one element in an ongoing process involving a number of other interrelated texts.

This is what science fiction has been, and this is what science fiction is.

What are the consequences of this realization?

Before addressing science fiction critics, I note that I am demonstrating by example a method for defining other literary genres: one examines all texts traditionally regarded as part of the genre; one studies all the commentaries that have accompanied and influenced those texts; and finally, one employs the shared traits of the texts and consensus of ideas in the commentaries to create a definition that describes all the texts typically considered part of the genre. To the greatest extent possible, the methodology eliminates the factors of personal opinion and judgement and is therefore, in my view, superior to other methodologies.

The particular results of this method seen in the case of science fiction implicitly propose a model for the creation and development of all literary genres, or at least all popular genres. That is, the genre begins when someone notices the emergence of the form, gives it a name, and proclaims its characteristics. Often, these characteristics are, as was the case with science fiction, the overall form of prose narrative, a characteristic language or *discours*, and a characteristic subject matter or *histoire*. Next, to broaden its appeal and resolve certain problems, the genre softens its original standards and creates, develops, or draws in other types of writing that meet only two of its three announced criteria. A stimulating tension then develops as the works of the original form struggle to hold the centre against works of the newer forms, while at the same time the entire genre collectively remains committed to the original criteria. The genre can die either by remaining too attached to its first standards and refusing to admit related forms, or by becoming too accommodating and admitting too many unrelated forms, causing the genre to lose its identity. Based on my limited knowledge of other genres, the model seems applicable to a number of them, and might serve as a stimulating premise for examinations of other genres.

While hesitant to move beyond my own area of expertise, I will venture a few tentative comments on other genres. The novel itself might serve as an example of a genre which destroyed itself by excessive absorption and amelioration; as the term came to apply to all book-length prose narratives, any sense of its original language of character development and focus on social issues was lost. Pirate stories and jungle stories are two embryonic genres which died because they remained overly specialized in their particular narrative styles and subject matters, and could not expand in a way that would ensure their survival. I cannot pretend to know anything about westerns, but I imagine that the genre has survived because it was more flexible: writers could move beyond its original locale, the nineteenth-century American West, forward to the present, backwards to colonial times, or geographically to countries like Argentina and Australia; and writers could shift from its original focus on the character of the cowboy and the theme of settling the frontier to explore other types of characters and other themes in other styles of language.

Since I can pretend to know something about detective fiction, I offer this sketch of its nature and development. Where to begin the story is a matter for critics who specialize in the field to establish, though I would begin somewhere between the time of Poe's 'tales of ratiocination' and the detective pulp magazines of the 1920s—excluding Sophocles, Shakespeare, and the like. If the literature is seen as emerging in this time frame, it appeared with three characteristic elements: the form of a prose narrative; the figure of an investigating detective, who in her thoughts and statements displays what might be termed the language of investigation—its typical *discours*; and finally, the depiction of a crime—usually a murder—which the detective investigates and solves, giving the genre a typical *histoire* or

THE MECHANICS OF WONDER

subject matter.

Next, one sees the emergence of three related types of stories which each contain only two of those elements. That is, if the characteristic language of investigation, and the figure of the investigating detective, are removed, one is left with what might be termed crime fiction: stories focusing on colourful characters on the wrong side of the law without the framing device of a detective or an investigation. Here, Jim Thompson's novels might serve as good examples, and there have been many other stories of this type that have appeared under the aegis of detective fiction.

Next, if the characteristic content—a crime to be solved—is removed, one might be left with something like spy fiction; spies, after all, are like detectives in their manner of thinking and speaking, but they are usually involved not in solving a crime but in preventing some kind of crime— infiltrating enemy organizations, foiling saboteurs, protecting political figures from assassination, and so on. Also, unlike the often limited geography of detective fiction—a city or a lonely mansion—spy adventures typically range all over the globe, further moving away from the common subject matter of the genre. And even since the beginning of the Cold War, espionage thrillers have been a popular branch of the field.

Finally, if the element of narrative is removed, one has true crime stories, descriptions of real detectives and investigations of real cases; 'true crime stories' have long accompanied detective fiction, and the Edgar awards for outstanding achievements in the field include an award for best nonfiction.

In addition, arguably dating back to Poe's brief comments, there has been a tradition of commentaries on detective fiction, though these have been less extensive than those regarding science fiction; but recently, and apparently as a direct response to the activities of science fiction fans, detective fiction fans have forged a community and have started to generate significant amounts of commentaries. Thus, at least in modern times, commentaries can be seen as part of the genre of detective fiction.

If one looks at the publications associated with detective fiction, these are all the types of writing you will find.

While the example of science fiction thus provides a stimulating model for the development of popular genres that might be fruitfully developed and expanded, there remains one more special issue raised only by science fiction: namely, the unusual purposes, first articulated by Gernsback, that appear to animate the machine.

Recall that Gernsback defined three functions of science fiction: to offer entertainment, scientific education, and ideas for new inventions or developments that might then actually be constructed by scientists. There is definite logic, then, in the three subsidiary forms that were attracted to science fiction, as I have already to some extent indicated. I have argued that the hidden agenda of Gernsback can be detected in countless texts of modern science fiction; one could also argue for the continuing primacy of that agenda, then, by considering the three types of texts that were generated by or absorbed into science fiction.

One hardly needs to point out that the goals of Gernsback are not the traditionally accepted goals of literature. Rather, the main purpose of literature, as articulated by William Faulkner in his Nobel Prize acceptance speech, has been regarded as this: to examine 'the problems of the human heart in conflict with itself which alone can make good writing because only that is worth writing about, worth the agony and the sweat' (cited in Renshaw, p. 378). A similar nexus of concerns is announced by Suvin: 'the basic purpose of fiction is to make human life more manageable, more meaningful and more pleasant, by means of selecting some believable human relationships for playful consideration and understanding' (*Positions and Presuppositions in Science Fiction*, p. 87). By this orthodox view, literary works have lasting value only if they offer some insight into the nature of humanity and human society; works without such insights are by definition ephemeral.

Thus, if much of science fiction is covertly dedicated to nothing more than harmless entertainment, scientific education, and ideas for inventors, it is by nature, apparently, devoted to ephemeral goals. Works that provide nothing but amusement are supposed to vanish as soon as new stories of a similar nature appear; works that present scientific facts are supposed to be superseded and made worthless by new discoveries; and works that propose new inventions are supposed to become obsolete, as their predictions are either realized—like Verne's submarine in *Twenty Thousand Leagues under the Sea*—or made foolish by later developments—like Gernsback's 'The Airplane of the Future' with its large propellers (*Air Wonder Stories*, September 1929, pp. 196–97).

Gernsback himself seemed to accept that works of science fiction lacked lasting value, either as entertainment, education, or prophecy, since he announced in 1932 that Verne's works were not:

> in the light of today's advance in science fiction... readable... Quite a number of them read so tamely today that the average reader would yawn. The incredible wonders in Jules Verne's day are commonplace today. The same is the case with a number of other older science fiction books. Time has caught up with them, and progress has been such that the authors' predictions have mostly been fulfilled, leaving the present-day reader with a very ordinary story on his hands. ('On Reprints', p. 5)

And yet, works like *Twenty Thousand Leagues under the Sea*, despite

Gernsback's views, are still read today, as are many other science fiction works that have been rendered obsolete. People still read Edgar Rice Burroughs's Mars novels, though they know that the real Mars is nothing like Burroughs's vision; and people still read Heinlein's *Rocket Ship Galileo* and 'The Man Who Sold the Moon', though they know that their depictions of the first flight to the Moon turned out to be wildly inaccurate. As many critics have pointed out, the works of Verne, Burroughs and Heinlein generally lack the normal qualities of superior literature, and works lacking those qualities are supposed to fade into obscurity; yet Verne, Burroughs and Heinlein endure. And the entire genre of science fiction, largely but covertly devoted to Gernsback's ephemeral goals, has also endured as an entity.

Why does science fiction endure?

This is not the occasion for probing the human condition, but one might note that the traditional goals of literature—to closely examine human nature and human problems—have not necessarily been goals of great importance in the lives of many people throughout human history. Many have lived long and happy lives without paying any attention to such concerns. But almost all people do bring certain priorities to their lives: to enjoy diversions from the routines of everyday existence and provide others with such diversions; to learn more about the world around them and convey what they have learned to others; and to develop methods for materially improving their lives and offer those ideas to others. While these goals can be seen at all times in the past, science has today apparently become the best mechanism for understanding and improving the world ('apparently' because, of course, the benefits of modern science can be hotly debated—a topic that cannot be explored here). So, one could argue, the purposes Gernsback embedded in science fiction are more universal, more fundamental to human existence, than traditional goals of literature.

And the aura of truly important priorities at work, one could further argue, accounts for the enduring popularity and relevance of science fiction. Why *do* people still read *Twenty Thousand Leagues under the Sea*? After all, there are many recent books that provide better entertainment than Verne's slow-paced narrative, that provide better information about life under the sea, that describe actual submarines that are more fantastic and interesting than the *Nautilus*. In terms of Gernsback's goals for science fiction, the novel is obsolete on all counts; and Verne does not seem to provide any of the values associated with high literature. But people still read *Twenty Thousand Leagues under the Sea*.

Glancing through that book today, I would tentatively suggest that there is something intoxicating, something fascinating, in the interplay of fundamentally human concerns that Verne brought to the writing of the book. *Twenty Thousand Leagues under the Sea* powerfully represents, and recreates for the modern reader, the spirit of a time when the undersea world was still an unexplored and mysterious realm, when scientific knowledge regarding that world was still limited and incomplete, and when scientific methods for exploring that world were still in their infancy. Similarly, *A Princess of Mars* represents and recreates the spirit of a time when, while all the frontiers of Earth were vanishing, other planets seemed to offer vast new vistas; and *Rocket Ship Galileo* represents and recreates the spirit of a time when manned flight to other planets first appeared to be an actual, realizable possibility in the near future. There remains something thrilling about these adventures, despite their outdated science and lack of other literary values; something thrilling about other older works of science fiction that embody these drives for entertainment, education, and prophecy; and something thrilling about a body of literature which announces a continuing devotion to those drives.

A paradox emerges from this line of thought: science fiction is usually celebrated for the glimpses it offers into the future; however, as literature, it may be most valuable as a window into the past—a record of human aspirations captured at crucial moments during their realization. Its works offer a sense of excitement, a sense of attention to basic human concerns, that is not available in works which strive to fulfil traditional literary goals.[10]

Of course, the goals that Gernsback emphasized were not, even for him, the *only* goals in writing science fiction. Time and again, he acknowledged the simultaneous importance of traditional literary values and urged writers to attempt to meet high literary standards; and his successors, to varying extents, have valued and supported these goals. Yet the apparently unimportant purposes that Gernsback introduced—entertainment, education, and stimulating ideas—have remained central to the genre; so science fiction writers have been urged to achieve both Gernsback's goals and the usual goals of literature. Thus, in the way it views itself, science fiction is neither popular literature nor high literature; rather, it has been, or it has attempted to be, both.

In validating as equally important a set of purposes that seem contrary to traditional literary values, one sees that science fiction is far more subversive than Suvin has ever realized. That is, the genre exists not simply to challenge or question the smug assumptions of the ruling class; rather, it also challenges and questions the smug assumptions of literary criticism itself.

In essence, Gernsback began the genre of science fiction by thumbing his nose at traditional literary values: he acknowledged their importance, to be sure, but argued that other qualities—entertainment value, scientific accuracy, imaginative suggestions for inventions—could be just as important, or even more important. Since Gernsback, one repeatedly sees his priorities embedded in science fiction texts, in the related forms which were absorbed into science fiction, and in the commentaries that accompanied science fiction—though some embarrassed practitioners have taken pains to deny the importance of Gernsback's agenda. Still, that peculiar agenda defined and motivated the genre, and the continuing success of the genre argues for the value of that agenda.

To apply the insights of Marxism to its critics, then, one can maintain that their general approach to science fiction represents a classic strategy of a dominant class—namely, an attempt to co-opt the revolution. Elitist critics committed to traditional literary concerns have carefully selected a few genuine science fiction texts which can be defended as expressions of their concerns; they have declared other genre texts to be lesser, unimportant works; and they have combined those few texts with a number of works from outside the science fiction tradition to build theories of science fiction that grow out of and apply solely to those carefully chosen works. Thus, they strive to reconstruct the genre of science fiction in a way that weakens and obscures its fundamental challenge to the values that inform literary criticism.

And, like the efforts of all representatives of a dying élitist class, their attempts to transform science fiction have failed. In the books and magazines of today, the genre of science fiction created by Gernsback continues on, oblivious to those who would define its priorities as ephemeral and valueless.

It is time, then, to stop twisting and distorting the genre of science fiction to meet traditional critical expectations; rather, literary critics must confront the genre of science fiction as it actually exists, in terms of the genre's own expectations.

Literary critics must embrace the entire body of literature that emerged under the name of science fiction—both good works and bad—as their central concern. They must examine those texts in the context of their relationships with each other, with related texts, and with the critical commentaries that have accompanied and continue to accompany those texts. They must stop declaring that certain approaches and works simply should not be interesting to intelligent people and must instead ponder the question of why those approaches and works are consistently interesting to intelligent people. And they must be prepared to consider the possibility that in certain significant ways, the agenda of traditional literary criticism may be flawed, and that in certain significant ways, the agenda of Gernsback may be worthwhile.

I am tempted to delete much of the above as pure speculation, for that is what it is. I really don't know why works of science fiction endure, or why the genre of science fiction endures. All I know is that the way to begin answering those questions is to look at the man who began science fiction: Hugo Gernsback.

As a telling image for all critics of science fiction, Theodore Sturgeon's 'Slow Sculpture' suggests the metaphor of bonsai sculpture. The bad tree sculptor approaches the tree with preconceived notions of what it should look like; ignoring how the tree is actually developing, she ruthlessly tries to force the tree to grow into that pattern, lopping off growths and twisting branches in strange directions to achieve her goal. More often than not, the tree rejects these arbitrary and unnatural dictates, and either resists them or dies. In contrast, the good tree sculptor begins her work by looking carefully at the tree and noticing how the tree seems to be growing. Accepting its natural inclinations, she then begins a slow process of subtly altering its growth, slightly improving upon its pattern of growth, working with the tree to make it a little more beautiful than it otherwise might have been. The result is a collaborative process, sculptor and tree working together to produce a work of art.

Too many critics of science fiction have been bad sculptors, elevating their personal preferences to doctrinal standards or borrowing theoretical models from other fields which they impose upon science fiction, ignoring works that do not fit the model, artificially celebrating those which do, and announcing a programme of priorities for science fiction with no real relationship to the genre's actual development and direction. In a sense, they have attempted to define science fiction without first describing it.

And their analyses have been properly rejected by the science fiction community, and have been without effect. Indeed, far beyond my power to condemn academic criticism, the fact that it has been universally condemned by those who should be most interested in it—people who write and read science fiction—is the most powerful indictment of their work that could possibly be offered.

A good sculptor of science fiction, as I have said, should begin by being descriptive before she is prescriptive. She must examine the modern genre and all its works, and the critical principles which engendered and shaped all those works, so that she can describe science fiction; then, and only then, can she embark upon a programme of deepening and extending those principles, looking for weak points or promising new directions, emphasizing particular texts within the genre which illustrate certain problems or potentials. In essence, this critic would be committed to working with science fiction, not working against it; and such a critic can expect to be listened to, and can expect to have some impact on the genre. David G. Hartwell may have best summarized the current state of science fiction and its ongoing requirements:

> SF, in the 1970s and today, is a capacious umbrella for a multitude
> of hybrid forms of fantasy, surrealism, weird tales, and pop retreads
> of all SF ideas. Another breakdown in definition is happening.
> Perhaps we need sympathetic, knowledgeable criticism, theoretical
> criticism, now more than ever to keep track of where we are.
> Certainly we need literary history for the first time, so that we do
> not forget where we have been. (*Age of Wonders*, p. 186)

Speaking as an informed participant in modern science fiction, Hartwell
argues for 'sympathetic' and 'knowledgeable' criticism; and academic
critics should be responding to these needs.

No reasonable person can be enthusiastic about all the works and all
the concerns observed in modern science fiction; a desire to change and
improve the genre is entirely admirable; and I certainly would not argue
that science fiction writers should return to the style of Gernsback, that all
literary values should be ignored, or that all science fiction critics must
abandon all efforts to achieve rigour and instead mouth Gernsback's ideas.
However, to change a genre, one must understand it; to understand it, one
must listen to the thoughts and opinions of those who have produced and
read its works. Without such knowledge, no critic of science fiction will be
listened to, and no critic of science fiction can have any effect.

Some day, another book about science fiction may be written. It may
be as imperious as *Trillion Year Spree* or as convoluted and filled with jargon
as *Metamorphoses of Science Fiction*; however, that book will be based on the
principles of Gernsback, Campbell, and their successors; that book will
grow out of those principles; and that book will be dedicated to exploring
the genre which actually emerged from those principles. For those reasons,
that book, unlike many of its predecessors, will be worth reading, worth
putting up with, worth learning from—and, not incidentally, one that
might actually have a beneficial effect on science fiction.

And that book will be an important step in an ongoing process.

This book is the first step in that process.

It is time for academic critics to help the idea of science fiction grow
some more.

Notes

1 And, I might add, I was never told that only scholarship from people with
PhDs should be examined; in fact, scholars of many literary eras regularly use
contemporary commentators from amateurs and others whose literary
credentials are suspect.

2 And, as a neophyte scholar, I began my study of science fiction with a

proposed project which Aldiss and Suvin might have heartily endorsed: the first volume of a proposed history of science fiction from Francis Bacon to Jane Austen (yes, Jane Austen, and please do *not* ask me to explain). However, as I began to harbour understandable doubts about this project's validity, I decided to add an introductory chapter defending my premises by discussing the origins and use of the term 'science fiction'—which led to Gernsback and *Amazing Stories* and, eventually, to the abandonment of that project and the completion of this one.

3 As, for example, in 'Hard-Core Science Fiction and the Illusion of Science'.

4 Of course, others have argued for such a definition; for example, Norman Spinrad said, 'There is only one definition of science fiction that seems to make pragmatic sense: "Science fiction is anything published as science fiction"' (cited in Jakubowski and Edwards, *The Book of SF Lists*, p. 258).

5 Two notes: first, while I call works of science fiction 'prose narratives', the genre easily extends into other narrative forms, such as films, television, comic books, and drama. There is also a sporadic tradition of science fiction poetry—a problematic matter, since these are not really narratives. As is often the case, Gernsback himself launched this tradition by publishing a few poems by Leland S. Copeland in *Amazing Stories*, and other magazines and anthologies since then have included them; still, because the form has never been popular, these poems appear more a matter of editorial indulgence than a response to reader interest.

Second, in these discussions I will avoid what is threatening to become a standard term for a non-mimetic element in science fiction—Suvin's *novum*—because it implies such elements can be identified, counted, and ranked in importance, and I do not believe this is possible. My description simply claims that something presented in the text does not exist in the environment of the author—whether it is major or minor, one element or several, and so on are matters of subjective judgement not worth addressing.

6 Of course, you may find other things, like science fiction poetry, and magazines may include other non-narrative extensions of science fiction like illustrations, cartoons, and puzzles. A few science fiction anthologies, like Theodore Sturgeon's *A Touch of Strange*, included realistic stories, with no scientific language or prophetic content. Some magazine nonfiction may veer into political issues with little concern for science or predictions—like the later Campbell editorials in *Analog* or the petitions regarding the Vietnam War that appeared in *Galaxy* in 1968. And there may be other exceptions; but these are relatively rare.

7 This distinction might be clarified by an analogy: speaking of early prose narratives that were considered 'novels', one notes that these typically featured a careful study of an individual character or characters and/or analyses of larger social problems and issues. This might be accepted as an accurate description. But that would not imply that there are three fixed categories of novels, 'character novels', 'social novels', and 'complete novels', or that all novels could be placed into such categories.

8 Of course, there are exceptions: for example, Ellison's *Again, Dangerous Visions* included Ben Bova's 'Zero Gee' and Barry Malzberg's 'Still Life', both prose narratives involving present-day science or readily predictable scientific advances.

9 I later found the same metaphor for science fiction as a single being in

Barry N. Malzberg's *The Engines of the Night*:

> Science fiction as a single, demented, multitentacled artist singing and painting and transcribing in fashion clumsy and elegant, errant and imitative, innovative and repetitious, the way the future would feel. Science fiction, born in 1926, dreaming through its childhood in the 1930s, achieving change of voice and the beginning of adult features in the forties with all of the misdirected energy and hints of promise, arriving at a shaky legal maturity at the end of the decade with the expansion of the market and the full incorporation of a range of style and technique. Young adult in the sixties with the knowledge turned loose in a hundred ways, some toward no consequence, others foreshadowing maturity. Science fiction at thirty-five, eligible to be President! Productive of fluency. Science fiction at forty in the mid-sixties with all the hunts of mid-life panic... Science fiction, settling from its decade of panic in the mid-seventies to pursue what it had passed over when young, reworking the familiar in thoroughgoing fashion. Science fiction now at the threshold of old age, the faint whiff of alcohol and decadence as it trudges toward the millennium. Science fiction, that demented artist of which we are all but cells and cilia. Blood and bone. (pp. 123–24)

10 Of course, it has often been said that human dreams provide a better record of human history than human actions; I only add that science fiction, as devised by Gernsback, provides an unusually powerful mechanism for articulating those dreams.

Works Cited

The following only lists works cited or discussed in the text; it is not a comprehensive bibliography of science fiction criticism and includes works with little direct relevance to that subject. To avoid pages filled with long dashes, I group together writings by Hugo Gernsback and John W. Campbell, Jr; unsigned materials attributed to Gernsback are marked '[unsigned]'. Almost all Campbell writings in *Astounding Science-Fiction* were unsigned, but since there is no authorship controversy, I do not label them as unsigned. Letters from *The John W. Campbell Letters, Volume I* are not listed separately. When referencing two or more stories or essays from one anthology, I list each item separately, stating the title, editor, and page numbers, and provide bibliographical data for the volume in an entry under the editor's name.

I. Works Cited by Hugo Gernsback

'The Airplane of the Future', *Air Wonder Stories*, 1 (September 1929), 196–97.

'Air Wonder Stories', *Air Wonder Stories*, 1 (July 1929), 5.

'Amazing Creations', *Amazing Stories*, 2 (May 1927), 109.

'The Amazing Unknown', *Amazing Stories*, 3 (August 1928), 389.

'Amazing Youth', *Amazing Stories*, 2 (October 1927), 625.

Baron Munchhausen's Scientific Adventures. *Amazing Stories*, 2 (February 1928), 1060–71, (March, 1928), 1150–60; *Amazing Stories*, 3 (April 1928), 38–47, 84, (May 1928), 148–56, (June 1928), 242–51, (July 1928), 346–57. Originally published in *Electrical Experimenter* in 1915, 1916 and 1917.

'A Different Story', *Amazing Stories*, 2 (August 1927), 421.

'Editorially Speaking', *Amazing Stories*, 1 (September 1926), 483.

'The Electric Duel', *Amazing Stories*, 2 (September 1927), 543. Originally published in *Science and Invention* (August 1923).

'The Electronic Baby', *Science-Fiction Plus*, 1 (May 1953), 59–61. Originally published privately in Gernsback's 1946 Christmas booklet, 'Digest of Digests'.

Evolution of Modern Science Fiction, New York: [privately printed], 1952.

'Experts Join Staff of "Amazing Stories"', *Amazing Stories*, 1 (July 1926), 380 [unsigned].

'Exploration of Mars', *Science-Fiction Plus*, 1 (March 1953), 4–11, 61–65. Originally published privately in Gernsback's 1949 Christmas booklet, 'Quip'.

'Fiction Versus Facts', *Amazing Stories*, 1 (July 1926), 291.

'The $500 Cover Prize Contest', *Amazing Stories*, 2 (June 1927), 213 [unsigned].

'Good News for Our Readers', *Wonder Stories Quarterly*, 4 (Fall 1932), 5.

'Guest Editorial', in *The H. G. Wells Scrapbook*, ed. Peter Haining (New York: Clarkson N. Potter, 1978), 140–41. First published in *Amazing Stories*, 36 (April 1961), 5–7, 93.

'Hidden Wonders', *Science Wonder Stories*, 1 (September 1929), 293.

'How to Write "Science" Stories', *Writer's Digest*, 10 (February 1930), 27–29.

'Idle Thoughts of a Busy Editor', *Amazing Stories*, 1 (March 1927), 1085.

'Imagination and Reality', *Amazing Stories*, 1 (October 1926), 579.

'The Impact of Science-Fiction on World Progress', *Science-Fiction Plus*, 1 (March 1953), 2, 67. Originally presented as an Address before the 10th Annual World Science Fiction Convention, Chicago, Illinois, 31 August 1952.

'In Our Next Issue', *Amazing Stories*, 3 (March 1929), 1058 [unsigned].

Introduction to 'Advanced Chemistry', *Science and Invention*, 11 (August 1923), 332 [unsigned].

Introduction to 'Advanced Chemistry', *Amazing Stories*, 1 (March 1927), 1127 [unsigned].

Introduction to *Baron Munchhausen's Scientific Adventures*, *Amazing Stories*, 2 (February 1928), 1061 [unsigned].

Introduction to 'Blasphemers' Plateau', *Amazing Stories*, 1 (October 1926), 657 [unsigned].

Introduction to 'The Crystal Egg', *Amazing Stories*, 1 (May 1926), 129 [unsigned].

Introduction to 'The Diamond Lens', *Amazing Stories*, 1 (December 1926), 835 [unsigned].

Introduction to 'Dr. Ox's Experiment', *Amazing Stories*, 1 (August 1926), 421 [unsigned].

Introduction to 'The Facts in the Case of M. Valdemar', *Amazing Stories*, 1 (April 1926), 93 [unsigned].

Introduction to *The First Men in the Moon*, *Amazing Stories*, 1 (December 1926), 775 [unsigned].

Introduction to *The Island of Dr. Moreau*, *Amazing Stories*, 1 (October 1926), 637 [unsigned].

Introduction to 'Just Around the Corner', *Amazing Stories*, 3 (July 1928),

358 [unsigned].

Introduction to *The Land That Time Forgot*. *Amazing Stories*, 2 (February 1927), 983 [unsigned].

Introduction to 'The Man from the Atom', *Amazing Stories*, 1 (April 1926), 63 [unsigned].

Introduction to 'The Man Who Could Work Miracles', *Amazing Stories*, 1 (July 1926), 312 [unsigned].

Introduction to 'The Man Who Saved the Earth', *Amazing Stories*, 1 (April 1926), 75 [unsigned].

Introduction to 'A Martian Odyssey', *Wonder Stories*, 6 (July 1934), 175 [unsigned].

Introduction to 'Mesmeric Revelation', *Amazing Stories*, 1 (May 1926), 124 [unsigned].

Introduction to 'Mr. Fosdick Invents the Seidlitzmobile', *Amazing Stories*, 1 (June 1926), 239 [unsigned].

Introduction to *The Moon Pool*, *Amazing Stories*, 2 (May 1927), 111 [unsigned].

Introduction to *The Purchase of the North Pole*, *Amazing Stories*, 1 (September 1926), 511 [unsigned].

Introduction to *Ralph 124C 41+: A Romance of the Year 2660*, *Amazing Stories Quarterly*, 2 (Winter 1929), 4 [unsigned].

Introduction to 'The Talking Brain', *Amazing Stories*, 1 (August 1926), 441 [unsigned].

Introduction to 'The Telepathic Pick-Up', *Amazing Stories*, 1 (December 1926), 829 [unsigned].

Introduction to 'Ten Million Miles Sunward', *Amazing Stories*, 2 (March 1928), 1127 [unsigned].

'Introduction to This Story', [*Off on a Comet*] *Amazing Stories*, 1 (April 1926), 4–5 [unsigned].

Introduction to *A Trip to the Center of the Earth*, *Amazing Stories*, 1 (May 1926), 101 [unsigned].

'The Killing Flash', *Science Wonder Stories*, 1 (November 1929), 486–487.

Letter to M. Craig, Secretary to H. G. Wells, 15 June 1926.

Letter to M. Craig, Secretary to H. G. Wells, 18 July 1927.

Letter to H. G. Wells, 4 May 1926.

Letter to H. G. Wells, 9 June 9 1926.

Letter to H. G. Wells, 5 October 1926.

Letter to H. G. Wells, 5 May 1927.

Letter to H. G. Wells, 3 December 1927.

Letter to H. G. Wells, 4 April 1928.

'The Lure of Scientifiction', *Amazing Stories*, 1 (June 1926), 195.

'The Magnetic Storm', *Amazing Stories*, 1 (June 1926), 350–56. First published in *Electrical Experimenter* (August 1918).

'The Most Amazing Thing (In the Style of Edgar Allan Poe)', *Amazing Stories*, 2 (April 1927), 5.

'The Mystery of Time', *Amazing Stories*, 2 (September 1927), 525.

'A New Sort of Magazine', *Amazing Stories*, 1 (April 1926), 3.

'On Reprints', *Wonder Stories Quarterly*, 4 (Winter 1933), 99.

'Our Amazing Minds', *Amazing Stories*, 3 (June 1928), 197.

'Our Amazing Stars', *Amazing Stories*, 3 (March 1929), 1063.

'Plausibility in Scientifiction', *Amazing Stories*, 1 (November 1926), 675.

'Predicting Future Inventions', *Science and Invention*, 11 (August 1923), 319.

'Pseudo Science-Fiction', *Science-Fiction Plus*, 1 (April 1953), 2.

Ralph 124C 41+: A Romance of the Year 2660, 1925 (New York: Frederick Fell, second edition 1950). Originally published in *Modern Electrics* in 1911 and 1912.

'Reasonableness in Science Fiction', *Wonder Stories*, 4 (December 1932), 585.

'Results of $300.00 Scientifiction Prize Contest', *Amazing Stories*, 3 (September 1928), 519 [unsigned].

'The Rise of Scientifiction', *Amazing Stories Quarterly*, 1 (Spring 1928), 147.

'The Science-Fiction Industry', *Science-Fiction Plus*, 1 (May 1953), 2.

'The Science Fiction League', *Wonder Stories*, 5 (May 1934), 1061–65.

'The Science Fiction League: An Announcement', *Wonder Stories*, 5 (April 1934), 933.

'Science-Fiction Semantics', *Science-Fiction Plus*, 1 (August 1953), 2.

'Science Fiction vs. Science Faction', *Wonder Stories Quarterly*, 2 (Fall 1930), 5.

'Science Fiction Week', *Science Wonder Stories*, 1 (May 1930), 1061.

'Science vs. Crime', *Scientific Detective Monthly*, 1 (January 1930), 5, 85.

'Science Wonder Stories', *Science Wonder Stories*, 1 (June 1929), 5.

'Skepticism in Science-Fiction', *Science-Fiction Plus*, 1 (June 1953), 2.

'Status of Science-Fiction: Snob Appeal or Mass Appeal?' *Science-Fiction Plus*, 1 (December 1953), 2.

'Surprising Facts', *Amazing Stories*, 2 (July 1927), 317.

'Thank You!', *Amazing Stories*, 1 (May 1926), 99.

'$300.00 Prize Contest—Wanted: A Symbol for Scientifiction', *Amazing Stories*, 3 (April 1928), 5 [unsigned].

'$300.00 Prize Story Contest', *Air Wonder Stories*, 1 (February 1930), 677 [unsigned].

Ultimate World, ed. with an introduction, by Sam Moskowitz, 1971 (New York: Avon Books, 1975).

'Wireless on Mars', *Modern Electrics*, 1 (February 1909), 394.

'Wonders of the Machine Age', *Wonder Stories*, 3 (July 1931), 151–52, 286.

'The World in 2046: The Next Hundred Years of Atomics', *Science-Fiction Plus*, 1 (June, 1953), 34–42. Originally published privately in Gernsback's 1945 Christmas booklet, 'Tame'.

'World War III—In Retrospect', *Science-Fiction Plus*, 1 (April 1953), 26–38. Originally published privately in Gernsback's 1950 Christmas booklet, 'Newspeek'.

II. Works Cited by John W. Campbell, Jr

'Atomic Age', *Astounding Science-FIction*, 36 (November 1945), 5–6, 98.

'Brass Tacks', [response to reader's letter], *Astounding Science-Fiction*, 27 (May 1941), 124–25.

'Brass Tacks', *Astounding Science-Fiction*, 28 (December 1941), 158.

'Brass Tacks', *Astounding Science-Fiction*, 30 (November 1942), 42.

Cloak of Aesir, 1952. (New York: Lancer Books, 1972).

Collected Editorials from Analog, selected by Harry Harrison (Garden City, New Jersey: Doubleday, 1966).

Comments added to 'The Reference Library' [book review column] by P. Schuyler Miller, *Astounding Science-Fiction*, 57 (September 1956), 152–53.

'Concerning Science Fiction', in *The Best of Science Fiction*, ed. Groff Conklin (New York: Crown Publishers, 1946), v–xi.

'Constitution for Utopia', in *Collected Editorials from Analog*, ed. Harry Harrison, 181–92. Originally published in *Analog Science Fact/Science Fiction*, 65 (May 1961).

'Contest', *Astounding Science-Fiction*, 21 (July 1938), 73.

'Editorial Number Three: Letter from the Editor', in *A Requiem for Astounding*, by Alva Rogers, xix–xxi.

'Editor's Note' following 'Solution Unsatisfactory', *Astounding Science-Fiction*, 27 (May 1941), 86.

'Foreword', in *From Unknown Worlds*, ed. John W. Campbell, Jr (New York: Street & Smith, Publishers, Inc., 1948), 3.

'Forgetfulness', in *Cloak of Aesir*, 15–46. Originally published (as by Don A. Stuart) in *Astounding Stories* (June 1937).

'Future Tense', *Astounding Science-Fiction*, 23 (June 1939), 6.

'History to Come', *Astounding Science-Fiction*, 27 (May 1941), 5–6.

'In Times to Come', *Astounding Science-Fiction*, 21 (May 1938), 92.

'In Times to Come', *Astounding Science-Fiction*, 22 (October 1938), 11.

'In Times to Come', *Astounding Science-Fiction*, 25 (June 1940), 50.

'In Times to Come', *Astounding Science-Fiction*, 26 (December 1940), 112.

'In Times To Come', *Astounding Science-Fiction*, 27 (May 1941), 87.

'In Times to Come', *Astounding Science-Fiction*, 27 (August 1941), 36.

'In Times to Come', *Astounding Science-Fiction*, 29 (August 1942), 98.

'In Times to Come', *Astounding Science-Fiction*, 30 (November 1942), 42.

'In Times to Come', *Astounding Science-Fiction*, 30 (December 1942), 74.

'In Times to Come', *Astounding Science-Fiction*, 32 (December 1943), 32.

'Introduction', in *Analog 1*, ed. John W. Campbell, Jr (Garden City: Doubleday, 1963), xv–xviii.

'Introduction', in *Analog 6*, ed. John W. Campbell, Jr, 1968 (New York: Pocket Books, 1969), xi–xvi.

'Introduction', in *The Astounding Science Fiction Anthology*, ed. John W. Campbell, Jr (New York: Simon & Schuster, 1952), ix–xv.

Introduction to *Beyond This Horizon*, *Astounding Science-Fiction*, 29 (April 1942), 9.

Introduction to 'Bridle and Saddle', *Astounding Science-Fiction*, 29 (June 1942), 9.

'Introduction', in *Cloak of Aesir*, 11–14.

'Introduction', in *14 Great Tales about ESP*, ed. Idella Purnell Stone (London: Coronet Books, 1970), 11–16.

'Introduction', in *The Man Who Sold the Moon*, by Robert A. Heinlein (Chicago: Shasta Publishers, 1950), 11–15.

'Introduction', in *Prologue to Analog*, ed. John W. Campbell, Jr (Garden City: Doubleday, 1962), 9–16.

'Introduction', in *Venus Equilateral*, by George O. Smith (New York: Prime Press, 1947), 8–12.

'Introduction', in *Who Goes There?*, 3–6.

'Introduction', in *A World by the Tale* [*Analog 3*], ed. John W. Campbell, Jr, 1963 (New York: Curtis Books, 1965), 7–12.

'Invention and Imagination', *Astounding Science-Fiction*, 23 (August 1939), 6.

The John W. Campbell Letters, Volume I, ed. Perry A. Chapdelaine, Sr, Tony Chapdelaine and George Hay (Franklin, Tennessee: AC Projects, 1985).

'Let's Make It Stronger', *Astounding Science-Fiction*, 25 (April 1940), 6.

'Night', in *Who Goes There?*, 206–30. Originally published (as by Don A. Stuart) in *Astounding Stories* (October 1935).

'Non-Escape Literature', in *Collected Editorials from Analog*, 227–31. Originally published in *Astounding Science-Fiction*, 61 (February 1959).

'Not Simply More', *Astounding Science-Fiction*, 26 (November 1940), 5–6.

'Of Things Beyond', *Unknown*, 1 (March 1939), 6.

'The Old Navy Game', *Astounding Science-Fiction*, 25 (June 1940), 6.

'Our Catalogue Number... ', in *Collected Editorials from Analog*, 65–68. Originally published in *Astounding Science-Fiction*, 49 (July 1953).

'Out of Night', in *Cloak of Aesir*, (Chicago: Shasta, 1952), 151–97. Originally published (as by Don A. Stuart) in *Astounding Stories* (October 1937).

'The Perfect Machine', *Astounding Science-Fiction*, 25 (May 1940), 5.

'The Place of Science Fiction', in *Modern Science Fiction: Its Meaning and Its Future*, ed. Reginald Bretnor, 3–22.

'Preface', in *Analog 2*, ed. John W. Campbell, Jr, 1962 (Garden City: Doubleday, 1964), vii–xi.

'Psionic Machine—Type One', *Astounding Science-Fiction*, 57 (June 1956), 97–108.

'Science-Fiction', *Astounding Science-Fiction*, 21 (March 1938), 47.

'Science Fiction and the Opinion of the Universe', *Saturday Review*, 39 (12 May 1956), 9–10, 42–43.

'Science-Fiction Prophecy', *Astounding Science-Fiction*, 44 (November 1949), 4.

'Science Fiction We Can Buy', *The Writer*, 81 (September 1968), 27–28.

'The Science of Science-Fiction', *Space Magazine*, 1 (Winter 1949), 4–7, 21. First published in *Atlantic Monthly* (May 1948).

'The Science of Science Fiction Writing', in *Of Worlds Beyond*, ed., Lloyd Arthur Eshbach, 91–101.

'Scientists Are Stupid', in *Countercommandment* [*Analog 5*], ed. John W. Campbell, Jr, 1965 (New York: Curtis Books, 1967), 9–17.

'These Stories May Upset You', in *The Permanent Implosion* [*Analog 4*], ed. John W. Campbell, Jr, 1963 (New York: Curtis Books, 1966), 7–12.

'Too Good at Guessing', *Astounding Science-Fiction*, 29 (April 1942), 6–7.

'Twilight', in *The Science Fiction Hall of Fame, Volume I*, ed. Robert Silverberg, 1970 (New York: Avon Books, 1971), 40–61. Originally published (as by Don A. Stuart) in *Astounding Stories* (November 1934).

'Unknown', *Unknown*, 1 (March 1939), 5.

'A Variety of Things', *Astounding Science-Fiction*, 22 (January 1939), 6.

'We Can't Keep Up!' *Astounding Science-Fiction*, 26 (October 1940), 6.

'We Must Study Psi', in *Collected Editorials from Analog*, 217–26. Originally published in *Astounding Science-Fiction*, 61 (January 1959).

'Who Goes There?', in *Who Goes There?*, 7–75. First published (as by Don A. Stuart) in *Astounding Science-Fiction* (August 1938).

Who Goes There? (Chicago: Shasta, 1948).

III. Other Works Cited

Adams, Percy C., *Travel Literature and the Evolution of the Novel* (Lexington: The University Press of Kentucky, 1983).

Aldiss, Brian W., Brian Stableford and Edward James, 'On "On *The True History of Science Fiction*"', *Foundation: The Review of Science Fiction*, No. 47 (Winter 1989/1990), 27–32.

Aldiss, Brian W. with David Wingrove, *Trillion Year Spree: The History of*

Science Fiction (New York: Atheneum, 1986). An earlier version, as by Aldiss alone: *Billion Year Spree: The True History of Science Fiction*. New York: Schocken, 1973).

Alkon, Paul, *Origins of Futuristic Fiction* (Athens, Georgia: University of Georgia Press, 1987).

Allen, L. David, *Science Fiction: An Introduction, Cliffs Notes* (Lincoln, Nebraska: Cliffs Notes, Incorporated, 1973).

'An American Jules Verne', *Amazing Stories*, 3 (June 1928), 270–72.

'The American Jules Verne', *Science and Invention*, 8 (October 1920), page numbers unknown.

Amis, Kingsley, *New Maps of Hell* (New York: Ballantine Books, 1960).

Anderson, Poul, interview with Jeffrey M. Elliot in *Science Fiction Voices #2*, 41–50. First published in *Galileo* in 1979.

Ash, Brian, *Faces of the Future: The Lessons of Science Fiction* (New York: Taplinger, 1975).

Ashley, Michael, 'Introduction: An Amazing Experiment', in *The History of the Science Fiction Magazines, Volume I: 1926–1935*, ed. Michael Ashley, 1974 (Chicago: Henry Regnery, 1976), 11–51.

———. 'Introduction: SF Bandwaggon', in *The History of the Science Fiction Magazines, Volume II: 1936–1945*, ed. Michael Ashley, 1975 (Chicago: Henry Regnery, 1976), 11–76.

Asimov, Isaac, *Asimov on Science Fiction*, 1981 (New York: Avon Books, 1982).

———, *Asimov's Mysteries* (New York: Dell Books, 1968).

———, (ed.), *Before the Golden Age* (Garden City: Doubleday, 1974).

———, *The Caves of Steel*, 1954 (New York: Pyramid Books, 1962). Novel originally published in 1953.

Bailey, J. O. [James Osler] *Pilgrims through Time and Space: Trends and Patterns in Scientific and Utopian Fiction* (New York: Argus Books, 1947).

Bainbridge, William Sims, *Dimensions of Science Fiction* (Cambridge: Harvard University Press, 1986).

Barron, Neil (ed.), *Anatomy of Wonder: A Critical Guide to Science Fiction* Third edition (New York: R. R. Bowker Co., 1987).

Bates, Harry, 'About Reprints', *Astounding Stories of Super-Science*, 1 (July 1930), 134–35 [unsigned].

———, 'Editorial Number One: To Begin', in *A Requiem for Astounding*, by Alva Rogers, viii–xvi.

———, 'Our Thanks', *Astounding Stories of Super-Science*, 1 (April 1930), 127–28.

Bayer-Berenbaum, Linda, *The Gothic Imagination: Expansion in Gothic Literature and Art* (East Brunswick, New Jersey: Associated University Presses, 1982).

Benford, Gregory, *Great Sky River* (New York: Bantam Books, 1987).

——, interview with Jeffrey M. Elliot in *Science Fiction Voices #3*, 44–52. First published in *Galileo* in 1978.

——, 'Plane in Fancy: Alien Lands for Human Drama', review of *The Science in Science Fiction* by Peter Nicholls, *Los Angeles Times*, 20 February 1983, Book Review, 2, 7.

——, *Tides of Light* (New York: Bantam Books, 1989).

——, *Timescape* (New York: Simon and Schuster, 1980).

Bester, Alfred, 'Science Fiction and the Renaissance Man', in *The Science Fiction Novel*, ed. Basil Davenport, 77–96.

Bleiler, Everett F. and T. E. Dikty (ed.), *The Best Science Fiction Stories: 1950* (New York: Frederick Fell, Inc., 1950).

Blish, James [as by William Atheling, Jr], *The Issues at Hand* (Chicago: Advent, 1964). Articles originally published between 1952 and 1962.

—— [as by William Atheling, Jr], *More Issues at Hand* (Chicago: Advent, 1970). Articles originally published between 1957 and 1970.

——, and Norman L. Knight, *A Torrent of Faces* (New York: Ace Books, 1967).

Booth, Michael R., *English Melodrama* (London: Herbert Jenkins, 1965).

Boucher, Anthony, 'The Publishing of Science Fiction', in *Of Worlds Beyond*, ed. Lloyd Arthur Eshbach, 23–42.

Brady, James T., Jr, 'History of Scientific Fiction', in 'Editorials from Our Readers', *Amazing Stories Quarterly*, 1 (Fall 1928), 571.

Bretnor, Reginald (ed.), *Modern Science Fiction: Its Meaning and Its Future*. (New York: Coward-McCann, Inc., 1953).

Brin, David, *The River of Time* (New York: Bantam Books, 1987).

Brooks, Peter, *The Melodramatic Imagination: Balzac, Henry James, Melodrama, and the Mode of Excess* (New Haven: Yale University Press, 1976).

Brunner, John, *Stand on Zanzibar*, 1968 (New York: Ballantine Books, 1969).

Budrys, Algis [as by John A. Sentry], 'Aspirin Won't Help It', *Astounding Science-Fiction*, 57 (September 1955), 52–59.

Card, Orson Scott, 'Afterword' to 'The Originist', in *Maps in a Mirror: The Short Fiction of Orson Scott Card*, by Orson Scott Card (New York: Tor Books, 1990), 268–270.

Carter, Paul, *The Creation of Tomorrow: Fifty Years of Magazine Science Fiction* (New York: Columbia University Press, 1977).

——, 'You Can Write Science Fiction if You Want To', in *Hard Science Fiction*, ed. George Slusser and Eric S. Rabkin (Carbondale: Southern Illinois University Press, 1986), 141–151.

Chapdelaine, Perry A., Sr, and George Hay, 'John Wood Campbell', in *The*

John W. Campbell Letters, Volume I, ed. Perry A. Chapdelaine, Sr, Tony Chapdelaine, and George Hay, 17–37.

Clarke, Arthur C., *Astounding Days: A Science Fictional Autobiography*, 1989 (New York: Bantam Books, 1990).

——, *Childhood's End*, 1953 (New York: Ballantine Books, 1967).

——, 'I Remember Babylon', in *Tales of Ten Worlds*, by Arthur C. Clarke (New York: Harcourt Brace Jovanovich, 1962), 1–14. Originally published in 1960.

Clarke, I. F. [Ignatius Frederick], *The Tale of the Future, from the Beginning to the Present Day*, 1960 (London: Library Association, 1978).

Clement, Hal, 'Whirligig World', *Astounding Science-Fiction*, 51 (June 1953), 102–14.

Cover, Arthur Byron, *Stationfall* (New York: Avon Books, 1989).

Cramer, John G., 'The Alternate View: Wormholes and Time Machines', *Analog Science Fiction/Science Fact*, 109 (June 1989), 124–28.

Curtis, Richard (ed.), *Future Tense* (New York: Dell Books, 1968).

Davenport, Basil, *Inquiry into Science Fiction* (New York: Longman, Green, 1955).

—— (ed.), *The Science Fiction Novel: Imagination and Social Criticism* (Chicago: Advent, 1959).

Davin, Eric Leif, 'Gernsback, his Editors, and Women Writers', *Science-Fiction Studies*, 17 (1990), 418–20.

Davis, C. L., *Utopia and the Ideal Society* (Cambridge: Cambridge University Press, 1981).

Day, William Patrick, *In the Circles of Fear and Desire: A Study of Gothic Fantasy* (Chicago: University of Chicago, 1985).

de Camp, L. Sprague, *Lovecraft: A Biography*, abridged by the author, 1975 (New York: Ballantine Books, 1976).

—— and Catherine Crook de Camp, *Science Fiction Handbook—Revised: A Guide to Writing Imaginative Literature* (New York: McGraw-Hill, 1975). An earlier edition, as by L. Sprague de Camp alone: *Science Fiction Handbook: The Writing of Imaginative Fiction* (New York: Hermitage House, 1953).

Delany, Samuel R., 'Time Considered as a Helix of Semi-Precious Stones', in *World's Best Science Fiction 1969*, ed. Donald A. Wollheim and Terry Carr. (New York: Ace Books, 1969), 87–126. Story originally published in 1968.

del Rey, Lester, *The World of Science Fiction 1926–1976* (New York: Ballantine Books, 1979).

'Discussions' [readers' letters and responses], *Amazing Stories*, 1 (January 1927), 973.

'Discussions', *Amazing Stories*, 1 (March 1927), 1180, 1181.

'Discussions', *Amazing Stories*, 2 (April 1927), 99, 102, 103.

'Discussions', *Amazing Stories*, 2 (June 1927), 308, 310.

'Discussions', *Amazing Stories*, 2 (July 1927), 412–15.

'Discussions', *Amazing Stories*, 2 (August 1927), 515, 516.

'Discussions', *Amazing Stories*, 3 (June 1928), 272.

'Discussions', *Amazing Stories*, 3 (July 1928), 370.

'Discussions', *Amazing Stories*, 3 (December 1928), 565.

'Discussions', *Amazing Stories*, 3 (January 1929), 957.

'Do You Want Science Fiction Movies?' [advertisement], *Wonder Stories*, 3 (December 1931), 904.

Edwards, Malcolm J. 'Desmond W. Hall', in *The Science Fiction Encyclopedia*, ed. Peter Nicholls, 252.

——, 'Hugo Gernsback', in *The Science Fiction Encyclopedia*, ed. Peter Nicholls, 270.

Elliot, Jeffrey M., *Science Fiction Voices #2* (San Bernardino, California: Borgo Press, 1979).

——, *Science Fiction Voices #3* (San Bernardino, California: Borgo Press, 1980).

Ellison, Harlan, *The Book of Ellison*, ed. Andrew Porter (New York: ALGOL Press, 1978).

—— 'Introduction' to '●', in *Again, Dangerous Visions II*, ed. Harlan Ellison, 1972 (New York: Signet Books, 1973), 9–12.

——, 'Introduction: Thirty-Two Soothsayers', in *Dangerous Visions #1*, ed. Harlan Ellison, 1967 (New York: Berkley Books, 1968), 19–31.

——, A Time for Daring', in *The Book of Ellison*, by Harlan Ellison, 101–15. Essay originally published in *ALGOL* (March 1967).

——, 'A Voice from the Styx', in *The Book of Ellison*, by Harlan Ellison, 117–40. Essay originally published in *Psychotic* (January and September 1968).

——, *The Other Glass Teat: Further Essays of Opinion on Television* (New York: Pyramid Books, 1975).

Eshbach, Lloyd Arthur (ed.), *Of Worlds Beyond: The Science of Science Fiction Writing*, 1947 (Chicago: Advent, 1964).

Farmer, Philip Jose, 'Riders of the Purple Wage', in *Dangerous Visions #1*, ed. Harlan Ellison, 1967 (New York: Berkley Books, 1968), 70–144.

Faulkner, William, 'Man Will Prevail' [Nobel Prize Acceptance Speech], in *Values and Voices*, ed. Betty Renshaw (New York: Holt, Rinehart and Winston, 1975), 378–79. Speech originally presented in 1950; text taken from *The Faulkner Reader* (New York: Random House, 1954).

Feinberg, Leonard, *Introduction to Satire* (Ames, Iowa: The Iowa State University Press, 1967).

Franklin, H. Bruce, *Future Perfect: American Science Fiction of the Nineteenth*

Century, 1966, revised edition (New York: Oxford University Press, 1978).

———, *Robert A. Heinlein: America as Science Fiction* (New York: Oxford University Press, 1980).

———, 'The Vietnam War as Fantasy and Science Fiction' (Paper presented at the Interdisciplinary Literature Conference on the Fantastic Imagination in New Critical Theories, College Station, Texas, February 1990).

———, *War Stars: The Superweapon and the American Imagination* (New York: Oxford University Press, 1988).

Frye, Northrop, *The Anatomy of Criticism: Four Essays*, 1957 (Princeton: Princeton University Press, 1971).

Garrett, Randall [as by David Gordon], 'There's No Fool...', *Astounding Science Fiction*, 57 (August 1956), 39–51.

Gibson, William, *Neuromancer* (New York: Ace Books, 1984).

Godwin, Tom, 'The Cold Equations', in *The Science Fiction Hall of Fame*, ed. Robert Silverberg, 543–69.

Gould, Stephen Jay, *An Urchin in the Storm: Essays about Books and Ideas* (New York: W. W. Norton & Company, 1987).

Grimsted, David, *Melodrama Unveiled: American Theater and Culture 1800–1850* (Chicago: University of Chicago, 1968).

Gunn, James, *Alternate Worlds: The Illustrated History of Science Fiction* (New York: A & W Visual Library, 1975).

Harrison, Harry, 'Introduction', in *Collected Editorials from Analog*, by John W. Campbell, Jr, v–x.

Hartwell, David, *Age of Wonders: Exploring the World of Science Fiction* (New York: Walker, 1984).

Hassler, Donald M., *Comic Tones in Science Fiction: The Art of Compromise with Nature* (Westport: Greenwood Press, 1982).

Hearn, Michael Patrick, 'Introduction', in *The Annotated Wizard of Oz*, by L. Frank Baum (New York: Clarkson N. Potter, 1973), 11–80.

Heilman, Robert Bechtold, *Tragedy and Melodrama: Versions of Experience* (Seattle: University of Washington Press, 1968).

Heinlein, Robert A., *Beyond This Horizon*, 1948 (New York: Signet Books, 1952). First published in *Astounding Science-Fiction* in 1942.

———, *Expanded Universe: The New Worlds of Robert A. Heinlein*, 1980 (New York: Ace Books, 1981).

———, *Grumbles from the Grave*, ed. Virginia Heinlein (New York: Del Rey/Ballantine Books, 1990).

———, 'If This Goes On—', in *Revolt in 2100*, by Robert A. Heinlein (New York: Signet Books, 1953), 11–129. First published in *Astounding Science-Fiction* in 1940.

————, *Job: A Comedy of Justice* (New York: Del Rey/Ballantine Books, 1983).

————, 'On the Writing of Speculative Fiction', in *Of Worlds Beyond*, ed. Lloyd Arthur Eshbach, 13–19.

————, 'Science Fiction: Its Nature, Faults and Virtues', in *The Science Fiction Novel*, ed. Basil Davenport, 14–48.

————, 'Solution Unsatisfactory', in *Expanded Universe*, 96–144. First published in *Astounding Science-Fiction* in 1940.

————, 'Waldo', in *Waldo and Magic, Inc.*, by Robert A. Heinlein (New York: Pyramid Books, 1968), 9–103. First published in *Astounding Science-Fiction* in 1942.

Highet, Gilbert, *The Anatomy of Satire* (Princeton, New Jersey: Princeton University Press, 1962).

Holman, C. Hugh, *A Handbook to Literature*, based on the original by William Flint Thrall and Addison Hibbard, third edition (Indianapolis: Bobbs-Merrill, 1972).

Horne, Charles I., 'Jules Verne, the World's Greatest Prophet', *Science and Invention*, 8 (August 1920), page numbers unknown.

Hubbard, L. Ron, 'Introduction', *Battlefield Earth: A Saga of the Year 3000*, by L. Ron Hubbard, 1982 (New York: Bridge Publications, 1984), vii–xv.

Huntington, John, 'Hard-Core Science Fiction and the Illusion of Science', in *Hard Science Fiction*, ed. George Slusser and Eric S. Rabkin (Carbondale: Southern Illinois University Press, 1986), 45–57.

'Important Announcement!' [no author given], *Wonder Stories*, 2 (October 1931), 581.

'In Our Next Issue' [no author given], *Amazing Stories*, 1 (November 1926), 673.

Introduction to 'The Red Spot of Jupiter' [no author given], *Wonder Stories*, 3 (July 1931), 215.

Jakubowski, Maxim and Malcolm Edwards, *The SF Book of Lists* (New York: Berkley Books, 1983).

Jameson, Fredric, *Marxism and Form: Twentieth-Century Dialectical Theories of Literature*, 1971 (Princeton: Princeton University Press, 1974).

Kaw, 'The Time Eliminator' [no other name given], *Amazing Stories*, 1 (December 1926), 802–05.

Keller, David H., 'Foreword' to *The Human Termites*, *Science Wonder Stories*, 1 (September 1929), 295.

————, 'The Revolt of the Pedestrians', *Amazing Stories*, 2 (February 1928), 1048–59.

Kelly, Frank K., 'Foreword', in *Starship Invincible: Science Fiction Stories of the 30s*, by Frank K. Kelly (Santa Barbara, California: Capra Press, 1979), 7–12.

Kevles, Bettyann, 'Truth Stranger than Science Fiction?' *Los Angeles Times*,

13 June 1984, Section V, 10–11.

Knight, Damon, 'Beauty, Stupidity, Injustice, and Science Fiction', *Monad: Essays on Science Fiction*, No. 1 (September 1990), 67–88.

———, *In Search of Wonder*, 1956, revised and enlarged (Chicago: Advent Publishers, 1967).

Le Guin, Ursula K., 'Introduction', in *The Left Hand of Darkness*, 1969 (New York: Ace Books, 1976), [xi–xvi].

Long, Frank Belknap, *This Strange Tomorrow* (New York: Ace Books, 1966).

Lowndes, Robert, letter, *Foundation: The Review of Science Fiction*, No. 35 (Spring 1986), 68–89.

Lundwall, Sam J., *Science Fiction: An Illustrated History*, 1977 (New York: Grosset & Dunlap, 1978).

———, *Science Fiction: What It's All About* (New York: Ace Books, 1971).

Luyten, W. J., 'The Fallacy in "Ten Million Miles Sunward"', *Amazing Stories*, 3 (April 1928), 25.

Malmgren, Carl D., *Worlds Apart: Narratology of Science Fiction* (Bloomington: Indiana University Press, 1991).

Malzberg, Barry N., *The Engines of the Night: Science Fiction in the Eighties*, 1982 (New York: Bluejay Books, 1984).

Merril, Judith, 'What Do You Mean: Science? Fiction?', in *SF—The Other Side of Realism: Essays on Modern Fantasy and Science Fiction*, ed. Thomas D. Clareson (Bowling Green, Ohio: Bowling Green Popular, 1971), 53–95. Originally published in *Extrapolation* (May and December 1966).

Miller, P. Schuyler, 'The Reference Library' [book review column], *Analog Science Fact/Science Fiction*, 67 (May 1961), 161–70.

———, 'The Reference Library', *Analog Science Fact/Science Fiction*, 68 (March 1962), 166–173.

Monk, Patricia, '"Not Just Cosmic Skullduggery": A Partial Reconsideration of Space Opera', *Extrapolation*, 33 (Winter 1992), 295–316.

Morgan, Chris, *The Shape of Futures Past: The Story of Prediction* (Exeter, England: Webb & Bower, 1980).

Moskowitz, Sam, 'The Early Coinage of Science Fiction', *Science-Fiction Studies*, 3 (November 1976), 312–13.

———, *Explorers of the Infinite: Shapers of Science Fiction* (Cleveland: World Publishing Company, 1963).

———, *The Immortal Storm: A History of Science Fiction Fandom* (Atlanta, Georgia: Burwell, 1952).

———, Introduction to 'The Way Back', in *Futures to Infinity*, ed. Sam Moskowitz (New York: Pyramid Books, 1970), 188–189.

———, *Science Fiction in Old San Francisco, Volume I: History of the Movement from 1854 to 1890* (Kingston, Rhode Island: Donald M. Grant, Publisher, 1980).

————, *Seekers of Tomorrow: Masters of Modern Science Fiction* (Cleveland: World Publishing Company, 1966).

————, *Strange Horizons: The Spectrum of Science Fiction* (New York: Charles Scribner's Sons, 1976.

Mumford, Lewis. *The Story of Utopias*, 1922 (Gloucester, Massachusetts: Peter Smith, 1959).

Nicholls, Peter, 'Futurology', in *The Science Fiction Encyclopedia*, ed. Peter Nicholls, 237–38.

————, 'Prediction', in *The Science Fiction Encyclopedia*, ed. Peter Nicholls, 473–74.

————, (ed.), *The Science Fiction Encyclopedia* (Garden City: Doubleday, 1979).

————, *The Science in Science Fiction* (New York: Alfred A. Knopf, 1983).

Nicolson, Marjorie Hope, *Voyages to the Moon*, 1948 (New York: MacMillan, 1960).

Orlovsky, V. [Vladimir], 'The Revolt of the Atoms', *Amazing Stories*, 4 (April 1929), 6–17.

'Over the Fence' [advertisement], *Astounding Science Fiction*, 23 (June 1939), 146.

Palmer, Ray, 'The Observatory by the Editor', *Amazing Stories*, 12 (June 1938), 8.

Panshin, Alexei, *Heinlein in Dimension* (Chicago: Advent, 1968).

————, 'The Short History of Science Fiction', in *SF in Dimension: A Book of Explorations* (Chicago: Advent, 1974), 19–29. Essay originally published in *Fantastic* (April 1971).

————, and Cory Panshin, *The World beyond the Hill: Science Fiction and the Quest for Transcendence* (Los Angeles: Jeremy R. Tarcher, Inc., 1989).

Parrinder, Patrick, *Science Fiction: Its Teaching and Criticism* (London: Methuen, 1980).

Pohl, Frederik, 'Astounding Story', *American Heritage*, 41 (September/October 1989), 42–54.

———— and C. M. Kornbluth, *The Space Merchants* [*Gravy Planet*] (New York: Ballantine Books, 1953).

————, *The Way the Future Was: A Memoir*, 1978 (New York: Ballantine Books, 1979).

Porges, Irwin, *Edgar Rice Burroughs: The Man Who Created Tarzan* (Provo, Utah: Brigham Young University Press, 1975).

Prince, Gerald, 'Formalist Narratology and Fantasy Literature', (presented at the Conference on the Fantastic Imagination in New Critical Theories, College Station, Texas, February 1990).

'The Readers' Corner' [readers' letters and responses], *Astounding Stories of Super-Science*, 1 (April 1930), 129.

'The Readers' Corner', *Astounding Stories of Super-Science*, 2 (June 1930), 422–23.

'The Readers' Corner', *Astounding Stories of Super-Science*, 3 (July 1930), 135.

'The Reader Speaks' [readers' letters and responses], *Science Wonder Stories*, 1 (May 1930), 1139, 1142–43.

'The Reader Speaks', *Wonder Stories* (June 1931), 132.

'The Reader Speaks', *Wonder Stories Quarterly*, 3 (Summer 1932), 576.

Renshaw, Betty (ed.), *Values and Voices: a College Reader* (New York: Holt, Rinehart, and Winston, 1975).

Review of *The Purple Cloud* by M. Shiel, *Wonder Stories*, 2 (December 1930), 761.

Rhodes, W. H. [William Henry], *Caxton's Book: A Collection of Essays, Poems, Tales, and Sketches*, ed. Daniel O'Connell, with an introduction by W. H. L. B. [William H. L. Barnes] (San Francisco: A. L. Bancroft and Company, 1876).

Robison, H. G., 'H. G. Wells—Hell of a Good Fellow—Declares His Son', *Amazing Stories*, 1 (February 1927), 1074–75. Originally published in the *New York World*.

Rogers, Alva, *A Requiem for Astounding* (Chicago: Advent Publishers, 1964).

Sagan, Carl, *The Dragons of Eden*, 1982 (New York: Signet Books, 1983).

Sargent, Samuel J., Jr, 'The Telepathic Pickup', *Amazing Stories*, 1 (December 1926), 828–30.

Scholes, Robert E., *Structural Fabulation: An Essay on the Fiction of the Future* (Notre Dame, Indiana: University of Notre Dame Press, 1975).

Scholes, Robert E. and Eric S. Rabkin, *Science Fiction: History, Science, Vision* (New York: Oxford University Press, 1977).

'The Science Fiction League' [monthly column of news and reports concerning the Science Fiction League], *Wonder Stories*, 6 (May 1935), 1519–20.

'The Science Fiction League', *Wonder Stories*, 7 (July 1935), 241.

'The Science Fiction League', *Wonder Stories*, 7 (August 1935), 371.

'The Science Fiction League', *Wonder Stories*, 7 (September 1935), 497.

'The Science Fiction League', *Wonder Stories*, 7 (November-December 1935), 753.

Siegel, Mark Richard, *Hugo Gernsback: Father of Modern Science Fiction* (San Bernardino, California: Borgo Press, 1988).

Silverberg, Robert (ed.), *The Science Fiction Hall of Fame*, 1970 (New York: Avon Books, 1971).

Simak, Clifford D., *City*, 1951 (New York: Ace Books, 1981).

Sloane, T. O'Conor, 'Acceleration in Interplanetary Travel', *Amazing Stories*, 4 (November 1929), 677.

———, 'Amazing Stories', *Amazing Stories*, 4 (May 1929), 103.

————, 'The Editor and the Reader', *Amazing Stories*, 4 (September 1929), 485.

Slusser, George, letter, *Foundation: The Review of Science Fiction*, No. 46 (Autumn 1989), 65–68.

Smith, Cordwainer, [Paul Linebarger] 'Scanners Live in Vain', in *The Science Fiction Hall of Fame*, ed. Robert Silverberg, 354–90. Originally published in *Fantasy Book* in 1950.

Smith, Everett C. (plot) and R. F. Starzl, (story), 'The Metal Moon', *Wonder Stories Quarterly*, 3 (Winter 1932), 246–59.

Spinrad, Norman, *Science Fiction in the Real World* (Carbondale, Illinois: Southern Illinois University Press, 1990).

Stableford, Brian, 'Anthropology', in *The Science Fiction Encyclopedia*, ed. Peter Nicholls, 37–38.

————, 'Marriage of Science and Fiction', in *Encyclopedia of Science Fiction*, Consultant Editor Robert Holdstock (Baltimore: Octopus Books, 1978), 18–27.

————, 'Proto Science Fiction', in *The Science Fiction Encyclopedia*, ed. Peter Nicholls, 476–78.

————, 'Science Fiction between the Wars', in *Anatomy of Wonder*, ed. Neal Barron, 49–63.

————, *Scientific Romance in Britain 1890–1950* (London: Fourth Estate, 1985).

Stashower, Daniel, 'A Dreamer Who Made Us Fall in Love with the Future', *Smithsonian*, 21 (August 1990), 44–55.

Sterling, Bruce, 'Preface', in *Burning Chrome*, by William Gibson, 1986 (New York: Ace Books, 1987), ix–xii.

————, 'Preface', in *Mirrorshades: The Cyberpunk Anthology*, ed. Bruce Sterling. 1986 (New York: Ace Books, 1988), ix–xvi.

Stewart, Frederick Dundas, 'Why We Believe in Scientifiction', *Amazing Stories Quarterly*, 2 (Winter 1929), 3.

Sturgeon, Theodore, 'Slow Sculpture', in *Nebula Awards Number Six*, ed. Clifford D. Simak (New York: Pocket Books, 1971), 25–47. Story originally published in 1970.

Suvin, Darko, *Metamorphoses of Science Fiction: On the Poetics and History of a Literary Genre* (New Haven: Yale University Press, 1979).

————, *Positions and Presuppositions in Science Fiction* (Kent, Ohio: Kent State University Press, 1988).

————, *Victorian Science Fiction in the UK: The Discourses of Knowledge and of Power* (Boston: G. K. Hall & Co., 1983).

Test, George A., *Satire: Spirit and Art* (Tampa, Florida: University of South Florida Press, 1991).

Tremaine, F. Orlon, 'About Brass Tacks', *Astounding Stories*, 18 (October

1936), 149.

———, 'Ad Astra', *Astounding Stories*, 18 (September 1936), 7.

———, 'Blazing New Trails', *Astounding Stories*, 17 (August 1936), 153.

———, 'The Door to Tomorrow', *Comet Stories*, 1 (July 1941), 123.

———, 'Editorial Number Two: In Absentia', in *A Requiem for Astounding*, by Alva Rogers, xvii–xviii. Based on materials originally published in 1950 and 1951.

———, 'Editor's Note Book', *Comet Stories*, 1 (December 1940), 125–30.

———, 'The Growing Consciousness', *Astounding Stories*, 19 (March 1937), 123.

———, 'In Tune with the Infinite', *Comet Stories*, 1 (January 1941), 81.

———, 'Looking Ahead', *Astounding Stories*, 17 (July 1936), 155.

———., 'Science Discussions', *Astounding Stories*, 18 (November 1936), 123.

———, 'Signposts in Space', *Comet Stories*, 1 (March 1941), 17.

———, 'Star Dust', *Astounding Stories*, 17 (March 1936), 65.

Tuck, Donald Henry, *The Encyclopedia of Science Fiction and Fantasy through 1968*, three volumes, 1974 (Chicago: Advent Press, 1982).

Turner, George et al., 'Melbourne University Science Fiction Association Symposium on John W. Campbell', in *John W. Campbell: An Australian Tribute*, ed. John Bangsund (Canberra: Ronald E. Graham and John Bangsund, 1974).

'Ultra-Violet Fluorescence' [advertisement], *Astounding Science-Fiction*, 28 (September 1941), 126.

van Vogt, A. E., 'Complication in the Science Fiction Story', in *Of Worlds Beyond*, ed. Lloyd Arthur Eshbach, 53–68.

———, interview with Jeffrey M. Elliot, in *Science Fiction Voices #2*, 30–40.

Varnado, S. L., *Haunted Presence: The Numinous in Gothic Fiction* (Tuscaloosa: University of Alabama Press, 1987).

Verrill, A. Hyatt, 'The Man Who Could Vanish', *Amazing Stories*, 1 (January 1927), 900–13.

Walsh, Chad, *From Utopia to Nightmare* (London: Geoffrey Bles, 1962).

Walters, Hugh [Walter Hughes], *Terror by Satellite* (New York: Criterion Books, 1964).

'Wanted: More Plots' [author not given], *Wonder Stories Quarterly*, 3 (Fall 1931), 5.

'Wanted: Still More Plots' [author not given], *Wonder Stories Quarterly*, 3 (Summer 1932), 437.

Warner, Harry, Jr, *All Our Yesterdays: An Informal History of Science Fiction Fandom in the Forties* (Chicago: Advent, 1969).

Weisinger, Mort, 'The New Thrilling Wonder Stories', *Thrilling Wonder Stories*, 8 (August 1936), 10.

Wertenbaker, G. Peyton, 'The Coming of the Ice', *Amazing Stories*, 1 (June

1926), 232–37. Reprinted in *The History of the Science Fiction Magazines, Volume I: 1926–1935* ed. Michael Ashley, 52–66.

Westfahl, Gary, 'Academic Criticism of Science Fiction: What Is, What It Should Be', *Monad: Essays on Science Fiction*, No. 2 (March 1992), 75–96.

——, '"A Convenient Analog System": John W. Campbell, Jr.'s Theory of Science Fiction', *Foundation: The Review of Science Fiction*, No. 54 (Spring 1992), 52–70.

——, *Cosmic Engineers: A Study of Hard Science Fiction* (Westport, Connecticut: Greenwood Press, 1996).

——, '"Dictatorial, Authoritarian, Uncooperative: The Case against John W. Campbell, Jr.', *Foundation: The Review of Science Fiction*, No. 56 (Winter 1993), 36–61.

——, 'Evolution of Modern Science Fiction: The Textual History of Hugo Gernsback's *Ralph 124C 41+*', *Science-Fiction Studies*, 23 (March 1996), 37–92.

——, 'Gadgetry, Government, Genetics, and God: The Forms of Science Fiction Utopia', in *Utopia: Past, Present, Futures*, ed. George Slusser, Roger Galliard and Paul Alkon (New York: AMS Press, forthcoming).

——, '"The Gernsback Continuum": William Gibson in the Context of Science Fiction', in *Fiction Two Thousand: Cyberpunk and the Future of Narrative*, ed. George Slusser and Tom Shippey (Athens: University of Georgia, 1992), 88–108.

—— '"An Idea of Significant Import": Hugo Gernsback's Theory of Science Fiction', *Foundation: The Review of Science Fiction*, No. 48 (Spring 1990), 16–40.

——, *Islands in the Sky: The Space Station Theme in Science Fiction Literature*, Preface by Gregory Benford (San Bernardino, California: Borgo Press, 1996).

——, '"The Jules Verne, H. G. Wells, and Edgar Allan Poe Type of Story": Hugo Gernsback's History of Science Fiction', *Science-Fiction Studies*, 19 (November 1992), 340–53.

——, '"Man against Man, Brain against Brain": The Transformation of Melodrama in Science Fiction', in *Themes in Drama: Melodrama, Volume XIV*, ed. James Redmond (Cambridge, England: Cambridge University Press, 1992), 193–11.

——, 'The Mote in Gernsback's Eye: A History of the Idea of Science Fiction', Dissertation (Claremont Graduate School, 1985).

——, 'On *The True History of Science Fiction*', *Foundation: The Review of Science Fiction*, No. 47 (Winter 1989/1990), 5–27.

——. *The Other Side of the Sky: An Annotated Bibliography of Space Stations in Science Fiction, 1869–1991*. San Bernardino, California: Borgo Press, forthcoming.

————, '"This Unique Document": Hugo Gernsback's *Ralph 124C 41+* and the Genres of Science Fiction', *Extrapolation*, 35 (Summer 1994), 95–119.

————, 'The True Historian Replies' [letter], *Foundation: The Review of Science Fiction*, No. 52 (Spring 1991), 69–71.

————, 'Words of Wishdom: The Neologisms of Science Fiction', in *Styles of Creation: Aesthetic Technique and the Creation of Fictional Worlds*, ed. George Slusser and Eric S. Rabkin (Athens: University of Georgia, 1992), 221–44.

————, 'The Words That Could Happen: Science Fiction Neologisms and the Creation of Future Worlds', *Extrapolation*, 34 (Winter 1993), 290–304.

————, 'Wrangling Conversation: Linguistic Patterns in the Dialogue of Heroes and Villains', In *Fights of Fancy: Armed Conflict in Science Fiction and Fantasy*, ed. George Slusser and Eric S. Rabkin (Athens: University of Georgia, 1993), 35–48.

————, 'A Zealous but Humble Reply' [letter], *Foundation: The Review of Science Fiction*, No. 49 (Summer 1990), 63–69.

'What Do You Know?' [scientific question-and-answer feature], *Amazing Stories*, 2 (November 1927), 759.

'What I Have Done to Spread Science Fiction: $500.00 Prize Letters', *Science Wonder Quarterly*, 1 (Winter 1930), 278.

Williams, Madawc, [letter], *Foundation: The Review of Science Fiction*, No. 50 (Fall 1990), 81–82.

Williams, Raymond, *Marxism and Literature* (Oxford: Oxford University Press, 1977).

Williamson, Jack, 'The Amazing Work of Wells and Verne', in 'Editorials from Our Readers', *Amazing Stories Quarterly*, 2 (Winter 1929), 140.

————, interview by Larry McCaffrey, *Science-Fiction Studies*, 18 (July 1991), 230–52.

————, 'The Logic of Fantasy', in *Of Worlds Beyond*, ed. Lloyd Arthur Eshbach, 39–49.

————, 'Scientifiction, Searchlight of Science', *Amazing Stories Quarterly*, 1 (Fall 1928), 435.

Wilson, Edward O., *On Human Nature*, 1978 (New York: Bantam Books, 1979).

Winn, Charles C., 'The Infinite Vision', *Amazing Stories*, 1 (May 1926), 136–39.

Wolfe, Bernard, 'Afterword' to 'Monitored Dreams and Strategic Cremations', in *Again, Dangerous Visions I*, ed. Harlan Ellison, 1972 (New York: Signet Books, 1973), 391–97.

Wolfe, Gary K., *The Known and the Unknown: The Iconography of Science Fiction*

(Kent: Kent State University Press, 1979).

Wollheim, Donald A., *The Universe Makers: Science Fiction Today* (New York: Harper, 1971).

Young, Louise B., 'Mind and Order in the Universe', in *A Writer's Worlds: Explorations through Reading*, ed. Trudy Smoke (New York: St Martin's Press, 1990), 443–48. First published in 1986 in *The Unfinished Universe*.

'Your Viewpoint' [readers' letters and responses], *Amazing Stories Quarterly*, 1 (Summer 1928), 431.

Index

Keller, David H. 9, 54, 140
Kelly, Frank K. 142
Kepler, Johannes 70, 73
Kevles, Bettyann 61
King, Stephen 250
Kipling, Rudyard 74
Knight, Damon 1, 50, 61, 177, 258,
    260, 278, 282
Knight, Norman L. 134, 185
Knight, Raymond 154, 295
Kornbluth, C. M. 134, 260
Kress, Nancy 10
Kreuziger, Frederick 88

Lasswitz, Kurd 28
Leiber, Fritz 259, 261, 266, 294
Leinster, Murray 76, 216, 258
Le Guin, Ursula K. 10
Lem, Stanislaw 302
Leonardo da Vinci 38, 70, 216
Lerner, Edward M. 305
Lewis, C. S. 9
Ley, Willy 297
Locke, Richard Adams 21, 24, 72
London, Jack 8
Lovecraft, H. P. 143, 177
Lowell, Percival 70, 138
Lucian 4, 15, 18
Lundwall, Sam J. 27, 92–3, 113, 135
Lupcott, Richard A. 251

McDermott, Dennis 176
MacDonald, John D. 250
MacHarg, William B. 295
McLaughlin, Dean 184
McNeely, Willis 199
Malmgren, Carl D. 293, 302
Malzberg, Barry N. 31, 262
Matheson, Richard 133
Mercier, Louis-Sebastian 81
Merril, Judith 1, 183
Merritt, A. 52, 69, 76, 80, 152, 216,
    294, 307
Miller, P. Schuyler 38, 73, 85, 156,
    160, 278
Milton, John 10
Monk, Patricia 178
More, Thomas 4, 10, 15, 16, 18, 63,
    115, 172, 214, 216
Morgan, Jacque 76, 80, 122, 123
Moskowitz, Sam 7, 19, 20, 22–3, 137,
    138, 140, 173–4, 177, 178, 191,

219, 254–5, 260, 263, 295
Mumford, Lewis 114
Murchison, Roderick 15

Nicholls, Peter 292
Nicholson, Marjorie Hope 86
Niven, Larry 249, 302
Nowlan, Philip Francis 209

O'Brien, Fitz-James 49
Orlovsky, V. 77, 150
Orwell, George 9, 216

Padgett, Lewis 209
Palmer, Ray 167, 170, 171, 175
Panshin, Alexei 7, 12, 19, 27, 30, 32,
    88, 161, 179, 230, 232, 243, 256
Panshin, Cory 7, 12, 19, 27, 30, 32,
    88, 230, 256
Parrinder, Patrick 32, 33
Plato 212–13, 214, 215
Poe, Edgar Allan 9, 21, 22, 46, 67, 68,
    71, 72, 79, 80, 81, 83, 85, 148,
    172, 208, 216
Pohl, Frederik 60, 116, 134, 143, 180,
    186, 256, 258, 260, 263, 264, 274,
    302
Prince, Gerald 13
Puttenham, George 2

Rabelais, François 4, 15, 18
Rabkin, Eric S. 29, 198, 199, 262
Radcliffe, Ann 108
Raphael, Rick 276
Repp, Ed Earl 9
Rhodes, William Henry 18
Richmond, Walt and Leigh 276
Rocklynne, Ross 191, 192
Rogers, Alva 157, 167, 169, 197
Rose, Mark 45
Russell, Eric Frank 209

Sagan, Carl 189, 202, 279
Sargent, Pamela 1
Schachner, Nat 157
Scholes, Robert 29, 198, 199, 262,
    302
Scott, Walter 110
Senarens, Luis 28, 79–80
Serviss, Garrett P. 28, 72, 216, 259
Shakespeare, William 9, 10
Sheckley, Robert 116